RANDOM HOUSE

LARGE PRINT

# TO WAKE
# THE GIANT

# TO WAKE THE GIANT

★

A NOVEL OF PEARL HARBOR

# JEFF SHAARA

RANDOM HOUSE
LARGE PRINT

**To Wake the Giant** is a work of historical fiction. Apart from the well-known actual people, events, and locales that figure in the narrative, all names, places, and incidents are the product of the author's imagination or are used fictitiously. Any resemblance to current events or locales, or to living persons, is entirely coincidental.

Copyright © 2020 by Jeffrey M. Shaara
Maps copyright © 2020 by David Lindroth Inc.

All rights reserved.
Published in the United States of America by
Random House Large Print in association with
Ballantine Books, an imprint of Random House,
a division of Penguin Random House LLC, New York.

Cover design: Carlos Beltrán
Cover photograph: US Navy

The Library of Congress has established a
Cataloging-in-Publication record for this title.

ISBN: 978-0-593-17206-3

www.penguinrandomhouse.com/large-print-format-books

FIRST LARGE PRINT EDITION

Printed in the United States of America

10  9  8  7  6  5  4  3  2  1

This Large Print edition published in accord
with the standards of the N.A.V.H.

This book is dedicated to Dan Martinez,
National Park Service Chief Historian for the WWII Valor
in the Pacific National Monument, which includes the
USS **Arizona** Memorial, Pearl Harbor, Hawaii.

His support and generosity opened the door to the
extraordinary resources and research that allowed
this book to be written.

"War is not an act of God.
It is a crime of man."

—Cordell Hull,
U.S. Secretary of State 1933–44

# CONTENTS

# LIST OF MAPS

# TO THE READER

**T**hroughout our history, certain dates have had enormous significance, serving as reminders or even symbols of an event that profoundly changed our world. In American history alone, there are those dates taught to every student: July 4, 1776. June 6, 1944. November 22, 1963. September 11, 2001. And there is one more: December 7, 1941. On that day, in a mere two hours, an aerial assault by the Japanese destroyed or damaged much of the American military fleet and air power in and around Pearl Harbor, Hawaii.

This story covers a full year, from December 1940 through the events and horrific tragedy of December 7, 1941. It is a story of sincere efforts to avoid a war confronting sincere efforts to start one, as well as a story of both heroics and blind incompetence. And it is a story about people on opposing sides, both old and young, who are men of character and courage, men with keen insight and brilliance; and others who are men of immense ego, incompetence, and an astonishing level of blindness. But there is no one villain, and no single hero.

One challenge in telling this story is to avoid judgment of the participants on both sides. Many, or even most, Americans were encouraged by the media to believe that the Japanese were "funny little people" or a "godless horde," as though they were a swarm of insects. I have inserted throughout this story actual quotes from various officials that, with our benefit of hindsight, display astounding ignorance. But such racism went both ways, as many Japanese viewed many Americans as rich, fat and lazy, spineless and weak, easy targets who would recoil in terror from any aggressive attack. And thus do wars start.

I did not expect how personal this history would become. My goal, always, is to dig into the minds of the characters so that I feel comfortable putting words in their mouths. My greatest priority is to do justice to those who earned it and to let those men or their families know they are not forgotten.

**To Wake the Giant** is told mainly from the points of view of three men in three very different locations.

In Washington, D.C., Cordell Hull is President Franklin D. Roosevelt's secretary of state, the diplomat responsible for bridging the dangerous gap between the United States and Japan. As such, he is exactly in the middle between Roosevelt, the American military chiefs, and the Japanese ambassador. Hull understands, more than anyone else in his government, that it is his duty to ensure good relations between the United States and every other country on earth—including, of course, Japan.

In Japan, Admiral Isoroku Yamamoto, a political moderate, is confronted by the growing power of the militants in his own government who advocate for war against the world's great powers. Knowing that Japan cannot win such a war, he must ensure Japan's survival by any means necessary. And thus Admiral Yamamoto devises a plan, a bold strike against the Americans that might grant Japan the time it needs to greatly strengthen its military.

In a small town in northeast Florida, Tommy Biggs is a nineteen-year-old with a talent for baseball and nothing else in his life. The Depression has crushed much of rural America, and Tommy's father is one of the victims. Enduring his father's chronic anger and his mother's despair, Biggs aches for a way out. The opportunity is unexpected, but Biggs suddenly finds an escape from the miserable poverty that engulfs his family and his community.

Throughout this story are several other points of

view and many names, known and unknown, yet all of them are important to these events.

I have taken liberties that must be mentioned (or you'll certainly mention them to me). In the Japanese language, names are given as last/first: Yamamoto Isoroku. In English usage, obviously, it is the other way around. Realizing that the number of Japanese characters in this story might cause some confusion, I have adopted the English standard, first name/last name. In addition, though the Japanese use the metric system (meters, kilometers, et cetera), for clarity's sake I have employed the American system of feet and miles. If this book is ever printed in Japanese, I'm certain they will make the necessary changes. I hope I am forgiven.

A total of three hundred thirty-five men survived the destruction of the USS **Arizona.** When I began working on this book in early 2019, there were exactly **six** of them still living. As I write this, there are **two.** As **you** read this, there could be fewer still. Or none at all. If there is one good reason for me to tackle this story, it is this: We must know, we must understand, and we must remember. Those who were there can no longer tell their own story.

Finally, my apologies for a bit of self-indulgence. The creation of this book has been a surprisingly difficult experience. Without trying to overdramatize this, there were times when the story simply became too emotional to write, or too consuming to stop. That has happened to me a few times in past books, but not as often as it happened here. I deeply appreciate the support and tolerance and affection from my family: my wife, Stephanie, and daughter, Emma. They've put up with a lot during the writing of this book. I hope I can make it up to them.

—JEFF SHAARA, APRIL 14, 2020

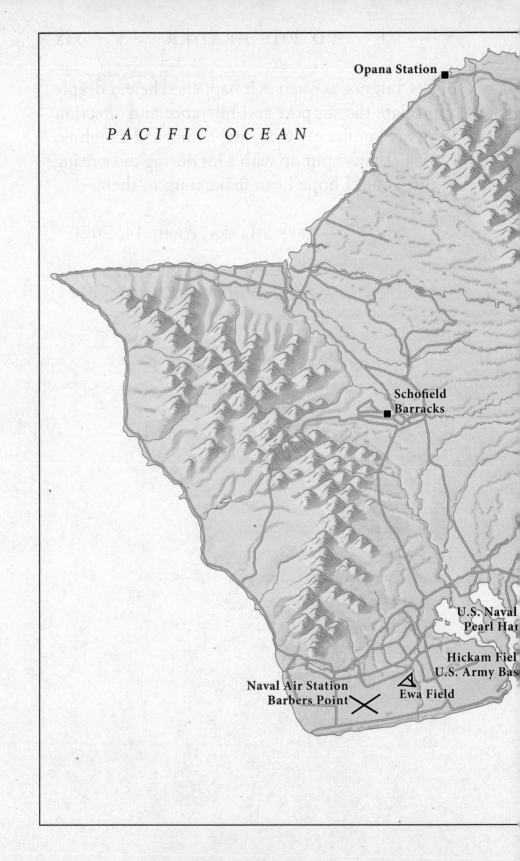

Map of Oahu in 1941

0          MILES          5

0          KM          5

■ Fort Shafter

HONOLULU

# INTRODUCTION

In many ways, World War Two in the Pacific begins with the Japanese victory over the Russians in 1905: the Russo-Japanese War. The level of swagger that results from Japan's decisive end to that war is passed on to a younger generation of officers, who embrace an unwavering belief in Japanese military superiority. In 1931, that belief is a primary justification for Japan to invade and occupy Manchuria, China. This blatant act of aggression draws immediate condemnation from the Western powers, though none is willing to commit military assistance to China's defense. The ease with which the Japanese secure such a large area of China (and insert their own puppet government) seems to justify the wisdom of their strategy. It is as though by accomplishing their goals, they prove those goals correct.

As the more militant voices take control of the government, Japan's Emperor Hirohito still holds sway, with a spiritual and emotional grip on his government and military. But the emperor, by all accounts a meek and mild-mannered man, will not insert himself directly into politics. Though he objects often to the practices of the more aggressive generals, he does little about them. This paves the way for nearly fifteen years of domination by Japan's military, leaving it free to push forward its own aggressive strategic planning.

Emboldened by its initial successes in China, the military plans a grand strategy that will spread Japanese influence, if not outright control, over most of Asia. It is driven in part by the need for natural resources, including oil, rubber, and metals, most of which Japan does not have within its own borders. But a growing racism also drives these goals, particularly the belief among many Japanese that they are a race superior to those they seek to conquer. These include the Koreans, who have already suffered under Japanese rule for decades; the Mongolians; the Southeast Asian peoples; and, of course, the Chinese. This notion of Japanese racial superiority extends beyond Asia as well; many in the Japanese military assume that the West lacks the courage to stand up to Japan's aggressiveness.

According to Japanese historian Saburo Ienaga, "the idea that 'all men are brothers' is simply missing" from the culture.

Over the next few years, the Japanese military continues to expand its conquest of China, and despite energetic condemnation from around the globe, Japanese resolve never wavers. Gradually, the focus of Japanese hostility turns more toward the United States, despite the fact that the Americans have been a primary trading partner, supplying Japan with the very raw materials it needs. According to Colonel Ishiwara Kanji, who authors a strategic report widely accepted by his superiors, "Japan must be willing to fight America to achieve our national objectives."

Despite the prediction from Colonel Kanji that "three or four divisions and a few river gunboats will be quite enough to handle the Chinese . . . ," the Chinese army, led by Chiang Kai-shek, begins to resist the Japanese invasion with more tenacity than expected. The result is a strategic slugfest that the Japanese military euphemistically describes as the "Chinese Problem." Although this is unknown to much of the outside world, the Japanese army commits a series of brutal atrocities against the Chinese, often against civilians. And despite a lack of any real gain in their costly campaign, the Japanese believe that withdrawing from China would be an admission of error, the kind of shame the Japanese find unacceptable. The cost of that campaign increases the need for Japan to pursue other conquests, meeting their need for natural resources.

On September 1, 1939, the attention of the world turns away from Asia as a new crisis rips through Europe, when Hitler's Germany invades Poland. In the United States, President Roosevelt and the American military leaders embrace the belief that Hitler is a far greater threat than anything the Japanese might be planning. The Western world is shocked as Hitler slices his way through northern Europe with relative ease, including a crushing victory over the French army that takes barely three weeks. Occupying Paris, Hitler spreads his brutality outward in several directions, from Scandinavia to North Africa. His most logical target now is Great Britain, which desperately seeks aid from the United States. As concern grows over Hitler's successes, there is enormous pressure within the U.S. government to pull its warships away from their primary base in Hawaii in order to add much-needed strength to protect shipping in the Atlantic.

But Roosevelt's pledge of assistance to Britain is not universally supported by the American people. For years, the movement favoring American isolationism has spread, and many insist that what happens **over there** should stay **over there.** Many isolationists view the great oceans to the east and west as impregnable barriers that will protect the United States from any real danger. It is the military chiefs who are quick to point out that oceans can also be highways—that in the modern world of 1940, no place on earth is safe from the submarine or the great warship. However, there is little objection to Roosevelt's push to remove ships from Hawaii. As they sit at anchor in Pearl Harbor, many, including high-ranking naval officers, believe their presence in the Pacific is simply a waste of time.

In 1940, the Japanese enter into the Tripartite Pact, which is essentially a treaty with Germany and Mussolini's Italy pledging joint cooperation as the war moves forward. Some in the American government are shocked by this unexpected alliance. The war that has been **over there** has just become far more complicated, and far more dangerous. The fear is that if the Japanese receive direct military assistance from Germany, they might be inclined to use it. Yet very few of America's leaders take that threat seriously.

At the end of 1940, the rhetoric from Tokyo becomes increasingly hostile, aimed at both the United States and Britain. If they hear it at all, the vast majority of American military chiefs and their civilian counterparts dismiss such talk with amusement: a tiny mouse roaring at a lion. The racism of the day only adds to the utter dismissal of the Japanese, with posters and cartoons depicting them with enormous buckteeth and inch-thick eyeglasses, incapable of walking in a straight line. Newspapers and Hollywood reinforce the stereotypes, lulling the public into a state of utter complacency.

In Hawaii sits the commander in chief of the U.S. Navy for the entire Pacific basin. His job is to protect American interests, including island bases spread throughout the ocean as well as those in the Philippines. On the island of Oahu, the U.S. Army also maintains a substantial presence, protecting the American naval fleet when it sits at anchor within Pearl Harbor. The two forces, logically, are expected to be mutually supportive and maintain a steady flow of communication with their chiefs in Washington. But these are regarded as frustrating, boring assignments. There simply is no threat.

"Should Japan go to war, one would have to resign oneself to it as unavoidable and throw oneself wholeheartedly into the fight."

—Admiral Isoroku Yamamoto, January 1941

"The Japanese are not going to risk a fight with a first-class nation. They are unprepared to do so, and no one knows that better than they do."

—Congressman Charles Faddis
(Pennsylvania), February 1941

# PART ONE

★

"All warfare is based on deception."

—SUN TSU, **THE ART OF WAR,** 500 B.C.

"Everything which the enemy least suspects
will succeed the best."

—NAPOLEON BONAPARTE

"Japanese sanity cannot be measured by
our own standards of logic. Japan's resort
to measures which might make war with
the United States inevitable may come with
dramatic and dangerous suddenness."

—JOSEPH GREW,
U.S. AMBASSADOR TO JAPAN, 1941

# ONE

## Biggs

PALATKA, FLORIDA—SATURDAY, DECEMBER 14, 1940

He knew he could hammer the ball when it left Russo's hand. The stripe of tape spun slowly, a lazy fastball, too lazy, floating toward him like a fat melon. He cocked the bat, then sprung forward, the bat meeting the ball, a hard thump, the ball now speeding away, rising. He began his run to first base, still watching the ball, hearing the shouts from the others, one voice, Clyde, the first baseman, "Holy mackerel. But it ain't staying fair. Too bad."

He touched first, curled toward second, his eye on the ball again, a quick turn in his gut. Beside him, Clyde said, "It's gonna hit your house."

Biggs watched it drop, a sharp punch through the

kitchen window. The others turned to him now, and Russo said, "Holy crap. You busted it to hell. Your folks home? Geez, Tommy, I ain't seen you hit one that far since high school."

Biggs looked at Russo. "You never pitched me a fat one like that. I was gonna kill it."

Russo turned again toward the Biggs house. "You killed it. Too bad it was foul."

Biggs didn't care about the game anymore, walked slowly off the field, past third base and the run-down lean-to that passed for the dugout. No one called him back, all of them silently grateful it was him and not any one of them.

He didn't turn back, couldn't hide the quiver in his voice. "I gotta make sure nobody's hurt."

His eyes stayed on the jagged hole punched in the window, and he moved with measured steps, in no rush to meet the wrath that would surely come from his father. At nineteen, Biggs knew there would be no belt, and his father had rarely used fists on his son. But there was anger in the man's words, the deathly glare from his eyes. No matter how old Biggs might be, his father's eyes showed a brutal viciousness, punishment enough for any offense.

Even before he graduated high school, Biggs had grown taller than his father, with broader shoulders, stronger arms. As he grew older, not one of his friends doubted that a nineteen-year-old with Biggs's athletic strengths could handle any of his father's mouthy brutishness. But Biggs knew that no matter the physical difference between them, his father was always to be obeyed. Or feared. His anger would often erupt for no apparent reason, a terrifying viciousness sometimes directed at Biggs's mother, the man's sharp voice carrying through the entire neighborhood.

As he grew older, Biggs finally began to understand just why his father seemed so angry. For so many of the men in the small community, the jobs had gone away, the lumber plant nearly shut down, one more casualty of the Depression. Some of those jobs had moved farther west, to another plant out in the Florida Panhandle. Men like Clarence Biggs seemed to live on hope and on pledges from the local politicians of the great efforts they were making to bring in more plants, factories, jobs for all. In every tavern, men repeated the optimism they heard from the newspaper—that the town would survive, even prosper, that Florida's celebrated boom of the 1920s would return, and with that, opportunity for all.

But in this neighborhood of ragged homes with clapboard walls, of vacant fields of sand and sandspurs, there was very little to be hopeful about. No matter what the men in the fancy suits promised them, Clarence Biggs had stopped paying attention to what Palatka was trying to be. What was here, now, were broken men. They knew what **poor** was, their pride as empty as their hope. Like most of them, Clarence had settled for work where he could find it. Every day, he spent long hours at a seafood plant near the St. Johns River. There was nothing elegant about scaling and gutting fish, the pay not enough to buy the fish he cleaned, and the stench he carried home on his clothes reminded them all that Clarence was too weary and too defeated to be embarrassed.

Biggs reached the front door, stood for a long minute, glanced back to the weed-infested vacant lot that was the ball field. His friends were gathered, watching him, and he waved them away, thought, Just play the damn game. He lowered his head now, let out a breath. No, I guess they can't do that. The only ball we've got is in Mom's kitchen.

The doorknob was flimsy, barely catching, and he turned it slowly, pushed the door open, heard the familiar squeal. He slipped inside, was surprised to see his father standing, arms crossed, near the opening to the small kitchen. Tommy saw the ball now in the man's hand, and his father held it out toward him.

"What kind of damned ball is this?"

He knew he was being baited, knew this would go however his father wanted.

"Only ball we got. The masking tape holds it together. Herman's father had a roll."

"Herman hit the ball through the kitchen window? Maybe one of those other jerks you play with? Maybe it was Babe Ruth, stopped by to play a couple innings."

"No. It was me."

"You? You actually hit the ball out of those weeds?"

"Yeah. Me. I'm sorry, Pop." He saw his mother, coming slowly out of their bedroom, standing quietly behind her husband. "I'm sorry, Mom. Didn't mean to bust your window. Hope nobody's hurt or anything."

She stared at him, shook her head slowly, a hint of anger in her tired eyes. She motioned toward the kitchen. "I had a head of cabbage chopped up in the sink. Making slaw for dinner."

His father poked a finger toward him. "And thanks to you, that cabbage is in the trash. Full of busted glass." Tommy looked downward, and his father said, "So, Mr. DiMaggio, unless you wanna chew your way through that mess, we got nothing else to eat tonight. Can't make soup out of this damned baseball. And let me tell you one more thing, slugger. Somebody's gotta fix that window, and right now. We got mosquitoes enough in this damn house."

"Yes, sir. You want I should go to the neighbor's, see if somebody can offer us something for dinner?"

His mother shook her head. "No need. I'll get something from Mrs. King. She's always offering collards from their garden. Mighty nice of her to help us out."

He waited, as though there might be more, something else he could say. He was used to the despair in both of them, saw it again now. But his father surprised him, tossed him the makeshift baseball.

"Put some more tape on it. It's coming apart. Maybe you can find some big-time ball scout to come watch you, sign you to some big deal with the Yankees. I bet **they** don't wrap their balls with tape."

"Hand me the yardstick. And thanks for helping me out."

Russo held it up to him. "Hey, I threw the ball. I'm a little bit to blame. You get all the busted glass outta there?"

Biggs scanned the edge of the window frame. "Yeah, best as I can tell. Okay, it's . . . sixteen by . . . twenty. But we gotta tack it on over the whole thing, so let's cut the board four inches bigger each way."

"You're the boss, Tommy."

He stepped down from the makeshift ladder, an old wooden crate. "I ain't the boss of much of nothing. I don't even know what I'm doing here. Tried to get a job over at the hardware store. Nothing there. I could sweep the floor at the damn barber shop. No pay, just a free haircut. My father lets me know every damn day how much work he has to do to feed us. Mostly me. I'm stuck, Ray. No other word for it."

Russo drew a pencil line on the old piece of clapboard, picked up the rusty hand saw, hesitated.

Biggs reached for the saw, said, "You want me to cut it? It oughta be my job anyway."

Russo handed him the saw, said, "I got something to tell you. Kinda important. I was gonna tell you after the game today. I wanted you to know before any of the others." He paused. "I joined the navy."

Biggs waited for the joke, but Russo's expression didn't change.

"The United States Navy? You mean like, the ocean and stuff?"

Russo smiled now. "That's the one. There was a recruiter set up in the city, at the post office. I got on the pay phone to my dad, talked it over. He said to go ahead. He said it made him proud. You know, he was a sailor back in the Great War. Said he fired those big damn guns. He talked about all that when I was a kid. I never give it much thought until I tried finding work, just like you. There's nothing around here, Tommy. Nothing at all. But now, I'm set to make twenty-one bucks a month, guaranteed. Think what you could buy with that."

Biggs stared at his friend, said, "What the hell? You mean all this? You really leaving? When?"

Russo seemed to inflate, pride on his face. "I damn sure do mean it. They say I'll take the train out of Jacksonville, heading up to some place in Illinois, north of Chicago. I leave in a few weeks."

"A few weeks? Jesus, Ray."

"I gotta tell you, Tommy, I went home, took the papers in so my dad could see 'em, and my mama, she starts bawling, **Oh Raphaele, Raphaele, stai attento.** She's always thinking I'm gonna step in something bad, always telling me to be careful. The more upset she gets, the more Italian she speaks. My dad's not like that, not at all. He wants me to do good, any way I can. He can't hardly work no more since he cracked his skull at that construction site, and I know that both of 'em need all the help I can give 'em. The navy's the way. Promise you that."

"Why the navy? Just 'cause of your dad?"

"Well, maybe one more thing. Doris is moving away. Her parents are heading up to Chicago. Her dad got a job with some hotshot somebody, and he's taking advantage."

Biggs wasn't sure how to respond. "You been dating her for more than a year."

"Year and a half. Hurts like hell, but she's gotta go with 'em. She's only seventeen. Can't blame her. She cried and all that, but I could tell she's excited to see the big city. Not too many are bigger than Chicago."

"Wow. I always figured you two to get married. You gave me hope." Biggs laughed. "I ain't had a steady girl since Jane, and hell, that was two years ago. There hasn't been anybody around here that's done anything for me. The good ones all run off to Jacksonville or Miami and find some jerk who wears a suit." He paused, could see how serious Russo was, none of his usual playfulness. "Jesus, Ray. The navy. Why not the army? That could be good too."

Russo smiled. "It's the right thing to do, Tommy. But I tell you what. Monday, let's take the bus into the city, and you can talk to this fella, this recruiter. He'll tell you anything you want to know."

Biggs took the hand saw, leaned low, perched the teeth on the edge of the board, eyed the pencil mark, his brain swirling with a strange energy. He started to cut, the saw grinding back and forth through the thin board. Russo leaned down, adding weight, steadying the board, and Biggs stopped now, looked at his friend, said, "Yeah, I'll go. Got nothing else to do. Guess it can't hurt."

JACKSONVILLE, FLORIDA—MONDAY, DECEMBER 16, 1940

He loved the big buildings, couldn't help staring upward at the massive banks, **Barnett, Atlantic,** and a huge sign across the street, **Walgreens,** a parade of people flowing in and out. Russo tugged at his sleeve.

"Come on. No time for sightseeing. That recruiter said he'd only be here until four."

Biggs's eyes stayed on the banks, fat buildings in every direction. "Guess it's easy to see where all the money is, huh?"

Russo ignored him, led the way across a wide street, cars halted at a red light to let them pass.

Biggs stared at the cars. "I'd like to drive one of those things one day. My pop says we'll never be able to afford one."

"Will you hurry? Don't matter how big a building is, it's just a pile of brick and stone. Cars are
just hunks of tin with a motor. You sound like
you're wandering in from the Okefenokee Swamp.
You can see every building in Palatka from your
back porch."

"Don't have a back porch."

"Oh. Yeah. Well, from **my** back porch."

"Your back porch is two boards set up on
concrete blocks."

"It's better than yours." Russo pointed down the
street. "There. Look, the post office. Christ, they
got a Christmas tree. But the navy sign's still there.
He's set up inside."

Biggs felt a rumbling discomfort, thought of
his parents. You should have told them, at least
mentioned where you were going. But he knew to
expect the worst, even a scolding for the quarter
he wasted on the bus fare. He could predict the
anger, just didn't want to hear it every day. It was
a sickening pattern, the best reason he knew for
telling them nothing at all. And if there was something here, something to excite him, the way it had
excited his friend? What would that do? How would
he tell them?

He stopped on the sidewalk, felt a chilly breeze,
pulled at his light jacket, couldn't avoid a shiver.
All around him, above him, were signs of the coming holiday, lights above the store windows, paper
images of Santa Claus, Christmas carols, what he

could only imagine was a shopkeeper's offer of good cheer, encouraging customers to spend their money. He was beginning to feel overwhelmed, and said, "I don't know, Ray. This sounds like a waste of time. It's all right for you—your pop knows all about ships and stuff. But I don't think this is gonna work out in my house."

Russo moved close to him, a hard stare. "Listen to me. You got nothing more than me. You got no more shot at college than I do. Look around you. Banks and insurance companies, drug stores and doctors' offices. You and me, we could go in there and maybe sweep their floors, empty their trash baskets. Except there's a dozen guys lined up for that job too. Dammit, Tommy, you're a hard worker, and you got guts. Except maybe right now. Just talk to the navy guy. It costs you nothing, and there's nothing to be scared of. They don't hog-tie people and haul 'em off in the back of wagons anymore."

"When did the navy ever do that?"

Russo thought a moment. "Well, not **our** navy, but somebody did it, somewhere. Let's go."

They moved up the shallow steps into the post office, the American flag high overhead, spread wide by the breeze. Russo led the way, Biggs's hands sweating, and he saw the recruiter now, white uniform, seated behind a narrow table. The sailor saw them coming, seemed to read them both, a broad smile, recognizing Russo.

"Mr. Russo, Raphaele, right?"

"Just Ray's okay, sir. I brought my buddy, thought he'd want to hear what you had to say."

The sailor stood, tall, gray hair at the temples. He held his hand out toward Biggs, kept the smile. "Chief Petty Officer Harvey Goodman. At your service, young man."

Biggs felt a strong handshake.

"Thomas Biggs, sir."

Goodman sat down again, motioned to the lone chair in front of him. Biggs sat slowly, still nervous, and Goodman said, "High school diploma, Mr. Biggs?"

"Yes, sir."

"Good. It's not required, certainly. Most of our younger recruits didn't get that far, but having the diploma can open some doors for you. For one thing, the navy hopes that all of its recruits can read. That always helps. I'm guessing that you're here because Mr. Russo has told you of all the advantages of a life at sea."

"Well, I suppose so, sir. He told me he's going to get twenty-one dollars a month."

Goodman laughed. "That's the least of it, Mr. Biggs. Yes, you'll get twenty-one dollars per month, which will increase if you're promoted, or if you qualify for one of the many specialties needed on every vessel. The longer you stay in the service, the greater your chance of that." He held up his left arm, several stripes on the sleeve of his jacket. "Twenty years, son. That's what these stripes mean.

And this patch on my arm? My rating. As I said, chief petty officer. Let's just say that I make a good bit more than twenty-one dollars per month."

The smile on Goodman's face invited a laugh, and Russo went along, a low chuckle. Biggs felt himself relaxing and Goodman said, "I've got plenty of literature for you to read, son, and I'm here to answer any questions. Don't be bashful."

Biggs looked down for a second, hesitated, then said, "Does the army pay any more?"

Goodman laughed again. "That's a good question, son. Let me answer it like this. You live in Florida, so I'll ask you . . . are you familiar with mosquitoes? Mud? Snakes? Maybe a scorpion or two? Ever sleep out on the ground, where ticks and redbugs bite you so bad you scratch for a week? Had poison ivy?"

Goodman waited for a response, and Biggs knew exactly where this was going.

"Suppose I have, sir. Most of it."

"Let me ask you this. You ever eat powdered eggs, powdered milk, plucked vermin out of your clothes, bugs in your water glass, chewed sand in your oatmeal? You ever march for miles through mud and sandspurs, maybe a swamp or two? Well, son, all of that, that's life in the army. Now, let me ask you this. You ever dream of seeing foreign lands, exotic islands, places more beautiful than you've ever known?" He didn't wait for the answer. "That's the navy, son. And there's more. You get free room and board, and when you're at sea, you'll be on the most modern and strongest ships in the entire world. You'll be given the best food Uncle Sam can provide, no sand in any of it. Hot meals, hot showers." Goodman paused. "You'll have the opportunity to train for a whole variety of specialties, from mechanics to electronics, plus working with the most powerful artillery the world has ever seen. You love your country, son?"

"Of course . . . yes, sir."

"There's a nasty fellow over there in Germany. He's already whipped the French, the Dutch, and a whole bunch of other good folks. Smart people in Washington are saying he's eventually gonna try to whip us. We've got the ships, the guns, and now we need good men, strong men. That sound like you, son?"

Biggs felt energized, sat up straight, glanced at Russo, who was nodding with a big toothy grin.

"I believe so, sir. But I don't know what to do."

"You eighteen?"

"Nineteen, sir."

"Can you prove it?"

The question was unexpected.

"Well, yes, sir. Birth certificate in a box in my mom's closet."

"Bring it to me, son. I've got papers right here, just like what Mr. Russo signed. When you enlist, the clock starts ticking on that pay. You'll do six weeks of basic training first, up in Great Lakes, Illinois. You'll go through all sorts of tests, physical and mental. The navy will help you find out just what you need to be doing, and just where you'll do it."

Russo punched him on the shoulder. "You might even get to serve on a battleship! That's what I'm hoping for."

Goodman tried to defuse Russo's enthusiasm. "Well, that's possible, certainly. But there are a great many other ships, all types, all sizes, and all of them important." He stood, held his hand out. "I'm happy to talk to you more, son. I'll be here at this location for three more days. You need to bring me that birth certificate. Then I'll take care of the rest."

Biggs stood, took the man's hand, a hearty shake. The smile was there again, and Biggs felt a wave of excitement, nothing like he had expected.

"I'll do what I can to get back here tomorrow, sir."

He led Russo down the steps toward the street, a congestion of traffic, a rush of people on the sidewalk. He remembered now all the reasons why he so rarely came into the heart of Jacksonville, could hear and smell it now. They moved toward the bus station, slow going, women in dresses, men in suits, all moving by, a mad rush to someplace Biggs never wanted to be. He pulled Russo out of the flow, a small square of green space, trees wrapped in colored lights.

"You're really doing this, aren't you?"

"Look at all this, Tommy. This is life in the city. Take away all the Christmas stuff and it flat out stinks, even more than it stinks at home. I can't wait to get out on the ocean, smell something a whole lot different than this."

PALATKA, FLORIDA—MONDAY, DECEMBER 16, 1940

"You're doing **what**?"

Biggs tried to keep his back straight, felt himself wilting under that too-familiar scowl of his father. "I'm joining the navy."

"Like hell you are. You know what the navy does? They fight wars. They're fighting one right now, over in England. We're helping out the damn Limeys against the Germans. Got no business doing any of that. None. That damn Roosevelt thinks he needs to jump in and help his buddy Churchill, and so Americans are off to a war that don't involve us. None of us. Not one bit! We got enough problems right here without sticking our noses into somebody else's mess!"

Biggs had heard the word "isolationist," knew that his father shared the belief of an enormous number of Americans. To them, the war in Europe was Europe's problem, and only Europe's problem. He had heard it from his father many times. If Hitler comes marching down Route 17, then maybe there's a fight worth having.

Biggs pushed against his father's tide. "Ray's signed up. His parents think it's a great idea."

"That damn Luigi?"

"His father's name is Luca."

"So what? One more Italian. I bet he pays a hell of a lot more attention to his buddy Mussolini than he does his country right here."

"He was in the U.S. Navy in the Great War."

"What? A spy? How do you know so much?"

The fury from his father was wearing him down, and Biggs looked toward his mother, sitting on the ragged couch, her head in her hands.

"Mom, this is a good thing. It's a real job. I got nothing else here."

She kept her gaze toward the floor, said, "I always hoped you might be a doctor. Make something of yourself, something we'd all be proud of. I always hoped there would be a way."

"Mom, I didn't have the grades for college. It's a nice dream, but I know better. Some people are meant for a big life. Some just aren't." He looked at his father again, saw the familiar stare, as much disgust as anger.

The older man glanced toward his wife, said, "Foolishness! Been hearing that crap for years. Big dreams, big wishes." He looked at Biggs again. "I know what your life is. The same as mine. You got no reason to think you'll ever be better than me. You ain't even got a damn job!"

"You don't have to tell me any of that, Pop. I've

put in for work at every store, every construction site, but there's no more room for somebody who doesn't have skills. I've looked for a chance every place I can around here. So, sure, you're right. I got nothing. You gripe because I live under your roof, and you have to feed me. Well, that'll change."

"Bull. You could be helping us out, paying for our damn groceries. There are jobs aplenty. You just have to get your hands dirty."

"Pop, I'm not gonna settle for a dead end. I'm not gonna gut fish for a living!"

His father seemed to stagger, the fury now driving him forward, the explosion coming, unavoidable, uncontrollable. Biggs tried to back away, the man's fist catching him on the chin, Biggs's head jerking hard to one side. He dropped, one knee, then back, sitting on the floor, bells in his ears. Now a new sound, the shrieking fury of his mother, rising up, full in his father's face, more screaming from both of them. Biggs shuffled through the fog in his brain, put a hand on his chin, checked his teeth, none missing. He focused on his father now, his mother sobbing, both staring down at him. His father leaned low, seemed energized by his **victory.**

"You son of a bitch. You apologize to me, or you get the hell out of my house. I'm not letting you join any damned navy, either. Nobody in this family is going off to fight someone else's war."

Biggs steadied himself, stood slowly, dizzy still.

"I'm sorry, Pop. I think you're wrong." He looked at his mother, said, "Mom, I can't keep living in this place. I got no future here." He looked again at his father, saw an odd weakness now, as though the man had used up all he had. "I need to do something for **me,** Pop. I can't just sit and wait for something to happen, playing baseball with a bunch of guys who are no better off than me. Ray's doing the right thing. His folks are proud of that, proud of him. You don't wanna give me none of that . . . well that's too bad. But it ain't gonna change my mind. And I'm sorry, Pop, but I'm nineteen. You can't stop me."

His father seemed tired, the same look of defeat Biggs had seen so many times before.

"You gonna run off and leave your mother behind. That's just swell. That make you a **man**?"

"Yes, Pop. It does. I can't just stay in this house forever. A man needs to make his own way."

"So, what you gonna do?" There was no hostility in the question, a surprise.

"What do you mean?"

"You're gonna join the damn navy, what the hell you gonna do? You ain't never been on salt water, you oughta be scared as hell. Ships **sink,** you know. It ain't like swimming in the river. Out there, you go straight down, maybe a mile or more. Bet you never thought of that, did you?"

Biggs had his first flash of doubt, saw smugness on

his father's face. He struggled to respond, thought of the recruiter, Goodman, reassuring words, and Ray, his excitement at whatever was to come.

"Well, Pop, I gotta find out. I gotta try, and they're gonna pay me to do it. And Ray says, if we're damn lucky, maybe they'll put us on a battleship."

# TWO

# Hull

**"T**he **admiral** is at it again. I talked to Stimson about it this morning. I may have to get Secretary Knox in here, Admiral Stark as well, lay all this out on the table. They're probably as tired of hearing Admiral Richardson's 'ideas' as I am. Sit down, you make me tired."

Hull sat, said, "I admit I'm a little tired myself, Mr. President. What's the unhappy admiral up to now?"

"You know, I wish you'd stop being so damn formal with me. We've been friends for too long, and unless there's a herd of reporters writing down everything we say, you should really just call me . . ." He paused. "Mr. President, **sir.**"

Roosevelt laughed at his own joke, and Hull smiled. He'd heard that one before.

"How about you call me Cordell, and I call you Mr. President? That way neither of us slips up in front of some foreign dignitary. Take the respect where you can find it. Some of your least favorite congressmen are referring to you as 'Old Three-Term.' Among other, um . . . interesting names."

Roosevelt nodded, hand on his chin. "I've heard some of those **other** names. Some of them quite colorful." He paused. "I didn't want three terms. I pushed you as hard as I could. You were the best man for the job, but you wouldn't take the nomination, and God help us if some isolationist from either party had won the election. The British are already in a load of trouble—Churchill's begging for our help. If we had elected somebody new, somebody who decided he'd rather listen to Charles Lindbergh's nonsense, that would have been a pure catastrophe for this country. I'm so sick of those congressmen who think they're representing their constituents by pretending that Hitler is only a problem **over there.** God knows what's going to happen to the French people, the Belgians, the Norwegians, Dutch, Danes, and anybody else who's already under Hitler's boots. And who's next? It scares the hell out of me, Cordell, that the British might cease to be a nation. All the while, big noisy voices in this country are telling the American people that it's none of our affair. I wonder how those fools will feel when German U-boats show up in every river on our coastline."

He paused again, seemed to catch his breath. "Sorry, I'm ranting a bit. But you've done a fair share of speechmaking on your own. There's probably a few over in the Capitol who listen to you more than they do to me—you're not quite as despised as I am. If you'd have accepted the nomination, I wouldn't be sitting here now raising my blood pressure."

"I'm older than you are. Best not talk to me about blood pressure."

Roosevelt smiled. "Fair assessment."

Hull debated saying anything else. He had endured enormous pressure from Roosevelt to run for president, so many in the Democratic Party believing that Hull was the best man available to carry on the policies they all saw as critical for the survival of the free world. But the isolationist sentiment was astounding, Congress split nearly fifty-fifty. Often, Hull had gone to Capitol Hill, speaking or lobbying for one of Roosevelt's programs, which seemed to him so obviously positive for the country. But closed minds fought every effort. The opposition to Roosevelt's policies came mostly from adversaries in the Republican Party. But even in his own party, there were those who insisted they spoke for the **folks back home,** insisting in their own public forums and local newspapers that as long as the world's problems remained **outside** the borders of the United States, they had no effect on anyone **within** those borders. And all too often, those voices were being believed.

But the secretary of state was not necessarily immune to the hostility that so many had directed toward his president. Hull was well liked and well respected, even among some of the most difficult members of the opposition. If that would have resulted in **President** Hull, no one could say, and he would not speculate. Once Hull had adamantly refused Roosevelt's push that he accept the party's nomination, Roosevelt had made the decision to run himself, seeking an unprecedented third term in office. Despite the howls of protest about what some called Roosevelt's blatant power grab, what the Republican opposition failed to understand, and certainly underestimated, was the positive sentiment toward Roosevelt among the American public. He won overwhelmingly.

There had been no doubt that Hull would continue as secretary of state. He was as much a confidant of Roosevelt's as an influential member of the cabinet. With Roosevelt's people preparing for his third inauguration on January 20, Hull couldn't avoid speaking out to Roosevelt about a serious concern.

"Please forgive me, but I've been chewing on this for a while now. You know that I fully support just about every program you've proposed . . ."

"You wrote some of them."

"Well, yes. Please, let me say this. I fully believe we need to support our allies and push back at our potential enemies. You sitting in that chair for another term was the best way to accomplish all of that."

Roosevelt seemed impatient. "Yes, yes. So, I'm here. The people said, 'Fine. Keep at it.' That's that."

"My concern is what might happen in the future. By you winning a third term, you've established a precedent. Down the road, twenty years, fifty, a hundred, someone who has his own interests in mind more than the country's, some demagogue . . . Well, you know what could happen."

"Have faith in the future, Cordell. Faith in the people. That's all we can do. I can't look that far down the road. What we are facing **right now** could be the greatest crisis the world has ever known; you know that too. It's one reason why the kind of bitching coming at me from people like Admiral Richardson just isn't to be tolerated."

"You were going to tell me what he's done?"

"Right, yes. So, Admiral Richardson was here back in October. You know that, of course. He sat right there in that chair and told me that the military in this country had lost faith in their civilian leadership, in **my** leadership. Didn't even couch it in friendly terms. Gave me all the same reasons I've heard before, why our naval base at Pearl Harbor is a gigantic mistake. He thinks that by having our fleet based out there, we're provoking the Japanese.

Why the hell would **they** want a war with us? I told him then, and I've been telling him since, that having our fleet in Hawaii is a cautionary symbol, reminding the Japanese that they simply can't gallop all over the Pacific as they please.

"You know better than I do that the Australians are with us on this. Hell, the British want us to send ships to Singapore; the Free French are afraid they're going to lose all of Indo-China. There are already Japanese troops around Hanoi, and we think they're building airfields. The Chinese have their hands full trying to win a war on their own land. Yes, I said war. The Japanese still refer to their invasion as the Chinese problem, as though Chiang Kai-shek caused the whole thing. If we have the fleet in Hawaii, at least we're showing that we care, for God's sake. Can you imagine what kind of message it would send to every single one of our allies, as well as to the Japanese, if we suddenly sailed away, pulled everybody back to California? But that's what Richardson insists we do. He beat me over the head with his so-called reasoning. The commander in chief of our entire Pacific fleet thinks the Japanese are too militant to be scared off by us having ships in Hawaii.

"I know something about the navy, Cordell. Big ships mean big power. So it seems to me that the more militant anyone is, including the Japanese, the more they'll respect someone else's military power. It should be simple, even to Admiral Richardson.

If you're stronger than the other guy, he'll mind his manners. Bringing the Pacific fleet back from Hawaii will look like a show of weakness. I do not understand how an experienced admiral cannot grasp that."

Hull said, "I've heard some of this. The secretary of war, the secretary of the navy, they've been harangued just like you were. When he was here in October, I ran into him at a dinner at the Willard. Admiral Richardson mentioned to me that he felt you were trying to bluff the Japanese, that we weren't serious about using the navy if a crisis erupted."

"Bluffs don't work, Cordell. This isn't about poker, it's about protecting our interests. The British, French, the rest of them, their survival's at stake. There is too much vulnerability in the South Pacific, and the Japanese seem entirely too interested in taking advantage of that. The only real naval presence south of the Philippines has been the British. But they can't afford to stand tall against the Japanese while they stand tall against Hitler."

Hull stretched his back. He was running out of fuel for the meeting, something he was becoming used to. "Mr. President, it has always been my policy when dealing with foreign ambassadors that we never issue any sort of threat unless we have the **strength** and the **will** to back it up. A threat without force behind it **is** a bluff, and as any card player knows, a bluff can be called with embarrassing results." He paused. "Since Japan entered into their Tripartite Pact with Germany and Italy, they made their intentions clear. I suspect Hitler has told the Japanese that whatever they choose to do in the eastern hemisphere is of no concern to the Germans. Hitler has already demonstrated that his goal is to subjugate as many peoples as he can, by brute force. I have no doubt that if the militant voices in the Japanese government were to believe that there would be no consequences from our side of the Pacific, they would begin the same kind of program in their half of the world. I assume Secretary Stimson agrees?"

"He wouldn't be my secretary of war if he didn't. You know better." Roosevelt pointed a finger at him. "Which is why our fleet must be maintained in Hawaii. I tried to explain that to Admiral Richardson, and he offers me insults, as though a mere civilian cannot possibly grasp such weighty military matters. It sounds to me as though you grasp them pretty well. Stimson said this morning that by keeping our fleet in Hawaii, at the very least we are communicating to everyone, friend and potential foe, that we're watching, we're paying attention."

Roosevelt paused, seemed to sag in his chair. "Richardson doesn't understand. I find that astonishing. Even if we're talking about our own territories, we're vulnerable ourselves, from the Philippines to Wake, Guam, Midway, and every other damn place in between. He just doesn't understand his role on this stage. The world, the entire world seems poised for some kind of explosion, and yet this man is hell bent on yanking our most valuable and powerful weapons out of Hawaii and hauling them back to California. And he's damned profane about how he talks to me about it."

"Mr. President, I heard much of this back in October. So, what stirred the pot now?"

"Right. Yes. This week, yet another damned letter from Hawaii, from Admiral Bloch, endorsed by Richardson. More of the same complaining, the same arguments, the same show of defiance." Roosevelt stopped, seemed to fight for energy. Hull had seen this before, knew to let the president take his time. "You know, Richardson served under me when I was secretary of the navy. Even then, I tried my damnedest to like the man. Didn't work. Now, I've given up **liking** him at all. Pretty certain he feels the same about me."

"That doesn't give him permission to disrespect his commander in chief."

"You're right. And so, right now, I have to perform the parts of this job that are both happy and miserable. I have the power to fire people who don't do what they're told. And sometimes I'm forced to fire someone who has served his country honorably for decades. In this case, it's the same man."

"So, you're going to relieve him?"

Roosevelt looked down, nodded slowly. "Hawaii is a long way away. We need a man out there who recognizes that there are capable people in Washington who know what they're doing, and when we tell him what to do, he doesn't bitch about it."

U.S. STATE DEPARTMENT, WASHINGTON, D.C.—
    TUESDAY, DECEMBER 17, 1940

He respected the secretary of war, could see the age in the man's face, the slow effort to pull himself up the stairs. Henry Stimson was four years older than Hull, and had even more experience in the highest workings of the government than Hull did. Stimson had been secretary of war for President Taft, secretary of state for Herbert Hoover, and in between had served in two wars, including a stint as governor-general of the Philippines. Now he was secretary of war yet again; in an unusual move by Roosevelt, he had chosen the man based on his extraordinary depth of experience, regardless of the fact that Stimson was a Republican.

Stimson was also staunchly in favor of Roosevelt's policies regarding the war, extremely aware that whatever the situation today, everything could change tomorrow, and probably would.

"Is he going to fire Admiral Richardson?"

Stimson leaned back in the chair, nodded slowly. "I believe the correct word is 'relieve.' Military people put a great deal of stock in those kinds of details."

Hull said, "Not sure if you know this, but there is a new ambassador from Japan. He'll be here next month sometime. Maybe we can reach some sort of understanding, find a way to defuse any potential problems."

Stimson laughed. "You still talk like a politician. Here's what you do. You meet with the Japanese ambassador . . . what's his name?"

"Nomura."

"Right. You meet with Mr. Nomura, and the first thing you do is smack him on the side of the head. Nice crisp shot. Knock his glasses across the room. I assume he wears glasses? They usually do."

"Actually, he has only one eye."

"Well, don't smack him too damn hard. Point is, you show him, **Look, Mr. Ambassador, this is what we do to our enemies. You wanna be our enemy?** Should work miracles in Tokyo."

Hull knew when he was being poked. "I assume that's what you did, when you sat in this office?"

"Oh, hell no. Might have started a war or something. But it looks to me like we're headed for a war anyway. Might as well get the first lick in."

Hull shook his head. "Or, I could talk to him first. Maybe **avoid** a war. Isn't that part of my job?"

Stimson stared at him. "Question is, is it a part of Mr. Nomura's job? Or is he just here to observe us, to see how we're observing him? Chess match. And I don't trust those bastards one bit. They've cozied up to Hitler, for God's sake. Whatever they're trying to do, it won't be in our favor."

"I suppose it's my job to figure that out, and if there's a bomb here, like so many of you military people seem to believe, it's my job to defuse it. That reminds me, I need to inform our own ambassador to Japan, Joe Grew, just what's going to happen with Admiral Richardson. If there is a front line to all this potential mess, Grew's on it."

Stimson thought a moment, said, "You know, it's one thing for a man to argue his principles, to defend what he thinks is right. You might even suggest a thing or two to your superiors. But Richardson made a mistake. No, he made two. First, he forgot that our president is an old navy man himself, that the United States Navy might as well be called Roosevelt's Boats. The president loves his ships, loves that service more than any other. If he could serve on a ship today, he would. Admiral Richardson treated his commander in chief like Roosevelt's sticking his nose in places it doesn't belong. That's mistake number one."

"Number two?"

"By God, Cordell, he did the worst thing he could have done to his commander in chief. He hurt his feelings!"

———

On January 5, 1941, the order was sent from Washington to the Headquarters of the Office of the Commander in Chief, U.S., at Pearl Harbor, Hawaii. If Admiral James Richardson had no wish to maintain his command in Hawaii, his wish was being granted. Though the fleet would remain, Admiral Richardson would not. He had been relieved.

His replacement was a man known well by the president, a former subordinate of Roosevelt's who had worked his way up the navy's chain of command by efficient, if not altogether brilliant, service. The fifty-eight-year-old was a Naval Academy graduate, which was almost essential for this level of command, an enormous stepping-stone to an even higher position. The command at Pearl Harbor would put him squarely in the spotlight, giving him the responsibility and authority for the entire Pacific fleet. Where Admiral James Richardson had tried to shape Washington's strategy in the Pacific by his own bluster, his replacement was seen by the War Department, and by his president, as a man who would be far more agreeable and would follow the instructions Washington wanted him to obey. His name was Husband E. Kimmel.

# THREE

## Biggs

JACKSONVILLE, FLORIDA—SUNDAY, JANUARY 12, 1941

He had followed the instructions sent by the navy, riding another bus up to Jacksonville, where he would board the train taking him most of the way north, a journey halfway across the country. It was more than two weeks after Christmas, but the grimy walls of the train station were still decked out with giant wreaths. There were other holiday decorations as well, and Biggs couldn't help asking himself if someone had forgotten to do their job. Maybe by March, someone would realize it was time to take them down.

The Christmas season had not meant anything to Biggs for many years. Like most children, he had embraced the joys that came from innocence and gifts, any gifts. With age came reality, that his father had nothing to celebrate. His mother had still tried, baking sweets, but even that effort had faded away, the small pie or cake now more likely owing to the generosity of a neighbor.

This year had been one more dismal experience, made worse by a visit from a pair of his mother's cousins, making the short drive from the coast, near St. Augustine. They came with presents that no one wanted, Biggs feigning gratefulness for a box of assorted fishing tackle. He offered up as much enthusiasm as he could, smiling promises that they'd serve him well on his next outing. Even his father had chuckled at that, a discreet wink between them, both men knowing that Biggs had never fished.

But useless gifts could be ignored. What was worse was the subtle message brought into the Biggs home by two women too judgmental toward the meager furnishings in their cousin's home, the lack of an automobile, and the unfashionable dress of Biggs's mother. Biggs despised one in particular, a large, jiggly woman who knew nothing of moderation when it came to perfume. Within minutes of her arrival, the entire house had been infected with the aroma that Biggs could only guess had been squeezed from flowers that prospered at the town's garbage dump.

They had stayed for two days, finding accommodations at one of Palatka's meager motels, reinforcing their arrogant sense of superiority about their place in the world. After two insufferable days, the women had slid into their car, with too many hugs and fake smiles. Biggs had satisfied his obligation to his mother by giving a brief hug to each, the perfume now a part of him. He had then made his own escape. He had nowhere to go, but he knew that once the two women were gone, his parents would erupt into their inevitable fight. It was completely predictable, his father blasting out the customary insults toward his wife's family. But she defended them, always, as though it were required, no matter their subtle insults to her, their self-satisfied **victory** over their station in life. No matter her own embarrassment, they were, after all, family. Even the hostility of her husband couldn't erase that.

As his father's voice had risen behind him, Biggs had wandered toward the Russo home, knowing that the Christmas season there had a far different meaning. Ray had always embraced the holiday, the notion of **family** meaning so much more to him. Even now, with the holiday past, there was a delicious aroma drifting out of the Russo kitchen. Ray's mother was a magnificent cook, and if there was little money for an elaborate feast, she created one from her own ingenuity and the wisdom handed her by generations of family from Southern Italy.

He was tempted, drawn by the smells, but he wouldn't just wander in. He could never avoid a sense that he was trespassing on the kind of joy he wasn't allowed to feel, though he knew that Ray and his entire family would have welcomed him. It was a spirit Biggs would never feel in his own home. There was always room, always a plate for one more.

As he and Ray waited for the train, Biggs had been surprised to see others waiting as well, young men sizing up each other. He didn't know them, some younger, likely right out of high school. Scattered about were teary-eyed parents, hearty handshakes from proud fathers. From Ray's family, the tears flowed, Luca Russo cradling his son's head between his hands, soft words, Ray nodding, tears of his own.

Biggs's mother had made the bus trip with him, an eye-opening experience for a woman who had rarely been outside Palatka. Biggs had not expected his father to come, but he saw him now, a sudden surprise. It was obvious that Clarence had taken the next bus, and Biggs watched him moving slowly, sheepishly through the entryway of the station. Biggs waved toward him, caught his eye, Clarence moving closer, no bluster, no anger, just a tired, em-barrassed man who rarely went out in public. As he drew closer, Biggs understood his father's hesita-tion. He smelled strongly of fish.

"Thanks for coming, Pop. I'm glad you did. It might be a while before I can see you again."

His mother said nothing to her husband, took Biggs's hand, an emotional squeeze. "We'll miss you, Thomas. It won't be the same with you gone."

He put a hand over hers, no words. His father ignored the gestures, seemed distracted, eyeing the crowd, as though some kind of threat might suddenly appear.

"Not been here in a while. Looks like they cleaned the place up a little."

Clarence still avoided Biggs's eyes, noticed the Russo family, said, "That your buddy, right? Italian kid?"

"Yeah, Pop. Ray Russo."

Clarence grunted, offered nothing more. The voices of the crowd seemed to drift over them like a blanket, hiding the awkwardness of their own silence. Biggs eyed the train schedule, flapping numbers on the wall.

"Looks like they're boarding." He looked at his mother, saw her tears. "It's okay, Mom. I'm gonna be great. It's a good place for me to be. And there's Ray, too. I already got a friend."

She squeezed his arm one last time, released it, said slowly, "You'll do real good. Make sure you write us letters. Tell us where you are."

"Sure thing, Mom."

He looked at his father, still gazing around the tall ceilings.

"I gotta go, Pop."

"So, how far does the train go?"

"I'll end up in Chicago. It's a bus the rest of the way."

"Long damn way. I thought the navy floated boats. Not sure what you're gonna do in Illinois, for God's sake."

"It's the training center, Pop. Basic training. I gotta start there."

There was another grunt, then a long silent minute. Biggs checked the board again.

"I need to go. They're boarding."

His mother clasped her hands in front of her, managed a smile. "Be careful, Thomas. You can come home anytime. We love you. Don't forget that."

Clarence looked at his son finally, seemed to struggle for words. "Listen . . . um . . . Look, I ain't never had nothing to give you. A man's supposed to take care of his family, and I know I ain't done such a good job." Biggs wanted to interrupt, something holding him back. **Let him speak.** "Your mother knows how hard it's been." Clarence looked down. "I'm nobody. I done nothing. I gave nothing to nobody. Except I gave **you** to her. You and her . . . you're all I got." His eyes came up again, and Biggs saw him blinking away tears. "Boy, I just want one thing from you. Do **good.** Do something you'll be proud of. Do something they'll remember you for."

GREAT LAKES, ILLINOIS—FRIDAY, FEBRUARY 28, 1941

"Take a good look around you! Look every man in the eyes. Do it!"

Biggs obeyed, the rest of the company as well, the faces so familiar, all those men who had been through so many weeks of the same ordeal. No one was smiling, every man expecting some arbitrary punishment merely for turning his head. They were used to that now, the part of basic training that served no more purpose than to remind them just who was in charge. Biggs stared again to the front, eyes on the man they all knew as the "Recruit Division Commander." He stood in front of them, hands locked behind his back, his winter jacket open to the brutal cold, a familiar display of toughness from the man nearly all of the recruits had grown to hate.

After a long moment, he said, "That's enough. Eyes front!" He paused, a quick scan through the formation. "Are you cold, pukes? Hell, it's damn near spring! You got your damn jackets on, so if I hear any teeth chattering, or anybody bitching, you can all strip down to your skivvies. Any complaints? Good. Now listen up!"

He crossed his arms now, his fierce expression mellowing. "This is a day every one of you will remember. Every man here has made it through basic training. You don't need a drill instructor, no more RDC. From now on, you will refer to me as Chief Monroe. But remember this. When you arrived here, there were a hell of a lot more of you. Some of you washed out. Just **quit.** They're back home now, crying to their mamas that this was **too hard.** Why? They weren't any weaker or any stupider than you pukes. They just didn't believe me. Six weeks ago, I told them, like I told you, **you can do this.** You want to be a sailor, you'll **have** to do this. The first day you were here, I told you that if you'd work, you'd make it through basic training. I told you that all you had to do was pay attention to **me,** and do what the hell you were told.

"Most of you, once in a while, you needed a boot up your ass. But every one of you, you had to learn to eat right, walk right, talk right, you had to learn what a **head** was, a **piece,** boondockers, swabs, the brig, chow, galley, and fish. You did enough push-ups to shove this ground halfway to China. You ran so many miles around this base, you coulda run back to your mamas. But you **didn't.** You've learned what the navy expects of you, what the officers will expect of you, what the men around you expect of you. When you arrived here, most of you thought a **ship** was just a big boat, and a **screw** was something you did in the back of your daddy's car. You've learned about mechanics, about gunnery, about what you need to do to function on a ship, any ship in the navy. And a hell of a lot more."

He paused. "The army's out there somewhere, ground-pounders getting all impressed with the rifle in their hands, playing with a bayonet, covering up their tender ears when a single artillery piece goes off. But you . . . a good many of you will either be serving aboard or serving alongside a floating weapon that is more powerful than your grand-daddies could ever imagine. A light cruiser today has more firepower than any **fleet** of ships from years ago. The entire Union Navy in the Civil War couldn't stand up to a single destroyer today. And even today, right now, there is no **modern** navy anywhere in the world superior to ours. To **yours.**" Monroe stopped, scanned them all. "It is my duty to inform you, all of you, no matter how useless you might be, that officially, my job is finished. Your basic training is complete. You may stand at ease."

The outburst was spontaneous, hands in the air, a hard cheer that Biggs shared. Monroe allowed himself a slight smile, but he wasn't done just yet.

"Listen up, you pukes. I got one more thing to say, and you better pay attention. Your assignments will come later today, and I had nothing to do with that. So don't come bitching to me if you end up on a garbage scow on Lake Erie. There's a good chance you'll be assigned to duty in the Atlantic, whether escorting cargo or helping find those damn Nazi U-boats. Some of you might keep in tight to the East Coast, but don't think that's easy duty. I'm hearing that in places like Miami or Charleston, Boston, even New York, there's more stupidity from civilians than even from you misfits. They won't shut down the city lights at night, and U-boats are taking advantage, using those lights to locate and silhouette merchant ships. A damn freighter goes up in a fireball, and Miami Beach gets all excited, like it's the damned Fourth of July. The war isn't just way the hell over in Europe. It's close by. So no bitching if you get assigned destroyer duty out of Norfolk, or Savannah, or anyplace else.

"Those of you who showed more brains on paper than you ever showed me, you might get assigned to engineer or radio school. If you put in for some other kind of specialty, you'll find out if you measured up, if the navy thinks as much of you as **you** do. Most all of you will leave here as an E-1. Bottom rung. Some will be notified they've advanced to E-2. Don't get a swelled head. Doesn't mean you outrank anybody, or you're gonna get a big fat raise. What it **will** do is give you a better chance at whatever job you're hoping to get.

"And hear this. Those of you who are sent out to deep water, you might end up in England, protecting the route that's keeping our **ally** from starving. This Hitler fellow is a bad problem. Your mamas don't want to see a bunch of Nazi bastards marching down Main Street. So do whatever it takes. Do your duty, and make sure the brass knows it was **me** who taught you how to do it. Unless you screw up. Then I never heard of you." He paused, an afterthought. "Oh, and some of you might get sent to the Pacific. Probably will. They say there might be some trouble in the Philippines, and that the Japanese are stomping hard all over China. But it's a big ocean, and one island's pretty much like another out there. At least you'll get a suntan."

He was straightening the sheet on his cot, perfect corners, and he looked toward Ray.

"The chief surprised me. I think he actually cares about us."

Russo laughed with the others around him. "Yeah, go tell him that. See how many push-ups he'll make you do."

Biggs straightened his dress shoes, made a mental note to polish them one more time. He said, "Any idea where you'll go?"

Russo shrugged. "I know where I **want** to go. But I'll go where they send me. You too. Doesn't much matter what we want. I put in a request for battleship duty. Not sure if they pay any attention to that. Been looking at 'em in a navy magazine. Huge, beautiful. And like the chief said, it's a war machine. It can level an entire city."

Biggs checked his locker again, neat perfection, and said, "Yeah, I put in for that too. I'm trying not to give it that much thought. Anyplace will be the navy. Hope they'll give me a chance to be a medical tech or something like that."

Ray looked at him, tilted his head slightly, as did others as well. "You really put in for that? I thought you were kidding. What the hell you wanna mess around with bandages and stuff? Blood makes me wanna puke. And you sure as hell ain't giving **me** any damn shot."

Behind Russo, another man, Parker. "Maybe he just **likes** giving **short-arm** inspections."

The laughter flooded the barracks, a good joke at Biggs's expense. His reasons wouldn't matter to most of them, and he just absorbed their humor, knew it was a gibe he'd probably hear again. They had already experienced the short-arm inspections when they first arrived at the training center, a doctor or corpsman examining their genitals for signs of venereal disease, or any other contagion they might have brought from home.

The men turned back to their own equipment, and Ray was still looking at him, serious now. "You know, corpsman's school could work for you. You're smart, for sure. Pay's probably a lot better too. You planning on going after that?"

"Not yet. If they let me, I'll start as a hospital apprentice, an HA, be assigned to help the ship's doctor. I guess the smaller ships might only have a corpsman, so I'd be there to help him. That could help me get into corpsman training, for sure. Either way, it might give me a chance at a good job later on."

Ray nodded. "Like I say, you're smart, Tommy. All those tests they gave us, I probably screwed up every one of 'em. I bet you did real good."

Biggs shrugged. "Maybe. We'll find out pretty quick. I'm just happy as hell we made it through. The chief was right: A bunch of 'em didn't."

The cots were made, the men checking the neatness of each other's, a friendly inspection to help anyone avoid a last dose of punishment from Chief

Monroe. The door slapped open at the far end of the barracks, a sharp voice.

"Ten hut!"

Biggs responded immediately, instinct now, moved to stiff attention at the foot of his cot. The voice was unfamiliar, and there was no sign of the chief.

"Listen up. When I call your name you will report to the clerks outside. They'll have your assignments. Stand at ease." The man paused, a nod of his head. "Congratulations, men. You're sailors in the United States Navy."

The names came alphabetically, Biggs fourth on the list. He stepped outside, following the first three men, saw a long table, alphabetical sections, those from other barracks lining up as well. Four clerks sat with boxes of envelopes, and Biggs moved to the first station, waited behind the others, beneath the sign in bold black letters "A-G."

The men in front of him gave their names, each man receiving a sealed envelope. One man moved back past him, said, "God, I'm nervous as hell. We supposed to open this right here?"

Biggs shared the man's anxiety, said, "Hell if I know." It was his turn now, and he said to the clerk, "Biggs, Thomas."

"Here you go. Good luck, sailor."

He moved away from the table, others still lining up, and fingered the brown envelope, thick enough to hold several papers. Details, he thought. They have to spell it all out. Well, open it. His hands were sweating in the cold, his breath a steady fog. The voice in his head pushed him again to tear the paper open, but he felt paralyzed, a hard thumping in his chest. He moved slowly back toward the barracks, saw Russo, falling in line at the other end of the table.

"Tommy! Where're you going? What's it say?"

Biggs looked at him, shrugged. "Don't know. Haven't opened it yet."

Russo was at the table now, and Biggs heard him.

"Russo, Raphaele."

Biggs waited for him, and Russo was there quickly, seemed to pulse with energy, his own envelope in his hands. "Well? What's yours say?"

Biggs tried to ignore the pounding in his chest. "Open yours first. I'm too damn nervous."

Russo didn't hesitate, ripped at the paper, said, "We're all nervous, Tommy. Might be the biggest day of my life." The contents of Russo's envelope slid out into his hand, and he read, seemed to sag. "What the hell? The **Curtiss**? I been assigned to some ship called the USS **Curtiss.** I'm rated an E-1, seaman apprentice. I report to Bremerton, Washington. I ain't going to the Atlantic? Well, hell."

Biggs was annoyed with his friend. "Hey! They coulda stuck you on that garbage scow, right? You're going on a navy ship, the real deal."

Behind them, Biggs heard whoops, a few curses, the full variety of responses to the assignments.

Russo said, "You're right. Just a little disappointed, that's all. But it'll be okay. Yeah, it's a real ship. I'll check it out—there's gotta be somebody around here can tell me more about it. Says here, **seaplane tender.** Well, that's okay. Taking care of airplanes. Go ahead, what's yours?"

Biggs took a long breath, the nervous chill still inside him. He tore open the envelope, thought of the **Curtiss** . . . seaplane tender. Yeah, that's good. I'd take that. The paper slid into his fingers and he hesitated, couldn't avoid thoughts of the chief's garbage scow. He opened the fold, read.

Russo grabbed his arm. "Damn it all, where're you going? You got a real ship?"

Biggs read the words again, his eyes wide in disbelief. "I made E-2. They're assigning me as a hospital apprentice. Just what I was hoping for." He read the next page, his eyes wider still. "Jesus God, Ray. I got a battleship. I'm going to the USS **Arizona.**"

# FOUR

===

# Yamamoto

BATTLESHIP NAGATO, ARIAKE BAY, JAPAN—
MONDAY, JANUARY 27, 1941

**❝I**t pains me to say this to you, Admiral. But at the Ministry, and elsewhere, there are some who feel you are insane. With my apologies, sir.”

Yamamoto looked up from his cards, smiled. “You cannot distract me, my friend. I raise your bet. Double it, in fact.”

He watched as Fukudome looked at his own cards, and Yamamoto could see from the blink of the man's eyes that Fukudome had nothing in his hand.

Fukudome laid his cards down, shook his head. “You have bested me again, sir. I fear I cannot defeat you at this game, or any other.”

“How about we play gin then?”

"Please, sir, no. I cannot offer you any challenge. Surely there is something I can request from the orderlies, some refreshment? Or surely there must be a report from some department on this ship that requires our attention."

Yamamoto had already spent the afternoon in grouchy boredom, and his usual relief, and greatest joy, was gambling. If there was no one else to engage him, and thus be victimized by him, Shigeru Fukudome, his chief of staff, would graciously endure the punishment. Yamamoto was grateful for the man's efforts, though he had little patience for an opponent who couldn't offer much of a challenge.

Yamamoto sat back, tried to ignore the anxiousness, a jittery coldness in his chest. "Where is Admiral Onishi? He is late."

Fukudome stood stiffly, made a short bow. "Sir, I shall check with the deck officer one more time. I will inform him that the admiral should be escorted to your wardroom with all haste."

Yamamoto waved him away. "Go. Just bring him to me."

Fukudome moved out quickly, with typical efficiency.

Yamamoto drummed his fingers on the table, ran his hands over the playing cards, a game forming in his mind, some kind of bet made just for picking up a random card. It was his constant exercise; if there was no game to be had, he would create one. And if there was a game, there had to be an opponent, anyone who could offer a challenge for Yamamoto, so that his victory, whether through skill or luck, would be so much sweeter.

Even as a young man, he had been drawn to games of chance, nearly any game or any chance. He bet on athletics, on random events in nature, on the efficiency of his deck crew, men who had no idea that their various duties around the ship were being tallied by their admiral. He was never far from the fantasy that one day he would retire from the Imperial Japanese Navy, move his family to Monte Carlo, become a professional gambler. He had traveled there before, seemed always to win, a handsome profit that he imagined could be parlayed into great wealth. But for now, there were duties, always duties, and these days, there was a frustration far more dangerous than boredom on his flagship.

The knock came now, the unmistakable rhythm of his chief of staff.

"Enter." Fukudome opened the door, then stood aside, allowing the other man to enter.

"Sir, Admiral Onishi."

Yamamoto managed a smile, thought, **Finally.** Onishi seemed to march into the wardroom, halting abruptly, standing tall above him. To the diminutive Yamamoto, Onishi seemed gigantic, with an athletic physique that made him an imposing figure in any group. He served as chief of staff of the Eleventh Air Fleet, and Yamamoto considered him a good friend, one who shared Yamamoto's enthusiasm for the airplane. Even more, Onishi was one of the few men with whom Yamamoto could safely discuss any topic, including those subjects that might bring down the wrath of the government in Tokyo. And to Yamamoto's delight, Onishi enjoyed gambling.

Yamamoto said, "You may be seated, Admiral. Now, you may tell me your thoughts. Hold nothing back. I trust your opinions, you know that."

Onishi removed an envelope from his jacket, spread the contents on the table. Yamamoto recognized his own writing, saw notes in the margins, said, "I can see that you do have opinions."

Onishi picked up a page, read for several seconds, and Yamamoto could see theatrics, a delay for dramatic effect. He would allow Onishi his game, but it was to be a short game. Onishi seemed to understand that as well.

"Admiral Yamamoto, you have designed a plan that for all purposes resembles the most intriguing game of chance I have ever seen."

Yamamoto smiled broadly. "That is why we must do it. It is why I must lead it. It is why you must assist me."

Onishi said, "I have concerns that we must discuss."

"That is why you are here, of course. I sent that proposal to the naval minister the same day I sent it to you. I have not yet heard anything of substance."

"Are you surprised?"

"I am surprised by very little that comes from Tokyo."

Fukudome had taken up his customary position, standing to Yamamoto's left, and Yamamoto looked that way, said, "Bring in the orderly, with a bottle of whatever decent spirits we have. My friend here is thirsty."

Onishi smiled. "Very much so, sir."

Fukudome returned quickly with the orderly, a small man named Omi, older, many years in service to the admiral. Omi poured from a porcelain bottle, filling a small glass. Fukudome pointed toward Onishi and the orderly gently set the glass in front of him. Onishi tasted, then gave an approving nod.

"I feel much better now. Thank you." He sipped again, said, "You must believe the Ministry respects your instincts, your experience. Surely they will respond approvingly to your plan."

Fukudome motioned toward the small man, a silent order. **Leave.** Onishi started to protest, but the orderly was already gone.

Yamamoto had watched the scene, said, "I am sorry, my friend, but I require you to keep a sharp mind."

Onishi put the glass to one side, Fukudome removing it quickly. Onishi laughed. "Ah, yes. I am in the presence of the admiral who does not drink spirits. I should have remembered that."

"Take no offense, Takijiro. I do not object to

anyone who enjoys a healthy drink. If we were in a card game right now, I would insist you fill your glass many times. Dull senses make for careless decisions. I admit that I once enjoyed a glass or two, but there was a time, years ago . . . My only memory of the occasion is that I woke up in a ditch beside a road. It was an experience I vowed never to repeat."

Onishi studied the maps again. "You realize that the Naval Ministry might believe that you had consumed a bottle or two when you created this plan. I admit, sir, I might agree with them."

Yamamoto had enough doubts as it was, knew that Onishi was simply speaking those doubts aloud. He looked down, chose the words he had rehearsed in his mind for weeks now.

"They are locked into the old ways. The Naval Ministry, the army, all of them believe that Japan's strength lies within the **man,** that it is the spiritual perfection of the samurai that wins battles. That if your enemy is not pure of heart, does not possess a warrior's heart, he will fall to you, just by your will alone. Perhaps in the days of the sword. But now . . . it is absurdity."

Fukudome seemed uneasy, and Onishi looked at him, laughed.

"You need not fear the words of your commander. No matter his blasphemy, or who might disagree with him, he is correct."

Yamamoto looked at Onishi. "My chief of staff has doubts about my ideas. He is wrong, of course.

But he is still my chief of staff. Sit down, Shigeru. No doubt you are among many who believe this plan is a measure of my foolishness. Or insanity."

Fukudome sat, after a brief bow. "Thank you, Admiral. I shall remain discreet."

"Of course you shall. There is no alternative." Yamamoto returned to the maps, pushed them aside, said to Onishi, "The Ministry, every high-ranking official of this government, **every one of them,** believes that Japan's destiny, its wise course, is to engage in an all-out war with the great powers, and defeat them by tactics that worked exactly once, more than thirty years ago against the Russians. The scale is much larger now, the entire Pacific Ocean; the enemies are far stronger, whether the British or the Americans. But our goal, our **methods** remain the same.

"They insist that we should commit some act of aggression against, say, the Philippines. But that is only a ruse. We hold our fleets back, waiting for the response. The Americans must respond, of course, and so they will send their mighty navy across the ocean, seeking justice, seeking to rescue the afflicted. But we have planned well. We pick at them with our submarines, we bite off small pieces of their fleet, reducing their strength as they cross the great ocean. Then, when they reach a place of our choosing, we attack them with all our forces. The Americans shall be utterly destroyed, their ships sent to the bottom of the ocean." He paused. "It is a grand story, is it not? We must surely be celebrated by our children, and their children, for centuries to come."

Onishi nodded, said, "I have been hearing much of this great strategy. There are few in the government or in the Naval Ministry who talk of anything else. They also speak incessantly about the power of our battleships, the finest in the world. With such beasts, such magnificent weapons, we cannot be defeated. Even now the Naval Ministry begs for the funding to build even more of the great ships, larger, more powerful. It is foolishness. But no one in Tokyo can be convinced of that. They insist that the larger the ship, the easier it will be to conquer the world. Perhaps the stars as well."

Yamamoto glanced at Fukudome. "His gift for sarcasm rivals my own. Admiral Onishi knows well of a man named Billy Mitchell, an American who fought to convince his reluctant military to accept the value of the airplane. They are still reluctant, so much so that Mitchell died without receiving the credit he was due. Like us, the Americans place extreme value on the great ships of their fleet, the mighty battleship. The days of those weapons have passed, but singing a new song only draws laughter, mockery. Mitchell suffered for it, and I regret that he did not live to see his ideas celebrated as they deserved to be." He looked at Onishi. "This is not a lesson I must teach **you.** That is why I revealed my plan to you even as I offered it to the Ministry."

He paused. "The Americans value their battleships as we do, but those will not win a war. The aircraft carrier is the greatest tool either of us possesses."

"I agree completely, sir. Time will prove that we are correct. The airplane is so inexpensive to build, we can fill the skies."

Yamamoto felt the familiar gloom, said, "Unfortunately, those who make such decisions are holding tightly to the old ways. They fantasize that it is still 1905, that we will once again fight the Russians, a glorious victory with our great ships. And that is why I designed this plan, and why I need your support, and that of many others, to convince the Ministry and the naval staff that they must look upward." He glanced at the papers again. "As it is for so many of us, the battleship is a **symbol** of great importance to the Americans. It is a beautiful mass of steel and guns that takes the breath away from civilians, from congressmen, that inflates their president with pride. I must convince the Naval Ministry that striking a blow against those **symbols** could have much more power than any salvo from our cannons."

Onishi seemed puzzled. "So, you are proposing we target only their heaviest ships? What of their aircraft carriers? You know my feelings—that if we engage in a war with the Americans, or anyone else, our airpower must be superior. I believe that right now, it is. Eliminating their aircraft carriers will win us the war."

Fukudome spoke up now. "Forgive me, Admiral. But what 'war' are we fighting? There is talk, certainly, all those speeches that come out of Tokyo, but we are not at war with anyone. Why do you speak as though we are?"

There was a silent moment, and Yamamoto said, "Because we **will** be at war. There is not enough wisdom in our government, in our army, to understand why they should avoid that. They speak too often of our pride, our rightful place, our **destiny** in this world. They believe the Pacific Ocean belongs to Japan, that it is our **right** to take what we require. They are already planning the occupation of Southeast Asia, of the Dutch East Indies. There are great resources to be had—petroleum, metals, as well as deepwater ports and airfields. Our destiny. No one seems aware that this entitlement might have a cost." He slid one paper toward Onishi. "Here, as I said, they are insisting on a plan to invade the Philippines, that perfect bait to lure the American fleet to its death."

Onishi said, "What would happen if the Americans did not respond? What if they conceded the loss of the Philippines, rather than put their fleet at risk?"

Yamamoto feigned amazement. "What absurdity! Such a thing is not possible. The plan will become reality, because the plan says it will happen. Those who have created this strategy cannot be wrong, because the plan says they will not be wrong. The plan says we will be victorious, and so, we will be victorious."

He sat back, crossed his arms. Onishi leaned his arms on the table, shook his head.

"And so, you offer them a different plan?"

"I am under none of their illusions that my plan fulfills some kind of destiny. Nor do I think their minds can be changed. We do require the resources of Indo-China, Sumatra, Bali, all the rest. The army has proposed that in time, we occupy India and Australia, and no one dares to disagree with the army. Of course, the Philippines cannot be left unmolested, since the Americans would threaten our left flank as we move southward. So, we must strike there. But I do not believe the fantasy that such a move will invite the American navy to its certain doom. They will not rush across the Pacific in a blind need for vengeance. They have not grown strong by foolishness. And so, I have suggested an alternative, to delay any interference from the Americans that would impede all of this 'destiny' we hear about."

Onishi shook his head, fumbled with the empty whiskey glass. "I am concerned that your goal is too ambitious. The Ministry will never believe you can create a plan to destroy the American fleet."

Yamamoto stood now, energized by the argument. "I do not believe we can destroy the American fleet. But I do propose that we damage it severely. I propose that we strike their battleships and their aircraft

carriers, their magnificent symbols. I propose that
the message we send to the American people and
their government is that we have these capabilities.
We must instill the fear in them that we are a mad
and unpredictable people, who could strike them
at any place, at any time. We do not have to attack California. We just have to convince them that
we **might.** This attack is not about victory, about
winning a war. It is about delaying them, keeping
them back, damaging their military might and their
pride. My duty as commander in chief of the fleet is
to use that fleet to support the strategies of others,
to allow us a more secure passage for all those lofty
goals to the south that Tokyo insists upon."

Onishi stared at the papers in front of him. "Sir,
surely you accept that the challenges are . . . well,
they are overwhelming. Consider the distance between our ports and Hawaii, the need for refueling
our ships, the number of aircraft carriers required
to transport sufficient numbers of planes. And, to
me, the greatest challenge of all: the need for absolute secrecy. How do we ensure that the Americans
do not learn of this plan, and are not waiting for
us? We would be sending an armada across an enormous span of open ocean. If we are spotted by a
single American submarine, a single reconnaissance
plane, even a merchant ship, the entire plan could
collapse, or worse, could result in annihilation of
our entire force. As soon as a declaration of war is
issued, they will come to full alert, in every way."

"Then there will be no declaration of war. The assault itself will be all the declaration required. Let us just say, it will be **obvious.** In the meantime, yes, the entire operation must be kept utterly secret. And you are correct in your appraisal. It is **challenging.**"

"What would you have me do? What is my duty here?"

Yamamoto pointed a finger at him. "Your duty is to create pilots: Choose them well, train them, teach them. They need not know what they are training for. That will come in time. You have an admirable passion for the airplane. Put that to practical use."

Fukudome stood, pacing slowly, eyes down. "I do not understand how you believe we can defeat the Americans. Such talk is foolishness." He paused, recognizing the bluntness of his words. "Please forgive me, Admiral, but I am concerned that you are putting yourself in great danger, that the government will use any defeat against the Americans as an excuse to remove you from your command. And this plan, it cannot succeed. Do you not see that?"

"I never suggested we would defeat the Americans, Shigeru. For several months we may prevail, achieve magnificent victories over unprepared opponents. But I am under no illusion that we have the ability and the resources to outlast the United States or Britain. We can damage great ships, and they will build more. We can shoot their airplanes from the sky, and they will build more. If the war should last for a year, two years, we will not prevail." He paused. "I know you do not support this plan, that you feel I am insane. But all I propose is an attack that will paralyze the Americans, for perhaps six months. That's all. My ideas are no more grandiose than that."

He paused, and Onishi seemed surprised.

"You say we will not prevail. And yet this assault would start the very war you don't think we can win. I have never heard you express such a contradiction, sir."

Yamamoto let out a long breath. "Never assume I favor war. There are decisions being made by men whose only talent is mindless ambition, and they have made a war inevitable. They believe that if they say anything loudly enough, it will become truth. We signed that absurd Tripartite Pact with the Germans, and now we mimic the ways of Hitler, and preach war with the United States. What do you suppose will happen if the Germans defeat the British, and the Americans defeat us? Does no one realize that the Germans will happily march into Japan and pick up the pieces for themselves? America is not a nation of conquest. Germany is. And now, because it is **exciting,** because we must establish our **greatness,** we will conquer as well. There will be a great cost in that, unless we are perfectly successful, unless we defeat everyone who will stand in our way. Where do we find that strength? Where do we find the money? Yes, **money.** It costs enormous sums of money to fight a war. America has money, a great deal of it, a great deal more than Japan."

Yamamoto looked down at his hands, flexed the three fingers on one hand, stretched the stiffness in his back. "I am fifty-seven years old, my friends. I carry the wounds of our great victory over the Russians. It cost me two of my fingers. But it cost Japan its humility. Those who hope for war only know victory. It is too late for me to lust after heroics, seeking medals and shrines. I have had a very good career; I have earned respect. I have taught young fliers their craft, and I have taught young officers how to lead."

He paused. "If we strike the Americans hard, if we so shock them from their complacent superiority, then it is possible they will turn away from making war. Or, at least, they will take their time. But for all those here who claim they are weak? I have been to their factories in Chicago and Detroit. In Texas, they have oil wells that stretch beyond the horizon. No, they are not weak. But a great many American civilians are passionately against a war. Perhaps there is a small chance to show those people how ugly a war can be. If we can damage and frighten them, they might persuade their government to keep away, at least for a while. That would make our army very unhappy, of course. They hope to charge with their bayonets at every nation on this earth. But it is the only hope Japan has to survive."

Onishi seemed to animate, fists pounding slowly on the table. "So many challenges. How can you believe this will work? I am very skeptical. There are difficulties even you cannot foresee."

Yamamoto was impatient now. "Of course there are challenges! Of course there are unforeseen difficulties. This is not a game of mah-jongg. We must strike the Americans where they are vulnerable. I do not intend to wait for them to understand the value of the airplane as you and I do."

"When do you expect to hear from the Naval Ministry? Do you believe they will approve your plan?"

Yamamoto sagged in his chair. "There is a fable, of a man pushing a boulder up a steep hill. Right now, I am that man."

Onishi leaned forward, his arms on the table. "I shall offer support as I can, sir. I can assure you that the air squadrons will accept this duty with enthusiasm."

Fukudome seemed frustrated, said to Onishi, "Then, you believe this plan is practicable?"

Onishi smiled. "I believe this plan is **possible.**"

Fukudome stood, moved closer to the map sketches on Yamamoto's table. "Sir, is there no other way to trap the American fleet? Why not attack them piecemeal on the open sea?"

Yamamoto had been through this with Fukudome before, had no patience for it.

"Piecemeal is useless. No one retreats from

piecemeal. The American Pacific fleet is headquartered in Hawaii, and there is nowhere in this hemisphere where they are as vulnerable as they are at Pearl Harbor. If you want the lion's cubs, you enter the lion's den. I want as many of those **cubs** to be as damaged as possible."

He was feeling exhausted, wanted a moment alone with Onishi. He looked at Fukudome, said, "Go, find Commander Isho—I owe him a dinner. He's the only man on this ship who has beaten me at bridge."

Fukudome bowed, moved out, the door closing. Yamamoto waited a long second, said, "I don't know how this will end, my friend."

"We can be successful, sir. But there are many details, much planning, training, all of it. This is not something that can be done in a week or two."

"I know. I need someone to plan the air assaults, to work with me on completing the details, who knows carrier aircraft, who understands the kinds of weapons we require."

Onishi smiled. "I've given it a good deal of thought. Are you familiar with Commander Minoru Genda?"

Yamamoto said, "Not sure."

"Perhaps you know him from his acquired nickname, Genda the Lunatic. He is a powerful advocate for air assaults."

Yamamoto shook his head. "We might all be called lunatics if this doesn't work."

"It will work, sir."

"You said it was only **possible.**"

"That just means it's a gamble, sir."

Yamamoto smiled. "Yes, it is. But I cannot escape the question. If it is destined for me to commit hara-kiri, I have always wondered: How much does it hurt?"

# FIVE

# Hull

It was called Magic, the result of an exhaustive amount of labor by a very small and very secret group of American cryptologists led by Lieutenant Colonel William Friedman. In August 1940, after more than a year and a half of examining Japanese coded messages, Friedman and his team succeeded in cracking the Japanese **Purple** code, the primary pathway for secret messages between the Japanese foreign ministry and Japanese embassies and consulates all over the world. For the first time, the men at the highest levels of the American government had access to the Japanese frame of mind, the vast trove of messages that filled the air to and from Tokyo. While Magic did not penetrate Japanese military codes, it opened a clear window into Japanese diplomatic communications.

The existence of Magic was a secret of the highest priority, and to limit the risk of discovery, the cryptologists created only eight decoding machines. One was sent to Admiral Thomas Hart, in command in the Philippines, a potential front line to any serious conflict with Japan. Three were given to the British, and the remaining four were divided between the American army and navy commands in Washington. As the intercepts of the **Purple** messages came through the various intelligence offices, they were translated, a slow and laborious process, then sealed and delivered by hand to only those few authorized to receive them, including the president, Secretary of State Hull, and Secretary of War Stimson. As well, the translations were made available to the highest level of the military: Army Chief of Staff George Marshall, Secretary of the Navy Frank Knox, and Chief of Naval Operations Admiral Harold Stark.

The Magic system was far from perfect, the intelligence officers often inundated with dozens of **Purple**'s messages, some completely innocuous, some of critical importance. The sheer volume often meant days of labor in decoding each message. Thus, when messages of even the highest priority were passed along to the necessary recipients, they might be days old, and so, in some cases, obsolete. But as an alternative to a complete void of information, the Magic intercepts could at least open the door to the thinking of the Japanese, to whatever instructions or cautions they were sending out to their diplomats. And, one of those included the newest ambassador to the United States, Kichisaburo Nomura.

THE CARLTON HOTEL, WASHINGTON, D.C.—
   SATURDAY, MARCH 8, 1941

Nomura had made his official introductions to both Hull and the president the month before. Now, with Nomura settled into the Japanese embassy in Washington, Hull invited him to a working meeting, and Nomura willingly accepted.

They met in Hull's own apartment, a comfortable set of rooms in the Carlton Hotel. Hull and his wife, Frances, had chosen the hotel as their residence for a number of reasons, comfort being a priority. But the Carlton had one other significant advantage for the secretary of state: It was situated barely two blocks from the White House.

It had become Hull's custom to welcome foreign ambassadors and their representatives in his apartment, rather than in the cold confines of the State Department. Often he scheduled the meetings after dark, adding another layer of intimacy and cordiality to the gatherings. The convenience of this was obvious for Hull: complete control of the surroundings, which might or might not include drinks or even dinner, depending on the guest and Hull's agenda. But there were other advantages as well. The comfortable setting, combined with an atmosphere of warmth, tended to blunt confrontations that might otherwise have been thorny. Hull soon learned that a comfortable sofa tended to loosen both the mood and the tongue of many of the foreign officials who settled into its soft cushions across from him.

Nomura was a heavy man, nearly six feet tall, a physical appearance that was very different from most of the Asians Hull had met. But he seemed to be permanently cheerful, with an endearing smile.

Nomura sat across from him now, hands clasped together, another gesture of politeness. Hull had noticed a pronounced limp, and knew from Ambassador Grew that Nomura had a glass eye. Hull avoided focusing on either, and Nomura said, "I wish to thank you for the invitation to your personal quarters. I am not happy with newspapermen, and they gather around my embassy like flocks of birds. However, they seem not to care where I spend my evenings, so they usually leave me alone when it appears I am simply retiring to my residence."

Hull nodded with a polite smile, and Nomura continued, "They seem not to realize that I am just an employee of my government, the same as you. I can offer them nothing for their newspapers, any more than you." Nomura smiled again. "If I might observe, Mr. Secretary, I notice that you are politely avoiding looking at my afflictions. Please be at ease, sir. The truth is that, about nine years ago, I was the victim of an assassination attempt, a bomb thrown by one of a radical element, a Korean gentleman who was unhappy with my government. I lost my right eye, and even today, my leg contains very many splinters. There were others beside me who were not so fortunate as to survive."

Hull was getting used to the thickness of Nomura's accent. Though Nomura had excellent command of English, his words could be difficult to interpret, and Hull was keeping as silent as possible, focusing his attention carefully on whatever Nomura said.

Hull knew from the Magic intercepts that Nomura's appointment to this position had come about primarily because of his past cordiality with Roosevelt and his previous experience as a naval attaché in Washington. Hull also knew that there was considerable skepticism in Japan that Nomura would actually accomplish anything of substance. It was likely that Nomura's sole task was to stress to the American government, especially Hull, that there was a longtime friendship between the two countries. But those days had faded away nearly a decade ago, especially with the Japanese invasion of China. Then, and now, Chiang Kai-shek, China's leader, was an ally of the United States, and consistently made loud and vigorous demands for American military assistance against the Japanese forces occupying his country.

Hull's patience for small talk had run its course. There were too many important topics to discuss.

"Your country has entered into the Tripartite Pact with Germany and Italy. That presents the United States and our allies with a difficult situation. I'm sure you understand that what Hitler has already achieved with his military is no less than the brutal subjugation of numerous peoples throughout Europe. It has been suggested by many around the world that your alliance with these two European dictatorships is nothing more than a plan to carve up the world into each of your spheres of influence. The American people have become aroused by the barbarity of German atrocities inflicted upon democratic peoples, and now, the American people are aroused by the words and deeds of your government."

Nomura glanced downward, then looked at Hull, spoke slowly. "Mr. Secretary, Japan is not committed to courses of conquest."

There was no emotion in the words, and Hull sat up straight now.

"As long as Japanese forces are all over China, as long as Japanese warships, troops, and planes are as far south as Thailand and Indo-China, accompanied by the kinds of bellicose threats that Japanese statesmen are making every week, there can only be increasing concern as to what we can plainly interpret as Japan's intentions for conquest."

"I would suggest, Mr. Secretary, that my leaders

are very willing to make peace with China. It is only necessary to combine the existing government in Nanking with the government of Mr. Chiang Kai-shek."

"You are referring to your puppet government in Nanking, whose strings are pulled from Tokyo? The fact that Chiang Kai-shek has been forced to defend himself from a Japanese army inside the borders of China should make it very clear that his government is not interested in your 'peace' proposal. On what basis do you feel that would lead to a peaceful solution?"

Nomura looked down at his hands, seemed to grasp for something to say. "Our nations enjoy warm relations. I see every reason why that should continue."

"Ambassador Nomura, there are loud voices in your government and in your military who are preaching hostility toward the United States, toward Britain, Australia, and France. Anyone reading a Japanese newspaper can find these speeches, interviews, documents created for your own people to consume. How should we interpret that? Whose voices are we to believe?"

Nomura seemed resigned to the obvious, said, "There are moderates in my government who wish nothing more than friendly relations with the United States. But too often, those voices of intelligence and reason are shouted down by the militants. I am sad to tell you that the militant factions have risen in power, and it is those voices you hear. My direct superior, Foreign Minister Matsuoka, has made numerous speeches in which he emphasizes that Japan will not kowtow to anyone, that our goal is a Greater East Asia Co-Prosperity Sphere, seeking only to protect Japanese interests. Your government, with its embargo of critical industrial materials, has put significant economic pressure upon Japan. Many in my government see that as an act of aggression."

"Mr. Ambassador, we have threatened no one, invaded no one, and surrounded no one. We freely offer cooperation in peace to all who wish it. But we cannot sit by while any government takes upon itself the mission to conquer free peoples. And I would emphasize to you, Mr. Ambassador, that it has been Japan's moves toward conquest, Japan's own acts of aggression, that force us to enact our shipping embargoes. The embargoes did not come first."

There was no anger in Nomura's face, and Hull could clearly see what Magic had already told him, the **Purple** messages having made clear that the man was doing a job he did not want. Nomura's instructions from his government were being carried out before Hull's eyes.

"Mr. Ambassador, you know that our embargo of goods is not absolute. We continue to sell you oil, which might be the single most valuable import for your economy. That is an act of hopefulness, that one day soon we may again see cooperation between our countries. That cannot happen as long as you are aligned with Germany."

"I share your hopes, Mr. Secretary."

Nomura offered nothing else, and Hull gathered his papers, the sign that the meeting had concluded. Nomura stood, made a deep bow, couldn't hide a hint of sadness.

Hull said, "Mr. Ambassador, we shall do all we can. No one wants a war."

Nomura bowed again but said nothing. Hull understood the silent message, the words Nomura would not say: In Japan, a great many people are hoping for a war.

THE WHITE HOUSE, WASHINGTON, D.C.—
    TUESDAY, MARCH 11, 1941

They sat facing the president, no one speaking, nervously waiting for the results of the vote in the Senate.

Hull glanced to one side at the scowling face of the treasury secretary, Henry Morgenthau. Hull had not always been friendly with Morgenthau, had bristled at his tendency toward intruding into the responsibilities and relationships that were rightfully the territory of the secretary of state. Roosevelt had wielded a careful hand, nudging Morgenthau to his proper duties at the Treasury Department. In the end, there was no serious friction, Hull accepting that Morgenthau was a passionate man who was doing all he could to guide American foreign policy through the morass of isolationism, especially in Congress. Even more than Hull, Morgenthau had pushed hard for an agreement between the United States and Great Britain that would go as far as possible to aid Britain's desperate war effort without the U.S. actually becoming an official participant.

The plan was called Lend-Lease, the Americans guaranteeing that all manner of supplies, including essential military materiel, be shipped to Britain, much of it on American merchant ships. The name said it all. The aid was neither a gift nor a purchase by Britain. As Morgenthau and his British counterparts had confirmed, Britain simply didn't have the financial resources to pay for billions of dollars in assistance.

Hull had already weathered protests from Germany, some in Berlin insisting that if the United States was to provide aid to Britain as a neutral observer, that same aid should flow to Germany as well. Very few in the American government took that demand seriously. Regardless of overwhelming sentiment throughout the United States that Britain be given assistance, in Congress the usual voices of isolationism were loud with protest. After considerable pressure from Roosevelt, and Hull's own vigorous testimony at various hearings, the Lend-Lease program had passed the House of Representatives with a sizable majority. But that was a month ago, and since then, isolationists throughout the country had applied pressure of their own.

The most influential voice from those vehemently opposed to any assistance to Britain was Charles Lindbergh. In 1927, Lindbergh had made a solo flight in a single-engine plane across the Atlantic, the first pilot to accomplish such a feat. Since Lindbergh was an officer in the Army Air Corps, the military recognized his extraordinary accomplishment by awarding him the Medal of Honor. Throughout the 1930s, Lindbergh had been regarded by most Americans as a genuine hero, his boyishly handsome face seemingly made for the newsreel cameras.

But Lindbergh had become a vocal critic of Roosevelt, and campaigned vigorously against American interference in the increasing turmoil, and horror, of the war in Europe. Lindbergh's celebrity had given muscle to the isolationist movement, and once the House of Representatives had voted in favor of Roosevelt's plan, the pressure from the isolationists and Roosevelt's various enemies had shifted toward the Senate. There, the vote would determine whether or not the Lend-Lease bill would pass.

Hull scanned the roomful of somber faces, in one corner the president's friend and perhaps closest advisor, Harry Hopkins. Hull looked toward Roosevelt, the president staring at the telephone on his desk.

Roosevelt said, "They should be voting now, right?"

One of his aides, seated behind Hull, said, "Anytime now, sir."

Morgenthau pounded one hand into his palm. "This is ridiculous. Why in hell is it so hard for those people to make the right decision? It's a simple equation, isn't it? Do you want the British to prevail, or the Germans? What kind of world do you expect there to be?"

Hopkins said, "According to Mr. Lindbergh, if the Germans win the war, we will have nothing to fear. It will not harm us at all."

Morgenthau grunted. "It will certainly not harm Mr. Lindbergh. He's friends with half of those people in Berlin."

Hull said nothing, knew that Morgenthau's anxieties went far deeper than politics. He was Jewish, a rarity in any president's cabinet, and Hitler's deadly animosity toward Jews of any nation was no secret.

Roosevelt sat back in his chair, his eyes still on the telephone. He looked at Hopkins now, then the others, settled on Hull. "The Germans are sweating this as much as we are, right? You told me that, right?"

Hull understood the president's nervousness, nodded, said, "They are. Our embassy in Berlin cabled me just before Christmas, expressing their **distaste** for our intentions. It seems that Hitler and his friends had convinced themselves that due to their military successes alone, we would do everything in our power to maintain our neutrality, perhaps offering them a nonaggression pact, in order to ensure friendly relations. We know now that peace with the Nazis means total surrender, but they are convinced that we are so afraid to stand up to Hitler, we will offer any concessions they require to maintain the peace."

Voices were raised throughout the room, angry dismissals.

Morgenthau spoke above the others. "Yes, it's nonsense. Utter nonsense. But that's how those people operate. Just because their own people have swallowed that load of bilge doesn't mean we should."

Hull said, "Quite right, of course. We're not paying much attention to anything that comes out of Berlin these days."

The silence returned, a long minute, broken by the jarring ring of the telephone. Hull saw a slight quiver in the president's hand as Roosevelt put the phone to his ear.

"Yes."

Hull studied the president's expression, was grateful to see a smile.

"Thank you, Missy."

Roosevelt placed the phone on the receiver, leaned back in the chair, a wide grin Hull had come to know so well. "Gentlemen, the vote was fifty-nine to thirty. We have prevailed."

The joy was immediate. Morgenthau held his hand out toward Hull.

"This was your party, Cordell. You convinced those blocks of wood in the Senate to vote with their brains. Fine work."

Hull took the hand, let out a long breath. "Thank you, Henry. We all still have a great deal of work to do." He looked at Roosevelt and his beaming smile.

"Mr. President, I should immediately cable our ambassador in London, and phone the British ambassador here. A great many others. The Turks have been anxious about this. Ambassador Grew in Tokyo, certainly. Well, it's a long list. I would imagine most every major newspaper throughout the world will make something of it, one way or the other."

Roosevelt motioned toward the door. "By all means. Go, go. I will telephone Mr. Churchill personally. This shall bolster his spirits considerably. The rest of you, see to those in your sphere who need to know as a priority."

Hull rose, made a short bow to the others, then moved out through the door to the Oval Office, with another nod toward Roosevelt's secretary, Marguerite LeHand. "It's a momentous day, Missy. This is history. He's as happy in there as I've seen him in months."

She shared the same smile as her president, said, "He deserves it, Mr. Secretary. This is an excellent day. I know that you and the president and so many others have been working so very hard toward this. Congratulations."

"Thank you. But this is not victory. There is great evil in this world, and it possesses great power. It is perhaps difficult for us to understand why others despise us so, why a free nation is anyone's enemy, why so many bad people need to make war."

"I am comforted, Mr. Secretary, knowing that men as capable as you are protecting us."

Hull shook his head. "Thank you, Missy, but you must not credit me with that. Protection comes from the sword, the cannon, the battleship. That's what today was about, that we may send the means for our allies to survive, the **power** they will need to survive. I fear that eventually, we may require that power right here at home."

# SIX

# Biggs

**W**ithin forty-eight hours of receiving his assignment, Biggs had boarded the train that would take him from Chicago to the port of San Francisco. The journey had been an adventure, the train winding past the kind of country he had never imagined, vast fields that stretched to the horizon, broken only by sad towns and the extraordinary stink of stockyards. With darkness, he welcomed the chance to find sleep, resting his head against the window, trying to ignore the astounding amount of snoring that drifted all through the car.

With the new day, he awoke to mountains and snow, as though the train had taken him to another world. But the astounding beauty of that was not to last, and as the train rolled into San Francisco he searched for different kinds of details. He had heard stories about the city, the odd mix of people and exotic food, the beauty of the bay and the ever-present danger of earthquakes. Until recently there had been a chance that he would remain there for as long as a week, while the navy found him a spot on a ship that would take him to Hawaii. Biggs had been optimistic that he would have time to explore the city, but that kind of adventure was not to be.

As the train completed its journey, a prominent sign greeted him in the train station: **Military Personnel This Way.** He was one of a dozen or more, mostly sailors and marines, who gathered alongside an unmarked bus. After a long ride along the shores of the bay, the men were deposited at the naval base at Treasure Island. The base spread along a part of the harbor that was populated by ships of all sizes, and Biggs searched for what would surely be a battleship. But nothing there seemed large enough, and he thought of Russo, by now onboard the USS **Curtiss.** Biggs still wondered just what a seaplane tender looked like, and if there were any in San Francisco Bay. But there would be no time to learn much of anything about Treasure Island. Within twenty-four hours of his arrival, more orders came. He was to report immediately to a mine-layer, the USS **Oglala.** The **Oglala** would be his transportation to Hawaii. An hour after he boarded her, the ship was under way.

At three thousand tons, she was barely a tenth the mass of the great battleships, but to Biggs she was enormous, an observation that drew howls of laughter from the crewmen who were now his hosts. They were good-natured in their ribbing of his utter lack of experience, since, of course, they had all begun the same way. And they took particular delight in warning him just how rough the seas could be across that stretch of the Pacific, on a ship this small, a prediction that came true almost immediately. But very soon the inevitable question had come—just why he was going to Hawaii. His assignment to the **Arizona** caused hints of jealousy. Biggs was surprised by their reaction, felt apologetic, though he was beginning to understand that his posting seemed to many others to be an extraordinary gift from the navy, even if he wasn't entirely sure **why.**

PEARL HARBOR, HAWAII—SUNDAY, MARCH 9, 1941

"Topside, gentlemen. Formation."

The **Oglala**'s crew seemed to know the routine, every man in his pressed whites moving up quickly, lining up shoulder to shoulder along the rails on the main deck. Biggs had been told of the ship's tradition, that entering port, the captain of the **Oglala** ordered the crew to turn out as a form of salute, a show of respect for the naval base's senior command.

Biggs stood with them, facing out from the

starboard side of the ship, his eyes scanning the variety of craft berthed along the shoreline. All across the harbor, he saw other ships anchored together, clusters of warships that seemed to be mostly destroyers. As the **Oglala** moved farther into the harbor, he could see a dry dock, an enormous box, holding a pair of ships larger than this one, embraced by all manner of heavy equipment. Beyond the dry dock he glimpsed the conning tower of a submarine, then another. He knew of several recruits in his class who had volunteered for that duty, drawing respect from Biggs and many of the others. What the training had taught him about submarines had led more to his claustrophobia than to any enthusiasm for service inside a steel tube that sank on purpose.

But his first real glimpse of the subs, like so many of the other ships anchored across this part of Pearl Harbor, was stirring something deep inside him, a new kind of nervous excitement, that everything he hoped the navy would offer him would be found right here. This was his new home.

Behind him, he heard a voice. "Seaman Biggs, about-face!"

He responded instinctively, was now face-to-face with a young officer.

"Sir!"

"Follow me, Seaman. Something you should see." The officer led him behind the others, toward the bow, then around, now on the port side of the ship.

"The **Arizona**'s over there, just off Ford Island, on the right, third one in. Thought you'd want to see what she looks like, even from this far away. Pretty impressive from any distance." He paused. "Good luck, sailor."

Biggs saluted the officer, turned again, eyes fixed across the open water of the harbor, a row of enormous ships berthed end to end. He scanned them all, focused now on the **Arizona,** one thought rising up in his mind. God, she's enormous. He tried to see every detail—the towers, the scout planes perched on her stern, as much as he could make out on every deck. But his eyes settled on the most impressive part of every battleship, and he said the words in a low whisper. "God almighty. Look at the guns."

Even from a distance, he could see the cannons, three each in four turrets, two forward and two aft. There were smaller guns as well, the details too far away to make out. I'll find out soon enough, he thought. He pulled his gaze away from the **Arizona,** searched the other battleships, each one slightly different. Massive and powerful, but in his mind, none was quite as beautiful as his own. He thought of Russo again. Wonder if he's here, or maybe he'll stay close to Washington. It's a big harbor, and I got no idea what the **Curtiss** looks like. Jesus, Ray. I understand now. I know why you wanted a battleship so bad. I've never seen anything so beautiful in my whole damn life.

ONBOARD USS ARIZONA—SUNDAY, MARCH 9, 1941

The launch had taken him across a calm patch of open water, and as he drew closer to her, he caught the smell of oil and paint, saw men dangling from ropes along the hull. The launch reached the heavy wood pier at Ford Island, jerked to a halt. One of the crewmen tossed a line to a man on the pier, who called out, "How long you be here?"

Behind Biggs, the coxswain answered, "Two minutes. Just bringing this **bubblegummer** to the **Arizona.**"

Biggs absorbed the insult, had expected this, one of the lessons from Chief Monroe back in basic training. Sailors had their own vocabulary, the new recruits onboard any ship the easiest targets. There was no reason for any new man to take offense. More new recruits would always follow, and of course, they would become the next targets.

The crewman in the launch said, "That way, sailor. The accommodation ladder amidships. Don't forget to salute the OOD."

Biggs nodded a brief thanks and climbed up to the pier. He hoisted the seabag on his shoulder, moved toward the ladder, saw others moving that way, coming from somewhere on Ford Island. No one seemed to notice him, and Biggs stayed back, waited for them to board, heard the formal greetings as they stepped onto the ship. Biggs had learned the formalities in basic training, but the reality was brand new, strange, made more strange by the massive gray steel that spread along the pier in front of him.

"You lost, sailor?"

The voice startled him, and he turned, saw an older man, an officer, saw the gold "scrambled eggs" on the man's hat, a row of gold stripes on his sleeve. Behind him were two younger officers. It was more brass in one place than Biggs had ever seen.

"No, sir. Um . . . just waiting to go aboard."

The older man smiled. "New recruit?"

"Yes, sir."

"What's your rating, son?"

"E-2, sir."

The man nodded, glanced back at the others. "Good. That means your RDC actually taught you something. I've seen too many E-1s come out of basic, and I wonder what in blazes they were being taught there. With all we have to be concerned about, we don't need to spend time teaching some green kid how to tie his shoelaces. What's your specialty?"

"I volunteered for medical training, sir. I've been assigned as a hospital apprentice. I'm hoping to be a corpsman someday. Nobody in my family's ever had an opportunity like this, sir."

It was more than he needed to say, and he was embarrassed now. But the older man nodded approvingly.

"Good for you. Most kids show up here and want

to do nothing but fire the guns. There's a lot more to running a ship like this than fireworks. You'll like Dr. Johnson, and there's a new man, Dr. Condon. Good men, both. I hope you stick with it. The navy needs well-trained medical personnel everywhere we go." He looked upward, Biggs as well, a row of men along the rail staring down at them. "This is a proud old ship, with a lot of history, son. Don't forget that. Now, go on up. Looks like you got some people waiting for you."

"Um . . . after you, sir." It seemed like the right thing to say, Biggs eyeing the audience above him still. A jeep appeared, carrying three men, all armed, and behind them, a huge black sedan. Both vehicles rolled to a dusty stop, and the two younger officers moved that way, one opening the car's rear door.

The older man nodded toward them, then said to Biggs, "That's my transportation. I'm headed the other way. There's a lot of **talk** that comes with this job. Meetings with admirals just about every day, and my aides are terrified I'll be ten seconds late. Even admirals can wait once in a while." He paused. "At least they serve a decent lunch."

Biggs's curiosity was overwhelming: a man with **aides.**

"Sir, if you don't mind me asking, are you one of the senior . . ."

"I'm your CO, son. Captain Van Valkenburgh. That's why you've got sightseers watching you up on deck. Best thing you can do is make it known up there that you got no idea who I am—you don't need those boys thinking you're the captain's buddy. It'll cause you too much grief. Just tell 'em I was asking you what time it was."

His guide was a chief petty officer, and Biggs followed him through a hatch, then down through another. All around him, men were moving, but there seemed to be no great urgency, as though for many it was a day off.

"Here. This is your billet, this compartment. You'll share this with all your new buddies."

Biggs was confused, saw a row of metal tables, a miniature mess hall. "I sleep here?"

The chief had his hands on his hips, as though tired of explaining this too many times. "The tables are folded up and stowed after dinner. You hang your hammock up there from those hooks. Make sure you put your spreader sticks at each end, or you'll roll up like a rug. The hammocks are hung three high, and you're the new man, so you get the top. Two things: Cinch it up tight so your ass doesn't bounce off the man beneath you, and don't fall out of the damn thing. First morning they wake up, most idiots roll over like they been spit out of a cocoon. That won't make you any buddies when you land on somebody. There are cots, too, but the new men never get those. Stay here long enough, you might be that privileged.

"Reveille's at 0530, and breakfast at 0600. Color ceremony is at 0800, on the stern. We got a band that thinks they can play the national anthem. It's debatable. You might get to hear that, or not; depends on what your duty assignment is. Some days you'll start work at 0700. You'll roll up your hammock and stow it in those cabinets right there. Leave it be until chow that night." He looked at Biggs's seabag. "You won't be needing a fourth of the crap you brought with you. I'll show you where the lockers are, and you can stow most of your gear there. There's shelves, over there on that bulkhead. That's where you'll stow your ditty bag, your shaving kit, toothpaste, whatever else you need to look pretty."

Biggs was overwhelmed again, inhaling the odd smells around him—fuel oil, cleaning fluid, grease, chow. The chief seemed to be running out of energy for this routine, said, "You bring any jugs of water with you?"

Biggs was puzzled by the question. "No, sir. Was I supposed to?"

The chief almost laughed. "That's a joke, sailor. On this ship, you're allowed three half gallons per day of clean water. Make it last. Shower, shave, wash your hands, whatever else. This ship generates its own fresh water from the ocean. It's some fancy process and I got no idea how it works. But it don't pump out enough to let you take some forty-minute hot shower. Try that, and your shipmates here will toss you overboard. The captain? Well, we let him do what he wants."

Biggs saw a handful of sailors drifting in through the far hatchway, wanted to offer some kind of greeting, but they ignored him, sitting down heavily at the closest mess table.

The chief paid no attention to them, said, "And one more thing. The laundry is below this deck. You're responsible for keeping your uniforms clean, whether you like it or not. Ignore that and Petty Officer Kincaid, who runs this little kingdom, will chew you hard. I don't recommend it. He likes to hurt people. Laundry costs fifteen cents for any size load, and it's a dime more if you want your whites pressed. I recommend that too. None of my petty officers, and, sure as hell, none of the brass will tolerate any member of this crew who dresses like a slob. You got that?"

"Yes, sir. Absolutely."

"Yeah, **absolutely.** I'll tell PO Kincaid you said that. We'll see how long it lasts. All right, that's about it. You missed lunch, but there's a gedunk stand one deck up, aft."

Biggs didn't want to ask, but his face betrayed the obvious question. The chief didn't hide his impatience.

"The gedunk stand is where you can get the unhealthiest junk on the ship, so naturally it's popular as hell. They got ice cream, candy bars, all sorts of other crap. Actually, I kinda like the Tootsie Rolls.

There's also a general store. All manner of useless stuff there; all you need is money. There's the post office, bakery. Hell, we even got a blacksmith shop, but I ain't seen a single damn horse on this boat yet. You'll figure it out soon enough. I ain't handing out maps. Make sure you get a good night's sleep tonight, though I bet you won't.

"We'll stand out in a couple days, expect to be at sea maybe a week, maybe less. That's the routine around here since we got a new hotshot admiral. Kimmel's his name. Never met him. Don't want to. But the orders come down every week. Most times, we stand out on Monday, come back to this glory hole on Friday night. Five days of running around in circles, shooting at targets we've already hit, blowing hell out of ships that shoulda been sunk years ago. We practice real difficult things like zigzagging, stuff you could do on your tricycle. Supposed to make us tough to hit in case some enemy submarine tries to torpedo us. A boat this big, I'm not too damn worried about some pissant sub. Not sure just who the enemy is supposed to be anyway. German U-boats are about four million miles from here.

"Weekends, a third of us get liberty, but don't get your hopes up. Let's just say that new men don't get much consideration. You keep your nose clean, and one of us will cut you a break. We got us a new ensign who's about twelve years old, so you can ignore him. Like I said, your immediate superior is

Petty Officer Kincaid. He's been around damn near as long as I have, and he knows the ropes."

"Can I ask, how long you served, Chief?"

The look on the man's face made Biggs regret the question immediately.

"Feels like three hundred years. Don't ask me again." He glanced at a piece of paper in his hand. "Orders say you're assigned as a hospital apprentice."

"Yes, sir. I been told that the doctors are good to work for."

The chief shrugged. "Maybe. Don't know them. But you wanna be a penis machinist, that's up to you. I try to stay away from folks like the docs. I ain't never had a short-arm inspection that was any fun. Well, whatever makes you happy."

"I've never actually performed those exams, Chief. They didn't drill me on that in basic."

The chief pushed his hat back, put his hands on his hips. "You know how they do them, right?" He didn't wait for a response. "A whole flock of us line up and drop our drawers while the doctors and numbskulls like you take a close look at what's going on between our legs. Me? I been lucky. Some of these jackasses get the clap every time they go into town. I guess we're fortunate that we've got professionals like **you** to make sure our loggerhead don't fall off."

Biggs had endured those inspections during basic training, had never really thought that he might be the one doing them. He didn't know what to say. The chief started to move again, then stopped. "What's so damn funny?"

Biggs didn't realize he had been smiling. "Sorry, sir. I never heard it called that. Guess I learned a new word."

"Sailor, by the time you finish your service on this boat, you'll be able to write your own dictionary."

# SEVEN

## Biggs

ONBOARD USS ARIZONA, PEARL HARBOR, HAWAII—
SUNDAY, MARCH 9, 1941

He was ravenously hungry; it had been hours since his tour with the chief. He was seated now on a hard bench, one of several tables in the mess area, directly below the hooks for his hammock. At one end of his table sat a petty officer, and Biggs couldn't avoid looking at him. He was an older man, with a hard creased face over wide shoulders and thick heavy arms. It was the only seat at the table's end, the other men seated along the sides. Farther down the compartment, the last of the men found their seats, and immediately, the mess orderlies brought large bowls, huge spoons protruding from each one, setting two down on each table. No one moved, and Biggs stared at the massive heap of white beans, the first meal of any kind that he'd experienced on the ship.

At the end of the table, the petty officer scooped a heaping spoonful onto his plate, then handed it to the man on his left. The procedure was repeated across from Biggs, then down along the far end of the table. Biggs had been warned against stepping out of place most anywhere on the ship, but here, he could sense a different kind of **off-limits.** As the beans crept closer to his white porcelain plate, he realized that eyes were on him. He responded with stiff-backed discipline, eyes front, waiting his turn. The closest bowl was slid noisily in front of his plate, and he paused, wary of what might happen next. He eased one hand toward the spoon, heard the growling voice of the petty officer.

"Wait a minute. Hold on." There was a silent pause, seconds ticking by. "Okay, now you can have 'em."

A chuckle came from most of the men around him, one man beside Biggs slapping him on the back.

"Enjoy this stuff, sailor. Two or three days a week, this is all we get. I'd advise you to use the ketchup, and sop it up with a hunk of that cornbread. Only way you can fool your mouth into thinking these damn beans taste good."

Biggs followed the suggestion, stirred the ketchup into the beans on his plate. From the end of the table, the petty officer clenched his teeth, said, **"Reserves,** right?"

Biggs realized the question was directed at him, said, "Um, no, sir. I enlisted."

The man seemed surprised, and Biggs saw a few nods from the others around the table. Beside Biggs, the man said, "Good for you. Most of us been here awhile. The damn reservists, they drop in to get duty pay or hash marks, anything they can take, then they flit off like moths to wherever they can go next. We kinda thought that was you, seeing as how you ain't got any dirty fingernails."

Biggs said, "No, I enlisted, my buddy and me. He went to the USS **Curtiss,** and they sent me here. I'm assigned as a hospital apprentice, second class. I start duty in the sick bay and dispensary tomorrow." He glanced at his fingers. "I guess the doctors wouldn't be too happy if I showed up with dirty fingernails."

The others seemed to ponder that, most of them with approving nods.

Another man said, "Tell you what, pal. You ever have to fix me up for something, I want you to re-member I'm your cabin mate. Don't be hacking off anything that ain't gotta go."

"I doubt I'll do any hacking. I'm hoping to get training to be a corpsman. But I'm not sure when that'll happen."

The petty officer sat back, arms crossed. "Oh, for God's sake. You all sound like a bunch of biddies at a tea party. Big dreams. Big talk. You're from the

South. I can hear your accent. But it ain't Mississippi or Virginia."

"No, sir. Florida. It's south I guess, closer to Georgia than Miami."

The petty officer stood now, said, "All right, enough of this kindergarten class. He passes muster. He's officially one of the rest of you worms. What's your name, worm?"

"Biggs, sir."

"Well, Mr. Biggs, just so you know, if you'd have dipped those beans out of turn, I'd'a broken your arm. Guess you coulda fixed it up yourself. All right, I've spent all the time I can stand with you turds. I'm back to my own comforts. You may resume eating your slop."

He moved away, the others staring down at their food until he was completely gone. As his footsteps faded, the men seemed to exhale in unison, the forks jabbing again into the red glop on their plates.

Biggs was curious, said in a low voice, "Who is he?"

The man beside him said, "Petty Officer Kincaid. He's what we like to call a son-of-a-bitch bastard."

Biggs recalled the name, the instructions from the chief.

Across from Biggs, a man said, "He comes in whenever we get a new recruit. Likes to bust chops, or arms or legs, tries to catch any kind of slipup. Then he goes back to petty office country."

"That like officer's country? I've heard of that."

Beside him, "It's probably a hell of a lot more cushy than officer's country. The petty officers run this ship. Maybe run the whole damn navy. I hear the captain's scared of the whole lot of 'em. He's got a marine standing guard outside his quarters in case one of the POs decide to take over."

The others laughed and Biggs said, "Name's Tommy Biggs."

Beside him, "Ed Wakeman. I'm from Sioux Falls."

Biggs wasn't sure just where that was.

Across from him, "Hank Mahone, Columbus, Ohio. You really from Florida?"

"Yeah, near Jacksonville."

Mahone said, "You left sunshine and beaches to join the navy? Hell, you had all the good stuff right out your window. Now you gotta put up with officers. And Kincaid."

Biggs was feeling more comfortable now, laughed along with the others. Another man spoke up, a small dark man with a distinctive northern accent.

"I got one thing to offer you, fella, what I tell all the new boys. I been here four years, and I learned a few things. The most important . . . never volunteer for nothing. Not never no how. They'll think you actually like doing all that stuff, and you'll never see the light of day ever again."

Wakeman waved a hand toward the man, said to Biggs, "Don't pay no mind to Vincenzo. He thinks 'cause he's from New York he's got the market cornered on brains."

Vincenzo feigned indignation. "It's Brooklyn, sport. Nobody's from New York unless they work on Wall Street. Or they sing in some Broadway show. I seen Jimmy Durante once . . ."

The protests came in a flurry, and it was obvious to Biggs that this story had been told before. Biggs finished the beans on his plate, said, "I was gonna head over to the gedunk stand, maybe get some ice cream. Anybody wanna go?"

Mahone said, "On purpose? You mean like, to eat?"

Wakeman leaned in closer. "A little advice, Tommy. Up there in sick bay, if you get some poor moron comes in with a broken bone, and you run out of whatever the hell you use to make a cast, you just get some ice cream from the gedunk stand. Better than any plaster."

Biggs saw nods around the table. It was a unanimous opinion. "Maybe I'll skip the ice cream. I heard there were Tootsie Rolls."

Wakeman said, "Come on. I'll go with you."

The mess was breaking up now, orderlies removing the dishes and everything else on the table. Biggs looked back, saw one man breaking down the tables, storage bays opening, the compartment once more becoming their sleeping quarters.

As they moved through the open hatches, Wakeman

said, "I'm sure glad you didn't give Kincaid a reason to bust your ass. He does it just for fun. Damn near broke my jaw once, then dared me to report him. He probably woulda tossed me overboard."

They reached the gedunk stand, where a crowd of men had gathered. Ice cream and cold drinks were being served by two men behind the counter. They waited their turn, Biggs paying a nickel for the candy, Wakeman doing the same. They moved away through the crowd, Wakeman leading Biggs up and out onto the main deck.

Biggs said, "What's your rating? If I can ask."

"Seaman first class. I do a hell of a lot of maintenance, painting, scraping, all the good stuff. My main job is to make damn sure the holystoning gets done right."

Biggs stopped, suspected a joke. "The what?"

"They didn't teach you about that in basic?" He looked down, pointed. "See? We got teak decks on this ship, and they gotta be cleaned about once a week. We got bricks with holes in 'em, and we use sticks to push 'em back and forth on the deck. They toss down some sand and lime so it gets real rough. After about a thousand pushes, we wash it all down, and then polish the deck. No idea who came up with the idea, but it works pretty damn good. They say it makes all the admirals real proud to see it. Don't know about that. I never asked them."

"Wow. I didn't know there was so much to do, so much more than just drills. When I got my posting to sick bay, I figured I'd never have much of a chance to learn all that other stuff."

Wakeman stared at him, then began to laugh.

"What? I say something dumb?"

Wakeman laughed harder, others gathering around, curious. Biggs felt foolish, though he wasn't sure why.

**"Biggs!"**

He turned and saw the imposing figure of PO Kincaid, sweat and muscles in a T-shirt.

"Yes, sir. Here."

"I see you. I had to interrupt my damn gym time to find you. I got orders from the ensign." He said the rank with a spitting growl. "You're new, so this is the only time I'm giving you the benefit of the doubt, ever. You're supposed to check your duty sheet every damn day. Yours ain't been checked."

"Yes, sir, I know my duty starts in the sick bay at 0800."

Kincaid put his hands on his hips, a hard glare that made Biggs back up a step.

"Hospital Apprentice Second Class Biggs, you are to report to the quarter deck aft at 0700, for paint and barnacle removal duty." Kincaid scanned the others, no one speaking. "Anyone else want to volunteer? We can always use more. Ah, Seaman Wakeman. Wondered where you ran off to. You are to report to holystoning detail, 0700, main deck, forward. The rest of you . . . get the hell out of my way!"

ONBOARD USS ARIZONA, AT SEA—
    TUESDAY, MARCH 11, 1941

Despite all the lessons from basic training, a part of him still expected salt air and sunshine. But he seemed to be learning a new lesson every hour. His first duty involved hanging from the port side of the ship, painting the hull. He learned quickly that the paint he was ordered to apply might be painted over again a week later. He also learned that the men who shared this duty came from nearly every kind of job on the ship, except of course for the petty officers. That was another lesson: Petty officers seemed to run everything, in every part of the ship, just as Wakeman had said. It seemed strange to Biggs that he rarely saw any of the actual officers, certainly not the captain. Biggs knew there were places off-limits to him—officer's country certainly, as well as some of the more technical areas, from communications to fire control centers. As curious as he was, he knew there was almost no chance that he would ever see the bridge or the engine rooms.

With the ship now at sea, Biggs had reported to his posting, and was scheduled to spend seven hours on duty in sick bay. There was another lesson he was learning, that on the first day out of port, sick bay was busy, long lines of men suffering the aftereffects of whatever adventures they had enjoyed during their liberty. A simple hangover didn't qualify a man to miss duty, so the doctor instructed Biggs to hand out aspirin and bicarbonate, the cure for nearly every ailment Biggs saw.

By late morning, the parade of misery had mostly passed. Biggs sat down for the first time at a small metal table. The doctor, Johnson, sat as well, said, "Busy morning. Some hooch joint in Honolulu must have had a sale on the fuel oil some of these guys drink. How about some coffee? I always have a pot going. It's better than fuel oil, I promise. And, it's better stuff than you'll get with your chow."

"No, thank you, sir. Never really drank it much. It was a little expensive for my mom to buy. We kinda did without a lot of that stuff."

Johnson seemed surprised at the answer. "Where're you from, Mr. Biggs?"

"Palatka, Florida, sir. Near Jacksonville."

"Can't say I've been there."

"Can't say anybody's been there, sir."

Both men laughed, and Johnson reached for the coffee pot. Biggs studied him, and Johnson seemed to notice, said, "You're guessing the details, right?"

"Not sure what you mean, sir."

"It's all right. I'll tell you. Been in the navy for nearly twenty-four years. My accent's a lot like yours. I grew up in Alabama, a town just like your Palatka. Graduated from Randolph-Macon, then went through med school at Vanderbilt. That's in Nashville. A few people **have** been through there. I turned fifty last year, and I made damn sure there was no party. Age is not something to be proud of, like a medal."

Johnson drank from the cup, stared into the coffee, made a sour look. "Too long in the pot. Need to make a new one. Or, even better, teach you to do it."

"Happy to, sir."

"Maybe later. I'll handle this one." Johnson dumped the grounds out of the tin pot, bent low, retrieved a canister of coffee from a cabinet. He filled the container, then added water from a small sink, closed the pot. He switched on a hot plate, said, "One of life's luxuries right here. The skipper allowed me to have it, since I insisted there were a good many **medical** reasons for me to heat water."

Biggs appreciated the doctor's humor, liked the man already.

Johnson rechecked the coffee pot, said, "I was assigned a new doctor couple weeks ago, not much older than you. Dan Condon. They only made him a lieutenant j/g, which seems a little nutty. He makes it all the way through Harvard Medical School and the navy puts him at the bottom of the damn ladder. Good doctor, I think, though he's only twenty-six. Makes me feel older than hell. Of course, I'm a full-blown commander, so I outrank him all to pieces. But where it counts, we're dead equals. Don't you forget that. I have more years of experience, but he runs circles around me when it comes to new surgical techniques. You'll meet him this afternoon, when he comes on duty. He'll relieve me at fourteen hundred hours." He paused. "So, you're . . . nineteen?"

"Yes, sir."

"High school diploma, right?"

"Yes, sir."

"They wouldn't have assigned you to sick bay otherwise. College degree and they make you an officer. I've known a good many high school graduates who are a hell of a lot better at command than some who have a sheepskin." Johnson glanced at the coffee pot. "I've got ten pharmacist's mates, most of them hoping to go to corpsman school. There are about fifteen corpsmen on the ship, but that number changes pretty often. That sound like something you'd like to do?"

"Maybe, sir. Not sure, not yet anyway." The words rose up in his head. **I just had to get away from home.** "The navy gave me good pay, I can see the world, good food, all of that. And, it's not the army."

Johnson laughed. "So, you swallowed everything some recruiter fed you, eh? Did he tell you that you'd be scraping barnacles off the hull, or polishing every piece of wood on the ship?"

Biggs didn't respond.

"I saw the duty sheets for this division, Mr. Biggs. I wondered why you hadn't reported down here, saw they assigned you to breathe paint for a few hours. Surprised you didn't stumble in here this morning, like the rest of those unfortunates."

"I don't understand, sir."

Johnson laughed. "It's called 'paint drunk,' Mr. Biggs. The paint they use on the hull has all sorts of wonderful chemicals in it. Has to, so it fights off the salt water and doesn't peel off the ship. You breathe that stuff all day, it can give you a good punch in the head. Nothing to do but let it pass. Beats me why they make you boys do that. Some of the gunnery people, the mechanic's mates, carpenters, firemen, the whole bunch of you. They probably told you they need to change the color on this ship maybe once a month. Blue, then gray, then white, then stripes for camouflage, then back to gray again. What color are we now? I'm waiting for purple."

"Gray, sir. I did feel a little dizzy last night. Didn't know why."

"Now you know why. I'd like to make sure you stay in here with me more than out there, doing God knows what job. I'll put the word in to see if I can exempt you from deck duties. They made me a commander, I guess I can act like one. You put in some good time here, and I'll recommend you for promotion. I have an instinct for people, Mr. Biggs, and I think you'll do just fine. You move up the ladder two more ratings, and you'll officially be a petty officer. That qualifies you to be a pharmacist's mate."

Biggs absorbed the words, said, "Not sure I'd do well as a petty officer. Nobody seems to like 'em."

Johnson laughed. "Nobody said you have to be one of **those,** Mr. Biggs. There are bullies and loudmouths everywhere in life. Don't allow a simple promotion to change who you are. Just do your job, be yourself, and be decent to people."

"Yes, sir. Thank you, sir."

Johnson moved over to check the coffee maker, the water beginning to percolate.

"Hurry up, for crying out loud." He looked toward Biggs now. "I was serious, what I said about the navy before. It's good duty, and it should pay off for you down the road. You need to appreciate that you're on one of the oldest and proudest battlewagons in the fleet. We have a good crew and a good skipper." He wrapped a cloth around the handle of the coffee pot, poured a fresh cup. "It's not quite ready, but I'm tired of waiting. You know, there's talk that we might be sent to the Atlantic. That's where the mess is. Rumors, anyway. I learned a long time ago, talk can be found anyplace you stick your ear."

Johnson checked his watch. "I've got one of the mates, Mr. Vaughan, coming on duty in about twenty minutes. Some of the new men will be joining us when we return to Pearl. Transferring from other ships. I lost a couple of the mates a few weeks ago when their enlistments ran out. Not much I can do to make 'em stay if they don't want to. You'll be helping out all of us at one point or another. As long as there's not some kind of plague spreading through the ship, it won't be that difficult."

He sipped carefully at the steaming cup. "Look, there's not much to do down here right now. Tomorrow, either Dr. Condon or I will give you a serious tour of the facilities here, show you the ropes as best we can. Why don't you go topside, take a good look around. Stay out of the way, though. And, if anybody questions what the hell you're doing there, mention me."

A sudden crash of thunder echoed through the bulkheads, the ship rolling slightly. Biggs jumped, felt a burst of panic, grabbed the table, steadying himself, said, "Good God . . ."

It came again, Biggs more prepared this time, a hollow rumble that bounced his stomach. He held a tight grip on the table, eyes on Johnson, who gave a sharp yelp, staring down at a spreading coffee stain on his shirt. Johnson blew out a long breath, said, "Well, that hurt like hell. Probably took the hair off my chest. Those fellows catch me every time, just as I'm about to drink from a cup of the hottest brew I've made all day. Damned if I don't have to change another shirt."

Biggs glanced around the sick bay, but nothing seemed damaged, no cabinets open.

Johnson smiled. "The big guns, Mr. Biggs, fourteen-inchers. Turret One is right above us. You'll get used to it. One of the reasons we put to sea every week or so is the firing drills. They're teaching the new fire control fellows how to do the job, the loaders, the men down in the magazines, all of it. You probably know all this, but we're floating near thirty-two thousand tons. We're hauling twelve fourteen-inch cannon, and they've got a range near twenty miles. Can you imagine that? We can hit targets none of us would ever see." He paused. "I guess it's unseemly for a doctor to talk like that. Although, blowing up things from so far away means the doc doesn't have to deal with it."

The big guns erupted again, the deck beneath Biggs's feet bouncing, the ship rolling again.

Biggs waited for more, said, "Wow. I bet it's really loud up top. Doc . . . um, sir, you think we'll get to the shooting war? I know the fight's in the Atlantic, and you've heard talk we might go there. But if we don't . . . I mean, I look at this ship, all those others back in Pearl Harbor, and I think, well, there's a whole lot of firepower, big-time weapons. It would sure do some good against the Germans. I'd just . . . hate to miss out."

Johnson was pulling a fresh shirt from a small locker. "One piece of advice, Mr. Biggs. Don't be in a hurry to go to war, no matter where you are. It's never like you expect it to be. And something I learned from some of the men in my family, who fought in the Great War: Men march off to war. They don't **march** home. If you survive a real war, you'll come home a very different man. Even on a ship like this one, don't ever convince yourself that war is easy, or that it's an adventure. The reason I'm here in this sick bay is not just to pass out aspirin to the drunk and penicillin to the reckless. We have bandages and tourniquets, morphine and operating kits. That drawer over there? There's an amputation saw. War can be a bloody horror, Mr. Biggs. Even on a battleship."

# EIGHT

# Yamamoto

Onboard Battleship Nagato, Ariake Bay, Japan—
Thursday, April 10, 1941

"I offer you most genuine congratulations, Mr. Fukudome."

Fukudome bowed. "It has been my honor to serve as your chief of staff. But the Naval Ministry has offered me an opportunity that I cannot ignore. I hope you understand, sir."

Yamamoto sat back, said, "What exactly is your new title?"

Fukudome inflated a little, with obvious pride. "Sir, they have assigned me as chief of the First Bureau. I will answer only to Admiral Nagano."

Yamamoto knew the details already, but he allowed Fukudome his moment, perhaps the only time the chief of staff would be allowed to impress his commander.

"Serve him well. You will, of course."

Fukudome bowed again, no words, and Yamamoto saw emotion on the man's face. Yamamoto stood, said, "Now go. There need be no ceremony here. You have earned your new post, and you must not disappoint."

"Thank you, sir."

Fukudome exited the wardroom and Yamamoto leaned forward, resting his hands on the wide table. Perhaps you will serve Admiral Nagano better than you have served me. Nagano is old, not long for the service, and he requires sharp minds around him. Perhaps I am old as well. How long will it be before they begin to speak of me as a mindless old fool? Some already do, no doubt about that. After all, I have strange and dangerous ideas, I dare to insult the **old ways.** Even some of the **new** ways—the insanity of the alliance with the Germans.

He had known of several plots to kill him, most of them clumsy, amateur assassins attempting to barge into his office, knives at the ready. But no one in the high command ever claimed responsibility for those threats. Yamamoto suspected the efforts came from farther down the navy's chain of command. There were an increasing number of younger officers who embraced the army's style of aggressiveness, or even something more extreme, actively promoting a more rigid loyalty to Germany. They kept mostly to themselves, their politics too radical for their superiors to tolerate. But their number was growing, alarming the highest levels of command. As a moderate, Yamamoto was a tempting target. Despite the clumsiness of the attempts to harm him, many above and around him were concerned that at any moment another attempt might be made on his life, perhaps the next time by someone more professional.

He stared at the entryway to the wardroom, smiled. At least, he thought, if there are assassins here, they would have to be from the crew, and that is called mutiny. I doubt that has happened before in this navy. No, I am at risk only if I am elsewhere. And why? Because I object to outdated strategies? Because I do not scream at newspaper reporters about our place in the world, how we must vanquish our enemies? Because I do none of those things, they send assassins to eliminate me?

He pondered the word. "They." Who are **they,** exactly? It would be easy to assume it is the army. There are those who actually believe Japan will be best served if the army and navy engage in a civil war, fighting for supremacy, seeking to gain favor with the emperor by their strength alone. The navy would not win that fight. The army controls too much, and has far greater influence over the government and the citizenry through its ability to create fear, to spread propaganda that serves its purposes.

So how would we fight the army? Sail our great ships into Tokyo Bay and destroy the city? Who thinks of such things? And yet, if I speak out, if any of us who are more moderate speak out, we will still be targets, fearing men in dark alleys who carry knives.

He picked up a small porcelain cup, the tea already cold. He drank it anyway, and thought, So now Fukudome has been promoted. He has always disagreed with my Hawaii plan, and now he will serve alongside others who feel the same way. How much power do they have to sweep me away, or to dismiss my ideas? Like the army, they plot to make war, no matter the cost. And so, a war is inevitable, no matter what any of us try to do to prevent it. Japan has never lost a war, not in our long history. So, when we lose this one, what will happen? How will our emperor explain this to his people? How will our culture survive?

Yes, that's the greater purpose: survival. If we can survive by my hand for another six months, another year, that will be my service to the emperor. And, likely, he will never know. He is already leaning toward the voices who insist it is our destiny to rule all of Asia, to spread our empire across the Pacific. I cannot change that. So, I must do what I am doing now, engage our new enemies with an attack that will keep them away, that will grant us more time, so that we may become stronger, so that Japan may survive.

YOKOSUKA HARBOR, TOKYO, JAPAN—
   THURSDAY, APRIL 17, 1941

The **Nagato** had moved northward, closer to Tokyo, accompanied by a fleet of smaller support ships. It was the usual practice, the Naval Ministry making a show for the public in various parts of Japan where the anchorages allowed. With the government making broad pronouncements about Japan's need for territory, with so many verbal attacks aimed at every potential enemy, the fleet's arrival had a predictable effect, was a reassuring and inspiring spectacle. For Yamamoto, berthing close to Tokyo had another enormous advantage.

He had made a brief visit to his home to see his wife, Reiko, and have a quick word with his four children. The visits were rarely comfortable for any of them—too much time apart, so many years, so much distance. They seemed to have very little need for him anymore; at nineteen, his oldest son, Yoshimasa, was very much the man of the family.

Reiko was a dozen years younger than her husband, their marriage arranged, as so often was the custom. Over the many years they had been together, he had grown weary of what seemed to him to be an aloof coldness, as though she didn't want him around. He had often described her as a powerful woman, capably managing life in his absence. But those close to her, including him, knew that she was sickly much of the time, one reason why having strong-willed children was so important to her. When Yamamoto would visit, he'd struggle to avoid the arguments, because no matter her physical problems, she often had more strength in her angry words than he could handle. And so, his visits would be short.

But Reiko was not the only woman in his life.

Her name was Chiyoko. When he met her nearly seven years before, she was a geisha, and the most beautiful woman he had ever seen. Older now, she still performed a geisha's duties, but also helped oversee the social education of several younger women. Yamamoto was the only relationship in her life that had nothing to do with her profession.

He was discreet, and protected her as best he could, as she protected him. It was not unheard of for a Japanese man to enjoy the company of a mistress, but Yamamoto was far too public a figure, and a highly admired one at that. Even more important to him, there were still too many nasty undercurrents running through both the army and navy high commands, and Yamamoto had plenty of enemies. Some would welcome a public embarrassment as the perfect cause for removing him from command, less messy than assassination, but just as effective.

He wore civilian clothes, his usual routine now when leaving the ship. The restaurant was dark and quiet, a place he had taken Chiyoko before, where the owners understood the necessities of discretion. They sat in the back, Yamamoto's favorite spot, but he faced the entrance, an old habit from being stalked by men with knives. Now, the caution was more to escape reporters and their questions about the dangerous issues in Tokyo, the conflicts between army and navy, the fragility of Prime Minister Konoye's government, and the increasing shortages of so many commodities. The government had already issued orders for people to conserve oil, gasoline, and some basic foods, such as wheat. The newspapers were voicing noisy speculation that all the shortages might force Japan to do more than merely talk with foreign powers, especially the United States.

Yamamoto hated reading the newspapers. It drilled hard into him that the delays and debates and arguments over his proposal for an attack on Hawaii might mean that Japan would be forced into a war it was not yet prepared to fight.

He kept his gaze on the curtained doorway, felt impatient. Chiyoko leaned closer, one hand on his arm.

"Be calm, Iso. Admiral Hori is always pleased to visit with you. And he can eat more than you, so he will be happy to try all the specialties."

He looked at her, the low light reflected by the silver threads in her kimono. "Where did you get that? It is beautiful."

"You finally noticed? It was a gift from Minister Kiro."

Yamamoto sniffed. "Don't know him. But if he wishes to dress you in finery, I cannot object."

He fought against jealousy, knew that her job was only that. She could always read him, and did now.

"He is a foolish little man who enjoys making speeches to geishas, since they will not walk out on him. He is generous, so I listen."

Yamamoto wasn't sure if she was telling the truth, but he knew she was trying to reassure him. "Thank you, my beautiful flower. Perhaps he will buy me a new pair of shoes."

She smiled, and he absorbed the beauty in her, thought, No man is more fortunate.

He saw motion at the curtain, the man bending low, slipping inside, a hand on the brim of his hat, eyes adjusting to the darkness. Yamamoto did not wave, knew he was seen, couldn't hold back the smile. He pulled himself to his feet, a bow, the other man moving close, a bow of his own, matching the smile.

Taikichi Hori had been Yamamoto's closest friend for most of their lives. They had attended the Naval Academy together, had moved up through the ranks in lockstep. But Hori had stumbled through the war of hostility that infected both wings of the military in the early 1930s. As moderate in his views as Yamamoto, Hori had suffered from the plotting of some of the same enemies who pursued Yamamoto. However, the assassins didn't attack Hori with knives, but with a more insidious tactic: They assaulted his character and his reputation, until the Ministry had no choice, so they said, but to place Hori on the naval reserve list. Regardless of the rank he continued to hold, there could be no active command in the field. His career was over.

The two men sat, and Hori gave Chiyoko a polite smile. He seemed uncomfortable, and Yamamoto knew why.

"It is all right, my friend. I will not keep secrets from her. And, I did not ask you here to discuss classified matters. Have you tried the blowfish?"

Hori relaxed, and gave Chiyoko a more genuine smile. He said, "No, I have not. Have you?"

Yamamoto said, "She enjoys it. She is trusting, because the chef here is her uncle."

Chiyoko said, "Cousin, actually. Yes, I trust him. You should try everything here, Admiral Hori. It is very good."

Hori nodded approvingly at her use of his title, said to Yamamoto, "She is still charming, Iso. A talent for flattery. Does she always know exactly what to say?"

"To me."

She said to Hori, "I suggest the blowfish, and the octopus. But it is all excellent."

Yamamoto said, "I just cannot bring myself to eat the blowfish. But the boiled eel is rather good."

Hori laughed. "So, I have come halfway across Tokyo to discuss the menu?"

The server was there now, and Yamamoto said, "Boiled eel, sea bream, salted. **She of the great courage** will attack your blowfish. And let us all hope it does not attack her in return. And for my friend?"

Hori said, "Same as him. I too am a coward."

Yamamoto smiled as the server moved away. "You have no imagination."

Hori said, "From everything I hear, you have enough imagination for all of us. Pure fantasy, I am told. You believe a small airplane can best a mighty battleship. How can that be?"

He knew Hori's sarcasm, but he also knew that Hori's skepticism was commonplace in the Naval Ministry.

"We shall learn soon enough. I have a crew of young men exploring that very subject."

"I am intrigued, Iso."

Yamamoto saw the server coming. "A conversation for another time. There isn't much I can tell you anyway. Work is being done. I am eager to see how that work progresses."

The server put his food down in front of him, and he tried to feel hungry, saw Chiyoko pick up the blowfish with her chopsticks. He couldn't avoid concern, the stories coming out at least once a week, the deadly poison in the blowfish claiming another customer, some incompetent chef jailed for carelessness in its preparation.

Yamamoto said to her, "You get along with your cousin? Good friends?"

She had been through this before, both men now watching her eat.

She shook her head. "Actually, he despises me. And he owes me a lot of money. He told me he wished I would just go away. Other than that, we are very close."

Yamamoto looked at Hori, who said, "You ask idiotic questions, you get appropriate answers."

Yamamoto poked at the eel on his plate. "She's used to it. It's an old habit of mine." He paused, more serious now. "With her I can be playful. But there is no play elsewhere. How many more times can I offer my suggestions, how many times can I tell them they are wrong? It makes me tired, my friend. How do I know when I am so tired it is time to stop all this, time to walk away?"

Hori looked at Chiyoko. "How often does he do this?"

"Every time I see him."

Hori said, "My good friend, I have heard doubts from you for years. And so has she. It is not time for you to walk away. You still have work to do. There are good people, good young people who require you to lead them. When they can lead as you do, then it will be time to walk away." He paused. "Besides, I know what is happening behind your closed doors, in your wardrooms."

"No you don't."

Hori smiled. "I cannot play poker with you. All right, I don't know. But I know you are developing a grand strategy, and when you have done the work, you will find a way to make it happen. There are doubts about you in the Ministry, and there is fear. But I would not bet against you, Iso. And neither would most of the navy. That's why they're afraid. You are punching a hole in their perfect view of the world."

Yamamoto put down the chopsticks. "Their perfect view of the world?" He looked at Chiyoko. "Do you know how they make decisions, form their plans about strategy? If they make a plan, it must be a good plan, because it is the plan. If they believe it, it must be true, and it is true because they believe it. Right now, their plan is that the Americans are to make an enormous blunder, and sail straight into our trap. And it will work, because they say it will work."

Hori leaned closer, lowered his voice. "It is who they are, my friend. Japan does not make mistakes. We are invincible. I have listened to that kind of reasoning for years."

Yamamoto poked again at his food. "I wonder if the Spanish believed they were invincible, when their armada sailed off to fight the English."

Hori sniffed. "They were the Spanish. They were not the Japanese."

Yamamoto knew his friend's sarcasm. "It doesn't matter to me what their 'reasoning' is. I am offering them the only chance we have to hold the Americans back. I do not pretend this will win us a war. Only the army is so foolish as to think we can rule our part of the world. They listen to Hitler's speeches, and believe that we are destined for such things. It is madness."

Hori leaned closer again. "Careful, my friend. That kind of talk is unhealthy." He looked at Chiyoko. "Enjoying the blowfish?"

She seemed to welcome the break in the tension, gave him a smiling nod, then glanced at Yamamoto, a show of concern. Yamamoto looked down at his plate, was finally hungry. He stabbed at the eel with his chopsticks, stuffed his mouth.

"I am seeking ways to curb my outrage. Sometimes I am better at it than at others." He dug into his rice with his chopsticks. "As I've grown older, I find I have less tolerance for those whose brains are made of this rice. It amazes me how so many of those people end up in the Naval Ministry. As for my unhealthy talk, it is why I value friends such as you." He looked at Chiyoko. "At least you know that I am not always such a grouchy beast. Oh, and you may tell your cousin he has excellent eel. But I'm still not trying the blowfish."

Hori cleaned the last bit of food from his plate, said, "Now that you have grown calm, I need to offer you a suggestion. I am not under instructions to do this, I promise you. But the talk is growing stronger."

Yamamoto looked at him, felt a sudden sense of dread. "What talk?"

"It has been suggested, by those who know such things, that your career in the navy might best be terminated. It has been suggested that you take a different course."

Yamamoto sat back, arms folded. "Go on."

"It is a certainty that you would be extremely popular with the civilian public, that you could easily be elected to a prominent political office. It has also been suggested that you could, in short order, become prime minister."

Yamamoto waited for the smile, then realized the man was serious. "Suggested? By whom? I am supposed to embrace this idea, that somehow becoming a politician is more fulfilling than commanding the fleet? That I can talk to reporters and make great speeches, and accomplish nothing at all? So that I might become one of the great mass of useless politicians in this country who cower before the power of the military? Who fed you this nonsense?"

Hori laughed. "Because I am **nobody** now, I often hear more than I'm supposed to. I learn things, I talk to people. I might be out of favor in the official buildings of the navy, but I still have some very good friends. There is concern about you, concern for what lies ahead."

"I have concern about me as well. It drives me toward retiring every day. But I am here for one reason. I am **concerned** about the future of our country. I cannot prevent the insanity of war. But I can try to provide us with some advantages." He paused. "Very soon, there will be very bright and very innovative young men accepting the challenges I have offered them, young men who understand and appreciate the value of the airplane, even more than I do. Their job will be to iron out the problems, the riddles. My job will be to patiently wait for them to complete their tasks, so that finally, I can take those details to those 'people' who 'suggest' things, and convince them that my young men are right, and that the old ways are simply wrong."

"And if you cannot convince them?"

"Then Japan will go down in flames much sooner than any of those fools can comprehend."

# NINE

## Hull

"**W**ho are the authors of this thing?"

Stimson was prepared for Roosevelt's question, had no need to consult any paper. "Mr. President, Rear Admiral Patrick Bellinger is a decorated naval pilot, saw considerable action in the Great War. Major General Frederick Martin commands the Hawaiian Air Force, the aviation unit under the overall command of General Short. Both men are considered to be experts in the area of military aviation."

"So, Mr. Secretary of War, do you take this seriously?"

Stimson shook his head. "Never said that. I respect these men. But I'm not taking this as seriously as some might hope. As **they** might hope. This report was ordered by Admiral Kimmel; thus, when it was completed, as a matter of protocol, it was sent to General Marshall, Mr. Knox, and me."

Roosevelt shuffled the papers, read aloud. "'The aircraft at present available in Hawaii are inadequate to maintain, for any extended period, from bases on Oahu, a patrol extensive enough to ensure that an air attack from orange . . .'" He paused. "'Orange' is Japan, correct?"

"Yes, sir."

"'To ensure that an air attack from a Japanese carrier cannot arrive over Oahu as a complete surprise.'" Roosevelt picked up another paper. "Oh yes, this one's a real gem. They insist any Japanese declaration of war against us shall be preceded by a surprise attack on oceangoing ships from submarines, plus a surprise attack on Oahu itself, including our ships and installations. They further insist that the most likely and dangerous form of attack on Oahu would be from the air, from aircraft carriers, who will, I presume, sneak up on us, perhaps in the middle of the night?"

Roosevelt's secretary of the navy, Frank Knox, spoke up now. "Mr. President, there is one accurate statement of which we are well aware. We do not possess adequate numbers of aircraft on Hawaii to effectively patrol a three-hundred-sixty-degree circumference, twenty-four hours a day."

Stimson said, "Overall, I feel that Martin and

Bellinger have done a bang-up job spelling out our weaknesses in Hawaii. But those weaknesses cannot be repaired at the drop of a hat, nor are they likely to become a priority as long as the Germans are winning their particular war."

Knox said, "Sir, I must respectfully disagree on one point. Eliminating weaknesses must **always** be a priority. We have established a powerful naval presence in Hawaii, as a deterrent to Japanese incursions in the central and south Pacific. But that deterrent is only as effective as the strength behind it. This report tells us that there are weaknesses which we must address."

Stimson looked at Knox. "We have never been prepared to fight wars both eastward and westward. Nor should we stretch our resources only to prepare for what **might be,** sometime down the road. Our priority right now is the Atlantic. It has to be. There is a **war** there. I am not aware of any activity by the Japanese which seriously threatens our security."

Roosevelt looked at Hull, said, "I agree. Mr. Secretary, has the State Department been in communication with the ambassador from Iceland?"

Hull sat up straight in the chair. "Yes. They're terrified. Their consul, Mr. Kuniholm, has expressed extreme displeasure that German U-boats regularly sail in close proximity to the Icelandic coast. Their government believes that it is only a matter of time before German troops land there, most likely to establish an airfield and naval base. There is little or nothing the Icelandic people could do to stop them. In addition, the British ambassador, Lord Halifax, continues to insist, as did his predecessor, that we station a number of warships at Singapore. The ambassador continues to offer the argument that such a show of force would stop the Japanese from any more aggressiveness toward Southeast Asia."

Roosevelt said, "I like that fellow, Lord Halifax. Good egg. But he can't possibly expect us to spread our fleet all over the world. We have plenty of concerns without that."

Hull checked his notes. "One more point, Mr. President. We have received correspondence from our people in Berlin. It seems that the Germans were caught completely off guard by our passing the Lend-Lease Act. In fact the word used was 'flabbergasted.' Apparently there is a baffling mental process at work in the Reichstag, the belief that if the British are defeated, the United States will be so terrified of any more war, we'll seal off our borders, and concede the rest of the world to whatever Hitler decides to do."

Roosevelt shook his head. "I am not surprised. I am certainly not flabbergasted. But more than the German attitude, I am concerned right now with their military incursions. Hitler has most recently invaded and secured positions in both Yugoslavia and Greece. The British have suffered a substantial defeat in North Africa and have been driven back to their bases in Egypt. With all that is currently happening, I believe it is time for us to shift some more of the naval strength away from Hawaii, and into the Atlantic. Lord Halifax won't object to that, I'm certain. And Churchill will give me a kiss on the cheek. The greatest danger we are facing right now comes from German submarines. They are distressingly effective at sinking our merchant ships, and even passenger ships have come under threat. Combating those U-boats has to be our priority. Does anyone disagree?"

Hull saw heads shaking, no one protesting.

"All right then, let's put this Martin-Bellinger Report to bed. Everyone agrees they did a fine, thorough job. And, from what I can tell, everyone agrees that they are describing a threat to Hawaii that simply doesn't exist. Or am I overstating that? I'd like to hear from my chief of staff. General Marshall, you have not yet offered us your opinion. I know that you have absolute confidence in General Short, and you believe Hawaii is in good hands."

Marshall spoke slowly, choosing his words with precision. "We believe that the greatest threat to our interests in Hawaii would come from the indigenous population, those Hawaiian citizens of Japanese descent. They number approximately one third of the population. We are confident that those people would take orders from Japan if the time should come for outright conflict. Thus, sabotage of our installations on Oahu and elsewhere is clearly a possibility. To protect against that, General Short is taking every precaution. Beyond this threat, it is my view that the island of Oahu is nothing short of a fortress, impregnable against external aggression.

"In addition, to enhance that strength, we are preparing to relocate thirty-five B-17 long-range bombers, thirteen medium bombers, and one hundred fifty pursuit planes. The B-17s have an effective range far out into the open Pacific, and thus will offer a formidable weapon of defense against any potential enemy. I believe the greater threat to our security lies in the Atlantic."

Hull was always impressed by Marshall's perfect command of whatever information was requested. He could see that Roosevelt was swayed by Marshall as well, but knew that the president was a navy man, and would let no decision pass without some word from the navy secretary, Frank Knox. Roosevelt's short nod was the only cue Knox required.

"Mr. President, I wish our fleet had the capacity to confront every danger we might face in every part of the world. But, as our resources are limited, and our staunchest ally under severe threat, I see no alternative. While I do not wish to denude the Pacific of our fleet, certainly we can selectively transfer a force that can turn the tide against the Germans."

Roosevelt turned to Hull now. "Anything to add, Mr. Secretary? Any observations?"

Hull glanced at the others. "I am not qualified to offer opinions on military matters. As the world crisis is primarily confined to one side of the globe, it should be easier to deal with. My only fear is that, with all the rattling of swords coming from Japan, we cannot be certain we won't find ourselves at war across two oceans and not one. It concerns me that we are so completely dismissive of the Japanese threat. The State Department is daily in receipt of some obnoxious chest-beating by many of their officials, including their foreign minister.

"While I do not disagree with putting our focus on the Atlantic, I am reminded of a tale of a man who was swimming away from a sinking boat, losing his pants in the process. When he reached the shore, and saw a crowd of people, he naturally pulled his shirt down to cover himself. But then the onlookers were pointing out that his behind was now exposed. So he pulled the shirt to cover that part of himself, and of course, he exposed the front. Perhaps my only fear, gentlemen, is that we will be exposed one way or the other."

Roosevelt looked at him with a smile. "Well, until we have two hemispheres' worth of trouble to contend with, we'll just put our energies toward the one that's urgent."

THE CARLTON HOTEL, WASHINGTON, D.C.—
    MONDAY, APRIL 14, 1941

"What's wrong?"

Hull shifted in the soft chair, tried to make himself comfortable. "My back. That's all. Giving me some problems."

"You're fibbing."

He waited for more, knew it was all Frances needed to say.

"Not really. My back is raising a riot when I stand up for any length of time. One more ailment. They seem to multiply daily. Fortunately, Mr. Roosevelt allows us to sit in his presence. It's the advantage of working for a president and not an emperor."

"So, is it your 'old age' again? How often do you complain about what cannot be changed?"

He knew the mischief in his wife's voice, and he also knew she was right. He looked toward her, her smile, the sharp eyes, the look she had given him for thirty-three years. She moved over closer to him, a hand on his shoulder.

"You know that very nice man from Scotland— Mr. Graham, I believe? He had a package delivered here this morning. I was going to open it, but thought I'd wait for you. I'm quite certain it's a bottle of something."

Hull shook his head. "That's just what we need here: more reasons to wake up with a headache. Well, I must be gracious. I'll have my staff respond to him accordingly. You're right, he is a good fellow. They are some very nervous people over there. They need us, desperately. Every morning, they stare across the English Channel, wondering if today is the day the Germans will come."

"Do you think the Germans will come?"

He thought for a few seconds. "There is no

predicting what Hitler will do. But if the Germans invade Britain, it will be a close thing. There will be no easy going, like the Germans had in Denmark. The number of casualties on both sides will remind us of the Great War, certainly. I'm not sure either Britain or Germany could recover from those kinds of losses. And, it will certainly force us to make a full military commitment to Britain, no matter what the isolationists in Congress say. It is a nasty business."

She moved behind his chair, put both hands on his shoulders. "I do not know how any of you can absorb this, day after day. I fear terribly for the British. What does this world become if the British and their empire simply cease to be?"

"I have no answer to give you. It would be a world few of us would be comfortable with. And that is why it cannot happen."

The shared anxieties were the price they both paid for his always confiding in her. It was no different now than it had been in every job and every elected office he had held. He had learned long ago that those who claimed to be your confidant rarely fulfilled the job with the kind of trust he required. Now, that trust was more critical than ever. There were so many secrets, so much intrigue, so many **words** that had the power to change the world.

He knew of so many in the president's cabinet, in Congress, whose wives seemed content to perch on some shelf, waiting for the necessity of appearing at social functions, as though their only purpose was to smile at those who smiled at them. But Frances had always been very different. Certainly, she could handle the social functions: organizing events for him, assisting his staff at the State Department in all of those necessary matters, things he had no idea how to address himself. But when the events were over, when the dignitaries went home, there was no shelf for her to perch upon, awaiting the next social obligation. If there was an issue that gnawed at him, she would detect it. If he was troubled by something far removed from their home, she would know that as well.

She probed his shoulders with her hands. "Is that why your back hurts?"

He ignored the question, said, "Harder, please. I have always admired the strength of your fingers. I should have digits with that much iron. I can think of a few senators whose eyes I might poke." He paused. "No, that's crude. There is enough of that kind of talk around the world. And not just Europe."

"So, is **that** why your back hurts?"

She worked his shoulders with steel efficiency, pushing him deliciously into the chair, then said, "I think I'll stop now. Someone isn't being honest."

He sat straighter. "For possibly the meanest woman on this earth, you are an exceptionally fine wife."

"I know. What happened today?"

"We received a report from Hawaii, from two of the top-notch aviation people out there. They prepared a document detailing a litany of problems involving our defensive preparations, our readiness, our inventory of aircraft, all of that. Of course, I would defer in judgment to those who know what the hell they're talking about: Stimson, Knox, and Marshall. There aren't three men in this country who know more about military matters. They dismissed the report as fantasy, insisting that there is no threat in the Pacific, that our only concern should be the Atlantic. They, or I should say we, have decided to shift some of our naval strength out of Hawaii, and move it to the Atlantic."

She moved around in front of him, sat, looking at him. "Is that a problem? You said the British need us terribly."

"They do. But the army chief of staff, General Marshall, and probably most of the War Department insist that there is no threat from Japan. It is as though everything the Japanese have done so far matters not at all: the move into Southeast Asia, the fighting with China, the bellicose nature of their threats toward us. We froze shipments of most raw materials to them. From our side we are punishing them for their indiscretions. But Ambassador Grew is right there, in Tokyo, and he knows the Japanese character. They will not just accept our punishment and go merrily on. Ambassador Nomura puts on a broad smile, and does his polite bowing, but his government is doing neither." He stopped, realized he was running out of breath. He saw the concern on her face, held up a hand.

"I'm sorry. I am not a military expert. But I know something about diplomacy." He paused. "Did I tell you about the message we received back in . . . God, I guess it was January or February, I don't recall. It seemed to carry very little importance, and the military people laughed out loud when they heard it. The Peruvian ambassador in Japan contacted our people there, with information that in the event of trouble with us, Japan was planning to attack our base at Pearl Harbor. I thought it sounded rather absurd, and Grew agreed, though he did place some confidence in the reliability of the Peruvian source. We passed the message on to the Department of the Navy, of course, and their intelligence people dismissed it as an utterly ridiculous rumor. They criticized Grew pretty severely for swallowing such a story. I've dealt with rumors ever since I stepped into this position. To me, it sounded like one more."

"Cordell, do you think the Japanese are intending to start a war?"

He shrugged. "They haven't confided in me. They're pushing their way south: Indo-China, the Dutch East Indies. They need natural resources, and that's where they'll find them. And they don't need to punch us in the mouth to proceed as they wish. We're not going to lift a finger to defend those places, as long as they leave us alone in the Philippines, in Hawaii, the Panama Canal. It just makes me a little uncomfortable that we're moving ships out of Hawaii. But the military men don't seem to care just how noisy the Japanese are becoming. That's my job, I suppose, to listen to the noise, and try to figure out what it really means. They can't react to noise. They have to wait for someone to punch us, and then, if we're fortunate, we're able to punch back a lot harder."

"You sound as though you're talking about a school yard."

He sat forward, his hands on his knees. "It seems that way sometimes. A world full of unruly children. And if that's true, here's my fear: Children don't always understand the consequences of what they do. Right now, that's a terrifying thought."

# TEN

# Biggs

**H**e was exhausted, nursing blisters from what seemed like an eternity pushing a mop across the teakwood decks. As promised by Petty Officer Kincaid, Biggs had been called out of the sick bay yet again. Biggs had rarely used the more graphic four-letter words he had often heard erupting from his father. But now there was a new one, "swab," that was fast becoming his newest profanity. The command to swab the decks brought joy to PO Kincaid, and misery to anyone unlucky enough to be handed the mop. With the ship at sea, and the other specialized crewmen going about their training, Kincaid had seemed eager to assign the tedious task to the newest man in his command. Biggs could sense that if he wasn't the new man, Kincaid would give him the duty anyway.

When Biggs wasn't pushing a wet mop, Kincaid had passed him along to a gunnery crew, ordering him to assist the gunner's mates at the ammunition transfer stations. Officially it was training in another skill, since most seamen were assigned to all manner of jobs. In a tight situation, every man had to know how to perform several tasks. For Biggs, this meant hours of hoisting belts of fifty-caliber shells to the machine guns as they fired their rounds into open air.

As fascinated as he was by the fourteen-inch guns, Biggs had been grateful not to be assigned that particular duty. The men emerging from deep below the turrets were inevitably plastered with filthy sweat. The farther down the men worked, the dirtier they became, their primary job hoisting the heavy bags of powder up onto the lifts that carried them upward toward the breeches of the guns deep inside the turrets. From all Biggs could learn, firing a single round from a single gun was a perfectly timed and carefully executed operation. In those drills, despite the hierarchy of rank, every man who did his job was a key part of the system. From gunnery officers and range finders to turret and fire control officers, a significant screwup from any one of them could cost lives.

For those not actually a part of that team, the blasts from their fire drew every man's attention, all eyes turned to the turrets. The shock of their thunder, the recoil that rocked the ship was even greater on deck than it had been for Biggs in sick bay, and in the open, there was so much more than just noise. As the guns fired, the fourteen-inch projectiles were actually visible, streaking away in a great arc until they disappeared over the horizon. The question had occurred to him, as it had to nearly every new recruit: How in God's name do you know if you hit something? But he kept that to himself, knew that even if the question seemed like a good one to him, Kincaid would think it was stupid, and no doubt some abuse would follow.

The training this week had included only gunnery practice for the antiaircraft guns and smaller deck guns. But Biggs still felt a sense of excitement over what the gunners were being trained to do. The exercises had gone on at sea for most of a week, the crew drilled in antiaircraft practice as well as in the entire range of critical duties they would have to perform in the event of an attack by torpedoes. The maneuvers needed to escape enemy submarines had seemed logical enough, but Biggs was surprised to learn that an even greater vulnerability was attack from the air, that enemy torpedo bombers could launch their "fish" at close range. The antiaircraft gunners, and all those assigned to the various gunnery stations, were schooled to focus special attention on low-flying enemy planes, so low to the water they might not be visible until they had time to launch their torpedoes. In basic training, Biggs and most of the others had experienced antiaircraft practice only by firing into the clouds above. But here, the experienced gunnery officers passed along a different kind of wisdom, that for a ship at sea, the enemy could come from anywhere.

With this week's drills complete, the **Arizona** had sailed back into Pearl Harbor, the tugboats easing her into her place along the east shore of Ford Island. Biggs was relieved to learn that he would return to his duties in sick bay, and that, for a few days at least, someone else could suffer the misery of deck swabbing.

"Coffee, Mr. Biggs?"

Biggs shook his head with a smile. "Still don't drink the stuff, sir. Thanks for asking."

It had become something of a game, though Biggs had begun to wonder if Dr. Johnson was truly that forgetful. At an open cabinet, one of the pharmacist's mates worked at organizing some of the smaller pieces of surgical equipment.

Johnson looked that way, said, "Mr. Block, don't get too detailed about that. Every time we go out for some kind of gunnery drill, this whole place shakes up again. Unless something's broken, don't spend much time on it."

"Yes, sir. Everything seems fine here."

At the other end of the largest room, another of

the mates was checking levels in various bottles, and Johnson said, "Mr. Corey, you can close that up. I think we're good for today. I had a call from a lieutenant up on the quarter deck that we've got a broken arm heading our way. A couple of the corpsmen are bringing him down. Seems one of the marines did something . . . Well, I'm not going to speculate. We can handle it. You three are dismissed."

The responses were immediate and joyful. Biggs glanced at the clock above the doctor's coffee maker: 1530. A half hour early. The two pharmacist's mates moved out quickly, both men with a smiling salute for the doctor.

"Hold on a minute, Mr. Biggs."

He felt a tug of dread, that something had changed the doctor's mind.

"How you getting along with the mates?"

"Just fine, sir."

"There's a custom—maybe not on this ship, but on some. Those boys are all petty officers. It's the required rating for them to be assigned to the post. Minimum is E-4. Almost always the apprentice is low man, and of course, everybody here knows it. I've seen that duty made pretty miserable, practical jokes and other idiocy. I try to stop that kind of nonsense, since I need you here as much as I need them, and I don't want some jackass bullying you so you transfer right out of here."

"No, sir. They've not done anything. I mean, they kinda stand aside when the dirty jobs come up. That patient yesterday, the fella who threw up his lunch in here. I know that's my job cleaning up, not the petty officers'."

"Good to hear. Block and Vaughan are both good men, Corey too, but he's new. I just need to know I can depend on the lot of you if we run into a jam." Johnson put his hand in a drawer, pulled out a paper. "I'm glad they're gone. They'll each finagle one of these anyway. Petty officers get pretty much anything they want. Here."

Biggs was curious, took the paper, his eyes wide. "Sir, this is a liberty pass."

"I know that, Mr. Biggs. That's why I gave it to you. You've earned a little time off. Get yourself cleaned up, a fresh uniform, make yourself presentable for the officer of the deck. They take that sort of thing seriously. You're representing this ship everywhere you go. You'll need to be back onboard by, whatever it says, 0100 I think. One piece of advice: **Don't be late.** They take that seriously too. I don't want to have to fish you out of the brig."

"Hey! You got liberty? Me too. What you gonna do?"

Biggs continued polishing his shoes, saw Wakeman running a comb through hair that wasn't long enough to matter.

"I don't really know, Ed. Never been into Honolulu at all. What's there to do?"

The men all through the compartment laughed,

and Biggs felt foolish, and as usual, he wasn't exactly sure why. Wakeman reached into his ditty bag for a small white bottle, sprayed a quick squirt down his shirt.

From down the compartment, Mahone was preparing for a shower, said, "Hey, Ed, you oughta keep him close to you. It's his first liberty. We don't need a problem, somebody stealing his dough, stuffing him down an alley. Some of those places are pretty rough. What say, Ed?"

Biggs held up his hands, didn't want to impose on Wakeman's plans. "No, it's okay, I'll be okay. I'll just walk around and stuff."

Wakeman cocked his head to one side, laughed. "Hank's right. You seem like a decent guy, and so far, you haven't done anything real stupid, or dangerous. And Kincaid hates you, so that's even better. Takes his attention off the rest of us. Yeah, sure, come along with me. I'll show you the ropes, keep you out of trouble."

More laughter behind Wakeman, and Mahone said, "Yeah, sure you will. Hey, Tommy, try to keep **Wakeman** out of trouble. He likes to pick fights with marines."

Wakeman played along, said, "Not on purpose. Sometimes I have to explain to those jarheads what 'marine' stands for: **Muscles Are Required, Intelligence Not Essential.** Just trying to be helpful. For some reason, they seem to take offense at that."

Biggs joined the laughter, wondered just how many marines Wakeman had fought, thought, It doesn't seem like the best idea.

Biggs said, "Sure, okay. You wanna fight a regiment of marines, I'll not get in the way."

Mahone pointed a finger at him. "You catch on fast. After his fifth beer, anything can happen."

Wakeman laughed again. "Six. Five just gets me warmed up. Come on, Tommy. Let's head up to the deck. The OOD likes his goodbye kiss."

"Yep, I'm almost ready. Thanks a bunch. Guess I got some things to learn."

Behind Biggs, there were footsteps in the passageway, a grunt as the man stepped through the hatch. Biggs could tell by the faces of the others that it was Kincaid. He turned, said, "Hello, sir."

"What the hell do you think you're doing? You got a date with the new ensign? He looks like he'd be your type."

Wakeman said, "He's got a twelve-hour liberty pass, sir. He's going with me into town."

Kincaid's face seemed to inflate like a hot air balloon. "Where the hell did you get a liberty pass? What tin-brained gap-jawed moron would give you . . . Give me the damn thing, right now."

Biggs hesitated, knew how valuable the pass was. But he also knew that if he tried to hold it back from Kincaid, it might cost him teeth. He reached into his shirt, handed the paper to Kincaid. Biggs expected the paper to be ripped to shreds, the dream of liberty vanishing.

But the petty officer read for a few seconds, said, "So the damn doctor did this. I wondered what went on in that sick bay. Lots of ass-kissing, it appears." He handed the pass back to Biggs, who stuffed it safely into his shirt. "You know how to tell time, lamebrain?"

"Yes, sir."

"Your liberty ends at 0100. You show up here five seconds late and I'll be at the head of the ladder to toss your ass in the drink. You hear me?"

"Absolutely, sir."

Kincaid turned, started for the hatch, stopped, faced them again. "Hell, this moron made me forget why I came down here. The captain's sent word that he expects us to do our part to compete at various forms of athletics with the other ships in the fleet. It's his way of improving our physical conditioning, and he's probably made some bets with the other skippers. There will be sign-up sheets posted in the passageway, and in the gedunk stand, for anyone who's got some kind of skill at some sport. If you're any good, then do your part. If you're going to embarrass the ship, the captain, and me, forget I said anything."

Behind Biggs, Wakeman said, "Excuse me, sir. What kinds of sports?"

"Athletic ones, dink whip. Football, boxing,

basketball. Hell, some others. Wrestling, rowing. And, I think, baseball."

Biggs smiled, then stifled it, but not fast enough for Kincaid.

"What're you smirking about?"

"Nothing at all, sir. Do you know when those sign-up sheets will be posted, sir?"

"They'll be posted when they're posted. I'm late for my nap."

Kincaid turned, moved out through the hatchway, and behind Biggs, Wakeman said, "What's up with you? You some kind of athlete?"

Biggs smiled, stowed the rest of his gear. "A little baseball. High school, a little after. I'm ready to go."

Wakeman looked at the others, said, "He's being cute. I bet you played a bunch of ball, huh? You pitch or hit?"

"Mostly hit."

Wakeman nodded, slapped Biggs's back. "Let's go, slugger. Maybe we'll run into Ted Williams."

# ELEVEN

# Biggs

PEARL HARBOR, HAWAII—SATURDAY, APRIL 26, 1941

He mimicked the moves of the others, a stiff salute to the officer of the deck, then a salute toward the Colors fluttering above the stern. Once down the ladder, Biggs followed Wakeman, who led him into a rapidly moving parade of men, all heading toward the launches that would carry them from Ford Island to the mainland. The trip took only a few minutes, each of the fifty-foot boats packed tightly with sailors, a chorus of enthusiastic chattering. Once across the water, Biggs could see a line of taxicabs, some painted in garish designs, probably to attract more business.

As he stepped up from the launch, another lecture was delivered by the shore patrol officers, the navy's version of the police. The lecture fell mostly on deaf ears: more grave warnings about consequences should they return after their passes had lapsed. He scanned the men around him, saw that none were paying any attention to the shore patrol. All eyes were on the taxis.

He tried to keep up with Wakeman, moving along with the crowd of white, but he stopped, surrounded by an extraordinary smell. For the first time in weeks, he was away from the stink of grease and paint, machinery and gunpowder, all a part of life on an enormous ship. Now, the air was sweet, a light warm breeze drifting down from the hills to the north. He saw the source of this new fragrance—vast seas of flowers, sprays of colors through the open fields, spreading down along the road itself.

But there was no time to linger. Wakeman was already calling out to him, motioning with a sharp wave.

Biggs joined Wakeman in the cab, was surprised that other sailors followed him in. The car seemed designed for five men, and seven had squeezed in, each one obliging the driver with the standard fare of twenty-five cents. As they drove out onto the road, Biggs stared across more of the wide-open lands, enormous fields of thick tall grass. His question was answered by Wakeman: sugar cane. There were more fields, rows of thousands of spiny plants, his question answered before he could ask: pineapples. The trip took no more than a few minutes, the distance less than ten miles, but the fields, and then the mountains beyond, made him understand what he had read about Hawaii, all the talk of **paradise.**

Beside him, one of the other sailors, staring out the other side, said, "Look at those beaches. I bet there's some honeys out there. You fools can go to the bars, I'm heading out to the sand."

Wakeman said, "Suit yourself. That just makes one less sailor lined up at the bar."

Biggs ignored the talk, tried to see the city coming into view. Wakeman seemed to read his mind.

"Those big buildings are hotels. That's the Halekulani, that one's the Royal Hawaiian. Forget them. We ain't dressed for it, and anything they got we can't afford. Those places are for the officers, **senior** officers. They put on their top-notch dress uniforms, sit out there under the moonlight with some high-class dames, smoke their Cuban cigars, and forget the rest of us are alive."

The others seemed to agree, and Biggs felt the car slowing, then pulling over into another sea of taxicabs. The cab driver turned to them as they unwedged themselves from his car. He was an elderly Asian man with brown skin more rugged even than Kincaid's. The accent was heavy, but the message clear: "Twelve-thirty. I be here only to twelve-thirty. You miss, they put you in brig."

Wakeman pulled Biggs from the car, said to the driver, "Plenty of time, grandpa."

Around them, others cabs were unloading their cargo, clusters of men in white, plus a scattering of marines. Biggs had a sudden dread that Wakeman might actually start something right off the bat. But Wakeman was already on the move. He looked back toward Biggs, said, "Come on. Clock's ticking."

Biggs kept up, the street crowded with sailors, most headed in the same direction. Wakeman tugged his arm, said, "I forgot to ask you. You got money, right?"

"Yeah. Seven bucks."

Wakeman said, "I got four. That makes you my best friend. Let's go get something to eat."

As they left the restaurant, Biggs rubbed his stomach, a soft groan coming from some very happy place. Wakeman shared his joy, the two of them walking out into the street, joining the parade of sailors.

"Ed, that's the best steak I've had in months, maybe years."

"Don't get used to it. That place cost us two eighty-five. At least their beer was cold. I need another one of those."

Biggs followed Wakeman's lead, moving silently through the throng of white-uniformed men. What he couldn't reveal to Wakeman was that he hadn't had a genuine sirloin steak his entire life.

"There it is. The Black Cat. Worst booze on the

island, but the beer's cheaper than that restaurant. Fall in with me, sailor. There's always a line."

Biggs followed, trying to absorb every detail. He could see a larger building off in the distance, a flow of sailors moving in and out.

"Hey, Ed. What's that place? Seems popular."

"That? It's the YMCA. That's for teetotalers and mama's boys. Anybody can't find anything better to do ends up at the Y. They got women in there you can dance with, for a price. But you better keep your distance. No lovey-dovey stuff. And after the dance, if you actually try to touch one, some goon breaks your arm. You're allowed to have a conversation, if you want, but I've always wondered why anyone would want to sit and talk to a dame, knowing that's all you're ever going to do with her. Hell, I heard some of 'em are married. They just go there to pick up a few bucks. You can get a hamburger in there, and they got cold milk, stuff you can't usually get on the ship. But I didn't come to town to get a glass of milk."

Biggs laughed. "For somebody who's not a teetotaler, you sure know a lot about the place."

"I'm not paying you any mind." The line for the beer counter moved quickly, and Wakeman said, "We're up next. Don't be bashful." A sailor in front of them moved away, and the Asian bartender waited impatiently. Wakeman said, "Hey there, my buddy and I will have two beers. Make sure they're cold."

Biggs saw no expression on the man's face as he dipped down, retrieved the two bottles from a watery bath behind the bar.

"Sixty cents. You want 'em opened?"

Wakeman put the change on the wooden bar, said, "We ain't marines, sport. We don't chew through the glass."

The bartender popped off the caps, and Wakeman said, "You still selling gin in this place that's half water?"

Off to one side, Biggs saw an enormous man, obviously Hawaiian, sliding slowly toward them. Wakeman seemed to notice as well, made a bow toward the bartender.

"Thank you, kind sir."

Wakeman handed a bottle to Biggs, the crowd of sailors behind them pressing forward, the bar doing a brisk business. They slid through the mass of white uniforms and out the door, Biggs holding the beer close, no chance of spilling on someone who wouldn't appreciate it.

"Hey, Ed. You see the size of that lunk that was eyeballing us?"

Wakeman glanced back at him, then moved off the street into a narrow clearing, a small bench occupied by a sleeping sailor.

Wakeman ignored the sailor, but Biggs couldn't avoid the man's aroma. Wakeman said, "I heard 'em called bouncers. You make an ass of yourself and they bounce you right into the street. There're a few of those big guys in just about every joint here. They can mess you up pretty good, even before the shore patrol gets there. Then, those boys will mess you up too. Hell, I was just playing back there. But the Black Cat's pretty well known for watering down their whiskey. Probably every joint does the same thing. That's why you get beer. Not much they can do to that."

He took a long swig from the bottle. "And something else you need to know. It's a good idea to stay close to where you see all the uniforms. Don't go wandering off down some side street. I've heard it said that the natives here aren't too happy having an islandful of sailors. Hell, there have been sailors based here for years, not sure why the natives ain't gotten used to it. We spend enough money, and drink a hell of a lot of their local brew. I ain't never had a problem, but I know some that have. Most of the trouble comes when somebody tries to get too friendly with a local girl. Their families get a little prickly about that. But that's why we got Hotel Street. Let's go over to the beach first; I'll show you where it is. Then, we can make our way over to **squack**-land. There's a trolley comes through over that way. We can hop on."

Biggs had no idea what Wakeman meant, but he followed along, moving only as fast as the mass of white uniforms around them, elbows and shoulders twisting past. He slipped off into a small open area, Wakeman following, and Biggs took a swig from his beer, felt his face twisting into a squint.

"Good God. What is this stuff?"

Wakeman shrugged. "Yeah, I know. It's called Primo, but there ain't nothing prime about this crap. They should call it 'pisso.' But unless you want to go to the Royal Hawaiian and pretend you're classy enough to be there, this is what we got. Trust me. You'll get used to it."

"Guess I got no choice."

"Now you're getting the picture. Come on— there's the trolley. I'll show you the beach, the classy part of town."

Biggs followed as Wakeman stepped up to the passing trolley, the car already packed with men in uniform. After a few short minutes, Wakeman motioned to him, **Get off.** Biggs obeyed, followed Wakeman again. The street wasn't nearly as crowded here, and Biggs saw a statue, nearly twenty feet tall, obviously of a native Hawaiian, a wide sandy beach behind it.

Wakeman said, "Waikiki Beach. Looks nice. But keep your shoes on. The sand will cut up your feet real good. It ain't Florida sand, I promise. Coral or lava or something. And any fool thinks he's gonna find some sweet bathing suit honey out there is dreaming. Those are at the hotels, and they're only looking for officers."

Biggs was absorbing all that Wakeman was telling

him, saw very few people out on the beach. He looked again at the statue. "Who the hell's that?"

Wakeman shrugged. "The head Hawaiian, I guess. Big cheese."

Biggs wouldn't accept that explanation, moved toward it, saw a cluster of sailors coming together, posing for a photograph around the base of the statue. He waited for them to finish, and Wakeman was there now, said, "What's the deal? It's just a statue."

"Hell, I don't know. Just curious. I want to see the sights." The sailors cleared away, and Biggs moved closer, read the plaque. "It's King Kamehameha the Great. I guess he used to own the place."

Wakeman said, "Yeah, okay, fine. You ever wanna come to the beach, get broken glass in your shorts, this is a good place to be. Tonight, we got other things to do. It's a little bit of a hike to Hotel Street, so the trolley is the only way to go. Come on. I told you I wanna see the squacks."

Biggs swigged again at the beer, still not used to the awful flavor. "What's a squack?"

Wakeman downed what remained of his beer. "Boy, you really don't know nothing. Hotel Street's the place to go for, um . . . some **friendliness.**" Biggs still seemed puzzled, and Wakeman shook his head. "For crying out loud, Tommy. Squacks are whores. And Hotel Street is where they live, or work. You can get just about anything else you want there too, including a tattoo."

"Why would I want a tattoo?"

"You could put something nice on your arm about the navy, like an anchor or something. Your mama's name maybe. Or even fancier, you could put a girl's name inside a heart. 'Course, if you ain't planning to marry her, that's dumb as hell. So, you got a girl back home?"

"No. I kinda gave up."

"Well, you got a world of opportunity right here. Not that you'd wanna marry one of the squacks. Although, she might be kinda rich. I hear they make stupid lots of money. Don't think I'd wanna sit around the dinner table and talk about her work, though. Come on, let's grab another beer or two along the way."

"Okay, but how many you figuring to drink?"

"Until the money's gone. That's kinda the way this goes." Wakeman waved him on. "Time's wasting, my friend. Wave goodbye to King What's-his-name up there and let's practice getting used to this genuine Primo beer."

He had suffered through more beers than he could recall, none of them going down any better than the first. But the fog in his brain stripped away the fear and reality of just what it meant to be on Hotel Street. The lines were long, the visits brief, the madams backed up by the menace of the bouncers, men eager to take your money. Once inside, Biggs was overwhelmed by the smell of perfume, and by the heavy haze from the beer. He had no idea what to do, how to act, what questions to ask. But the girl took his hand, helping him as he staggered unevenly to some place he had never expected to be. She had dark hair and dark eyes, and she spoke to him with a soft voice that reminded him of that girl he always hoped to find. And then, with his three dollars gone, it was over.

Wakeman staggered along with him, past the snaking lines of sailors, marines, and soldiers, all of them waiting their turn at the various doorways. They stumbled over each other's feet, Wakeman keeping his eyes glued to the path straight ahead. But Biggs still wanted to see it all, blinked through bleary eyes in drunken fascination as they moved past small shops selling jewelry and trinkets, souvenirs and pinball parlors, barber shops and clothing stores. He knew that Wakeman had done this often, and, more important, that Wakeman knew how to get back to the taxis. Biggs had no idea where they were, or how they had gotten there. He realized he still had a beer bottle in his hand, pulled it up to his face, said, "Hey, Ed. There's a little bit left."

"Drink it."

Biggs nodded. "Right."

He obeyed, the brew as warm as the air around him. He felt the sudden rise of a volcano, deep in his gut, his eyes widening in a desperate glance toward a narrow gap between two ramshackle buildings.

"Oh God. Gotta puke."

He made it to the narrow space, blind darkness in front of him, and his knees gave way, dropping him hard onto broken concrete. There was no holding back what came next, no thoughts of a good meal wasted. He let it go with pure abandon, then felt a hand on his back.

"Good job, Tommy. You're officially a drunken sailor."

Biggs stood slowly, Wakeman assisting. He put one hand against the small wooden building and tried to stop the swirling in his head, a useless effort. Wakeman said, "Come on. Taxi's over there. Maybe."

Biggs focused as well as he could on Wakeman's directions, saw Wakeman stumble, try to right himself, and Biggs said, "Christ, you're no better off than I am. You sure which way is right?"

Wakeman said, "What time is it?"

"Hell, I don't know. I ain't got a watch."

"I'll find out."

Biggs saw a pair of marines, one with a watch on a muscular tattooed arm, Wakeman moving their way in a crooked line. "Excuse me, gentlemen. Can you tell me the time?"

The larger marine eyed them both with a dangerous smirk. "What's your ship, swabby?"

Biggs moved closer, alarm bells in his head, felt a wave of impending doom.

Wakeman said, "The **Arizona.**"

"Woo-hoo. Hotshot battleship swabbies."

Wakeman seemed to run out of words, and Biggs said, "Sorry, just asking the time."

The marines seemed disappointed they hadn't gotten a rise out of the two sailors, and the one with the watch glanced at it. "It's 2350."

Wakeman seemed too far gone to be paying attention, and Biggs said, "Thanks, marine."

Biggs pulled Wakeman with him, let out a breath, felt as though he had just avoided losing his teeth. Wakeman seemed to come awake, pointed, said, "And there they be. Told you."

Biggs saw the taxis, and both men staggered toward them. They reached the first cab in line, the driver another old Asian man with a gap-toothed smile.

"We wait for more sailors. More coming."

The wait wasn't long, five more staggering in, most smelling as bad to Biggs as he knew he did. The quarters changed hands, Biggs now completely broke. This time, the ride covered the nine miles with a speed that would have drawn praise from a race car driver. Biggs held his arms tightly around his middle, willing himself not to be sick again. He stared out through the fog in his brain, focusing on the ships at their anchorage, blurry clusters of lights. He kept his eyes on the lights, the row of battleships, feeling a desperate need to focus on anything but the jerking motion of the taxi.

The cab disgorged them at the pier, no one more grateful than Biggs. Immediately, the shore patrol gathered them up, directing them onto one of the fleet of shore boats. Biggs held on to Wakeman's shirt, stepped down unevenly into the launch, was suddenly packed tightly alongside several dozen more men, most in the same condition he was. The boat moved out quickly, most of the men silent, others moaning in outright misery. The atmosphere was distinctively different than earlier that evening, the raucous enthusiasm for the adventure replaced now by sailors suffering the consequences.

The launch reached Ford Island in a few minutes, some of the men climbing out on their own. Biggs tried to help Wakeman, fell on his backside, Wakeman now bending low to help him. A hard hand gripped Biggs's shoulder, a harder voice barked in his ear, "Get your ass out of my boat. Come on, move."

The hand lifted him up, and he fell forward, another pair of hands pulling him up and out of the boat. He stood on his own, wavered slightly, heard Wakeman, "They were certainly polite. Come on. We're there. Kinda almost."

Biggs saw the lights along the berth, the massive shape of the **Arizona.** He followed Wakeman, who followed the slow river of men, all of them bound for the same place. At the ladder, the men climbed in slow single file, some helped by others, some climbing up on hands and knees. Biggs waited his turn, his mind drifting everywhere at once, until he felt a shove in his back, the ladder clear in front of him. He gripped the rails, blinked, took the first step. Behind him, he heard the voice of Wakeman.

"You can do it, Tommy. Don't look at the water. No thoughts of the water. Try not to feel the ship moving."

There was laughter above and below, and even through his fog, Biggs knew what Wakeman was doing. He said nothing, thought, **I'll get you back. You'll see.**

He reached the top step, forced himself into a straight-backed stance, his eyes finding the OOD, his words coming in a gummy slur.

"Report my return aboard, sir."

The officer of the deck waved him aboard without looking at him, seemed weary and impatient. Biggs thought, I bet he got this job because he did something stupid. Who the hell would volunteer for this?

Wakeman was aboard now, repeating the same formality. Behind them, at the top of the ladder, a pair of men stumbled onto the deck, one man throwing up. Biggs looked at the OOD, wondered what would happen, but the officer waved toward a pair of men standing to one side, stationed there for exactly this purpose. The drunken men were propped up, struggled to say the required words, the OOD waiting patiently, one of them finally offering some coherence.

"Report my return aboard, sir. Mister officer, sir."

He broke into sloppy laughter, and the OOD waved him aboard.

Biggs started forward, staggered, his knees not cooperating. Wakeman said, "Hey, do you need to go to sick bay? You look awful. Stink too."

Biggs's knees buckled again. "Maybe."

"Then go. I'm not holding your hand. I gotta find my hammock."

Behind him, Biggs saw more men coming aboard in perfect shape, a bounce in their steps, no hint of any impairment. Biggs tried to focus on those, the only conclusion: YMCA. He turned, looked for Wakeman, saw him leaning against the rail of the ship. Wakeman blinked hard, said, "Go on . . . sick bay. You look like hell, and you don't need to be puking out the top of your hammock."

"What about you?"

"I'm below you, remember? Won't nobody care."

The dizziness seemed to be getting worse, and Biggs tried to respond, no sounds coming from his mouth. He managed a slight wave of one hand, then looked for the hatch that would lead him forward, toward sick bay. He passed one of the hatches, knew he had to reach one more. There was a grunt beside him, and he jumped crookedly, saw a man just inside, hidden by the dark. The man stepped forward now, the ship's lights catching his face. It was Kincaid. The sight of the man's glare startled Biggs into a brief second of sobriety, and he said, "Hello, sir."

Kincaid said nothing, just looked at his watch, then stared for a long second at Biggs. Then he turned, back into the darkness, and was gone. Biggs felt the icy butterflies in his stomach, not a sensation he wanted. Well, he thought, he said he'd be checking. So, he checked. Maybe that'll piss him off too, that I'm on time. He'd'a been more pissed off if I'd puked on his shoes. The thought struck him as supremely funny, and he steadied himself, tried not to laugh out loud. No, he'll hear me, and read my mind. Sure as hell.

Biggs continued forward, made it to the hatch, stepped into the passageway, started up the first ladder, slow careful steps. The familiar smells came up toward him, disinfectant. Somebody's gotta be there, he thought. He paused on the ladder, gripped the rail tightly and took a long breath, tried to settle everything that was so unsettled. He continued up, saw a light from sick bay, felt desperately grateful. He was there now, said aloud, "Hello? Sir? Who's on duty?"

The face appeared, Dr. Condon, a smile of recognition, turning to concern.

"Good Lord, Mr. Biggs, what happened to you?"

"Liberty happened, sir."

Condon laughed, tempered it with a quick glance up and down to assess Biggs's condition.

"Come on in here. Let me check you out. You get into a fight?"

"Oh, no, sir."

"What did you drink?"

"Six beers, sir. Um . . . no, there were more."

"Was it that green Primo stuff?"

Biggs nodded silently. He liked Condon as much as he liked Dr. Johnson. Now he was just embarrassed, and was beginning to feel supremely stupid. "I'm sorry, sir. I never did anything like this before."

Condon laughed again. "It shows. Let's get you cleaned up. You smell like something I'd usually toss over the side. Let me guess. You and your buddies went to Hotel Street."

"Yes, sir."

Biggs sat where Condon directed him, removed his shirt, saw for the first time the stains, realized he looked as awful as he felt.

"Hotel Street is a pretty seedy area, Mr. Biggs. Not advisable to spend much time there. Are we going to have to include you in the short-arm inspection?"

Biggs dropped his head. "Guess so, sir. But God, she was beautiful. Never done that before, never. Not sure I ever will again."

Condon laughed. "You will, probably. Just be careful, take precautions. But don't make a habit of that sort of thing. There's plenty more to do out there."

"Yes, sir. Thank you."

He felt his stomach turning over again. "Uh, sir, is there something you can give me to settle my belly?"

Condon handed him a clean shirt, said, "Put this

on, and then, if you can manage the ladder, head down to the gedunk stand." Condon reached in a pocket, searched, pulled out a dime. "Here. Go drink a Coca-Cola. Best remedy there is. But next time? You're buying."

# TWELVE

# The Spy

The ship was the **Nitta Maru,** arriving like so many others in the commercial harbor close to Honolulu, a passenger list of tourists and businessmen, some American, most Japanese. They passed dutifully through U.S. Customs, the few Americans familiar with the routine, many of the foreigners finding their way with the help of passengers who spoke English, or even of the customs agents. As the Japanese tourists passed out into the warm fragrant air of Honolulu, some marveled at the green, softly rolling hills, while others were drawn to the city and its nearby beaches.

One man carried papers that passed him through customs without complication: the official documents of the Japanese foreign ministry. He was met and assisted by an official of the consulate, the usual practice for a new government employee serving his country. The documents listed his name as **Tadashi Morimura.**

Immediately upon his arrival at the Japanese Consulate, introductions of this new man were made to the staff. The consul general himself, Nagao Kita, seemed unusually enthusiastic welcoming Morimura, assuring all who served there that Morimura would be a valuable and useful asset to the duties of the consulate.

With introductions complete, the two men withdrew into the consul general's office. To the rest of the staff, Morimura seemed to be distracted and unfriendly, but not rude. But the staff had greater concerns, struggling with mountains of paperwork, a variety of official tasks both serious and mundane. Any new man, especially an assistant to the consul general himself, was welcomed for whatever load he might bear.

What no one but the consul general could know was that Mr. Morimura was not remotely who he seemed to be. His name was in fact Takeo Yoshikawa, and he had been sent to Honolulu with a very specific mission, which had nothing at all to do with managing the Japanese Consulate. He was a spy.

Kita sat, pointed to a chair, but Yoshikawa stood, staring out a window.

Kita said, "You do realize we must maintain the appearance that I am your superior, that you are here to perform all manner of services for this office, on my authority. No one will be told any more than that."

Yoshikawa glanced around the office, showing mild interest in the documents, plus a photograph of a family, which he presumed to belong to the consul general.

"Nice photo."

There was nothing genuine about the compliment, but Kita was accustomed to the shallow politeness of diplomats.

"Why, thank you. I have been in this post only for a few weeks, and my predecessor advised me to decorate my office with sentimental artifacts as I saw fit. My family is to join me here in several weeks, for which I am very pleased. Do you have any such photographs, or other mementos? If so, please decorate as you wish. You will be housed in the compound here, a cottage among several out back. The Ministry suggested in strong terms that you not establish a residence outside our walls. I concur. Here, you are free from observation."

Yoshikawa was already bored, said, "I have nothing to hang on walls. All I require is a bed, and perhaps a small stove."

Kita tried to maintain the smile, and Yoshikawa looked at him now, could see the strain it required.

"Mr. Consul General, you need not accommodate me in any other way. I know my instructions, what the Naval Ministry expects of me. My job is straightforward, and I shall approach it as that."

"Very well. I appreciate bluntness." Kita leaned to one side, pulled an envelope from the bottom drawer of his deck. "This came for you by special courier. No one here is aware of the contents."

He handed it across the desk, and Yoshikawa said, "No one except you."

Kita did not respond, and Yoshikawa tore open the envelope. When he saw the contents, he couldn't avoid a smile.

Kita said, "Is it what you were expecting?"

Yoshikawa counted the hundred-dollar bills. "Six. That is what I was told to expect. It will cover my expenses for a good while."

Kita leaned back in his chair, seemed perplexed. "That's a substantial amount of money. I don't know what kind of expenses you would incur here. Nearly everything you should need is within the compound, at your convenience. If you need anything else, we have staff who can secure it for you."

He paused. "I wish to ensure that you and I understand your role here. I have confirmed my own instructions with Tokyo. Will you please tell me what Tokyo has authorized you to do here? It is possible, certainly, that questions could arise which could fall upon this office. The FBI in particular makes it a practice to monitor our activity, though they have not yet come inside our compound. But that could change. My people here are excellent at what they do, jobs that can be challenging: dealing with Japanese immigrants, all the necessary paperwork for imports and exports, and any other matter that might arise. If there is some activity that is suddenly embarrassing to them, if your duties or any other activity were to attract unwanted attention, it could be most unfortunate, to your mission and to mine. In other words, if you are planning anything that could be dangerous to our relationship with Hawaii or the American military, I wish to know about that in advance. I believe that is a reasonable request."

Yoshikawa folded the currency, slipped it into his pants pocket. He turned again to the window, said, "I am here to observe the American fleet, calculate their numbers, and observe their movement. I am to do the same with the military aircraft. I am not here to light fires or blow up bridges."

Kita said, "That is much the same as I have been told. I must ask, for my own curiosity, why does the Ministry require this information?"

Yoshikawa ignored the question, picked up his small suitcase. "Do you have the key to my cottage?"

Kita handed him a small envelope, and Yoshikawa said, "Have one of your secretaries show me where

I am to stay. You need not concern yourself with my well-being or my activities from this point on. I will do all I can to convince your staff that I am performing consular duties here. But I do not answer to your authority, nor to anyone in your office. Are we clear on that?"

Kita's pleasantness evaporated. He stood, waited for Yoshikawa to offer the bow appropriate to Kita's position. Yoshikawa ignored him, and moved quickly out the door.

PEARL HARBOR, HAWAII—SUNDAY, MAY 4, 1941

Yoshikawa stepped off the road through tall grass, the hillside falling away in front of him, flowers bathing him in their scent, the soft buzz of a thousand bees the only sound he could hear. He stepped carefully over rocks hidden beneath the grass. He carried nothing in his hands, nothing in the pocket of his white linen pants, nothing in the lone pocket of the bright blue Hawaiian shirt he now wore. For anyone who happened by, Yoshikawa was one more in a vast horde of tourists, each one clamoring to see the beauty that was Hawaii. It was all around him, but as he stepped closer to the slope, he ignored all of that. He was focused on the water, and the great ships of the United States Navy.

He stood for several minutes, no one approaching him, no one driving past on the road, where his taxi and his specially chosen driver waited, a man with patience and no questions.

Yoshikawa backed away from the steep hillside, stepped again through the grass, crushing flowers, scattering the bees, reached the car, opened the door.

"Take me to the teahouse. You mentioned it before."

The driver turned, an older man with a naturally friendly face. "The Shuncho-ro. Yes, I take you. Many nice girls there."

Yoshikawa said nothing, and the driver started the car, pulling out quickly onto the gravel road. They rode in silence, Yoshikawa visualizing the details of the harbor in his mind. The ships had been farther than he had hoped, the details not as clear as he had needed. The driver seemed to read his mind.

"I can get you some binoculars, if you wish. It makes for better sightseeing."

"No."

Yoshikawa had gone over those kinds of details long ago. There could be nothing to make him stand out, nothing more than the typical tourist, gazing at fields of flowers, the presence of the great ships just a part of the fascination with such a beautiful place. Binoculars would draw attention, the military security perhaps, or even the FBI. He knew that there were many Japanese on the islands under surveillance, suspected as potential saboteurs. That most of them were resident Hawaiians seemed not to matter to the authorities. He wanted nothing to do with those people, considered most of the Japanese residents to be ignorant trash, untrustworthy, with loyalties that were at best suspect. The notion that he could recruit islanders to assist him as an army of potential observers had been dismissed completely in Japan.

His role was solitary, and his manner innocuous, even buffoonish. If there were police, he would bow too many times, maintain the mindless grin, play directly into the Japanese stereotype. And all the while, he would practice what he had been trained to do: notice what was important, ignore what was not. There would be nothing written down, nothing to incriminate him as anything beyond the simple-minded tourist, dazzled by so many impressive sights. The first rule he had learned during his training in Japan was clear enough. **Don't get caught.**

He stared out the window of the taxi, caught more glimpses of the harbor, the ships closer. The taxi passed several houses, small shops, but soon they arrived at the teahouse. The taxi pulled over, stopped, and Yoshikawa noticed one other car out front. He said nothing to his driver, bounced quickly from the cab, stepped inside. The smell of tea and tobacco was overwhelming and delicious, and his eyes settled immediately on a pair of geishas at one end of a narrow bar. They responded by shuffling toward him on their wooden shoes, made their short bows.

"Hello, sir. May we offer you tea? Would you like to sit? We are happy to talk to you."

"Got anything stronger than tea?"

They seemed confused at the request, but behind them, an older man said, "I have sake and beer."

Yoshikawa was disappointed, had heard much about the variety of alcohol the Americans had brought to the islands, had hoped to discover just how much it was possible to consume. That would have to wait for a different kind of bar.

"Sake, I suppose. But you should get something better. Not everybody wants to come here just to find Japan."

The man motioned to the geishas to move away, seemed to sense trouble. "We are a Japanese teahouse. I do not try to be anything else."

Yoshikawa didn't want to anger the man. "I'll take the sake. That's good."

He looked around, found nothing to see but tall grass outside the windows. He saw stairs now, said, "What's up there?"

The man was still wary, handed him a cup of sake, one of the geishas carrying the bottle on a tray.

"Upstairs is our second floor. Nice observation deck. Beautiful scenery."

"I'm going up there. She can come too."

He started up the stairs, heard the owner say something to the girls. They're probably his daughters, he thought. You dress them like geishas, and you had better expect them to be geishas. All I want is someone to pour my drink.

He reached the top of the stairs, a balcony, was surprised to see the harbor spread out before him, much closer than it had been from the grassy heights. There was a pair of men seated at the center table, the only other customers there. He ignored them, the geisha setting the tray down on a small table, then standing to one side. He was familiar with the routine. If he wanted her to sit, to talk, it would cost more. He downed the sake, and she stepped forward, quickly refilled the small porcelain cup. He downed that one as well, and she obliged him again. He allowed himself to relax, took his time with the drink, looked over toward the other two men, who were standing now, ready to leave. But his eye caught something behind the men, something he hadn't seen before.

"What is that?"

He knew the answer already, but she said, "It is a telescope. For a small price, we allow our guests to use it, to look at the ships, the airplanes. It is most beautiful, and very interesting."

He stood, moved that way, put his eye to the lens. He swept the telescope from side to side, could see Hickam Field, could see the details of every one of the large ships and some details of the smaller ones. He focused on one of the nearest battleships, saw sailors moving about on the decks, and nearby, shore boats and service barges. Another movement caught his eye, and he raised the telescope slightly, saw a trio of planes taking off from a field on what he already knew to be Ford Island. For the first time since arriving in Hawaii, he flashed a genuine smile.

"Yes. It is interesting. It is **very** interesting."

# PART TWO

———————— ★ ————————

"Japanese cannot be effective pilots because
as babies, Japanese children are carried on the
backs of their mothers, or their older sisters,
and their older sisters play hopscotch, (so
that) the baby's head bounces around and it
destroys the balance in the inner ear."

—As told to Captain Arthur
McCollum, U.S. Navy, 1941

"The Japanese, as a race, have defects of the
tube of the inner ear, just as they generally
are myopic"; [thus they have] "a defective
sense of balance and are less mechanical than
any other race" [and are not capable of
flying aircraft].

—Fletcher Pratt, historian, 1939

# PART TWO

# THIRTEEN

## Biggs

Onboard USS Arizona, at sea—
Thursday, May 22, 1941

**H**e had no idea why Kincaid had left him alone, but knew better than to ask stupid questions. All he knew was that others had been chosen for swabbing duties, which was just fine with Biggs. His duties now were what he had been trained for: remaining belowdecks in sick bay, working alongside the doctors and the pharmacist's mates. Each day that passed, Biggs had learned something, some small piece of medical expertise, learning to distinguish the serious from the superficial. The mundane ailments of most of the crew quickly faded away once at sea, the aftereffects of overindulgence usually cured with a good night's sleep. Most of the problems now involved physical injuries, often affecting the men who toiled deep below, whose duties put them around the heaviest machinery.

This shift, Dr. Condon commanded sick bay. Biggs had detected the subtle hint from the mates and some of the corpsmen that they felt Condon was just a bit too young and a bit too green to hold sway over them. It was an informal system that Biggs was becoming familiar with, that anyone new, regardless of his rating or whether or not he was an officer, had something to prove before any of the veterans would take him seriously. Biggs's exploits during his first liberty seemed to satisfy some, as though getting drunk or seeking out a prostitute earned a man a badge of honor.

He was still the newest man in sick bay, but the pharmacist's mates now mostly left him alone—no practical jokes, no games. They seemed to accept him for the efforts he had made to fit in, his acceptance of just where he stood in the medical hierarchy, which of course was at the bottom. His willingness to accept his place, performing the most unpleasant jobs, had earned him an odd sort of respect, even from the doctors. Biggs knew it was just the job, and that one day he might have the opportunity to climb the next step up the ladder.

He was wiping down one of the metal countertops when he heard voices, Condon responding. The voices were louder now, full of urgency and pain, Condon calling his name. He tossed his cloth into the small sink, hurriedly washed his hands. He moved quickly, saw two corpsmen and two sailors supporting an injured man, the man whimpering, then a long shout. Biggs saw the injury now, one arm blistered red, its flesh seared and a smear of blood on the man's pants, dripping onto the deck. One of his sailors turned away, overpowered by the smell, and Biggs stepped forward, the corpsmen now taking charge, laying the man flat on the deck. Condon grabbed a hypodermic needle, jabbed it into the man's uninjured arm, said, "Okay, I've given you morphine. You hear me, sailor? Talk to me."

The injured man looked up at Condon, already bleary-eyed. Condon said, "We're going to lift you up onto this table. Don't worry, sailor, you're in the right place."

Condon directed the others to lift the man, Biggs helping, careful to avoid the man's arm. They rocked him back, all arms supporting him, eased him up onto the table, laid him flat. Biggs was engulfed by the smell of the man's wound, made himself look at the bloody horror, knew it had to be a part of his job.

Condon said, "What happened?"

One of the sailors, an older man, wiped the back of his hand on a sweating brow.

"Antiaircraft gun, a blowback. This one's pretty bad. He gonna be okay, Doc?"

Condon was eyeing the injury, making a soft probe with his fingers, gently moving damaged skin. He looked toward the injured man's face, said, "He's out. Won't feel anything now. He'll have some scars, and it'll be a while before he returns to duty. When we get back to Pearl, I'll send him over to the hospital. They'll be able to fix him up there, better than I can here."

Biggs understood the term "blowback," someone firing a round before the breech was fully sealed. Inside the turrets of the largest guns, an ignition like that, from any source, could kill a man. At least, he thought, the antiaircraft guns are smaller, far less powerful, with far less powder to ignite. It didn't mean the man's pain was any less, just that he was still in one piece.

Condon said to Biggs, "Cabinet over there, on the end. White tube of salve."

Biggs moved quickly, handed the tube to Condon, stepped back out of the way, awaiting whatever might come next. Condon looked to the sailors, said, "You boys can return to duty. Nothing else you can do here."

One man seemed grateful to be let go, but the older sailor stood still, stared at the injuries. Biggs saw his insignia: chief gunner's mate. He had a touch of gray hair, wore the fierce expression of a man who had seen this before. The first sailor moved away, waited at the hatchway, but the chief didn't move, said, "I knew this would happen.

Damn it all, they keep sending us out here, doing God-knows-nothing. Same routine, over and over. The officers say it's supposed to teach us to be perfect, but all it does is bore us to death. Torpedo drill, antiaircraft drill, every stupid damn drill they can think of. I'm sorry, Doc, don't mean no disrespect. I appreciate what you're doing for Sam. But he's like the rest of us. Same thing, day after day. Instead of making us sharp, it's doing just the opposite. It's hard to take any of it seriously. We go to sea on Monday, go back to Pearl on Friday. I might as well be working in a damn hardware store. I've been in the navy for twenty-six years, and it scares me to hell that if there's ever a shooting war, we're gonna tell the enemy, **Oh, excuse me, hold on there, we gotta do this the way we practiced it.**"

Condon handed the salve to one of the corpsmen, motioned to the wound, and the corpsman went to work on it. Condon looked at the sailor, said, "I don't have anything to tell you, Chief. If nothing else, this ought to push all of you to pay more attention to what you're doing. I'm not gonna lecture you on that, not at all. It's just a fact."

The chief put his hands on his hips. "You're kinda young. How long you been a doctor?"

Condon kept his eye on the corpsman's work, said, "Long enough so I know how to do that."

The chief lowered his head. "Yeah, I guess so. Look, sir, I ain't blowing off steam about the officers on this ship. They're doing what they're told.

This whole task force out here, a dozen ships running around in circles. Yesterday we did a drill to
dodge bombs, like the bombs are always gonna
come from the same direction, at the same speed,
and be the same size. It's the admirals, sir, playing
with us like this is their own big-assed bathtub and
we're just toys."

Condon looked up, said, "That'll be all, Chief.
You can return to your station."

The chief seemed to understand he had gone too
far, put a hand on the patient's chest.

"Get better, Sam. The doc'll take care of you."

Condon watched closely as the corpsmen dressed
the wound. He looked at the chief. "He probably
can't hear you. Be grateful for that."

The chief kept his eyes on his man. "He can hear
me. I've reamed his ass so many times, he hears me
in his sleep." He looked at Condon now, a glance
at Biggs, the others. "Sometimes it's not practice,
eh, Doc?"

Condon said, "Not in here."

USS ARIZONA, PEARL HARBOR, HAWAII—
    SATURDAY, MAY 24, 1941

As they were eased back into Pearl Harbor, the rumors began. Biggs saw what they all saw, that ships
that should have been in their moorings were gone.
The officers knew the schedules for maneuvers,
which task forces were out, which were in port. This

time, something was very strange, the rhythm of each week's drills upset. The scuttlebutt was vague, and no one below the captain seemed to know who had given the orders, or why. But the rumors were confirmed not long after the **Arizona** tied up to a mooring of its own. Every man on the ship could see for himself that the fleet had become smaller, that three of the battleships, the **Mississippi,** the **Idaho,** and the **New Mexico,** along with the carrier **Yorktown,** had simply vanished.

The questions came quickly, a handful of officers digging for information, confirming that those ships, plus a number of destroyers and other support craft, had been ordered away from Pearl Harbor. They were to make their way through the Panama Canal to strengthen the Allied power in the Atlantic.

Biggs didn't understand anything about the kinds of naval strategies some of the men were tossing about with feigned expertise. But knowing that four of the great ships were simply gone didn't reassure anyone, Biggs included. Pearl Harbor just seemed a good deal more empty.

USS ARIZONA, PEARL HARBOR, HAWAII—
    THURSDAY, MAY 29, 1941

They had tried to play cards, but Kincaid interrupted them with what seemed to be a carefully calculated plan to annoy everyone.

"Listen, you turds. You've got a half day's rest, but don't get used to it. Orders have come down that we're painting the hull again. I asked for rose-petal pink, to please all you little girls in here, but the skipper likes gray, so I was overruled. Until then, enjoy sitting on your ass."

Kincaid moved out through the hatch, followed by a collective groan from the men around Biggs. The griping came now, the dread of hanging on ropes, smelling the harsh stench of paint.

Biggs sat at one end of a mess table, a sheet of white paper in front of him. It was his most recent effort to write to his mother, but the words weren't coming. The infuriating thought distracted him, as it had every week before, that whatever he said to his mother would be intercepted by his father, inspiring some kind of abusive criticism toward her. His mother had responded to his letters, though not as often as he would have liked, and thankfully, she'd made no mention of his father. Her letters were mostly meaningless chatter about everything that was happening with distant relatives, all their various ailments, all those who were aging badly. It was painfully mundane, and he loved every word of it.

This time, as always, he agonized over the right reply, something she would enjoy hearing, maybe even an emotion they could share. But, he thought, how do I send a note just to her? Simple answer to that one. You don't. He slid the paper aside, decided he would come back to it later.

At the other mess tables in the compartment, the men were involved in various activities of their own, some of them writing letters, some polishing shoes, idle chatter and the usual griping. As usual, the big talk and cursing was aimed at Kincaid, but no one had the idiotic courage to say anything to the PO's face.

Closest to him, Wakeman and Mahone were playing cards, what seemed to be a game of gin without any rules. Biggs slid that way, watched for a long moment.

Wakeman offered the invitation. "Okay, you look like a hurt puppy. You can join in the next hand. I'm wiping the floor with him in this one."

Mahone crossed his arms, careful to hide his cards. "Your ass, Ed. Got you on this one. Just wait. I need a six. Maybe a ten too."

"Thanks for telling me, numbskull."

Biggs was laughing, not sure if he wanted to join in the chaos.

The boatswain's whistle cut through the talk, then the loud voice on the speaker nearby.

**"Now hear this!"**

The sounds jolted him, the slight echo telling them it was ship-wide. Biggs sat up straight, looked toward the speaker, most of the others doing the same. Some of the talk continued from men who ignored the messages, as though they had heard it all before.

The loudspeaker came again.

**"Now hear this! To all hands. Notice received from the United Press in London. On twenty-seven May, 1941, the German battleship** Bismarck **was engaged in combat with ships and aircraft of the British Royal Navy and the Royal Air Force. After receiving considerable damage from British battleships** HMS King George V **and** HMS Rodney, **the** Bismarck **was sunk with much loss of life. That is all."**

Biggs heard cheers drifting through the ship, but not many. He looked to the others, said, "That's good, right? I mean, really good?"

Wakeman seemed oddly subdued, had stopped his card game and was staring into space. Mahone put down his cards, shook his head. Biggs was confused, saw Kincaid move in through the hatchway. Biggs wanted to ask him the question, thought better of it. He assumed Kincaid had something to say.

"You worms hear that? You suck that in?"

The responses were muted, and Biggs still didn't understand, waited for more. Kincaid said, "You know how big that son of a bitch **Bismarck** was? No need to guess. She was better than forty-one thousand tons. A third bigger than this whale. Now she's on the bottom of the ocean. Anybody thinks we're too tough, that nobody can kick our ass? Well, worms, the toughest ship in the world just got **its** ass kicked. Chew on that one."

Kincaid moved back out through the hatch, and Biggs looked again toward the others, saw no hint of cheering or gloating over what he imagined to be a great victory. Two tables away, Lorenzo said, "I loved that ship. Read all about her. She had fifteen-inch big guns, and she was a hell of a lot bigger than us. **She was eight hundred feet.** And she could make thirty knots. On our best day, we do about twenty-one. Any ship in this navy ever tangle up with her, it might have been 'Good night, nurse.' I guess the Limeys got lucky."

Biggs was still confused, said, "But she was the enemy, right? I mean, we're buddies with the English . . . the Limeys, right?"

Wakeman slid his cards aside. "Tommy, something you ain't learned yet. And I hope you do pretty quick. You know, when you play on a ball team, like maybe the Tigers, and you're playing the Yankees. Sure, you wanna win. But over there in that dugout, maybe there's Lou Gehrig and Babe Ruth. You'd respect that, right? You'd respect them? And, you'd try like hell to strike 'em out."

"Yeah, guess so, sure."

"Well, the **Bismarck** was Babe Ruth. She was a bigger, faster, and stronger battleship than this one. We respect that, Tommy. If we ever had to fight her, would we try like hell to sink her? Damn right. But now she's sunk. And you can cheer if you want to.

But I'll take my hat off to her. And even more important, we learned something today, that we better not forget. There ain't a ship on this earth that can't be sunk."

It was quiet in sick bay, Dr. Johnson reading a book in one corner of the smaller room, two of the pharmacist's mates playing cards. Biggs had taken advantage of the calm, knew that by tonight, as liberty ended, the place would likely fill up with the afflicted, as happened every night the ship was in port.

He stared at the paper again, pen in hand, wrote the date at the top. He was still annoyed with himself, thought, You're out of excuses, Tommy. Just write her the damn letter. He glanced over at the doctor, whose eyes were buried in some novel. He looked again to the blank paper, pondered the date, did the simple math in his head. Her birthday's in ten days, he thought. Wonder if Pop will do anything for her, if he'll even remember. The neighbors will know, I guess. Maybe. But he won't let them do anything for her, **no fussing.** Anybody spends a nickel on her, he takes it like a damn insult. Well, I'd fuss if I could. I guess this is the best I can do.

Dear Mom,
    Back in port now, after most of a week at sea.
We did a bunch of maneuvers, fired a whole

bunch of antiaircraft shells. Not much for the gunners to shoot at, maybe a seagull. (that's just a joke). Sorry to hear about Aunt Edna's poodle. And Cousin Barney's leg. If he was here, we could fix him up. I like the doctors a lot. They're teaching me all about working in sick bay, and they say I could go to corpsman training in a year or so, if that's what I want to do. I think it is, Mom. I'll never go to college, pretty sure of that. This is as close as I'll come. I'm sending you some pay, a money order, to help out. Also, maybe you can buy yourself something nice for your birthday. Don't let Pop talk you out of that. You deserve it, maybe something pretty. So, happy birthday. And don't ever forget that I love you. Pop too, I guess.

Love, Tommy

He reread the letter, saw Johnson looking at him. "Her birthday, right?"

Biggs nodded, had forgotten he'd mentioned it. "Yes, sir. Thank you."

"You sending home your pay? A lot of the men send something."

"Most of it, sir. I keep enough to go to town maybe once a month. That's all I need."

Johnson shook his head, smiled. "If you say so, Mr. Biggs. But most of the sailors I know think of liberty as the only reason they joined the navy. I know the phar-mates feel that way. Three of them are going ashore tonight, and probably half the corpsmen. Mr. Vaughan went last night. But you? It feels like I have to pry you out of here."

Biggs looked again at the letter. "I'm sending her enough to buy herself a nice present, if Pop don't grab it all." He paused. "I guess you're right about liberty. It's been a long week. Geez, sir, I sure wish I had a liberty pass."

Johnson laughed. "Don't go all hangdog on me, Mr. Biggs. Hand me that pen."

Biggs obliged, and Johnson reached into a drawer, pulled out the paper, went to work. He handed the pass to Biggs, said, "Just try to be a little more civilized this time, Mr. Biggs. You're supposed to **clean up** the messes, not become one."

It had already become more routine, Biggs falling in with the others, stuffing into the taxis, impatiently enduring the journey to town. Once in Honolulu, he moved with the flow of sailors toward the obvious places, the more popular destinations. This time, he ignored the street that led to the beaches, to the enormous statue of King Kamehameha. He knew exactly where he was going, saw it now: the Black Cat.

The beer was awful, something he was trying to get used to. He still had not acquired the taste for Primo, but the other labels, even familiar ones, were considerably more expensive. He moved outside, saw sailors tipping their bottles skyward, some not pausing until the brew was gulped down. Then, they returned to the bar, to do it all again. Biggs felt a certain admiration for that. He had seen men drink a half dozen brews in quick succession, a feat he would never attempt.

As he fought to swallow his way through his first bottle, he thought of Wakeman. No liberty for him tonight, he thought. That afternoon, Wakeman had been assigned to swab duty on the quarter deck. Kincaid happened to catch Wakeman reading a letter from one of his girlfriends, still with the mop resting on his arm. Kincaid had done what he always did, reacted to Wakeman's self-indulgence with his usual profane fury. When Kincaid ripped the letter into pieces, Wakeman naturally enough took offense, but Kincaid took much bigger offense. It wasn't the kind of thing that would put Wakeman in the brig, but sometimes Kincaid's punishment was worse. And so now, Wakeman was still swabbing the quarter deck, and might be doing that all night long.

Biggs finished the beer, the last gulp going down just a little more smoothly. He stood to the side of the current of sailors, eyed the Black Cat again. It's thirty cents, he thought. Mom won't mind if I hold back a little money for me. It's just beer. The guilt slipped away with thoughts of the next bottle. At least it would be cold.

"Hey!" The voice carried toward him above the

din of the mob, and he ignored it, focused on making his way into the Black Cat.

"Hey! Tommy! Hey!"

The voice was closer, and he tried to see the source, but the flow of men was carrying him along. He eased his way off the street, his back against a wooden building, and heard it again.

"Hey, Tommy! Hey, over here!"

He smiled now, knew the voice, searched the crowd, saw the small man struggling to get through the mass of white uniforms. Russo was there now, offering a strong handshake, both men enjoying the moment.

"I'll be damned, Ray. I wasn't sure where the hell your ship sailed off to. Besides that, I figured you drowned by now."

"No more than you."

"Yeah, but at least I can swim."

"You mean that splashing around we used to do in the river? I know your mom did her damnedest to teach us both how to swim. All I did was drink nasty water and stick my feet in the mud. At least you can doggy-paddle, Tommy. I can't even tread water."

Biggs laughed. "I guess that's why they put us on ships and not under them."

Russo showed the wide smile Biggs knew well, but the razzing came in a steady flow.

"Well, my boat's a hell of a lot smaller than yours,

so when I fall overboard, it'll be easier finding me. I hear they use battleships to teach those guys in the circus—you know, the ones who get shot out of a cannon? You training for that?"

"Nah, we're taking target practice on all those little ships around the harbor. Yours is probably next."

They stared at each other with wide smiles, a long few seconds, and Russo said, "Damn, Tommy, it's good to see you. So, how you doing? Hawaii looks pretty nice. Navy life okay?"

"Better than that. I'm assigned to sick bay, when I'm not painting the hull. I work for really good doctors. They want me to go in for corpsman training."

Russo nodded, still the big smile. "Proud of you. Knew you'd do good. Hey, you hear about the **Bismarck**?"

"Yeah. Hell of a thing. Bunch of my shipmates feeling kinda bad about it."

"Why? They German or something?"

Biggs realized that Russo wouldn't understand, but he wouldn't push it. "Nah, they just like battleships. So, how about you? How you doing?"

Russo shrugged. "Made it to seaman second class, so I figure I'll make it to admiral in about four hundred years. I paint the hull every week, swab the deck about ten times a day. I like the airplanes we serve, though—big noise, a lot of fun watching them take off on the water."

Biggs said, "Hey, come on. You want a beer?"

Russo made a face. "Nah. Nasty stuff. I'm still trying to find a place that has Chianti. And speaking of nasty stuff, what the hell are you doing in this part of town? I never figured you for Hotel Street."

Biggs laughed. "You're here too, right? Hey, it's something to do. One of my shipmates introduced me to the place. But never mind about that. How's your family?"

Russo's expression changed, the smile gone, a long pause. "I didn't want to tell you. Didn't want you upset. My papa died, Tommy. That construction accident last year . . . He was hurt in the head more than we knew."

Biggs felt a cold shock. "Jesus, Ray. I had no idea. I'm so sorry."

"Mama's trying to get by, and my sisters are helping out. I think, when my hitch is up, I gotta go home, try to find a decent job close by. The navy experience might help that. The chief on the **Curtiss** said that there could be a lot of seaplanes in a place like Jacksonville. I'm trying to learn what it takes to work on 'em, a mechanic maybe. Sounds like a job somebody might need."

Biggs stared at him, one thought punching him. Mom didn't write about that? Well, no. Pop didn't have much use for "that Italian fella."

Biggs wasn't sure what else to say. "You can't just stay in the navy? Make a career? You could make a decent wage if you move up a little, go for machinist or fireman or something. Hell, I'm making thirty-six bucks a month now. The petty officers make a hell of a lot more than that. And nobody's gonna toss you out the door when times get tough."

Russo shook his head. "Been all through this with my CO, and the chief. My family needs me close to home. My sisters are too young, Mama's only forty-five, but she's got no skills, and you know there's nothing in Palatka. She can't make it being a waitress, and I'm not having that anyway. Anything better than that? Hell, she didn't even finish high school."

"You could get out early then, like a hardship discharge?"

"No. I want to finish my hitch. I send home what I can every payday, but Mama don't want me quitting. I guess I don't either."

Biggs felt supremely depressed, completely detached from the mindless celebration that drifted past the two of them. "I don't know what else to say, Ray. You got me into this, and I gotta say, it's the best decision I ever made."

Russo grabbed his arm, gave it a hard squeeze. "Then I'm happy, Tommy. Something good came out of this. I'm happy for you. And I'll push hard to learn something useful on the **Curtiss.** You're right, there's a lot of technical stuff on any ship, and the guys seem willing to help me out."

Biggs thought, Because you didn't quit. "It'll work out, Ray. Give it time."

Russo managed a smile. "I gotta stick around regardless. I'm curious as hell how long it's gonna take you to fall overboard."

# FOURTEEN

# Hull

For several weeks, he had been coming into the office at the department more frequently. Too many dispatches were flowing in from the offices overseas, a level of heat he could feel coming from too many foreign capitals. The war that Japan was waging in China had continued with as much ferocity as ever, with no indication from Japan that it had any thoughts of agreeing to a withdrawal or even a temporary cease-fire.

He turned the chair around, faced the large window, and stared out toward the Washington Monument. He thought of Washington the man, so decisively handling a crisis that was utterly unique. There is very little that is unique about war these days, he thought. Entire countries are consumed, populations displaced, or worse. It is all too common. So what can we do now to be decisive, to repair so much that is broken?

He turned the chair back to the desk, and his perfect view of the portraits of Lincoln and Grant. Interesting pairing, he thought. Lincoln would charm, and Grant would fight. So, they have predicted our future. We tread ever so carefully down the middle of those paths. Clearly, I am the charmer. He smiled at his joke. There are warriors aplenty in this town. Stimson, for one. Age has hardened him, made him inflexible. If the president suggested that tomorrow we attack Germany, Henry would be the first to give a cheer.

He ran his gaze over the desk, stacked high with folders, papers, all manner of documents. So, is this what age has to done to **you**? You push papers? Not much charm to **that.**

He glanced at his watch, saw it was nearly two P.M. He tried to clear a space on the desk, thinking he should appear organized. He heard one of his assistants pounding on a typewriter, and Hull glanced at his watch again, thought, Will he be late? Not like a navy man. Or perhaps it is. The only navy man I can predict is the president, and I'm awful at that.

He heard a voice, the clack of the typewriter quiet. Hull tried to look busy, saw the young man now at the door of his office.

"Excuse me, Mr. Secretary. The chief of naval operations is here, Admiral Stark."

"Send him in."

Stark was there quickly, standing at attention with his usual smile. He wore the dress blue uniform, unusual in the summer's heat, offering Hull the impression that this meeting was some kind of singular honor for Stark. Hull felt he should stand, not sure why, and he pointed to the plush leather chair to the left of his desk.

"By all means, Admiral, let's not make this a dress ball. They put these soft chairs in here for a reason."

"Thank you, Mr. Secretary. This is the first time I've been in this office. Extremely impressive. Your view across the Mall is enviable. I rather admire President Jackson, and your portrait of him is a wonderful likeness. Magnificent fireplace too. I imagine in the winter, this becomes a most inviting place to be."

"I hope not. Shorter conferences are generally the best kind."

Stark kept the smile, and Hull tried to read him, admired the shock of wavy white hair over wire-rim glasses: a man who looked less like an admiral and more like a friendly bank president. Hull guessed him to be about sixty. He still wore the odd smile, but Stark's silent pleasantness was becoming tedious.

"So, Admiral, you asked to see me. What might we discuss?"

Stark raised a hand. "Ah, yes. Mr. Secretary, I am

not sure if you are aware, but you and I have been on the same side of an argument that we seem to have lost. I refer of course to the transfer of a portion of our fleet from Hawaii to the Atlantic theater. I know that you made significant arguments to the president, as did Secretary Stimson. The secretary had assumed I would cast my vote with him, so to speak, but after considerable thought, I concluded that the fleet should remain strong right where it is. Or, was."

Hull had endured these discussions, knew that Stimson's aggressiveness would almost always prevail with Roosevelt. "I was not aware that the decision had been made. I am not usually briefed on matters within the War Department. I was also not aware of your position on the matter, Admiral."

Stark lost the smile for a moment. "Are you acquainted with Admiral Kimmel?"

"Only in passing."

"Mr. Secretary, the admiral is a good friend of mine. He is also a great believer in the strength of our navy, which is one reason the president chose him to be commander in chief, Pacific Fleet. He and I have had considerable correspondence about the reduction of his fleet, and the implications of that action."

"So, how badly have they weakened the Pacific fleet?"

"Blunt. Good—no need to waltz around the matter. Three battleships, one carrier, four light cruisers, seventeen destroyers, and assorted non-combat vessels."

Hull absorbed the numbers, said, "That sounds like a fleet all by itself."

"Well put."

There was a pause between them, and Hull said, "Why exactly are you bringing this to me, Admiral? This is your area, and you answer to Secretary Knox and Secretary Stimson. I suppose you know that."

"Sir, you are more familiar with the Japanese mind than anyone in this city. You speak to their principals directly, you are privy to their press releases, you directly supervise Ambassador Grew. Do you believe the Japanese are sincere in what they say? Can they be trusted?"

It was an odd question, and Hull said, "Is it not your job, sir, along with Admiral Kimmel and everyone else in that uniform, to be prepared in any event? My job is to reach agreements, to breach differences, to find a common solution to a problem. Your job is to provide the security that allows me to do all of that. When I meet with diplomats from any of the Axis countries, they appear to be looking me in the eye. But in fact, I know them to be looking over my shoulder at the strength of our armed forces. My bargaining position, if I can use that term, comes directly from the strength that you command.

"My one fear, which I expressed to the president, is that by reducing the fleet in Hawaii, we have sent a signal to the Japanese that we are not as prepared to meet their threats as we once were. The counter-argument, which Secretary Stimson voiced so force-fully, is that beefing up our might in the Atlantic sends a strong message to the Germans that we are willing to commit ourselves to meet their threats."

Stark smiled again. "You are indeed a diplomat, sir. You lay plain both sides of the argument."

"Admiral, there is nothing 'plain' about what is going to happen in the Pacific. All we can say for certain is what the Japanese have already done, not what they are going to do."

"Perhaps. To that end, I have summoned Admiral Kimmel to Washington. He is in transit, and will arrive here tomorrow. Naturally, reducing his fleet did not go down smoothly with the admiral's com-mand. You are aware, certainly, of what resulted when Admiral Richardson voiced his displeasure at the orders coming from my office and others. As I said, Admiral Kimmel is a friend. I'm hoping to calm his concerns, and perhaps have him meet with the president himself. Perhaps then the admiral will realize that reducing the Pacific fleet is in the best interests of us all."

"Even though you don't agree with that."

Stark looked down. "It's the president's show, Mr. Secretary. I'm hoping that by bringing him here, Admiral Kimmel may be convinced of that. I do not wish to see him end up like his predecessor. As I said, sir, he is my friend."

WASHINGTON, D.C.—SATURDAY, JUNE 21, 1941

Hull occasionally had brief morning meetings at the White House while the president was still in bed. He wasn't sure how often Roosevelt allowed that kind of personal interaction, but Hull took it as a compliment. And, if Roosevelt nodded off in the midst of any discussion, Hull took no offense. The man was, after all, in bed.

"Admiral Kimmel's a pistol. Not as abrasive as Richardson, but he speaks his mind." Roosevelt paused, lit a cigarette. "I don't think he cares a whole lot for me. He came here expecting me to disregard all the decisions that have already been made, and do everything his way. But he didn't swear at me, like Richardson did. And when I told him it was done, that was that. He took his medicine, and is headed back to Hawaii."

Hull pointed to the lit cigarette, resting now in an ashtray beside Roosevelt. "Is that the best idea?"

Roosevelt seemed to notice the cigarette for the first time. "You sound like Eleanor. She'll give me hell for that. She gives me hell for most everything else. Things get a little touchy around here, I just pull the sheets up. Very convenient."

Hull could feel Roosevelt's mood, a strange buoyancy, as though all was right in his world. There had been a considerable outpouring of support for the president's fireside chat on May 27, a lengthy dose of reality aimed at isolationists in Congress, who continued to resist the necessity of aid to Britain. Hull had participated in the authorship of the speech, and had received his fair share of praise. But Hull was keenly aware, even if few others paid attention, that the entire address was focused on Germany, emphasizing to the American people, and the world, the dangers that Hitler and his military portended for the western hemisphere. Japan had not been mentioned.

As Roosevelt snuffed out the cigarette, Hull said, "I wonder if you should prepare a fireside chat that addresses our problems and possible threats in the Pacific."

"What threats?"

Hull wondered suddenly if he was on a fragile piece of ground. "The Japanese threat."

Roosevelt waved at him. "Yes, yes, I've heard all of that. Admiral Kimmel made all kinds of pronouncements to me about the great threat we face in the Philippines. But will you please tell me just how anything out there compares to what we will face in the Atlantic if Hitler invades England? Ask Churchill, he'll tell you straightaway. The Germans have run over every country they've attacked. No one has been able to fight them off. Hell, when France went, we should have realized just how much worse it would get. You look at the countries Hitler's military has conquered, it looks like one of those old maps of the Roman Empire, for Christ's sake. Except for one difference: He hasn't taken

England. You know damn well how important that is, how much is at stake."

Hull rubbed his chin, nodded slowly. "I know. But the Japanese are sure to occupy all of Indo-China, all of the Dutch East Indies, and they'll likely hit us in the Philippines along the way. I'm no military strategist, but I'm fairly sure they won't let our people there just sit on their flank."

Roosevelt smiled. "Oh, you strategize just fine. But I'm ahead of you. Sometime next month, we're appointing a new commander in the Philippines, Doug MacArthur. General Marshall has already planned to transfer a flock of B-17s out that way as well. The Japanese won't dare come near us."

Hull looked down, both hands on his knees, thought of Admiral Stark. **Not everyone agrees.**

Roosevelt said, "Look. I know there's bitching about the fleet in Hawaii. I heard it straight from Admiral Kimmel, and half the other admirals around here. But the fact is, we have to stand up tall in the Atlantic. It's not like I stripped Hawaii bare. They've got eight battleships still, and I promised Kimmel he'd get the next two off the line, the **North Carolina** and the **Washington.** They should be seaworthy in a few months. You just keep doing what you're doing. I've pretty well handed you most of the responsibility for any dealings we have with Japan. We've got a lot more eyes on Europe. It just has to be that way."

THE CARLTON HOTEL, WASHINGTON, D.C.—
    FRIDAY, JUNE 27, 1941

He unbuttoned the white shirt, saw the stain before she did. But there was no place to hide.

"You did it again, didn't you? How many times? How many shirts are you going to ruin?"

He looked at the red blotch on the shirt pocket. "It usually washes out, doesn't it?"

She looked at him with arms crossed, her head tilted slightly. "It never comes out. We just buy you new shirts. We should get them by the crate, instead of wasting so much money at the Men's Shop."

Hull stared at the stain. "Might be a good idea. I'd go through a pile of them before you noticed."

It was the usual scolding, what they both were used to. Hull could never break the habit of sliding red grease pencils into his shirt pocket. The pencils were his own affectation, what he used to edit the documents that came across his desk.

"You know, at least they're not pens. That would be worse. I think."

"Yes, then you'd ruin your jackets too. Honestly. Give me the shirt. I'll try yet again to get it out. I assume you still have shirts to wear."

He smiled, handed her the shirt. "I have plenty. I wouldn't dare run out."

He heard a knock at the door in the next room. Frances said, "Who on earth could that be?"

"Somebody who needs to see me, no doubt. I sent everybody home too early."

He moved into the front room, pulled open the door. The man was young, wide-eyed, obviously surprised that the secretary of state would open his own door.

"Sir. Oh. Sir, I have a message for you from the White House. I was told it was most urgent."

He took the sealed envelope from the young man, who seemed relieved to have completed his mission.

"Thank you, young man. You may leave."

The man moved down the hallway with quick steps, and Hull saw the presidential seal on the envelope, nothing else. Frances was waiting for him in the office, said, "The president?"

Hull turned the envelope over in his hand. "Yes, I assume. Unusual. There's no **Eyes Only** mark. Maybe they were in a hurry to get this over here."

"Well, open it. I have things to do, like cleaning your shirt."

He pulled a letter opener from a drawer on the desk, slid it through the flap. He saw several paragraphs, read slowly. His hand began to shake just slightly, a slow boil of anger. She waited a few seconds, then said, "What has happened? Is it the president? Is he all right?"

He knew Frances could read him well, but this time she was wrong. He shook his head. "The president is fine. The White House is passing along a bulletin from the United Press in Berlin. It's the Germans." He paused, tried to take a breath. "They have invaded Russia."

"Cordell, I'm not sure what this means."

He looked at her, then moved closer, put his hands on her shoulders. "It means, my love, that everything has changed. The entire world has just become a different place, and perhaps, a much more dangerous one."

THE CARLTON HOTEL, WASHINGTON, D.C.—
   SATURDAY, JUNE 28, 1941

Hull was in the worst foul mood he had experienced in a very long time. He sat across from Ambassador Nomura, avoided looking at him, fought to control the anger he couldn't ignore. Nomura had been escorted into Hull's comfortable space, but Hull made no effort to rise, offered no handshake, indulged in none of the pleasant formalities of diplomats. Nomura had made his customary bow, had waited for the invitation to sit, Hull responding by pointing to the sofa, no other sound. There was silence for a long minute, and he could sense Nomura fidgeting. He looked at him now, a cold stare, fought to keep his voice low.

"I am not inclined to offer platitudes, nor am I interested in any pleasant discussions about world events. Yesterday, Germany sent one hundred fifty army divisions—approximately three million men—and thousands of armored vehicles, and crossed the border into the Soviet Union. **Three million men.** A military operation this size would have been planned over a period of months. Japan has an alliance with Germany. You are partners, **friends.** Exactly how do you expect the United States government to react to this, to Japan's certain involvement in this outrage against the Russian people?"

He had run out of breath, waited for a response, could see that Nomura was actually sweating. Nomura avoided his eyes and kept his head down. He said, "Mr. Secretary, please accept my most solemn promise that I had no knowledge of the German action until last night, when I heard it on the radio news. If my government is a participant in this action by the Germans, I was not made aware."

"'Action'? That's how you are describing this? It is an invasion. As we speak, men are dying as they try to defend their country."

Nomura looked down again, nodded. "Yes. Invasion. But I know of no one in my government who had a hand in this . . . invasion. We have no other desire in our hemisphere than to promote peace. We have no aggressive goals toward the United States."

Hull focused on Nomura's demeanor, what seemed to be genuine sadness. The thought burst into his mind, Good God, he believes he's telling the truth.

Hull said, "Well, then, Mr. Ambassador, what will you do now, in the name of peace? Will you talk to your foreign minister in Tokyo, ask a few questions? Will you come back to me with some sort of meaningless apology? Will you describe what the Germans are doing the way you describe what you are doing in China? And, since your ally has now chosen to make war with the Russians, will you do the same? Is Vladivostok your next target? Surely, that would please Hitler. You can roll Russia up between you, share the spoils. Is that not the game being played here?"

Nomura let out a breath, seemed willing to accept Hull's anger. "Sir, I will speak with my foreign minister, and I will carry out his instructions. That is my job, is it not?"

Hull couldn't keep up his anger toward Nomura. All he saw now was a man with wounded honor. He is a decent man, Hull thought, working for an indecent government. But he will do what he must. He will do his job, while his government tells him only what it wishes him to know. And I must pretend that I believe him.

# FIFTEEN

# Yamamoto

He had thought of inviting Hori onboard the **Nagato,** his friend visiting often when the ship berthed close to Tokyo. Yamamoto was nursing a boiling fury, and couldn't just sit in his wardroom, couldn't abide the confines of his quarters. At first, he had paced the wide teak decks, the crew knowing to keep their distance, the scowl on his face telling them just how much space they should give him. Now, Yamamoto felt only like leaving the ship, taking a walk on grass, and screaming out loud at his friend, a man who would understand his temper.

The launch had deposited him on the pier, Yamamoto in civilian clothes. He did not look back at the great gray beast, ignored the low roar of the launch as it pulled away. He stepped up away from the water, saw the wide swath of green, a beautiful park where he had walked with Chiyoko many times. But she would not be here, not today. He did not want her to hear him so angry.

"Iso! Over here."

He was relieved to hear Hori's voice, saw him now, offering a cheerful wave. Yamamoto moved that way, enormously grateful to have a confidant, someone who would listen to his ranting without reporting him to those who would send him to prison.

"Thank you, my friend."

"For what? You asked me to meet you. I'm here."

"Let's move farther away from the water."

They walked silently, Hori waiting for whatever Yamamoto wanted to say. Yamamoto stopped now, turned to him, a glance past him, cautious of any listeners.

"Have you heard anything from the Naval Ministry, or perhaps from the prime minister's office?"

Hori shook his head. "Should I? What have you heard? Has something happened?"

"There is a surplus of stupidity in this world, my friend. Dangerous stupidity. The Germans have invaded Russia. And not just some noisy little invasion. Three million men."

He saw Hori's eyes widen. "That is incredible, Iso. They had a nonaggression pact, a treaty. They had already carved up Poland between them. Hitler and Stalin . . . It was as though they had a partnership."

"There is another partnership we must be concerned about. Hitler is supposed to be our ally as well. There is enormous concern throughout the government—no, call it **fear**—that we might now be drawn into a war not of our making. I share that concern." Yamamoto glanced around, saw no one else within earshot.

"There is speculation that because of our magnificent alliance with those people in Europe, by Germany's invading Russia we might be compelled to do the same. There are already plans being tossed about for an invasion of the Russian ports right here, Port Arthur and Vladivostok. It is suggested that the other two partners of the Tripartite Pact will expect us to do our share to support whatever decisions Hitler chooses to make."

Hori nodded slowly, and Yamamoto knew he understood. Yamamoto said, "It is one thing to hold the reins of the horse. It is quite a different thing when you merely ride in the cart. Hitler's cart."

Hori smiled. "I had forgotten you have been to Texas."

Yamamoto appreciated his friend's attempt at levity. "It would be humorous if it wasn't so outrageously stupid. What Hitler has done is attack the nation with the largest landmass on earth. This makes as much sense to me as loading up the Japanese army and ferrying them over to California to invade the entire United States. I'm quite sure we don't have the perhaps eighty million soldiers it would require to do that. How many more soldiers does Hitler have to send into Russia, if they get bogged down? Apparently, no one in Germany has ever heard of Napoleon."

"Iso, this government has a great many options for committing suicide. But taking orders from Berlin? No matter what they decide to do? It will not happen. I might be confined to the shadows, but I still have friends. The emperor is not pleased with the Tripartite Pact, no matter what you might hear from the Ministry. You have your own challenges, and you should use more energy to push through your own plans. If Hitler defeats Russia, his army is still a very long way from here. Worry about that when it is time."

"And when will it be time? When Russian bombs fall on Tokyo? Or perhaps German bombs? And if the Ministry ignores the American fleet in Hawaii? It might be American bombs."

BATTLESHIP NAGATO, YOKOSUKA HARBOR, TOKYO, JAPAN—SUNDAY, JUNE 29, 1941

The officers filed slowly out of the wardroom, the men saluting him with smiles, grateful for the invitation to a lunch far fancier than they were accustomed to. It was a gesture of appreciation from their admiral, who so rarely offered flattery to any of his subordinates. This time, the men had been handpicked for their outstanding performance in their specific stations on the ship. Yamamoto believed that this kind of recognition was likely to inspire others to increase their own efficiency.

The room was empty now, the table a display of culinary carnage, empty china plates and silverware. It was unusual on a Japanese ship, though his senior officers were used to it by now, that he ordered the table set not only with traditional Japanese touches, but with Western items as well, including small porcelain finger bowls. Most of the others had left theirs untouched, but he dipped his fingers into his own, his orderly at his side quickly, offering a fresh napkin.

"Thank you, Omi."

Yamamoto rubbed a hand on his belly, straining his shirt. "I fear I am eating too much, or too often. Perhaps too well."

Omi stood back, a short bow. "Oh, no, sir. You are most fit."

Yamamoto stood slowly, his hand still on his belly. "You are a poor liar. But you are forgiven. I am the only one here who is expected never to lie. Even if the truth is dangerous."

More orderlies were moving in now, efficiently cleaning the table, stripping off the white cloth. He knew he was in their way, stepped out through the door, walked along the steel rail and stared out at the harbor. There were a half dozen destroyers moored together, one aircraft carrier along a pier to his right. Three light cruisers were lined up in a formation of their own, and beyond, smaller patrol boats and service vessels. He looked to the sky, thought, A fleet of dive bombers would do . . . what? Destroy what we have anchored here? What would be the odds of their success? How many would be shot out of the sky? I am tired of asking these questions. I want answers.

For more than three months, the details of Yamamoto's attack plan had been discussed and debated, Admiral Onishi seeking out the counsel and opinions of the men he trusted. They were men who placed their faith in the airplane, who shared Yamamoto's belief that airpower was the only equalizer that Japan could rely on in any fight against a major power. But as Onishi had told Yamamoto, the man chosen to be the chief planner believed in airpower even more passionately than Yamamoto himself.

Commander Minoru Genda served as the staff officer for the First Air Carrier Division, and had hands-on experience with nearly every combat plane in the Japanese arsenal.

He was in his mid-thirties, a handsome man, well spoken, with a self-confidence that Yamamoto could sense immediately. As well, Genda had a particular physical trait that gave the impression of a man who exuded perhaps too much energy: The man's eyes seemed to burn when he spoke, a piercing stare that even Yamamoto found difficult to watch.

For weeks now, Genda had consulted with Onishi and others, hammering out details of Yamamoto's attack plan, analyzing what might work and might not. As Yamamoto considered the arguments, some directly opposing his own, he couldn't avoid the weight of his age, that he was an old man offering a plan that only young men could carry out. Even now, it was the young men who were fine-tuning the details, solving problems with solutions that even Yamamoto had not considered.

They filed into Yamamoto's wardroom, filling the seats around the long table. Yamamoto acknowledged Onishi with a smiling nod, but his focus quickly settled on Genda.

Yamamoto was drawn to the young man's hard stare, said, "You would do well at cards, Commander."

Genda seemed puzzled, but accepted the compliment. "Thank you, sir. I do not often have the time."

"No, I would imagine you do not. Perhaps we shall change that one day. I suspect you would be an excellent opponent."

He knew that Genda didn't grasp the observation, thought, A pity. Poker with him could be interesting. Genda's expression didn't change, a hard stare around the room, as though establishing himself as their spokesman. No one seemed to object.

Genda said, "Sir, Admiral Onishi and I have made every effort to eliminate those details we believe are simply impractical or too dangerous. And we believe we have put our greatest emphasis on those details which will guarantee success."

Yamamoto saw approval from the others, said, "'Guarantee' is a risky wager, Commander. I dare not use that description when I seek final approval for this operation from the Naval Ministry, or even the prime minister. There is only one outcome when you predict perfection, and nothing is perfect."

Genda nodded vigorously. "Yes, of course, Admiral. You are quite correct. I misspoke."

"So do we all, Commander. Please say what you came to say."

Genda pulled a short stack of paper from a folder, read briefly, then said, "Admiral Onishi has emphasized to us all that this operation must be carried out with the greatest secrecy, in order to catch the enemy by surprise. If the enemy is aware we are coming, the results could be catastrophic. Our fleet, and thus our aircraft, would be a long way from safety, and we might very well find ourselves sailing into a devastating trap. In every way possible, we must ensure absolute secrecy."

Yamamoto had agonized over this point from the beginning. "Commander, I agree, but there is no possibility that we can plan and execute this operation without confiding in other departments, over which I have no authority. It is a fact of life, I am sorry to say, that I do not personally command every support facility we require. I do not control the fuel depots, the armament stores, nor any other department that does not fall under the authority of the combined fleet. In addition, there can be nothing withheld from the Naval Ministry, from the combined Chiefs of Staff, or for that matter, from Emperor Hirohito."

Genda seemed chastened, bowed his head briefly. "I understand, of course, sir."

Yamamoto pointed toward the papers in front of Genda. "You may continue, Commander."

"Yes, sir. We believe the enemy's aircraft carriers are the primary targets. I understand the value of their battleships, but if we can eliminate their carrier force, we would have the advantage over their battleships virtually anywhere they would go. Without air protection, the enemy would be extremely vulnerable."

Yamamoto was surprised, said, "Commander, one primary purpose of this mission is to destroy American battleships. The message we must send to the Americans is that we have the capability to destroy even their most formidable weapons."

"Sir, are not their carriers formidable weapons?"

"Absolutely. And we shall attack them with the

same energy as we attack the battleships. But unless I instruct you otherwise, the American battleships are your first target."

"Understood, sir. If I may continue."

Yamamoto nodded.

"Next, we must make every effort to destroy the enemy's aircraft on the ground, if possible. There are several air bases in proximity to Pearl Harbor. If we are successful in our secrecy, the enemy's planes will still be on the ground when we arrive. We must prevent them from launching an airborne response as much as possible." He paused, glanced at the others. No one spoke up, Genda very much in control. "Next, sir, we are insisting that this attack be made with six aircraft carriers, not the four that have been suggested. The added air strength they would provide would make our assault all the more damaging to the enemy."

Yamamoto smiled, thought, I had suggested only four. These young men are indeed ambitious in their thinking.

"The next point, sir, is a concept I am not completely comfortable with. But there is a majority consensus among us that the attack be made with four types of aircraft: torpedo bombers, high-altitude bombers, low-altitude dive bombers, and fighters."

"What is your argument against that part of the plan, Commander?"

Genda took a deep breath, the hard glare in his eyes digging into Yamamoto. "I am a great advocate of the torpedo bomber, sir. There is no greater weapon against a ship at sea, no matter how powerful the ship. But Pearl Harbor is shallow, our estimates say no more than forty to fifty feet deep. The torpedo requires much deeper water even if launched from a plane flying no more than twenty feet above the water. The torpedoes would not have sufficient depth to straighten their trajectory. I fear they would just lodge themselves in the bottom of the harbor. It is also likely that the American ships are protected by some type of torpedo obstruction, such as netting. It is hard to believe that they would anchor the heart of their fleet in any harbor and not provide such protection."

"Well, then, that is a challenge we must consider. As you are aware, Commander, high-altitude bombing is haphazard at best, with a low percentage of success. Dive bombers are far more effective, but their bombs are likely not powerful enough to inflict serious damage against larger warships."

Yamamoto saw deep concern on the young faces. He looked at Onishi, who said, "We are examining all of those concerns. There are challenges, certainly."

"Then we must meet those challenges. Continue, Commander Genda."

"Sir, we believe that our fighter aircraft should play a significant role. First, they would serve as a protective escort for our bombers. And, of course, should the enemy launch their own fighter aircraft against us, we would likely shoot them out of the sky. If the enemy does not have fighters in the air, ours can perform well in strafing runs against many land-based targets, ground facilities of every kind. It is my opinion, sir, that our A6M Zero carrier fighter is superior to any other such aircraft in the world."

"I hope you are right. Go on."

"We are convinced that the attack must be made in daylight. We are suggesting that our carriers launch their planes at a distance of no more than two hundred miles from the target. Thus, the planes can be launched before dawn. That way, if the enemy locates our armada, and there is a significant naval engagement, it would most likely come after dawn, and the planes will already be on their way to their targets. But we cannot send the planes too early. As you know, sir, we do not possess the kind of instrumentation for accuracy in nighttime assaults. Another challenge, sir, is that we must refuel our ships while they are at sea. The navy has not achieved proficiency at this, which is regrettable. Between now and the scheduled time of the assault, I would emphasize training in this area. There is no alternative, since we do not have any island bases close enough to meet the range of the armada."

"I agree. We shall pursue that immediately."

"Thank you, sir." Genda paused. "And finally, sir, I suggest that we petition the army to approve the deployment of fifteen thousand troops to accompany our armada. Once our air assault is under way, these troops would land upon and occupy the island of

Oahu. Capturing the enemy's base would force them to withdraw completely from Hawaii, retreating to the bases on their west coast. Hawaii then would become our own forward base for launching every variety of attack against the Americans, wherever we might choose."

Yamamoto laughed. He looked toward Onishi, who sat with his arms crossed, shaking his head.

"I've heard of this plan. Admiral Onishi has told me already that you are advocating for an invasion, as well as the air attack. Very energetic of you, Commander, but it is not practical. Our goal here is not all-out war with the Americans, despite the nature of this assault. It is my hope, perhaps it is my fantasy, that our attack so terrifies the American civilian public, that those people will demand of their government that war with Japan must be avoided at all cost.

"That is also why I have advocated that our planes make a one-way assault. If we move our carriers much farther away from Oahu, perhaps four hundred miles, the Americans will be far less likely to detect us with any reconnaissance patrols. As that would place us at the maximum limit of our planes' fuel supply, we would make our attack, then ditch in the ocean close to the coast of Oahu. The pilots, many of them, would be rescued by our waiting submarines. I know American newspapers. They will describe this as a 'suicide assault,' and the American public will embrace that description. It will add to their perception of us as fanatical, and so, much more dangerous. It will add so much to the mythology of the Japanese warrior as being dedicated to total destruction, regardless of the loss of his own life."

Genda stared at him, his head cocking slowly to one side. "Sir? Do you truly believe this? The morale of our pilots would suffer from such an order. No matter how many submarines we deploy, a great many well-trained men would disappear into the sea. And, would not the submarines risk detection, by being so close to the island?"

"I said it was my fantasy, Commander. Perhaps the same way an invasion of the island is your fantasy. So, let us examine that question. How many army officers are you closely acquainted with, that you would trust to secrecy?"

Genda glanced downward. "Truthfully, sir, I'm not closely acquainted with any army officers at all."

"And why is that, Commander?"

Genda hesitated, looked toward Onishi. "I don't really trust the army, sir."

Yamamoto smiled. "Neither do I. Neither should the entire civilian population of Japan. And neither should the emperor. But we have a prime minister, Mr. Konoye, who can best be described as having the spine of a jellyfish, and no one is fooled when the decisions that come from his high perch seem to have been written for him by the army. It is the army that pursued this ridiculous war in China, and it is the army that wants us to grab every part of the Pacific. I promise you, if you sent fifteen thousand army troops, with their officers, into Hawaii, our navy would very soon find ourselves serving as their ferry boat service, hauling troops wherever they felt like going. California, perhaps? Mexico? The Panama Canal?"

He glanced at the young faces across from him. "There was a time when we had many allies in the Naval Ministry. Now my former chief of staff has joined them, and like so many of the others, they are dismissing your efforts, laughing at the foolishness of this entire enterprise. There are some, Commander, who would delight in burning those papers of yours as a tribute to our friends in Germany."

"That is outrageous, sir. Surely you speak only of the army. I know of no naval officer who would advocate such foolishness."

"Don't delude yourself, Commander. There are many officers, young, like you, who believe our path is too cautious, that we should follow the army's wishes, that we should emulate Germany and simply take whatever we want. That, Commander, is what you should find to be foolishness." He paused. "And since we're offering fantasies, here's another one. If there is a full-scale war, you can be certain that in time the Americans will send their bombers over Tokyo. I imagine the entire city in flames. That's the **purchase** we are making. This operation should buy us the luxury of time. **Time** might allow us to increase our defenses, so that when the war comes to Japan, we can prevent our own annihilation."

The faces stared at him, Onishi with his arms still crossed.

Genda shoved his papers into his folder, said, "Sir, I have added my voice as much as possible to call for an enormous increase in our production of aircraft. Fighters and bombers, and every other type as well. Our planes are the finest in the world. We can continue to improve them. We can use that force to prevent anyone from bombing our homes, or our ships."

Yamamoto looked down, shook his head.

"The optimism of youth." He looked at Genda now. "I agree with you, Commander. My voice is among the loudest advocating an enormous increase in aircraft production. Admiral Onishi feels the same way. And yet the Naval Ministry, the naval high command, they dismiss us, as they happily trumpet **their** fantasy. Right now, this day, two great new battleships are being constructed. The **Yamato** and the **Musashi,** more than sixty thousand tons each, double the size of this ship beneath our feet. Eighteen-inch guns, gentlemen; none like them in the world.

"But no matter what anyone in Tokyo tells you, those ships won't win a war any more than those American ships docked in Hawaii. And sadder still, for what we are spending to build those ships, Commander, I could give you most of the airplanes you ask for."

"What should we do, sir? How do we protest?"

"Very carefully, Mr. Genda. A better choice is to go and do your job. Look at your plans again. Make them better. Sharpen the points, remove the blemishes, train your pilots. And then, find a way to launch a torpedo in forty feet of water."

# SIXTEEN

# Biggs

ONBOARD USS ARIZONA, PEARL HARBOR, HAWAII—
WEDNESDAY, JULY 16, 1941

They had been in port for nearly two weeks, Biggs wondering if it was some kind of punishment for the men who had spent so much time complaining about the endless training exercises. But now, moored against the pier on Ford Island, the ship was undergoing extensive maintenance, most of it performed by the crew themselves. They applied yet another coat of paint, and performed service on what seemed to be every moving part, from pipe fittings to gunnery. With so much ongoing labor, liberty was being parsed out in small doses, adding to the frustration and boredom that were now becoming excruciating.

Captain Van Valkenburgh's push to organize

teams for the various athletic competitions had been a respite for some, but the vast majority of the crew were not athletes, and many of those men were veterans who found little excitement in cheerleading the competitions on Ford Island's ball fields. Men went about their duties with grumbling acceptance, some even grateful for whatever down time they were allowed. Others vented their frustrations in more destructive ways. With each day that passed, the number of fights had increased. Some were no more than shoving and shouting matches, exercises in creative profanity. But others were bloody and dangerous, the pent-up hostility leading to injuries more serious than a black eye.

The two marines brought the man into sick bay with a firm grip on each shoulder. Biggs was sweeping the deck back in one corner, and he stopped, called out, "Doctor? We have a patient."

Dr. Johnson emerged from the small office, said, "What's the problem here? Oh, a nasty one. Bring him over here, gentlemen." He looked toward the far end of the compartment. "Corpsman!"

The man came quickly, rushing past Biggs, and the doctor said, "Watch the arm. Grab some gauze and a tourniquet, in case we need it."

The corpsman moved away quickly and Biggs saw the patient's blood, the man cut down one arm, a wide scrape wrapped with the torn remnants of a T-shirt.

Johnson guided them to a table, said, "Lie here, sailor. Let's take a look." The sailor looked toward the marines, as though afraid to speak. One of the marines was much older, wearing the insignia of a first sergeant. He was a burly man with thick arms, a contrast to the other marine, a private, much younger.

The older man handed a paper to the doctor and said, "Here you are, sir. Both parties signed it. Explains it all right there."

The doctor looked at the marine. "I don't pay much attention to official paperwork, Sergeant. I want to hear it from you. Tell me what happened."

The sergeant looked at the doctor dismissively and said, "This fool decided to pick a fight with one of my men. I'm pleased to report that my man is not injured, but this one took a fall into some equipment."

Biggs hadn't crossed paths with any of the marines onboard, but he couldn't avoid thinking of Wakeman's favorite joke, **Muscles Are Required, Intelligence Not Expected.** He kept his distance, didn't care for the scowl coming toward him from the first sergeant, as though the man was reading his mind. The younger private moved back toward the hatchway, stood with no expression, hands clasped behind his back, the look of a man accustomed to long shifts standing guard.

Johnson removed the bloody rag from the arm, and the sailor finally spoke.

"Is it gonna be okay, Doc? It don't hurt much."

"Just lie there. We'll get it fixed up pretty quickly. What's your name?"

"Cockrum, sir. Machinist's mate first."

Johnson looked toward the secure closet, called out, "Mr. Hankins? Any time now."

The corpsman appeared, bandages in hand, and Johnson said, "Mr. Biggs, there's a tube of ointment in that cabinet behind you. Right now, please."

Biggs obeyed, handed the tube to Johnson. With the rag removed, the blood came again, dripping down onto the deck. Biggs kept back, no room yet for him to do anything else.

As they worked, the doctor said to the older marine, "Just about have the bleeding stopped. You're Sergeant Duveene, right? I've seen you in here before."

"Yes, sir. Just doing my job."

"Are you filing the report on this incident, Sergeant?"

"Yes, sir. Colonel Fox has already been informed, and is waiting on my paperwork. The colonel has already reported the incident to the captain. Your machinist here will spend four or five days in the brig—bread and water. That's the usual punishment for assault."

Johnson backed away from the patient, said to the corpsman beside him, "Mr. Hankins, finish wrapping the wound. I'm prescribing antibiotics for ten days. Let me put Mr. Block to work on that. Mr. Cockrum, we're going to give you some pills. Make sure you take one every day until they're gone. You understand?"

The patient looked at Johnson with bleary eyes, nodded slowly. "I'm gonna be okay, Doc? You sure?"

"I'm sure." He looked at the marine now, said, "Wait here. I'll give you my own report. You'll need that."

"I know the drill, Doc."

Johnson went to his office to work on the necessary papers. Biggs stayed back, watched the corpsman wrapping the patient's arm in white gauze. Hankins seemed to take his time, and Duveene noticed.

"Hey. Get on with it. He's due for the brig, and I'm not waiting all damn day."

Hankins said, "You want him fixed up right, Sergeant? He starts bleeding down in the hole and you'll have bigger problems. And you need to make sure he takes the pills."

Duveene said, "You ever been in the brig, son?"

Biggs saw Hankins clench his hands, but the corpsman kept his composure, finished the last bit of work on the man's arm.

"Not recently. I prefer to hear about it thirdhand."

The marine looked back at the young private standing behind him.

"They got a corpsman who talks like a college boy." He turned again to Hankins. "Just get it done. Any dumb son of a bitch decides to punch it out with one of my men deserves as much time in the hole as they give him. He'll learn to love it back down in the engine room after a few days eating dust and licking the floor clean." He leaned closer to Cockrum. "Hey, mouth. You can't talk? You did plenty of talking an hour ago."

Cockrum stayed silent, flexed the fingers protruding below the thick white bandage. After a few seconds, he said, "Didn't mean to get into it, Sergeant. He said some things ought not be said."

"Listen, machine head. Doesn't matter what anybody says to you, you don't haul off and swing at a guy. You're lucky he didn't take that arm clean off. You're also lucky that Lieutenant Hollis stepped in when he did, or you'd have been tossed overboard."

The corpsman did a final examination of the arm, said, "He's all yours, Sergeant. Just know that if our good work gets torn all to hell down there, we'll write **that** up too. He's taken enough punishment."

"You and the doc just worry about mopping up puke and curing jock rot. The marines run the brig and we don't need any help."

Dr. Johnson emerged from the small office now, gave the marine a hard stare. "First Sergeant Duveene, I don't appreciate any abuse of my men, including big talk. You go on and take this man to the brig, but I'll be sure to check on him. He's not guilty of anything more than being stupid, and that doesn't warrant any ill treatment by you or your guards. Do you understand me?"

"Understood, Doctor. I'll try to keep my men out of sick bay, and you keep your men out of my brig."

"Fair enough. One of my people will be down there in a while to check on his wound."

"Whatever you say, sir."

The marines moved to either side of Cockrum, took hold under his arms. Cockrum offered no resistance, moved with the men toward the hatchway, and out.

Biggs had kept to his corner, the broom still in front of him, as though he needed some kind of shield. He looked at Johnson.

"Wow, sir. I wouldn't wanna cross eyes with that first sergeant. He's one of those marines that scares people just for the fun of it."

Hankins laughed. "He's a plank owner. I don't think he's been on land in thirty years."

Biggs leaned on the broom. "A what?"

"A plank owner. An old-timer. I think he's been on this ship or one like it since he was born. Pretty much owns the brig, which is one very good reason to stay the hell out of there."

"I plan to."

The doctor said, "Yep. Best stay clear of him. More than one man has been brought in here with a pretty severe injury because he thought he should try proving his point to the marines. I've had some come up here straight from the brig with cracked heads and busted ribs. I don't approve of that sort of thing, but . . . well, it's the brig. Not much different from the county jail back home."

Biggs said, "So, you think the marines are as tough as they say?"

Both men laughed now, and Hankins said, "If you ask **them**? Sure. I guess that's what they're taught, that they can lick anybody on earth. But they're not so different from any sailor on this ship. I do remember a short-arm inspection where some of the marines took pride in every case of the clap they could bring us. Not sure I'd want my sister dating one."

They all laughed, but Johnson held up his hands.

"All right, no further. There's a reason they're trained like that. All of us might end up needing them one day, and if we're ever in a nasty scrap, you're likely to be in here patching them up. We're all on the same ship."

The laughter faded, and Biggs returned to his broom.

Hankins said, "Hey, sir, who'd Cockrum try to knock out?" He glanced at Biggs with a smile. "So I'll know who to steer clear of."

Johnson looked at the clipboard beside him. "PFC Finley."

Hankins seemed surprised, said, "Woody Finley?"

"It says Woodrow. Guess so. Why?"

Hankins shook his head. "Glad Cockrum didn't damage the guy. He's supposed to be an ace right-handed pitcher. Lieutenant Janz put the word out to assemble a decent baseball team, and Finley would sure as hell be the anchor."

Johnson said, "There's no team yet? I thought that was already happening."

"Well, sir, the football boys are practicing, and the rowers have been out in the harbor pretty regular. But the baseball team just hasn't come together."

Biggs stopped the broom, said, "Petty Officer Kincaid gave us the word about athletics, and he mentioned baseball, but nothing else was said. I thought the idea had been dropped."

Hankins said, "Not according to Lieutenant Janz. I guess the captain said **Do it,** so he's doing it. Why, you interested?"

Biggs said, "You bet. I love it. I'm too skinny for football, and my old man gave me too many boxing lessons growing up. The kind you never win. I always played baseball."

Hankins said, "Well, I can tell you, I thought about boxing, had a few amateur fights when I was fresh out of high school. But there's a guy on the **West Virginia,** Negro named Doris Miller. He takes people's heads off. Guess he had to learn to fight, growing up with a girl's name. I figured out pretty quick I needed to stick to sick bay. A few other fellas have climbed into the ring with him and found out what an ass-kicking is. So, you any good at baseball?"

Biggs shrugged. "I used to be, maybe. So now? I'd sure like to find out."

The schedule had finally been posted outside his compartment, a call for any interested players to report to the upper deck, forward at 1400 hours. Permission for him to leave sick bay early was granted by Dr. Johnson, all of the sick bay crew wishing him well. He could tell exactly what they were thinking; even the doctors were wondering if their apprentice could actually play.

It was clear and bright on the upper deck, the stretch of teak between the forward gun turrets and the bow of the ship. He gathered with the others, roughly thirty men, some jostling each other with noisy boasts of who would strike out who, who would be mouthy enough to take a pitch in his ear. Biggs eyed them all, tried to pick out the true athletes. He saw one marine, barrel-chested, thick arms, wondered if he was Finley, wondered why the machinist, Cockrum, had chosen to pick a fight with him.

Lieutenant Janz was there now, another officer beside him, an ensign. Janz held a clipboard, a sheaf of papers.

"Men, you signed up for the USS **Arizona**'s baseball team. Our goal is to field a team that will be competitive with every other team in the fleet.

We're not sure how many that will be, but if the turnout for football and other sports is any indication, we should have a healthy number. Captain Van Valkenburgh believes strongly in athletic competition, and he has expressed his confidence that every time we take the field, we will do honor to our ship."

He turned over the pages on his clipboard, the ensign talking to him in a low voice. After a full minute, Janz said, "Some of you have done this before, and I will count on you for leadership on this team. I see some familiar names, and I thank you for returning. From your sign-up sheets, I see we have a few pitchers, a couple of catchers, a few who specialize in fielding, and of course, as is always the case, most of you think you can hit home runs."

There was laughter, and Janz said, "You pitchers, fall in up close to the bow. We've got a box of baseballs there, and a makeshift rubber. Gloves are in that larger box. Find one you like. There's a few for lefties, just dig for 'em. All right, Seaman Harrington, front and center. Good to have you back. You'll catch for the pitchers. Home is marked with that steel plate over there; help 'em warm up. You fielders, spread out along the bow rail, do your best to keep the balls from rolling into the harbor."

Biggs watched a half dozen men move out, picking gloves, fists slapping the leather as they moved into position.

Janz looked toward the pitchers, seemed to

acknowledge one man in particular. "The first pitcher is PFC Finley. Most of you know that he's played some minor league ball, and might still have a chance to go to the majors." There were scattered hoots, a few claps. "You might also know that he's probably struck out nearly everybody in the fleet. Mr. Finley, take your place at the rubber and warm up. You hitters, take note. This might be the best way we know to determine who among you has the goods. Don't be embarrassed or insulted if you can't make contact. We'll work on that best we can, and you'll get plenty of chances. Once we put together most of a team, we'll head out onto Ford Island, where there are some fields drawn up. For now, there's not a lot of room up here, but most of you won't need it."

The teasing seemed to animate the men, but Biggs was focused on Finley, studying his warm-up, the speed, the pop of his pitches in the catcher's mitt. More men were watching as well, the talk quieting.

Finley called over to Janz. "I'm ready, sir."

Janz looked over his papers. "In alphabetical order, the ones who claimed to be hitters . . ." He stopped and looked at the gathered men. A man behind Biggs said, "Lambs to the slaughter."

"All right, first up, Hospital Apprentice Biggs. Front and center."

Biggs stepped out, and Janz didn't look at him, pointed to a tall crate.

"Bats are there."

Biggs dug through the bats, some with deep scars, most badly used. He slid one from the crate, tested the weight, tapped it on the deck, making sure it wasn't cracked.

Janz looked at him now, impatiently. "Batter up, Mr. Biggs."

Biggs moved to the plate, glanced at Finley, saw a smirk, saw the same look on the faces of the other five pitchers. He stood in, took two warm-up swings. Finley made ready, a slow wind-up, the ball coming hard and fast, and straight down the middle of the plate. Biggs kept the bat on his shoulder, let the ball rip past into the catcher's mitt.

Janz said, "What's wrong, sailor? You did see it, didn't you?"

There was general laughter now, even Finley smiling. Biggs stood in again, took one practice swing and waited. Finley wheeled around, the ball coming again, same as before. Biggs could see the laces, the backward spin, no movement on the ball at all. He whipped the bat forward, perfect contact, a loud crack, the ball in a high line drive straight over Finley's head, then far over the rail, disappearing into the harbor. There was no sound, all eyes watching the path of the ball. The faces began to turn back toward him, and he saw Lieutenant Janz staring at him. Biggs looked toward Finley, the marine with his hands by his side, a curious look on his face.

Janz waved toward Finley. "Give him another one."

Finley seemed to bear down, hard anger on his face. Biggs smiled at him, then stopped that, knew that taunting a pitcher could be a dangerous thing to do. **A ball in your ear . . .**

Finley stared hard past him, the catcher ready. Biggs thought, I tested him. Maybe embarrassed him. Now he's going to test me, and sure as hell, embarrass me. If he can.

The pitch came now, and Biggs could see the seams spinning sideways, the curveball, hanging, settling in right where Biggs wanted it to be. He swung again, but too low, the ball flying in a high arc back behind him. He turned, saw the ball coming down well astern. Janz and several of the others turned that way, and Biggs heard the ball impact the teakwood deck with a loud **whack,** saw a high bounce, a few men there scrambling out of the way, the ball coming down again into a cluster of white-suited officers. Biggs looked that way, past the huge gun turrets, nervous now, the bat still resting on his shoulder. The commotion continued on the main deck, sailors coming to formal attention, the gathering of officers looking up his way, one man pointing.

Beside him, Janz said, "Jesus, kid, you almost hit the captain. They might toss you in the brig for this."

Biggs watched two of the officers moving along the main deck toward the bow, climbing up now, the men on the upper deck snapping to attention. Biggs stiffened as well, the bat by his side. Only one was familiar: Biggs recognized Captain Van Valkenburgh from the first day he boarded the ship.

Van Valkenburgh had the ball in his hand, saw the bat, looked at Biggs with no recognition.

"Somebody lose this, Lieutenant?"

He tossed the ball to Janz, who said, "My apologies, sir. We were just starting with batting practice."

The lieutenant looked sharply at Biggs, the meaning clear. **Say something.**

Biggs said, "I'm very sorry, sir. I got under it a little. It was a foul ball. The first one went out the right way, I promise, sir."

Van Valkenburgh looked at the pitcher, Finley, acknowledged him with a sharp nod. He glanced at Janz, who said, "He nailed the first one, but I think it was a fluke. Mr. Finley's just getting warmed up."

The captain seemed to ignore Janz, said to Biggs, "I'd like to see that. Do it again."

Janz said, "You mean, you want him to hit it again?"

Van Valkenburgh looked at Janz. "That's precisely what I mean, Lieutenant."

Finley went back to the pitcher's rubber, and the catcher settled in.

Janz tossed the ball to Finley, then called out, "Strike him out, Private. No more flukes."

Biggs saw Finley staring at him with embarrassed fury. He stepped to the plate, thought, He knows he made a mistake. He hung that curveball. I just missed it. So, this one will be fast, to impress the captain. Okay, Tommy, just see the ball.

The pitch came, fast and low, at the knees, and Biggs swung, another hard crack, the ball in a high arc straight over the bow, far beyond the rail of the ship, the fielders turning, watching the ball disappear again into the harbor. The sounds came from the others now, whistles, a few hands clapping. Finley's anger changed now to surprise, and then, a nod of respect toward Biggs. Biggs looked toward the captain and Van Valkenburgh stepped toward him, stood in front of him, said, "I'm looking for some people to represent this ship on a ball field. I think you'll do just fine." He turned to Janz. "I would suggest, Lieutenant, that if you're going to have this man hit batting practice, you do it out that way, toward Ford Island. He'll run us out of baseballs."

ONBOARD USS ARIZONA, PEARL HARBOR, HAWAII—
    THURSDAY, JULY 17, 1941

Dr. Condon had completed his shift, Dr. Johnson now taking over. Biggs was learning that the routine for the doctors meant that his own shift might not be coordinated with either one of theirs. He didn't mind. He enjoyed working with both men, was already learning far more than he had expected to in such a short time.

He noticed a faint bloodstain on the floor beneath

the operating table, thought, Good God, I missed
that one. He knelt low, rag in one hand, disinfectant in the other. He rubbed the area with the wet
cloth, the harsh smell of the cleaner burning his
nostrils. He straightened up, still on his knees, and
cursed to himself, attacked it again.

The voice surprised him: one of the mates,
Bill Vaughan.

"Hey, Tommy. You working on that stain?"
Vaughan laughed now. "Every damn one of us has
tackled that thing ever since we got here. Let it go.
Nobody knows how it got there, or even what it
is. Dr. Johnson thinks it's been there as long as he
has, thinks maybe it's grape juice. Block thinks
somebody dropped a piece of cherry pie."

Biggs climbed up to his feet. "Thanks for letting
me know. I'd have worked on that stain all day. I
figured it was my fault."

Vaughan laughed. "That's what we've all thought."

Dr. Johnson emerged from the office, saw the rag
and bottle in Biggs's hands. "Going after that stain,
eh? Well, the first one of you gets it cleaned up earns
a Navy Cross; I'll sign the paperwork. Personally, I
think it's been there since they were building the
ship. Some high-flying bird took offense and left
his mark."

Biggs heard an odd noise, looked up toward
the turret above them, then toward the hatchway.
"What's that?"

Johnson stared at the ceiling. "It's music."

Vaughan looked up as well, shook his head. "Somebody's in Dutch. Radios were labeled contraband a while ago. Anybody caught playing one lands in the brig."

The doctor kept his eyes toward the direction of the sound. "I don't think that's a radio. It's too loud. Could be our band, but they don't play anything with that much . . . jump."

Vaughan said, "Other than Colors, I've never heard our band play anything worth listening to. A bunch of highbrow stuff."

Johnson continued to look up, said, "Careful, Mr. Vaughan. That highbrow stuff is what some of the old boys like to listen to."

Vaughan said, "You actually listen to that stuff, sir?"

The doctor smiled. "No. I said the 'old boys.' I'm an 'almost.' And I agree. I can't say I've ever heard our band do anything that sounded like that. Mr. Biggs, why don't you go topside, try to find out just what's going on."

"Certainly, sir."

He moved out through the hatchway, and the sound grew louder. Others were around him now, moving in the direction of the music. He heard questions, puzzled men moving up the ladders, following each other to the upper deck. The music grew louder still, and he stepped out to bright sunshine and a lively tune. The deck was crowded with crewmen, officers sprinkled through the crowd. The music came from nearly two dozen musicians, all in uniform. The songs came one behind the other, lively jazz, then a modern pop song, some of the men singing along.

Biggs scanned the musicians, most of them young, playing instruments of every kind: trombones, saxophones, clarinets, cornets, drums, and bass. The instruments were polished and perfect, every note as professional as anything Biggs had ever heard. He knew he should go below, report back to the doctor. But he was riveted, the music holding him in place, the sheer pleasure of the sounds overwhelming.

As a song ended, he asked a man beside him, "What's going on? Who are these guys?"

In the group closest to him, he saw an officer, an ensign, turning toward him, smiling with him, and the man said, "They just came aboard, sailor. The **Arizona** just got a brand-new band."

# SEVENTEEN

# Hull

THE WHITE HOUSE, WASHINGTON, D.C.—
FRIDAY, AUGUST 1, 1941

As Hull moved toward the Cabinet Room, he could still feel the weakness, his recovery not quite whole. For most of the past month, he and Frances had secluded themselves at White Sulphur Springs, in West Virginia. He knew the symptoms of exhaustion, and his wife had seen it more clearly than he had. She'd insisted he take time off and so, with no protest from him, they had journeyed to the pleasant coolness of the mountains, the hot springs, and a great deal of pampering. As much as the trip was recuperative for him, he knew she would appreciate a bit of pampering herself.

His appointments had been handled mostly by his undersecretary, Sumner Welles, a man who clearly

saw himself as capable of filling Hull's shoes. Hull
had no real problem with Welles's obvious ambition, but Welles had the unfortunate habit of going
over Hull's head, offering various pieces of information directly to the White House without con-
sulting Hull in the process. Roosevelt didn't seem
to mind the breach of protocol, as long as what
Welles provided him was useful. Hull didn't necessarily dislike Welles, but he had detected too often
that Welles, a much younger man, had his eye on
Hull's chair. As far as Hull was concerned, Welles
could wait his turn.

Now back in Washington, Hull had made it a
point of visiting with a number of reporters, if only
to demonstrate that he was completely healthy and
back to work. Rumors that he might be suffering from some affliction would help no one, and
Hull knew that with the extraordinary amount of
tension rolling through the capital, the president
would need him.

The men had filed into the Cabinet Room, low
banter between them. Hull took his place behind a
chair immediately to the right of the space Roosevelt
would occupy.

He saw Frances Perkins coming in, the men making way with smiles and empty chatter. Perkins was
the secretary of commerce, the first woman ever to
occupy a position in any president's cabinet. Hull

acknowledged her with a friendly nod, though he knew she would keep her smiles to herself. If any of them regarded her presence as less than serious, she might remind them that her position was no less significant than their own. A few of the less experienced cabinet members had been subjected to her devastating jabs.

Hull put his hands on the back of his designated chair. He waited for the rest to take their places, and met their glances with polite acknowledgment. Stimson was there now, and Hull was not surprised that the secretary of war had very little cordiality to offer any of them. While Hull and his wife had enjoyed their weeks in the West Virginia mountains, Stimson had been working harder than ever.

Roosevelt entered, today using his crutches instead of his usual wheelchair. Hull knew it was often a personal challenge, the president doing whatever he could to strike back at the effects of the polio. Behind Roosevelt, a young marine followed, keeping his distance. The president made his way slowly, finally reached his chair at the center of the table. Hull knew, as did they all, that no matter Roosevelt's discomfort, he would not allow anyone to lend him a hand.

Hull ached to assist him, thought, He must be feeling pretty chipper today to use the crutches. Or at least, he wants us to think so.

Roosevelt slid into the chair in an awkward maneuver and, as always, Hull stood prepared to assist.

On Roosevelt's left, the treasury secretary, Henry Morgenthau, did the same. Roosevelt settled in and the marine discreetly removed the crutches. The president spread his arms out on the table as though the effort had been perfectly routine.

Roosevelt said, "Be seated, please, Miss Perkins, gentlemen. I want to get right to it." He looked past the end of the table at two young men, the recording secretaries, seated at small desks. "You ready?"

The two men had pens in hand, both offering the president a crisp response, "Yes, Mr. President."

Roosevelt scanned the members of his cabinet, then pulled a small stack of folded papers from his coat pocket, spread them out in front of him. "As you all know, it is unusual for me or the secretary of state to bring to this cabinet matters of foreign relations. That has never been a reflection on any of you. Most of you have important duties and responsibilities within your own areas of authority. However, today, I will make an exception. There are events now occurring which could eventually involve all of you in one way or another."

He looked at Hull. "Proceed at your convenience, Mr. Secretary."

Hull cleared his throat, looked down for a moment, then over to the papers in front of Roosevelt, which were a handwritten copy of what he was about to say. He let out a breath. "Thank you, Mr. President. As you know, on July twenty-fourth, this cabinet approved a measure whereby the president would issue an order freezing Japanese financial assets in the United States. That order was put into effect, and was stated publicly two days later. This action was in response to an agreement reached between the government of Japan and Marshall Henri Pétain, president of the government of occupied France, which we know as Vichy. That allows the Japanese to occupy French Indo-China with whatever strength she wishes to employ there, without any resistance from France.

"By freezing Japanese assets in the United States, we have sent a stern warning to Japan that we do not approve of this formal incursion. It was our hope that the Japanese could be persuaded to avoid the occupation of that part of Asia by diplomatic means. We have been severely disappointed in that effort. We did not anticipate that Vichy would, in effect, hand over their colonies in Southeast Asia free of charge.

"In any case, our greater concern is that the Japanese will not accept this **gift** from Vichy and stop there. This permission granted to Japan by the French allows the Japanese to build air and sea bases, and to establish troop bases without any restriction or limitation on their size or disposition. From all we can determine by the various means at our disposal, the Japanese have clear designs on the Dutch East Indies, Thailand, Singapore, and would likely expand their belligerence aggressively toward any nation that might offer easy pickings.

One has to look no further than Nazi Germany to understand how this practice takes shape. There is a considerable threat to our own territories as well, including our islands in the South Pacific, and the Philippines."

He paused, his voice straining, his heart pounding. He took a drink of water from a glass in front of him, and began again. "The Empire of Japan has received notice from us of our severe displeasure at their recent actions, and we have presented them with a complete explanation of our justification for freezing their financial assets. Their response continues to be one of belligerence and bluster. In other words, there does not appear to be any hope of altering the dangerous course they are pursuing."

He looked toward Roosevelt, who had followed his comments on the paper.

"Thank you, Mr. Secretary. Based on the knowledge we now have of these and other Japanese actions, and their likely intentions, and with no sense that their government has any intentions of reversing course . . . in accordance with the Act of Congress of June second, 1940, I am exercising the authority granted the president to order a complete freeze on all goods and products from the United States to the Empire of Japan, most specifically, oil, gasoline, and other petroleum products. This total embargo shall go into effect immediately."

The reaction was swift and vocal, most of the cabinet reacting with enthusiastic approval. But that response was not unanimous. Hull scanned the faces and saw Frances Perkins looking down, a couple of the others reacting with disappointment or uncertainty. Hull wanted to reassure them all that this was not the end of anything, that it did not tie anyone's hands, nor cut off dialogue, but there was nothing he could say, unless the president asked him to.

He stayed in his seat, ignored the boisterous reactions of the majority. He couldn't avoid feeling a certain gloom. No matter the support for this kind of action, for Hull it represented a failure. And Congress will not be so enthusiastic, he thought. There will be baseless accusations toward the president of warmongering, and on the other side, there will be noisy shouts that we have not gone far enough.

He looked at Stimson, the man staring quietly toward the blue sky outside the window, betraying none of his thoughts. All through the spring and early summer, Stimson had increasingly pushed for the Pacific fleet, possibly the **entire** Pacific fleet, to be shifted to the Atlantic, still insisting there was no threat in the Pacific. But the aggressiveness of the Japanese over the past couple of months had forced Stimson closer to Hull's point of view. As hawkish as Stimson might have been, an attitude shared by Secretary of the Treasury Morgenthau, both men had seemed to come around to Roosevelt's way of pressing the issue: diplomacy first, and action, if necessary, to follow. No matter what we tried to believe, Hull thought, the Japanese have ignored every effort we made for a reasonable solution. Their goals are very specific and very inflexible, and to us, very dangerous.

He looked at Roosevelt, who was basking in the positive responses from most of his cabinet. No, Hull thought, we had no alternative. If conversation and reasonable compromises wouldn't reach the Japanese, the president had to get their attention another way.

THE CARLTON HOTEL, WASHINGTON, D.C.—
SUNDAY, AUGUST 10, 1941

Hull sat at his desk, had given up trying to work. He fought through his fatigue, stretched his back, suddenly caught her in the corner of his eye. It was her usual perch, just outside his door, leaning, arms crossed, watching him. He did his best to keep his back straight, scrolling now through a stack of papers, pretending they mattered. Sometimes that was enough to satisfy her, but this time, she wouldn't leave. He gave up, turned to her, said, "What? Something wrong?"

"Do you know what day it is?"

He had a sudden panic that it was her birthday, searched his brain. She stepped into the room, hands now on her hips, said, "It's Sunday."

"Well, yes, it's Sunday. Hell, I knew that."

"Nice language on a Sunday. Are you aware that Sunday was designed as a day of rest? You have one of your assistants sitting out there with a deskload of work, and he's here only because you would toss him to the wolves if he objected. But dear husband, I wish you would go outside and look down the street. You'll see visitors wandering around, enjoying the summer day. If you go into the office buildings around here, except perhaps **yours,** you'll find them mostly empty. People are home, with their families, enjoying time away from their work."

He looked back toward the papers, said, "What's your point?"

She laughed, as though too familiar with the brick wall she was up against. "My point, dear man, is that it's Sunday."

He stopped pretending to study the paperwork, sat back, looked at her. "Well, I am certainly with my family—**you,** right here. I'm home, too. But that's the best I can do, I'm afraid. These are not good times, my dear.

"I have always said that in the eight years I have served as Franklin's secretary of state, I was never without a crisis. But this is different. I'm not sure just **how** different, but it seems very much as if the entire world is at risk. Bad people, **very** bad people have too much power and too many weapons. I would not want to be the president, with the re-sponsibility he has for protecting the innocent, for straddling the line between reason and insanity. In some parts of the world, the insanity is winning. And if we are not careful, it will spread to every other part of the world. That is a terrifying possibility. But never in my life has it been as **real** as it is now, so frightening. And none of us can afford to make mistakes."

She moved to him, put her hands on his shoulders, probed in her usual comforting way with her fingers. "And, I suppose that is why you must work on Sundays."

He looked up at her. "That is why."

She had gone out for lunch with the wife of some consulate official from Venezuela. He sat at his desk still, fidgeting, tried to relax. His energy was precious now, and he knew what lay ahead might consume everything he had left today, whether it was Sunday or not.

He glanced at the clock above his bookcase, at the slow sway of the pendulum. Thoughts swirled through his head, another product of the weakness he couldn't avoid. You're not too old for this job, he thought. Stimson's older; so are several of the others. But weakness is not acceptable, not in any form. And sure as hell, not with Nomura coming here yet again.

His gaze settled on the pendulum, his eyes falling closed.

"Sir?"

He jolted back to consciousness, his aide at the door.

"Oh, sir, I'm so sorry. I didn't know you were sleeping."

"I'm not sleeping, Mr. Yancey. I was examining the workings of my clock, testing its accuracy."

Yancey looked up at the clock. "Is it accurate, sir?"

"Of course it is. What do you want?" He knew the answer before the young man could respond. "Nomura's here, right?"

"Yes, sir. Shall I show him in?"

Hull looked around, saw nothing that required tidying. "Send him in. I'm ready for him. And Mr. Yancey . . ."

"Sir?"

"There's nothing else on today's calendar. You may go on home. It's Sunday, after all."

"Thank you, sir."

Yancey backed out of the room, and Nomura was there quickly, the usual gracious smile, the immediate bow, his friendly greeting.

"Good day, Secretary Hull. I am grateful to see you, especially on Sunday."

Hull thought, What is this attachment everybody has to Sunday? There are only seven days to get things done. One's as good as the other.

"Sit down, if you please, Ambassador. You may assume your usual position on the sofa there."

Nomura sat in the lushness of the large sofa,

spread himself out just a bit, lounging without going too far. He kept up the smile but seemed to be waiting for something. Hull thought, He's wondering if I'm going to drop another bomb on him.

"Ambassador Nomura, I have heard no formal response from your government, or from any other channel, so I must ask you directly: Is there a response you wish to offer regarding our freezing of Japanese assets? Is there a reaction to our export ban on all products to your country?"

Nomura dropped the smile. "We are hopeful that President Roosevelt will agree to a meeting with Prime Minister Konoye. There is much that can be discussed, and many issues that can be solved to the satisfaction of both gentlemen. It has been suggested that Hawaii would be an excellent venue. This might allow President Roosevelt a level of comfort, being on his own soil."

Hull had guessed this was coming, rumors swirling around Ambassador Grew in Tokyo. But Grew had cabled Hull not to expect miracles. Nomura's smile returned, the picture of optimism, and Hull said, "We shall consider this proposal, certainly. I am curious what your prime minister would hope to accomplish. Have the angry voices in your country grown quiet? I have not heard anyone else in your government offer any sort of olive branch to the United States. Quite the opposite."

Nomura lost the smile, stared down for a brief moment. "I am not sure how to explain this to you,

Mr. Secretary. In Japan right now, there is a great deal of conflict between the civilian government and the military. So, when you ask about the attitude of those who control so much of what is happening in Japan, yes, there is conflict, there is anger. Many of us had hoped that the relationship between my country and yours would remain cooperative, perhaps even as allies."

The word seemed miserably inappropriate.

"We stopped being allies for two reasons. You invaded China, who is also our ally, and you signed a Tripartite agreement, which created alliances between you, Italy, and Germany. We have cautioned you against the course you seem intent upon following. We may also assume that because the Germans have pushed their armies into the Soviet Union, that you might do the same from your side of the world. Such are the obligations of allies."

Nomura held up his hands. "I regret, Mr. Secretary, that again I can offer you no information on our intentions regarding the Soviet Union— those are matters far beyond my knowledge. But please, since you mention the subject: Why have you aligned yourself with the government of China, with Mr. Chiang Kai-shek? He is no friend to you, yet you continue to support his efforts against my country's difficulties there."

"I don't have to like someone to respect his position. Chiang might be difficult at times, but he is the rightful head of the Chinese government, until the Chinese people wish otherwise. That's how civilized governments function, Ambassador. You are the invader. You are in the wrong."

"My government would disagree with you, of course. I cannot contradict what course they wish me to take."

Hull knew this was a serious admission for Nomura. Hull shuffled the words in his mind, had thought through this argument for days now. "You are certainly aware that when Hitler began his rise to power, and then when he put that power to such destructive use against peaceful countries, it was hoped that peaceful nations could rely upon reason and decency, that the laws of man and of governments would have an effect, and that Hitler could be made to understand that he had gone far enough. As we now know, that was optimistic, to the point of being naive. So, what are we to believe now about **your** government? You sign a pact with Hitler, embrace his hateful talk. Now, you are making deals with other governments to take possession of land for yourself, for purposes of expanding the reach of your military."

Nomura stared at him for a long moment, and Hull knew the man was searching for words.

"Secretary Hull, I can only communicate to you those things which my government orders me to do. I will tell you . . . many in my government were very confused why you had such objections to the Tripartite Pact."

"Are you among them?"

Nomura was animated now. "No. Not at all. I tried to make the foreign ministry understand that the course they were following was unwise. There were many discussions about that single subject, how the United States and Britain would react. It became apparent to me that I was what you would call . . . a lonely voice. I warned them that there would be consequences, and I was dismissed for being a fool. It is one reason that I am here, in Washington. The ministry thought it convenient to get me out of the way. I was becoming . . . a bother."

Hull wasn't sure how to respond, could see in Nomura's face that he was being honest. It is rare, he thought, that he reveals something of himself.

Nomura leaned forward, arms on his knees, unusually informal. "Secretary Hull, I must ask you a question."

"Certainly."

"The actions by President Roosevelt, the embargoes . . . You have taken an aggressive, harmful action against my country. We need not argue about the reasons. But there is no argument about the possible consequences. You frequently mention Hitler. Hitler pulled Germany out of the ashes of the Great War, convinced the German people they were still strong, that they could regain all they had lost. In the 1930s, as Germany grew stronger still, nations everywhere grew cautious. As Hitler used that strength to fulfill his ambitions, many nations responded by severing relations, by embargoes on goods, by sanctions, by freezing assets. I would suggest to you that such actions only helped to make him stronger, and more determined. What the world took away from him, he now takes from others as he wishes. How useful were all those embargoes and all those sanctions?"

Hull felt a twist in his stomach. "Are you saying that the actions we have taken against Japan will ensure war?"

"I most certainly hope not. I am suggesting only that it is possible that by taking such actions against the Japanese government, you may have increased the **enthusiasm** among powerful men in my government for finding other means of replacing what you've taken away. I fear that none of us may enjoy the results."

# EIGHTEEN

# Hull

The White House, Washington, D.C.—
    Thursday, August 28, 1941

They sat in a semicircle in front of the president's desk, Stimson reading the document aloud. Much of it was basic information, a consulate relating various activities to their foreign ministry in Tokyo. Stimson stopped, wiped his glasses, said, "Now we get to the important part. I quote the following. **'The recent general mobilization order expressed the irrevocable resolution of Japan to put an end to Anglo-American assistance in thwarting her natural expansion and her indomitable intention to carry this out, if possible, with the backing of the Axis, but, if necessary, alone.'** And, the conclusion. **'We will endeavor to the last to occupy French Indo-China peacefully, but if** resistance is offered, we will crush it by force, occupy the country and set up martial law. After the occupation of French Indo-China, next on schedule is the sending of an ultimatum to the Netherlands Indies. In the seizing of Singapore, the Navy will play the principal part. We will once and for all crush Anglo-American military power and their ability to assist in any schemes against us.'"

Roosevelt kept his chin resting on one hand. "That's it?"

Stimson said, "Yes, sir. It was sent from the Japanese Consulate in Canton, China, to the foreign ministry in Tokyo. Magic intercepted it several days ago, and unfortunately, it took some time to translate and sort out from the mountain of documents that we're receiving."

Roosevelt looked at Knox, at General Marshall beside him. "Don't we have translators? Isn't anyone capable of separating the important messages from useless garbage? Did it take somebody's particular genius to figure out the importance of this cable?"

Knox said, "Sir, the Office of Naval Intelligence is charged only with forwarding these messages to the Navy's War Plans Division, to Admiral Turner. Several of that office's translation crew have been on vacation. That was with Admiral Turner's permission, of course, sir."

Hull stayed quiet, sat in the last chair in the row, watched the reactions of the others. He knew that

Turner was one of Washington's least-liked military chiefs, but it would never be appropriate for the secretary of state to mention that.

Hull could see that Roosevelt was annoyed. Roosevelt said, "General Marshall, what of the army's intelligence people, your G-2? Are those people on vacation as well, sunning themselves on some beach?"

Marshall kept his gaze straight ahead, said, "Mr. President, as you know, the army and navy intelligence units are separate entities, and they divide their authority for handling the Magic intercepts on an alternating basis. This document happened to be intercepted on a day when the navy was handling the mail."

Hull looked at Frank Knox, knew that the secretary of the navy was feeling a knife planted firmly in his back. Knox didn't wait for Roosevelt to unload on him.

"Mr. President, I must point out that this document was sent via their **Purple** code at least a week or more prior to your announcing the embargo against Japan. This only reinforces why your embargo was so completely appropriate."

Roosevelt didn't seem swayed. "Wonderful. So the Japanese were giving us a good reason to do what we were going to do anyway, but for entirely different reasons. I suppose if there is a silver lining to this bargeload of inefficiency, it is that. Or, perhaps the embargo doesn't matter a hoot in hell to those people. It was our intention to squeeze their resources so they would no longer have sufficient raw materials to make war. Apparently we've had the opposite effect. In other words, gentlemen, no one here knows what the hell is going to happen, in Japan or anywhere else. Does that about sum it up?"

None of the military men seemed willing to answer the question. Roosevelt lit a cigarette, sat back in his chair, waiting for any response at all. After a long silence, Hull could see Stimson preparing his words, and he spoke now with an unusually soothing tone, something Hull had rarely heard from him.

"Mr. President, I assure you, as do Secretary Knox and General Marshall, that we shall do everything possible to tighten up the operation of both army and navy intelligence channels, including an increase in the number of interpreters. None of us will tolerate this kind of lax efficiency."

Roosevelt's expression didn't change as he glared toward all three men. "There is very little tolerance right here, Henry. There is too much at stake. You may return to your offices. I would hope that you would begin work on 'tightening things up' this afternoon."

They stood, and Roosevelt said to Hull, "Remain a moment, Cordell."

He caught a glance from Stimson, could see that he was not at all pleased to receive the president's dressing-down. Roosevelt waited for the door to the office to close, said, "Did I overreact?"

Hull was surprised by the question. "We already knew the information gained from the intercept. I don't believe that either army or navy intelligence cost us anything. As they get more efficient with Magic, they should prove themselves far more useful. Surely you agree."

Roosevelt smoked the cigarette, a cloud of smoke swirling above him. "You know, when Stimson was secretary of state under Hoover, he made quite a nuisance of himself to the military people. He insisted that intelligence intercepts were immoral, as though we shouldn't read someone else's mail. Of course, back then, half the world wasn't at war, or about to be. There aren't too many people around Washington who can stake a claim to as much service to his country as Henry Stimson. You're right there with him, of course. But I'm not certain he appreciates the value of this Magic thing."

"I'm not certain that I do."

Roosevelt seemed surprised. "Why the hell not? It tells us exactly what the Japanese mind is up to, and what they're telling their foreign offices. There should be no fog in their messages, no need for veiled talk. They're talking to their own people, for God's sake, so you'd assume they were being factual."

"Yes, we're listening in to what they're telling their diplomats. Ambassador Nomura is one of them, and they're telling him only what they want him to know. Surely that's the case all over the world."

Roosevelt held up the paper with the intercepted dispatch. "Did he receive this?"

Hull thought a moment. "Nomura? I'm not sure, actually. I get your point."

"Look, Cordell, we already know that he's over here as a puppet, a mask for what the Japanese are really thinking and planning. I know you trust him, and from my own contacts with him, I think he's a decent man, a man who is loyal to his country. But his usefulness to us is one-way. If we're intercepting what he's being told, we'll already know anything he can tell us. But we need him for the opposite reason. We tell him exactly what we want him to communicate to his government, and see what the response is. Obviously, we keep listening to him, giving no hint that we're getting the same memos he is."

"Certainly, Mr. President."

"God, I wish you'd stop that. We're alone. Call me any damn thing you want."

Hull smiled. "No, Mr. President. As long as you're on that side of your desk, and I'm over here, I'm playing by the rules."

Roosevelt sniffed. "I bet you're the only one who thinks that way. Stimson probably goes home and tells his wife exactly where he wants me to go."

"Oh, I do that too, sir."

Roosevelt laughed. "See? You're an honest man.

That's why you were a lousy politician. And if you'd have run for this office like I wanted you to, by now you'd be as good a liar as the rest of us." Roosevelt snuffed out the cigarette, slid the dispatch aside, flipped through another sheaf of papers. "What's happening with Prime Minister Konoye? Any word yet on whether we're going to meet face-to-face? And don't tell me we're waiting for Magic to tell us. I'm growing old as it is."

"We don't need Magic to tell us anything. The Japanese have a very different perception of leadership than we do. They expect that if you and Prime Minister Konoye meet, you can single-handedly solve every problem that exists. With a handshake, you can make policy, establish agreements, and, probably, negotiate treaties. We know that their military is making the real decisions, and that anything Konoye offers us comes with their approval. And frankly, Mr. President, it is my opinion that those people running things are as crooked as a bag of fishhooks."

Roosevelt thought a moment, then said, "What of my role in this? What can we gain?"

Hull had considered that question already. "Please allow me to relate a story, sir. I am reminded of a man I once knew in Tennessee. He was confronted on his travels by a highwayman, and the two agreed to talk. My friend, having a very chivalrous nature, unstrapped two revolvers from his belt and laid them on a stump seventy-five yards from where they would have their conversation. I leave it to you to guess how the conversation ended."

Roosevelt smiled. "Yes, yes. Make your point."

"Mr. President, we can go to Hawaii, make our demands that Japan pull out of China, pull out of Southeast Asia, bring their ships back home, and so on. Prime Minister Konoye would return home with his fur up, claiming we are unreasonable and interfering in the internal affairs of Japan. Or, instead, we agree that Japan is entitled to all they have taken thus far, but we express our sincere hopes that they go no further, even throwing in a 'please' or two; Konoye goes home trumpeting his success in backing down this powerful giant, and you, sir, come home to read every newspaper in the country comparing you to Neville Chamberlain. You would have handed Japan exactly what Chamberlain gave Hitler in Munich. We know how that turned out."

"Jesus, Cordell." Roosevelt sat up straight. "I have given this a great deal of thought. There will be no meeting with Prime Minister Konoye. That acceptable to you?"

"I will communicate that to Ambassador Nomura. And, yes, it is acceptable. And by the way, I do not believe you bear any resemblance to Neville Chamberlain."

As word of Roosevelt's embargo order spread through Japanese-held territory, the angry reactions were entirely predictable. But one particular reaction overshadowed the rest. As a squadron of Japanese fighter-bombers flew toward a routine mission over the city of Chungking, China, one of the planes separated from the others and executed a bombing run directly toward the American Embassy, the bomb impacting dangerously close. An American gunboat, the **Tutuila,** was anchored close by, and the plane's second bomb struck close enough to damage the boat. In his cable to Hull, Ambassador Grew was very explicit that the bombing was deliberate, and that casualties were averted only by good fortune.

To Hull's relief, the Japanese owned up to the mishap fairly quickly, the foreign ministry offering an official apology for the error. Hull accepted the apology, despite the obvious hostility behind the act. It was one more way the American government was doing as much as possible to prevent the harsh disagreements from boiling over into war.

On September 4, Nomura returned, this time to meet with both Hull and the president. A few days before, Nomura had sent a message back to Tokyo, transmitted via the **Purple** code and intercepted by Magic.

**"Japanese-American relations have reached a stage in which anything might happen at any moment, and they are likely to grow worse suddenly as Japan makes her next move . . ."**

From Chief of Staff George Marshall's office,

army intelligence presented a detailed report, sum-
marizing much of what was already known—that
Japan was closely adhering to the Tripartite Pact,
that the Japanese were aggressively pursuing the es-
tablishment of the Greater East Asia Co-Prosperity
Sphere, and that Japan had an intense desire to
end the "China problem"—and offering details
of Japan's intentions to occupy Southeast Asia for
both economic and strategic reasons. The report
concluded that, in light of these goals, the Japanese
**"would resort to every means available to keep
the United States out of the war."**

THE WHITE HOUSE, WASHINGTON, D.C.—
   THURSDAY, SEPTEMBER 4, 1941

Nomura wore the same gracious expression that
Hull was so familiar with. He made his deep bow
toward the president, accepted the invitation to sit.
He scanned the Oval Office, as though impressed
to be surrounded by so much American history.

Nomura waited politely and took his cues from
Hull, who always allowed the president the first
word.

"So, Ambassador, what do we have to do to smooth
over all the torn places in our relationship?"

Hull knew it was a useless question, but it would
require some kind of response from Nomura that
might reveal an opening.

"It is my hope, Mr. President, Mr. Secretary, that

we find the formula that allows us to put our differences aside. We should do what we can to reverse those issues which have so injured our relationship. Both of our nations seek only a road to peace."

Hull knew a good dance when he saw one.

Roosevelt seemed to read Hull's mind. "So, is it your position that if we would drop our embargoes against Japan, the Japanese government would agree to cease their aggressive actions against our allies and other free peoples in Asia and the Pacific. Is that it?"

Hull knew Nomura would never answer that question. Nomura forced a smile, said, "I shall communicate your question to the foreign minister. I must ask, though, why do you object so strongly to Japan placing troops in Indo-China? Those forces are of no threat to you."

Hull looked at Roosevelt, then said, "If Japan should establish bases of any kind in that part of the world, it opens up very convenient doors for your military to take the next step. We have many allies in that part of the world. Their best interests are our best interests."

Nomura seemed surprised. "But I am assured that my government would possibly agree to a non-aggression pact with you, Mr. President. This could be the pathway to peace between our nations, the peace that seems to be more elusive every day."

Hull and Roosevelt had received hints of this kind of offer before.

Hull said, "I understand the magnitude of such an offer. However, by tying together an agreement only between Japan and the United States, you leave open the possibility of a conflict breaking out where Japan might attack another country who we are also in alliance with, and we would be unable to respond as an ally should. Should you start a war with Australia, for example, we could not intervene without violating our agreement with Japan. Mr. Ambassador, that is unacceptable."

Roosevelt had kept his eyes on Nomura, said, "Surely you know that."

Nomura looked down, then up at Roosevelt. "I thank you for receiving me, Mr. President. I shall look forward to our next meeting."

Roosevelt seemed as eager to end this brief conversation as Nomura. He picked up the phone on his desk, the link to an aide who would escort Nomura out. But Nomura suddenly held up a hand, as though a new thought had crossed his mind.

Roosevelt hung up the phone, said, "Something else, Mr. Ambassador?"

Nomura's smile returned. "I understand your Congress has approved a draft of young men for your army."

Roosevelt said, "It was in the newspapers, yes. Very pleased about that. It authorizes the military to make significant increases to the number of troops in the field."

Nomura looked at Hull. "Yes, and I also read in your newspapers that the Congress almost declined to pass that measure, that it was only approved by a few votes."

Roosevelt looked at Hull, cautious now. "That's correct, Ambassador. Nonetheless, it did pass. It is now the law of the land."

"I see, yes. But it seems the isolationist element here is as formidable as ever, perhaps more so. It is very apparent to me that there is considerable sentiment among your Congress, and among your people, that they do not wish to fight a war."

Roosevelt had no humor in his face now, said, "Ambassador, there is 'sentiment' against fighting a war right here in this room. The issue of the draft was not a vote on American intentions, or American resolve. Anyone who interprets it that way would be making a truly regrettable miscalculation."

Nomura stood now, with a smile and a bow. "I completely agree, Mr. President."

Roosevelt's mood had turned sour, and he picked up the phone, said, "In here, now. Escort the ambassador out."

The door was opened immediately by a young marine. Nomura made another bow toward Hull, then left without speaking. The marine closed the door, and Roosevelt sat back, rubbed a hand across his forehead.

"Christ, Cordell, what's with that fellow? I felt

like I was in an interrogation room, where if I said the wrong thing, made a mistake, he'd shout at me, **Hah, got you!**"

There was no humor in Roosevelt's tone.

Hull said, "He's walking a tightrope. He has to keep good relations with us—you and me—or he might as well go home. He has to keep his government believing he's effective here, or, well, he might as well go home."

"We need him, don't we?"

Hull nodded. "Yes, Mr. President, we do. As belligerent as the Japanese are, we have to keep talking."

"So, why do you think he brought up the draft vote? Was he just digging at us?"

Hull thought a moment. "I have to believe that somewhere in Tokyo, some council chamber, some ministry, they know a war is coming, because they're planning it. What they do not seem to grasp, even if Nomura tells them, is that if **we** believe a war is coming, we will prepare for it. And that is why the Japanese will still talk to us. They don't want a war with us, a war that they know they will certainly lose."

# NINETEEN

# Biggs

USS Arizona, Pearl Harbor, Hawaii—
Thursday, September 11, 1941

**"S**o, you think we're going to war?"

Biggs looked up from his half-written letter. "Why?"

Wakeman turned the pages of his magazine, said, "Well, somebody's writing here about how the damn Japs are talking about kicking our asses, since they've already invaded China and someplace else in Asia. There's an article says we might have to send ships and planes and whatever else, in case the Japs try to invade there. This guy's saying that if the Japs keep grabbing places in Asia, they'll likely keep going south, maybe invading Australia. I met an Australian fellow once. Nice guy. Anyway, I ain't saying this fellow knows donkey squat about what he's talking about, but it sure sounds a lot like there could be a war, and not just in Europe."

Farther down the compartment, Mahone held up his own magazine, a copy of **Collier's.** "I ain't worried about none of that, Ed. I'm betting we'll sit tight right here. This fellow here, Walter Davenport, he says he's interviewed all kinds of admirals in Oahu, and with the fleet we got here, that we're . . . impregnable. That means 'strong,' right?"

Wakeman looked at Biggs, shook his head, then said, "Yes, numbskull, it means 'strong.' More than strong. It means nobody's gonna come marching in here unless we let 'em. Let me see the **Collier's.** I'd rather read that one than this crap from some pessimist. The guy's wife must be a Jap or something."

Behind Biggs, he heard the grunt and the footsteps he was beginning to hate. He turned, saw Kincaid, and another older man with him. Kincaid said, "See? They're a worthless bunch, for damn sure. Only way I get any work out of 'em is to kick everyone in the ass."

The other man laughed, and Kincaid said, "Listen up, children. This is Petty Officer Nichols. Old friend of mine. Been in the navy longer than me."

Nichols slapped him on the back. "Jack, nobody's been in the navy longer than you. Hell, you were on the first ironclad."

Biggs sat as still as the others, had never seen Kincaid anywhere close to a good mood, no one around him wanting to change that.

Kincaid said, "PO Nichols is a TC. Turret captain.

He's back after a long stay ashore. None of your business why. But I wanted to show all you jellyfish what a real sailor looks like. If we get into a nasty scrap, while you're running around pissing on yourselves, this is the kind of man who's gonna make a difference. Now, go back to playing marbles."

"Sir?"

Biggs saw that the question had come from Wakeman. Kincaid lost any hint of friendliness.

"What the hell do you want?"

"Well, sir, I been reading that the Japs are getting all angered up and stuff, that there might be a war in the Pacific, maybe right here."

Kincaid glanced at Nichols beside him. "You see? I told you about these morons." He put his hands on his hips, a familiar pose. "Listen to me. Every officer in this fleet will tell you what I'm telling you. If the Japs are stupid enough to start up with us, we'd sink their whole damn navy in three weeks. This ship, and every one just like it, would push right into Tokyo Bay. If the Japs didn't give up by then, PO Nichols and his big guns would turn that entire city into matchsticks. A war? Let me say this one time: I hope we do have a war, and not some damn sub-chasing nonsense in the Atlantic. I look forward to seeing what this ship can do. And I wanna see for myself which one of you little girls might actually turn into sailors."

Biggs thumbed through the magazine, glorious photographs of the hills and fields not far from the taxi stand that serviced them all on their liberty. He stared at one page for a long minute, the magnificence of the Royal Hawaiian Hotel, a handful of sunbathers and a neatly attired waiter, serving drinks in tall glasses.

Behind him, Phar-Mate Corey said, "I thought you were writing a letter."

Biggs turned, embarrassed to be caught. "Yes, sir. I finished the cleaning around the cabinets, wiped down the gurney, made sure the gauze was rolled tight."

Corey laughed. "Relax, Tommy. I'm not busting your chops. Just didn't know where you got the magazine."

"Well, sir, I was trying to write a letter to my folks, and I guess I got distracted. Dr. Condon got this copy of the **Saturday Evening Post,** and there was this article on Hawaii. It's funny, I can tell where the photographer took about half of these pictures. There's even a picture of the fleet. Well, some of it."

Corey leaned closer. "Let's see."

"Here, sir, take it. Doc Condon will probably want it back, though."

He handed Corey the magazine, turned again to his letter, one more wrestling match to find the right words to please his mother, while not causing an eruption from his father. He stared at the paper, his mind drifting. Corey sat down, thumbing through the magazine, and Biggs said, "You know, I think I'd like to live here someday. I don't know how long I'll be in the navy, but someday I'll be retired. This would be a hell of a beautiful place to make a home."

Corey laughed, Vaughan now joining in from the far side of the dispensary.

Vaughan said, "You know who lives in Hawaii? People rich enough to buy this ship, that's who. It's like the visitors who stay in the Royal Hawaiian. Unless your daddy's got a bunch of oil wells, the best hotel room you'll have here is that hammock you sleep in. The only other shot you got is to find some filthy-rich widow, looking for a plaything. Sorry, Tommy, but you ain't good-looking enough for that."

The two mates laughed, and Biggs felt a sour disappointment.

"Gee, I never thought of it like that."

Vaughan came closer now. "The best chance any of us has to live in Hawaii? A room up above a whorehouse or some other hellhole on Hotel Street. That's all any of us can afford. Enjoy what you've got here, Tommy. Use your liberty time to wander around, see what there is to see. These fools who get sent down here blind drunk, they think they're having a good time because they throw up. And how many girls have you seen out there? I don't mean those squacks, I mean a real girl, like you'd want your mama to meet. You go into town, wade through the crowd of sailors and everybody else, then come back and tell me how many actual females you saw."

Corey leaned closer to Biggs, said with a smile, "He does this about once a week. Go on, Bill, let it out."

Vaughan ignored him. "When I heard I was going to Hawaii, I was like you. I could hardly wait—all those hula girls and sunny beaches. Well, then you find out that if you look cross-eyed at a native, a **real** hula girl, her brother or her old man might rip you in two. You'll find out pretty quick that the folks who live here don't like us one bit. The bars and the squack joints will take our money, but the rest of these **citizens** will be damn glad when we sail out of here." He pointed at the magazine in Corey's hand. "You wanna drop in, take a peek at the Royal Hawaiian, or the other one, the Halekulani? Get ready to pay three dollars for a drink, and more than a buck for a beer. That's the facts of life, Tommy. The sooner we get the hell out of this place, maybe head back to Long Beach or Bremerton? It won't be soon enough for me."

Vaughan moved back to his side of the dispensary, busied himself with some task Biggs couldn't see.

Biggs said in a low voice, "Wow. I never thought of Hawaii like that. I guess there's a lot I don't know yet."

Corey looked through the magazine in his hands,

said, "Just do what you have to do, Tommy. There's plenty to do on this ship, from movies to concerts by the new band, all kinds of games and contests. Hell, I don't have to tell you anything about sports, you know that already. And if that's not enough, there's plenty to do in town, and it doesn't mean you have to wander around Hotel Street—you don't have to puke out a gallon of crappy beer to convince anybody else you had a good time. And no matter what all these pictures show you, nobody joined the navy because they wanted to marry a hula girl. This is a battleship, not some fancy ocean liner. Every man on this ship knows what she was built for, what those big guns are for. If we start shooting at a real enemy? Chances are they'll start shooting back. So enjoy what you're doing right now."

Biggs thought of Kincaid. "I've heard talk from some who are hoping we get into a hot fight. But then, Dr. Johnson told me not to get too excited about all that. I'm not sure how I feel. Some of the guys in my compartment, they talk about how bored they are, pissed off about going to sea and doing the same drills over and over. I don't like painting or swabbing worth a damn, but being out there, on the open ocean? That's aces. Until I did that, I wasn't really sure why I joined the navy. I kinda got talked into it by a buddy back home. But I love this ship, and I love being out on the ocean. Never expected that."

Corey moved away toward the doctor's small

office, tossed the magazine onto the desk. "You're doing just fine, Tommy. You're no different than me. I love the sea, I love this ship. It's home. The longer you're here, the more you'll feel that way."

Across the larger room, Vaughan called out. "Hey, Biggs, when's your next ball game?"

"Tomorrow at 1400, field number two on Ford Island. We're playing the team from the Marine Barracks."

Vaughan looked over his way. "I'm not on duty. Maybe I can swing a liberty pass. How about you, Ernie?"

Corey said, "Nope. I'm right here. Dr. Condon and I have to give a safety lecture to a group of new recruits."

Vaughan went back to work, said, "Sounds like a real hoot. Okay, Tommy, I wanna watch you bust a couple over the fence. If I don't cheer you, it's only because I'm surrounded by jarheads. They got no sense of humor."

————

**"He's in the army now.
He's blowin' reveille.
He's the boogie woogie bugle boy of
    Company B."**

Biggs clapped along with the rest, kept his eyes on the singer, standing out in front of the band, the voice of a professional. All around Biggs, feet were tapping, hands slapping knees, the smiles contagious. The song ended now, and another began, a slower piece, by Glenn Miller. The singer sat, picked up a trombone and began moving the brass slide. Too soon, the music ended. The singer stood up again, took a low bow, and held both hands high in the air.

"Thank you all! That's it for now. We have duties to attend to. My name's Jack Scruggs, and we are damn glad to be your band. We will see you at 0800, as always, for Colors."

The applause was loud and long, the sailors starting to rise, moving out to wherever they were supposed to be. Biggs still sat, kept his gaze on the instruments, marveled at the talent it took to make that kind of music. There was a hand on his shoulder, and he turned, was surprised to see Vaughan. Vaughan called out toward the band, "This way, gentlemen. You've got an appointment in sick bay."

Biggs looked at the band members, saw no signs of any ailment, but Vaughan was already down the ladder. Most of the musicians zipped a thin cloth around their instruments, some placing them in custom cases. They moved quickly, followed Vaughan off the upper deck, down the ladder. Biggs wasn't on duty for another hour, but he had too much curiosity, fell in behind them.

They reached sick bay, and Biggs kept back, saw Vaughan leading them in, packing the men along one bulkhead. Biggs ducked, could see into the hatchway now, was still baffled why these men were there.

Johnson emerged from one end of the compartment, saw Biggs, motioned him inside. The doctor scanned the room and said, "Gentlemen, I am Commander Samuel Johnson. I am one of the medical doctors on this ship. First, I want to say that your performances have given a lift to this entire crew, all the way up to the admiral. I commend you all. However, you are here today because one of your most important stations on this ship, in the event of any serious combat or other emergency, is to assist the medical staff in any way they may require, though primarily as stretcher bearers. We all hope you will never need the training you will receive here. But the plain fact is that, in an emergency, you could be responsible for saving the life of one or more of your crewmen. Some of what you might be asked to do is common sense, but there are duties you might not expect.

"Let me offer you one example. You come upon a situation where two men are wounded. One man has a cut on his arm. He's holding his hand on the cut; maybe his shirt is wrapped around the wound. The second man, he has a major stomach wound, so that his intestines . . . his insides are plainly visible."

The doctor paused, the musicians giving him their full attention. After a long moment, Johnson said, "You might not agree with what I'm about to tell you. But it is critical that you obey this protocol. If you are facing this situation by yourself, no corpsman around, your first efforts should go to the man with the wounded arm. It is a wound that is relatively easy to repair. Any bleeding can be stopped with pressure, wrapped up, even if you use the man's shirt. In other words, this man can be patched up, and he can return to duty. He might have to perform a critical function for this ship, and putting him back at his station might save lives. The second man . . . his wound will require major surgery. Nothing you can do will allow him to return to duty, and worse, it is possible that nothing you can do will ensure his survival."

Biggs saw heads drop, gloom spreading over the band members, and over Biggs as well.

Johnson continued, "Your job could be to assist one of my men, or one of the doctors. It is unlikely you will be called upon to administer any medical treatment beyond first aid. But that is not guaranteed. If there are casualties anywhere on this ship, it is far better for you to know what to do and what to expect. Staring at a wounded man wringing your hands makes you a liability. That's what this training is for—not to teach you to be corpsmen, but to perhaps save a life on your own, if one of us can't reach you in time to help."

The lecture from Johnson lasted another half hour, ending with the promise of more to come. Just like the drills at sea, the training was never-ending.

They filed out through the hatchway, Biggs moving closer to the doctor.

"Holy cow, sir. I can't really get used to that. The first time you gave me that talk, I guessed the other way around—attend to the belly wound. It seems like the right thing to do."

"Most people feel that way, Mr. Biggs. It's instinctive. But this isn't a lesson in compassion. In a combat situation, nobody can afford to be kind."

"Yes, sir. I guess so."

Vaughan moved over, said, "Don't worry about it, Tommy. First time I heard that, I went crazy. Thought it was cold as hell."

Johnson said, "It might be. But it has to be that way. The welfare of the ship has to come first."

Vaughan stepped away, the doctor moved into his office, and Biggs was surprised to see one of the band members at the hatchway.

"Excuse me?"

Biggs said, "Yeah, sure, come in."

"Could I get the doctor to look at my hand? Well, it's my finger, actually."

Johnson emerged from his office, said, "What's the trouble, sailor?"

"Sir, I play the clarinet and saxophone. After the last concert, I got a pretty bad blister. Fortunately, it's not where I have to put the most pressure. But it hurts pretty bad."

Johnson said, "Right over here, sailor. Have a seat. You have a name?"

"Yes, sir. Jerry Cox, sir, musician second."

"Nice to meet you, Mr. Cox. I love the reed instruments."

"Thank you, sir. I suppose I do too. I play a few others too, even the Hawaiian guitar."

Johnson said, "Mr. Biggs, hand me that tube of ointment, and the thin gauze. This won't be any problem at all, Mr. Cox. It might be sore for a while, but we'll keep any nasty bugs out of there. The last thing we want is an infection. Hawaiian guitar? That's a strange one."

"Yes, sir. We've found out that most of the crews who have spent time in Hawaii aren't too keen on hearing that one. I think they get enough as it is."

Biggs brought over the ointment and gauze, and Johnson went to work. He said to Biggs, "Aren't you curious where this man is from?"

It was a familiar cue, to occupy the patient's attention.

"Yes, sir, I am. Where are you from, Mr. Cox?"

"East Moline, Illinois. Not many people have heard of it, I guess."

Biggs and Johnson both laughed. Cox was obviously baffled by their response, and Biggs said, "I'm from a place in Florida that would fit inside the

Moline Post Office. And, the doctor's hometown would fit inside that."

They all laughed, the distraction working like it was supposed to. Biggs kept his eyes on Cox's face, felt a hint of recognition.

"You go through basic at Great Lakes? Back in February?"

Cox said, "Yeah. Finished up in March."

Biggs smiled. "I knew you looked familiar. I was there too. Not sure if we bumped into each other, but after six weeks you remember some faces."

Cox said, "You play an instrument?"

Biggs sniffed. "I wrapped a paper napkin around a comb once. Played 'Yankee Doodle' for my mom on her birthday. My buddy, Ray, slapped a cardboard box for the drums. He's on the **Curtiss** right now, seaplane tender."

Cox laughed. "I guess we might use a comb-player in the band once in a while."

Johnson held up Cox's hand. "All done, Mr. Cox. It was a little worse than you described it. I wanted it cleaned out to keep any creatures from sneaking in. And, like I said, it'll be tender, but you can still use it, if you don't press too hard."

Cox looked at the gauze wrapping his finger. "Thank you, sir. I might take a day off. We've got the band contest on Saturday at Bloch Arena. If you can get liberty, you oughta come out."

Biggs said, "Where's that?"

"New place built over near Hickam Field, right

across the harbor. Supposed to be real nice, holds a bunch of people. There's gonna be four bands, and we're competing for a pretty nice trophy. Our director, Mr. Kinney, says that if we win, he'll get us all promoted to ensign. Kinda doubt that. But it'll be fun."

Biggs looked at Johnson, who nodded. "Sure, I'll write up a pass. I think I'll go myself."

ONBOARD USS ARIZONA, PEARL HARBOR, HAWAII— FRIDAY, SEPTEMBER 12, 1941

He was soaked through with sweat, the dirt from the ball field invading every part of his body. He climbed the ladder slowly, made his formal greeting to the officer of the deck, who stood back, seemed to give Biggs a wide berth. Biggs knew he had to be carrying a fragrant aroma no one wanted to experience, but he was too tired to apologize. He stepped inside the hatchway, stayed back as an officer came up the ladder, a lieutenant Biggs had never seen before. The man looked at him with a frown of disapproval.

"What's your problem, sailor? You ever hear of a shower?"

Biggs stiffened, said, "Yes, sir. I just came off the baseball field, sir. I'm headed down for a shower now."

The officer's mood changed, a smile. "Good. How'd we do?"

"Um, sir, we played the Marine Barracks boys. They won."

"Hmm. Well, get 'em next time."

"Yes, sir."

The lieutenant moved down the passageway, and Biggs didn't hesitate, quickly descended the ladder, then the next one until he reached his compartment. He stepped through the hatchway, was startled by the angry scowl of Kincaid.

"So, here's one of our losers right now. You know what you did today, Biggs? You let the damn marines embarrass us. I'm just giving the word to all your shipmates here." The others were sitting along the sides of the mess tables, and Kincaid pointed at Biggs. "This worm let them score fourteen runs. I guess the whole team must have pissed themselves when they saw those jarheads." He turned to Biggs again. "You too, I'll bet. Too scared to come out of your dugout, right?"

Biggs was in no mood for this. He wondered how Kincaid already knew about the game.

"I hit two home runs and a double, sir."

That seemed to pause Kincaid's harangue, but he summoned the disgust again. "Sounds like you're awfully proud of yourself. Well, it wasn't enough, was it? All right, since you embarrassed this ship today, tomorrow at 0800, you will report to holystoning duty on the main deck, starboard. You may or may not have any help, but I don't care. You'll work until 1600, or until I tell you to stop."

Biggs thought of the band concert. "Sir, the doctor gave me a liberty pass for tomorrow. Our band is playing, a contest with other bands."

The look on Kincaid's face didn't change. "I don't care if you're going dancing with Ginger Rogers. You will report as ordered."

Biggs was too exhausted to hold back, his anger rising. "Sir, I really want to go to that concert. Dr. Johnson says I'll have a pass. You have no reason to be such a son of a bitch . . ."

Kincaid seemed to light up. **"I been looking forward to this."**

He stepped forward, the fist coming straight at Biggs's nose. Biggs ducked quickly to one side, Kincaid's blow missing him completely. Kincaid rose up, a low growl, "You little bastard. You talk to me like that . . ."

"What's the trouble here, Petty Officer?"

The voice came from behind Kincaid. Biggs saw the white uniform, the rank, recognized the lieutenant as the man he had just seen in the passageway.

Kincaid hesitated, then turned around, said, "There's no problem here at all, sir. Just teaching one of my men some respect."

The lieutenant looked past Kincaid to Biggs, said, "No shower yet, Mr. Biggs?"

"No, sir. On my way."

"You did a fine job out there, Mr. Biggs. Our pitching was a little off, that's all. I spoke to Lieutenant Janz. He says that without your bat, it would have been even uglier. They've never voted an MVP before, but you're in the running, for sure."

"Thank you, sir."

The lieutenant said to Kincaid, "It would be a real problem if our best hitter had some kind of mishap. There are a lot of people on this ship who are pretty happy with this sailor's contribution to our baseball team. Do you understand, Petty Officer?"

The words came out slowly, barely audible. **"Completely, sir."**

"Good. We'll be going into dry dock on Monday. Just some minor repairs and maintenance for a few days, but I would guess there will be ample opportunity for liberty."

Behind Biggs, the others responded with low sounds of approval.

The lieutenant said to Kincaid, "Petty Officer, I would suggest that you take advantage of the opportunity as well. From where I stand, I think you could use a little down time. As you were, gentlemen."

The lieutenant moved out through the hatchway, the compartment deathly silent. Kincaid turned to Biggs, spoke with the snarl of a vicious dog. "When does baseball season end, worm?"

Biggs felt the heat from Kincaid's wrath, said, "Don't know exactly, sir. They haven't posted the full schedule yet. December, I think."

Kincaid started for the hatchway, took a look back toward him. "I'm counting the days."

# TWENTY

# Yamamoto

TOKYO, JAPAN—SATURDAY, SEPTEMBER 13, 1941

His impatience had been increasing daily. There were still so many roadblocks put in the way of his plan by his superiors, who dismissed his strategy as outrageously risky. But Yamamoto was still commander in chief of the combined fleet, and did not need anyone's approval to order the training programs for ship captains, air commanders and pilots, and everyone else who would be a part of his attack plan. Even now, Commander Genda and several of Genda's subordinates were analyzing and debating the possible routes the fleet would take on its approach to Hawaii. As well, Genda was selecting the appropriate air commanders, mapping out their potential flight paths, and increasing the training for the pilots, men who still had no idea just what they were training to do.

As Genda and his men labored, Yamamoto continued to confront the naysayers. Most were admirals, some above him in rank and seniority, men with the power to terminate the operation altogether. Others had served under him, including Fukudome, his former chief of staff.

Yamamoto couldn't truly fault anyone for their doubts. He had plenty of his own. What he railed against was the utter lack of imagination among the men who were charging ahead with their own plans for war, a foregone conclusion that it would involve the United States and Britain, if not the Dutch and the Soviets. The sheer magnitude of what they were trying to accomplish had caused some of the most vocal among them to pull back just a bit, as though they were finally taking seriously that all-out war against everyone in the Pacific Rim might be a disastrous mistake.

He knew that the skepticism toward his plan could become contagious even among the men who now supported it. There was one effective method for quieting much of that, while solidifying the numbers and statistics that could buoy his case. On September 2, he had scheduled war games, a traditional exercise usually called for later in the year. But Yamamoto wouldn't wait. He knew that Japan was entering a precarious time, and with the embargo now in effect, the prime minister and the Naval Ministry would quickly bend to the noisy will of the army. To the army, war was no longer a point of discussion—it was happening. The only variable Yamamoto could see was just how much time it would take for the Japanese military to adequately prepare.

Yamamoto understood the power he had over his war games. Unlike the exercises as staged by so many other nations, these games took place not on the open ocean, but at the Naval War College, in Tokyo. Instead of ships at sea plotting their movements and firing patterns, these games took place on a large table, with questions and answers on paper and the naval officers standing close by, offering suggestions. The games involved a large number of senior officers, who plotted out their proposed assaults against a great variety of targets from the Philippines to Burma, the Netherlands East Indies to Malaya, as well as a number of islands throughout the South Pacific, including those held by the Americans. But Yamamoto's plans for Hawaii were staged separately, in a room where access was restricted to those few men already aware of his plan.

The first set of games had been judged by the officers present to be something of a failure. Unhappy with that outcome, Yamamoto scheduled a second game, focusing mostly on his Hawaii plan, and once again held in relative secrecy. The conclusions this time were considerably more positive, the judge concluding that the attack stood a 50 percent probability of success. Though some who took part in the exercise were nervously unhappy with those results, Yamamoto considered them acceptable. It was not a difficult conclusion for him to reach, since, in this exercise, Yamamoto had been the judge.

ONBOARD BATTLESHIP MUTSO, TOKYO BAY—SATURDAY, SEPTEMBER 13, 1941

His temporary command post was now on the **Mutso,** a battleship very much like his beloved **Nagato** but closer to the offices and meeting rooms where he needed to be. It was no secret that with the American oil embargo, it was not wise for the larger ships of the fleet to make journeys just for the convenience of their commanders, not even the commander in chief.

He had finished his lunch, enjoying the meal by himself. He sat back and allowed the orderlies to do their job, rapidly cleaning the table, removing any crumb he had left behind. The solitary meal was a luxury—no urgent meetings, no discussions that produced indigestion. As he watched the orderlies, he thought of tomorrow, smiling in anticipation of Chiyoko's being there to share a meal with him. With his flagship anchored this close to Tokyo, it had become customary for her to visit him. No one among the crew or the officers dared to offer a disapproving glance. He knew as well that when she retired with him to his quarters, she would do as she always did, clean and straighten up, as though the orderlies were never performing to her standards. There would be no protest from him, that lesson learned long ago. If she insisted on performing the task, she **would** perform the task. He had learned as well that watching her scurry around his quarters like a manic squirrel was a pleasure all its own.

As the orderlies completed their task, he focused on his favorite, Omi, said, "Go out, down the passageway, locate Admiral Ugaki. He should be in his office."

Rear Admiral Matome Ugaki was his new chief of staff, had accepted that position a month before. He was an extremely tall man, another of those around Yamamoto whose height only emphasized to Yamamoto how diminutive he was.

Ugaki appeared at the door, his hat clamped under his arm. "May I be of service, sir?"

"Do we have any outstanding appointments yet today? I know our ship's captain had suggested some sort of gathering in my honor. I would appreciate it if you could dissuade him. I wish no sign of disrespect. We are, after all, his guests."

"Sir, if I may suggest, you are no one's guest. This is your ship, as it is your fleet."

Yamamoto thought, No, actually the fleet belongs to the emperor. But he kept the words inside, said, "Your graciousness is appreciated, Admiral. As is your obedience. So, I will be more direct. Please inform

the captain that I will be unable to attend a gathe-
ing. Offer him my respects. Make that 'sincere' respects. You may do that now."

"As you wish, sir."

"Oh, and please have someone check with the
mail room. I am expecting a small parcel."

"As you wish, sir."

Ugaki was out quickly, and Yamamoto sat back
in the chair, thought, What will all these years of
obedience do to me when I retire? Everyone who
speaks to me grovels. I don't insist on that, even if
they feel that I do. But soon, I will be an old man
with no one to obey me. Instead, there will be tolerance, or perhaps even rudeness. When was the last
time anyone was ever rude in my presence? Well,
perhaps my wife. No, do not think on that. Never
think on that.

There was a light rap on the wardroom door, and
he said, "You may enter. I will not bite you."

The door opened slowly, a young officer peering
in. "Sir? I did not understand what you said."

"Good. What do you want?"

"Sir, Admiral Ugaki asked me to bring you your
mail. It just arrived, sir. Just the one package."

Yamamoto saw the roll of brown wrapping.
"Excellent. Drop it right here on the table, Ensign.
You are dismissed."

The young man obeyed and was quickly out the
door. Yamamoto felt the heft of the rolled paper,
smiled, thought, Yes, at least I have **something** to

do this afternoon. He stood, hurried out toward his temporary quarters, but couldn't wait, tore one end off the packet. He stopped in the passageway, unrolled the contents, thought, I don't know why this so brightens my day, my entire month. It was another piece of his American experience, pages of stories and advertisements, so many lessons on just who his adversary was going to be. It was the latest issue of **Life** magazine.

He heard heavy footsteps behind him, a guard climbing up, now in the passageway. The man seemed relieved to find him, said, "Sir, you have a visitor. I was not certain where to escort him."

Yamamoto was annoyed, glanced at the cover of the magazine, rolled it up under his arm. "Who is it?"

"Sir, it is Admiral Tomioka. He just arrived on a launch. The officer of the deck said he was not expected."

"No, he was not. But admirals think they belong anyplace that suits them. Have him escorted to my wardroom."

The man offered a sharp salute, then quickly disappeared through a hatchway below. Yamamoto scowled, reached the entrance to his quarters, tossed the magazine inside. He returned to his wardroom, the long table cleaned to a shine, sat down heavily in his chair at the center of the table, drummed his fingers on the metal. The knock came now, and he said, "Come in, by all means."

The door opened slowly, and he saw the guard, and behind him, his surprise visitor.

Sadatoshi Tomioka was commander of the First Division, First Section of the Navy General Staff. Yamamoto was curious just why he was there. Tomioka was not his friend.

Yamamoto said to the guard, "Thank you, Petty Officer. You are dismissed. Please close the door."

The guard backed away, the door closing.

Yamamoto pulled himself up to his feet, made the obligatory formal greeting, a bow that Tomioka returned.

Yamamoto said, "Is the wardroom acceptable? We could retire to my personal quarters."

"It is not necessary, Admiral. I will be brief. I am here on behalf of the Navy General Staff. There is concern that you are continuing to advocate your plan to attack the American base in Hawaii, against all advice to the contrary."

"And you do not approve?"

"No, I do not. Many others in the Naval Ministry and the General Staff believe it is a foolish gambit."

Yamamoto began to feel a game brewing. "How foolish?"

Tomioka clearly did not expect the question. "Well, I have heard estimates that the probability of success is no more than fifty percent."

Yamamoto rubbed a hand on his chin. Yes, he thought, news of the estimates has traveled quickly. As I'd hoped.

He returned to his chair. "Those are very satisfactory odds, better than you would receive at any casino. I am pleased to receive such support from the General Staff."

He could see Tomioka growing flustered, exactly the reaction he was hoping for.

"No, you do not seem to understand."

Yamamoto thought, The game is over. He made a fist, pounded it slowly on the table, stared hard at Tomioka.

"No, it is **you** who does not understand. There will be a war, yes? It has been decided already, and not by me. My plan is the best one we have to keep the Americans back, out of our way, until we can secure strongholds throughout the South Pacific."

"Admiral Yamamoto, that is your opinion. There are others who believe the Americans will sit by and avoid any involvement. They do not have the stomach for a conflict. It has been suggested that when the first blood spills, the Americans will most likely sue for peace."

Yamamoto fought the urge to laugh. "Suggested by whom? Never mind. Have you been to America?"

Tomioka shook his head, and Yamamoto sat back, said, "I have. I truly enjoy every part of that vast country. Let me offer you some history, perhaps more than you received in school. For any of you who believe the Americans are not worthy of a fight, that they do not have the stomach for blood, perhaps you are familiar with the American Civil

War? In the 1860s, they divided and fought each other in the bloodiest war in their history. They did not require any enemy to inspire them. They fought **each other.** Are you familiar with football?"

Tomioka sat down slowly, another shake of his head. "I'm not certain. No."

"Football is a game between two teams, on a grass field. I attended a contest near Chicago, between Iowa University and Northwestern University. Iowa won the game, but that's not the point. The entire contest was a magnificent show of raw violence. We have nothing to compare to it. So if there is no enemy beyond their borders, they create one at home, for their amusement. Are you familiar with the sport of prize fighting?"

Tomioka seemed utterly uncomfortable, shook his head again. "Sorry, no."

"Two men stand inside a roped square, with light leather gloves. They pummel each other until one man is knocked unconscious. It is literally a fist-fight. This sport goes back to the ancient Greeks, and yet, in our modern world, it is the Americans who have made it their own." He paused. "So, I would suggest, Admiral Tomioka, with all respect to you and your naysayers, that you not try to convince me that the Americans will cower or run terrified from a fight. From any fight. If my plan is successful, they might back away for a few months, to regroup and repair, allowing us a window of time. That might be our only advantage, because when we start a war, with either the Americans or the British, we do not have the resources to outlast them. It must be a rapid, decisive blow that will allow us to build our strength. And that is what I will accomplish in Hawaii."

Tomioka stood again, composed himself, said, "I am not often lectured in such a way, Admiral. It is of little concern what the Americans claim as their cultural heritage. The General Staff has determined the best strategy for executing the inevitable conflict. We have made plans that are consistent with our beliefs that the war can be won only by the great battle as we have designed it. The navy shall lead the effort to obliterate the American presence in the Pacific, which will support the bases that the army has established throughout Southeast Asia."

Yamamoto fought the urge to scream at the man. He knew that if he stood, he might be tempted to climb over the table. After a long moment, he said, "What are you going to do for oil? How far from our shores can the fleet wage this war of annihilation?"

He saw the smugness now, Tomioka tilting his head with a half smile. Tomioka said, "That is a simple problem, Admiral. We shall draw the enemy close to our shores, where we do not have to expend valuable fuel. Once he is here, he shall be destroyed. Having our ships so close to home, it will allow us to refuel, refit, rearm, as need be. I would think a man of your experience should understand the simplicity of that."

Yamamoto fought to keep his temper under control. He hated smugness as much as he hated incompetence. He took a moment, controlled his breathing and his anger. "Admiral Tomioka, has no one considered that by bringing the enemy's navy into our waters, we will also bring the enemy's aircraft, and possibly his troops? By staying close to our shores, we will invite the war to our shores. We will have handed **them** the gift of logistics. They will not have to sail away across a wide ocean to refuel and refit and rearm. They will be close enough to destroy our cities with their first blow."

Tomioka seemed to absorb what Yamamoto said, then shrugged, as though it was an entirely alien concept. "Admiral Yamamoto, I do not see any difficulties with our overall strategy. Why are you proposing that we strike the Americans so very far away, with all the challenges of distance, of refueling and communication?"

"I have explained myself to every one of you. Every challenge is being dealt with. The sharpest minds in the fleet are working every day to solve those things you would so easily dismiss." His voice was rising, so he stopped, fought for calm. "I have said this to the Chiefs of Staff, to the Ministry, many times. If we damage the American fleet in Hawaii, it will grant us **time.**"

Tomioka seemed to ponder the concept. "I suppose there is much to discuss."

"Admiral Tomioka, I believe that to be the worst

word ever created. 'Discuss.' No one ever has to offer an idea, an original thought, no one ever has to make a decision. They can just . . . discuss."

Tomioka looked down for a brief moment, and Yamamoto saw a look of profound gloom.

Tomioka said, "Perhaps I shall visit with you again, Admiral."

Yamamoto made himself stand, the appropriate show of respect. "Thank you for visiting me, Admiral Tomioka. Please offer my respects to the navy chiefs, and to the Naval Ministry. I am happy to say that there are some among the Ministry, as there are some among the Chiefs of Staff, who are more flexible in their thinking than others. Once the plans have been assembled in detail, once the challenges have been successfully addressed by my officers, then we shall present our plans in their final form. Then, you and the other skeptics may decide if a fifty percent chance of success is a respectable gamble. Or perhaps you would wait for the Germans to decide if we will be a part of their war, and then they will instruct us how we will fight it."

The message came to him in a plain envelope, delivered by a courier who offered nothing about who had sent him.

Yamamoto sat on the small bed in his quarters, his chief of staff standing in the hatchway, politely patient. Yamamoto scanned the paper, said, "Not sure why anyone made such a fuss to be secretive with this. It's just a diplomatic message. I suppose I shouldn't be surprised. I've been warning them, the Naval Ministry and anyone else who would listen, that we have made a terribly bad wager."

Ugaki said, "I do not understand, sir."

Yamamoto looked again at the paper. "It's a note passed from the German military attaché in Thailand. The message is as plain as it can be. **You cannot trust Japan. Germany will settle with Japan after she has won the war in Europe.**"

Ugaki seemed puzzled. "Sir, does this mean that our ally is speaking ill of us behind our back?"

Yamamoto laughed. "That might be the most polite way of expressing disgusted outrage I've ever heard. Congratulations, Admiral. The fact is, we have made an alliance with a back-stabbing psychotic. The moment Hitler believes us to be weak or vulnerable, we will fall under the same steel wheels that are grinding through Europe. And no one in Tokyo can seem to understand that."

ONBOARD BATTLESHIP NAGATO, TOKYO BAY—
THURSDAY, OCTOBER 9, 1941

The meetings were growing more intense. Yamamoto was directly confronting the staunchest opponents of the Pearl Harbor plan. To his enormous dismay, his friend, Admiral Onishi, one of the first men to hear of the plan back in January, and the man who had recommended Commander Genda, had now turned against the idea. As it was with Admiral Fukudome, Yamamoto's former chief of staff, a number of those men close to Yamamoto were now in opposition to him.

The arguments continued with the same simple theme. Those opposed to Yamamoto's plan insisted that if the Americans stayed out of the war, Japan would have free rein in the South Pacific. Yamamoto's counter was as it had always been, that you would not keep America away from helping her allies, and that in any protracted war, Japan was destined to lose. By attacking the American fleet at Hawaii, there could be a window of time opened for the Japanese to complete a great deal of her plans southward, including the capture of a major source of new oil in the Dutch East Indies.

As the meetings dragged on, a frustrated Yamamoto made a new argument: If the Japanese put their focus only on Southeast Asia and the South Pacific, they would still draw the wrath of the Americans, who had staunch allies all over that part of the world. With Japan's military energy focused southward, how vulnerable would Japan be to air strikes from American aircraft carriers, strikes that could devastate Japan's major cities? At least an attack on Pearl Harbor could delay that possibility.

Yamamoto's senior aide was by all definitions an odd duck. Captain Kameto Kuroshima was very well known among Yamamoto's circle of officers for his utter lack of personal hygiene. The man bathed perhaps once a week. This fact was only enhanced by his obsession for smoking, which produced a trail of ash through anyplace he spent time. To men like the rigid Ugaki, Kuroshima inspired dread, not to mention a fog of unpleasantness anytime he was in the room. Fortunately for those with such sensitivities, Kuroshima spent most of his time in his own quarters, working feverishly on those parts of Yamamoto's Hawaii plan as he was assigned. Yamamoto trusted him implicitly, and relied on the man to sort through several aspects of the air assault, working in partnership with Commander Genda. When Kuroshima tackled a task, any task, he would lock himself in his quarters, often not emerging for several days. It was just as well that no one made any effort to disturb him. When alone, Kuroshima rarely wore clothes.

As the details came together and so many of the questions were finally answered, Yamamoto chose Kuroshima to present the Hawaii plan directly to the heart of the Navy General Staff. The final arguments were of course Yamamoto's own, but he knew that Kuroshima would drive home the message with considerable vigor. Yamamoto added the postscript himself, the message to all those admirals as clear as it could be: He was absolutely determined to carry out this mission, and he would stake his career and his position on its success. And if that would not sway them, he had instructed Kuroshima to offer one final argument in favor of the plan: If it was not approved, Yamamoto and his entire staff would resign.

Despite his respect for Kuroshima, Yamamoto wasn't immune to the man's unpleasant aura, and couldn't ignore the stub of a cigarette that dangled precariously from his mouth. Kuroshima was yet another tall man among so many around Yamamoto, thin, almost wispy, leaning toward Yamamoto like a sapling that might fall over.

Yamamoto pointed to the chair across from him, but Kuroshima seemed content to stand.

Yamamoto said, "Who spoke? Who made the first response?"

"Chief of Staff Nagano. He offered no objections. I think he understood the tone of your message, and he acknowledged that you should be given a chance to see it through."

Yamamoto was surprised, but couldn't take his eyes off the cigarette, the stream of ash growing longer.

"He said that? I'm being offered a **chance**? Well, of course. Not quite a full commitment. But that's an excellent turn, which I did not expect. That old man has a habit of digging in his heels against any idea he's ever heard."

Kuroshima shrugged, the ash dropping away, falling somewhere around his feet. "Your former chief of staff, Admiral Fukudome, had his say. He said he would no longer express his objections. He seemed to fall in line with his superior."

Yamamoto sniffed. "I was his superior once. He didn't fall into any line with me. But, that's good. Either you changed his mind, or he just got tired of fighting with me. What about Tomioka, Onishi, the rest of them?"

"The only argument of any force came from Admiral Tomioka. Among the others, there were no real arguments against you, sir. Or, they have objections still and they just don't want to talk about them anymore. That seems curious to me."

"Why?"

"You sent me there expecting an argument from every one of them. But they just seemed to . . . roll over."

"Except for Tomioka."

"Yes, sir. However, I persuaded him."

Yamamoto smiled. "How?"

"As you directed, sir. I said your dedication to this plan was absolute, so much so that if it was not carried out, neither you nor your staff would accept any responsibility for the survival of the empire. That seemed to have the effect you anticipated. So, to conclude, sir, I'm pleased to report that the Navy General Staff has dropped its opposition to the Pearl Harbor attack. They have authorized you to conduct training as you feel is necessary."

"I'm already conducting the necessary training."

Kuroshima shrugged, lit another cigarette. "I didn't feel the need to mention that, sir. They behaved as though they were granting you a huge concession. I didn't want to upset them."

Yamamoto sat back, took in the aroma of Kuroshima's cigarette, a treat he had not allowed himself in years. "So, there it is, Captain. Just like that. They've fought me, and schemed behind my back, they've convinced my friends that I'm out of my mind. And then, just like that, they tell me to go ahead and do it."

"I'm not sure it's like that, sir. They're saying they won't oppose you anymore. They know how popular you are within the navy, how many officers are working for you. They may be stuck in the dirt like dead bamboo, but they do pay attention once in a while."

Yamamoto had heard enough. "Thank you, Captain. It's possible we'll have to do this all over again. As you discovered, minds can change, even stubborn ones. You are dismissed."

Kuroshima saluted, knocking another stream of ash from his cigarette. He turned with no hint of formality, an orderly holding open the door. Yamamoto could feel the air clearing. He smiled now, wading through the report in his mind.

Fukudome, my friend, my once–chief of staff, turns against me, and now, changes course. And Onishi. Someone convinced him to turn his back on a plan he knew was a good one. Now, he has come back as well. And the others, some of them old men, useless, past their time. But they have power, and that can be a deadly combination. Still, for now anyway, they will grant me the opportunity to hang myself.

ONBOARD BATTLESHIP NAGATO, TOKYO BAY—
SATURDAY, OCTOBER 11, 1941

He felt weak, energized only by the thought that she would be there later that afternoon. He looked around his quarters, saw nothing too out of place, then reached into a cabinet, removed a clean shirt, and tossed it over a small chair. He smiled at the thought of her scolding him for his slovenly ways. And I will scold her for her scolding me. The thoughts slipped away, and he looked at the small desk. The letter was almost finished, but the words had run dry, his thoughts too gloomy. The black ink was still wet, his brushstrokes neat and elegant. I just take my time, he thought. People make such a fuss, as though I am an artist with the brush. Hori pretends I have great talent. It is one reason he is my friend. But he is not nearby. And so I must write this letter to him.

He sat, moved the paper, shook his head, couldn't escape the strange gloominess. Hori, I hope you can understand what I'm feeling through the ink on the paper. There are not many who can know such things.

**"I find my present position extremely odd—obliged to make up my mind to pursue unswervingly a course that is precisely the opposite of my personal views."**

ONBOARD BATTLESHIP NAGATO, TOKYO BAY—
FRIDAY, OCTOBER 17, 1941

It was unusual for Ugaki to do anything in tandem with the slovenly Kuroshima, or even to stand close to him. But they were there now, a pair of opposites standing tall with idiotic smiles, no explanation why.

Yamamoto had no idea what was happening, was impatient for answers. "Do you two wish to go into the wardroom and sit down?"

Ugaki said, "It is not necessary, sir."

Yamamoto looked at Kuroshima, who flicked an inch of ash from his cigarette to the deck beneath him.

"I'm happy to stand right here. I think you'll want to stand for this too, sir."

Yamamoto was tired of the mindless grins. "All right, enough of this. What are you two so giddy about?"

Ugaki said, "Sir, we have received a message from the naval staff. It seems that since our forces have successfully occupied a number of important bases in Indo-China, including a network of airfields, the army has now secured its position so effectively that they no longer require the support of our aircraft carriers. Therefore, the naval chiefs have agreed to your request, made some time ago, for two additional carriers to be added to your task force for the Hawaii operation. You will now have—"

"Six."

"Yes, sir. Six."

Yamamoto saw the grins again. He tried to share their good moods, but couldn't shed the weariness. "Please cable this information to Commander Genda. I should imagine he will receive this news with the same moronic smile that you two have now."

Ugaki saluted, turned away, was met at the ladder by an aide. Yamamoto saw the aide hand him a paper, said, "What is it now? Two more carriers?"

Ugaki had lost the grin, said, "No, sir. This is from the prime minister's office. Prime Minister Konoye has formed a new government, as ordered by the emperor."

Yamamoto had no interest in the civilian government, said, "Yes, this is his third attempt. He will have no more success this time."

Ugaki handed Yamamoto the message, said, "That is certainly true, sir. He is no longer prime minister."

Yamamoto read through the bureaucratic jargon, the names chosen to fill slots in the new government, men who likely would never be heard from again, except in their own towns. But he stopped now, focused on one name.

"So, the new prime minister is General Hideki Tojo. Well, I see the army has sealed its grip on the government. And now the navy has surrendered to his power. Our new naval minister is Admiral Shimada. He commands the Yokosuka Naval Station. He has no experience, not with politics, not with standing tall against the wishes of the army. He is an office boy, and Tojo will slap him around like an unruly child."

He handed the paper back to Ugaki. "So it goes, gentlemen. We are rolling downhill faster than I ever believed. I wish I could predict what lies at the bottom."

# TWENTY-ONE

# Hull

The ball clanked rudely against one side of the wire wicket. Hull stood straight, shook his head.

"You would think after all this time, I'd play this game with at least a flicker of skill."

"Stand back, Mr. Secretary. I'll show you how it's done."

Hull backed away, and Casey leaned low. His mallet struck the ball with a loud crack, the ball glancing off Hull's, then rolling through the wicket. Casey put one fist in the air.

"I told you, did I not? Is that the skill you're referring to? I believe the rules allow me to launch your ball somewhere toward the Potomac River."

To one side, Wood laughed, said, "Easy, Richard.

Cordell Hull plays croquet with more false modesty than any man in the American government. He's setting you up for a thrashing, I guarantee. Therefore, Minister Casey, as a fellow representative of His Majesty's Commonwealth, I would offer you one bit of advice. Before too much longer, both England and Australia might require a significant amount of assistance from our American friends. Thus, it would be unwise to offend their secretary of state by brutalizing his croquet ball."

Casey looked at Hull, then at Wood. "Are you suggesting we should let him win?"

Wood laughed now. "I wouldn't go that far. No cause to give him a swelled head."

Casey approached his ball, struck Hull's lightly, the ball rolling only a few feet. "Does that maintain our alliance, Mr. Secretary?"

Hull smiled. "You had your chance, sir. In the game of croquet, generosity can be fatal." He pointed toward Wood. "You're up. Try to hit Richard's ball. And then, if you'd like, I'll assist you in sending it to the Potomac."

Casey feigned outrage, but they all laughed now, as Wood sent his ball on an errant path, opening the door for Hull's inevitable victory.

Casey said to Wood, "I've come to understand that competition seems to bring out a particular brand of American viciousness. This is what happens when they no longer enjoy the rule of a monarch. They become savages."

Wood stood with his hands on his hips, looked at Hull. "Very important savages. So, Cordell, will Secretary Stimson be joining the game?"

"Never does. He's perfectly fine with any of us using his lawn, but he's not interested in the game. He is most generous in allowing me to escape here when I feel the need. It's something of a sanctuary. My own residence offers nothing like what Stimson has here. He's content to let others enjoy the benefits."

Casey lowered his voice. "Is he all right? Is it age, then?"

Hull stopped, looked up toward the imposing mansion. "He just turned seventy-four. I can't say he's any worse for it. Hell, I just turned seventy. Anything that afflicts him would certainly be afflicting me."

He knew that wasn't quite accurate, that Stimson had a variety of ailments that seemed to sap his strength, limiting his mobility. But Stimson would never reveal that, and it wasn't up to Hull to be indiscreet about it.

Hull was comfortable in any gathering with both these men, among the closest allies the nation had, and two of the most agreeable representatives Hull had to consult with. Edward Wood, the First Earl of Halifax, was Britain's most recent ambassador to the United States. Lord Baron Richard Casey was Australia's minister to the United States, a post carrying the same level of diplomatic importance.

Hull watched as Casey missed badly, and Wood resumed the needling.

"Really, Richard. You would allow us to be beaten yet again by a colonist? All right, go on, Hull. Humiliate us yet again."

Hull struck his ball for the final time, colliding with the wooden stake and ending the game. He smiled. "Well, I was a bit off today, but things turned out in the end."

Casey took the mallets, placed them in the nearby rack, and Wood said, "More false modesty. You were toying with us." He gazed up at the house. "I must say, this is rather a pleasant residence for a government man."

Hull said, "Woodley has been the home to two presidents. I suppose you would call them government men. And Stimson has earned a little luxury in his life." Hull saw a maid emerging through a patio door, carrying a silver tray. "Gentlemen, you should meet Violet. She runs the place. Every time I'm here, I insist she not go to any trouble—after all, I feel like I'm trespassing. But around here, she outranks me. So, she goes to whatever **trouble** suits her. We're the better for it."

The short, round woman set the tray down on a wrought iron table, three chairs already set in place. She stood back, with polite smiles toward all three men. "I have some tea for you here, gentlemen, and some cookies. They're homemade, of course. If you wish something else, the secretary has suggested that I offer you some of his prized spirits from his cellar."

Hull looked at the others, saw temptation in both their faces, but he spoke up first. "The tea is perfect, Violet. Please offer our regards to the secretary. Has he returned, by chance?"

"Oh, no, sir. He has meetings. Mrs. Stimson expects him home very late. If you need me, I'll be in the kitchen, through the doorway right there."

She backed away, and the men sat, a silver teapot between them. Wood said, "Fine work, Hull. She was all set to bring us twelve-year-old Scotch."

Hull smiled. "And Stimson would have made you pay for that for months. You'd be reminded of it every time your paths crossed. He takes that sort of thing personally. No, I'll settle for tea. That's known as 'diplomacy.'"

They filled their china cups, the other two sampling Violet's cookies with approving nods.

Wood grew more serious now, which Hull had expected. Wood stared down at the steaming tea and said in a low voice, "I have to tell you, Cordell. The prime minister is still hopeful I can convince your president to send some of your fleet to Singapore. Lord Casey and I are in agreement that such a move would deter the Japanese."

Hull had heard this before, sat back in the wrought iron chair. He knew that the croquet match was always a prelude to a serious conversation. "Deter them from doing what? What Mr.

Churchill is hoping is that we apply additional pressure on the Japanese to prevent them from doing what they're going to do anyway. I received a cable from Ambassador Grew, in Tokyo. He understands the Japanese mind better than any other man in my service. He is most definite in his opinions that the Japanese will not succumb to pressure of any kind. If the Japanese do not get whatever it is they are seeking by negotiation, they are likely to react in a most unpredictable and violent way. The term 'saber rattling' has no meaning to them, and we would only waste our time by issuing them empty threats. According to Grew, they interpret any display of power not as something they should fear, but as a provocation to make war. They won't back up. They'll just attack."

Casey said, "Do you agree with him?"

"I suppose I have to. I trust Joe Grew. The one counter to all of that pessimism is that Stimson and the military heads have insisted that we are deploying a great many B-17 bombers to the Philippines. I'm assured that they have the range to provide exceptional air protection to Singapore. And that would not simply be saber rattling. It's protection of our interests, no matter how the Japanese interpret it."

He saw Wood glance at Casey, and Casey said, "I assume you know, Cordell, that so far, you have landed just nine B-17s in the Philippines. It is said that there are many more to come. But there has been no timetable announced. Forgive me, but there is skepticism in Australia that your government will deliver on its promises. Too much of your energy is being directed toward the Germans."

Hull was embarrassed that these men had military information that was outside of his jurisdiction. "I'm certain that Stimson and General Marshall are making the necessary arrangements to beef up our forces in the Philippines. The place is, after all, American territory."

Wood said, "Cordell, if the Japanese have no respect for a show of force, what good are those B-17s, no matter where you park them?"

"That's not a question I have the expertise to answer. If the Japanese attack the Philippines, I assume we shall order retaliation. If they sink our ships, we shall certainly do likewise. But we are not at war, and we will not **start** a war. Chiang Kai-shek has demanded that we position troops and artillery, all of that, inside of China, to attack the Japanese forces that he is fighting, to drive them out. How do you think that kind of move would be received in Tokyo? It's an easy answer. We will have started a war."

Wood said, "Chiang will insist on anything that will help Chiang. I assume you were as firm with your **no** as he was with his demand."

"Of course."

Hull sipped from his teacup, soothing warmth against the cool fall air.

After a long moment, Casey said, "My government is feeling a considerable sense of unease. We don't know just how far the Japanese intend to go. Indo-China is not so far away from Australia. We have a lengthy and often indefensible coastline. We would of course require considerable assistance from you both. That is self-evident, I suppose."

Wood said with a smile, "See? That's why it was unwise to punish his croquet ball."

Hull appreciated the levity, Casey nodding with a smile of his own.

Casey said, "Quite so. Cordell, you will relay that to the president, I would hope."

"Certainly."

The somber mood settled in again, and Casey said, "Geographically, we are very much alone in the world, and we have to see the Japanese as a threat, no matter their intentions. Forgive me, but nine B-17s parked in the Philippines offer us very little assurance. There have been those in my country, many of them minority politicians, who over the past two years have spoken out about our need for neutrality in the war with Germany. It's all so very far away, no threat whatsoever, and I have heard so often, 'What do we care what happens to Europe?' But now? The Japanese have changed our world. We are very, very afraid."

Hull set the teacup aside, said, "There are still a great many in the U.S. Congress who claim to speak for their constituencies, and who believe that all we need do is pull down the shades, and all will be well. The infuriating argument the president must endure so often is that we are protected by two great oceans, as though all that water is a perfect barrier against danger. I have heard Stimson say more than once that though the oceans might be barriers, they are also highways. And yet so many people in the U.S. seem to be oblivious to what Hitler could do to us, and now, the Japanese."

Wood said, "What of this Tojo fellow? He seems a bit of a blast furnace, wouldn't you say?"

Hull pondered the question. "The Japanese have always presented themselves and their government as a perfect balance. One half is peaceful, friendly, eager to cooperate with us, and with you. The other half is militant, aggressive, angry, and dangerous. Whether in Tokyo with Ambassador Grew or right here with their Ambassador Nomura, it has constantly been suggested that this careful balance could only be upset by **us,** that it would be our actions that would topple the comfortable peace. I honestly don't know if they actually believe that. Is it all just a tactic, to keep us hoping that all will be well if we just accept every demand they issue?" He stopped. He knew that Wood had access to the Magic intercepts, but Casey very likely did not. "Despite what the Japanese government will have us believe, if Hideki Tojo is now in control, there is no balance at all. I just don't know what this means for us, for all three of us."

Wood set his teacup aside, a cloud of gloom on his face. "We thought that Konoye would keep things going in a more moderate direction, that he could maintain . . . well, that balance you're talking about. He might have been too weak to stand up to the military, but at least he seemed to be a voice of reason."

Casey said, "I'm beginning to believe that when it comes to Japan, there is no 'reason.' Tojo has been one of the loudest voices pushing for a war. If the emperor has allowed him to take that post, it means the war faction has won. And that means we are all under threat. What do they want? Are they seeking land? Seaports? Or is it just to extend their borders, plant their flag anywhere they can? Are they mimicking Hitler, or intending to outdo him? God, I hate asking these kinds of questions. The answers, whatever they may be, are terrifying."

He looked at Wood. "My apologies, Edward. I do not overlook that England has already experienced this war. But that serves as a warning to us all. I said before, my country is very frightened of what will come next, on any day, any week. We are desperate for the kind of protection only you two can provide."

Hull felt a sinking depression. "I cannot make any pledges. It isn't my place. I continue to place my hope in communication, that there has to be time for us to talk. There have to be reasonable men somewhere in that country who will insist on

reasonable solutions to our differences. I'm beginning to believe that it's the only hope we have left."

THE WHITE HOUSE, WASHINGTON, D.C.—
    WEDNESDAY, OCTOBER 22, 1941

"Gentlemen, we have beaten this subject to death,
and none of us has the slightest idea what we're
talking about. I didn't bring you in here to get hard
answers—I'm aware there are none. What I was
hoping for is something exactly like this." Roosevelt
held up a paper. "Options. Hard-case possibilities.
It's what we need in order to make a plan, a contin-
gency." He looked at Marshall. "General, who's the
author of this brief?"

Marshall said, "Sir, this is from Lieutenant
Colonel Bicknell, from G-2, the intelligence office
under General Short, commanding our army force
in Hawaii."

Roosevelt absorbed that. "G-2, Hawaii. I would
suppose they're watching the Japanese pretty closely?"

Stimson said, "Quite. Short is a good fellow, handles things out there pretty well, in concert with
the navy."

"That's Admiral Kimmel, right?"

"Yes, sir."

"I assume they can read the **Purple** codes, that
they have access to Magic machines, like they do in
the Philippines?"

Stimson looked at Marshall, who said, "Surely they do, Mr. President."

"All right, General Marshall, please enlighten us as to what your G-2 fellows have concluded about Japanese intentions."

Marshall said, "Mr. President, Colonel Bicknell suggests, after careful analysis, that the following actions could be taken by the Japanese. One, they will attack Russia, likely their port at Vladivostok. Two, they will add pressure to Indo-China and Thailand, forcing those nations to grant them greater access to naval and air bases, and press them for economic cooperation, which certainly means that the Japanese would take whatever resources are available. Three, they'll attack the British possessions in the Far East, notably Singapore. Four, they will mobilize to defend themselves against an attack by the United States, in the event we come to the aid of the British. Five, they will simultaneously attack the territories of the British, Dutch, Chinese, and the United States, at whatever points might promise Japan its greatest tactical, strategic, and economic advantages."

Roosevelt said, "Is this accurate? We have spies in the Japanese government figuring all this out?"

Marshall said, "I cannot offer a guarantee of accuracy. This is intended to be an assessment of possibilities of what the Japanese might do."

Roosevelt seemed to flash a familiar anger,

something Hull had seen often. "In other words, General, who the hell knows what the Japanese intend to do?"

Stimson said, "Mr. President, this simply outlines the most likely paths of action, allowing us to make preparations."

Roosevelt looked at the others, said, "Thoughts? Opinions? Everybody awake in here?"

The men glanced at each other, and after a long pause, Marshall said, "The attack on Russia is the most likely, in my opinion. That, plus the pressure they can apply to Thailand. The French have already buckled in Indo-China, and the Japanese have established a strong presence there, so they can take whatever they want. Logically, Thailand would be next. It would not be a major military undertaking for the Japanese."

Roosevelt looked around the room, still impatient. "Anyone else? What about that number three, the possibility of attacks on the British possessions? Churchill is raising holy hell that we're not doing enough to help them down there. I keep pointing to the Atlantic, telling him how many U-boats we're sinking. That quiets him down for a half hour or so."

Marshall said, "If Japan were to attack Singapore, or any other British possession, they would invite a full-scale war with Britain, which we do not feel the Japanese want."

Roosevelt said, "According to Churchill, the

British are stretched pretty thin dealing with Hitler, the North Atlantic, North Africa, and God knows what else. I believe him."

Marshall glanced at Stimson, who said, "It is our intention to send all available power to the assistance of the British, wherever that might be required."

"You think you might advise me of that when it's going to happen? And, doesn't it seem to any of you, especially Secretary Knox, that 'all available power' means pulling naval strength away from any possible confrontation with the Japanese?"

Hull could feel the condescension oozing out of Stimson, a trait often shared by Marshall. The words **"united front"** flashed through his mind.

Stimson said, "Mr. President, we would certainly include you in any discussion of a timetable for assisting the British. We of course do not presently have the arsenal at our disposal to protect the entire world. And, I would point out, sir, that the Japanese possess far less of an arsenal than we do. There simply is no threat in that theater."

Roosevelt sniffed. "All right, what about the last one, number five?"

Hull spoke up now, surprising the others. "Mr. President, that last possibility means that the Japanese would simultaneously declare war on the U.S., the Dutch, the British, and the Australians. As they have already taken what they want from the French, it seems possible that it is their intention to strike as hard and as quickly as they can, to establish their footholds in those places they intend to occupy. From there, they could possibly spread outward even farther."

Roosevelt looked at him, his head cocked to one side. "You know something we don't?"

"I'm sure not, sir. I've been studying the same Magic reports you all have. I've read what you've read about Prime Minister Tojo. Their move southward into Indo-China is not an isolated occurrence, one mission to inhabit one obscure piece of territory. There is certainly a plan at work, and their intentions are far from honorable. From our own point of view, it seems that the Philippines are extremely vulnerable."

Stimson said, "What the hell do we do about that? Hit them before they hit us? We can't just start our own war to keep them from starting theirs. Besides, we need to commit as much power as we can to the Atlantic. We can't have a war in both directions."

The others seemed to agree, Marshall and Knox still scanning their copies of the report.

After a long pause, Marshall said, "With all due respect, Secretary Hull, we are making moves that will provide significant protection for the Philippines and our islands in the South Pacific. Once the air squadrons are in place, and fully manned, the Japanese will strike us there only at a severe cost to their own cities. I assure you, we have that situation firmly under control."

Hull heard the condescension in Marshall's voice.

He also knew he had none of the information Marshall was offering. But Hull couldn't ignore what he continued to learn of the Japanese duplicity with their negotiations, their offers of friendship, and now, the kinds of men who had taken control of their government.

He looked at Roosevelt. "I'm not sure that we're in control of any part of this."

Marshall said, "Mr. President, it is our estimate that, with their ongoing deployments and subsequent losses in China, the Japanese would be incapable of any wide-scale assaults until early next year."

Hull sat back. He had no choice but to accept intelligence that he didn't have access to.

Roosevelt said to him, "You meeting with Ambassador Nomura anytime soon?"

"Tuesday, sir."

"Good. It's likely that we knew about Tojo before he did. Curious what he has to say about that."

"I'd be surprised if the ambassador says much at all. I'll go through the usual dance moves with him, but I don't hold hope for anything of substance, certainly not any significant changes to our relationship."

Stimson said, "Does he not understand how dangerous things are? He can't just spread on all that diplomatic butter like it's the same old show."

"I suppose I'll find that out."

THE CARLTON HOTEL, WASHINGTON, D.C.—
   TUESDAY, OCTOBER 28, 1941

"Our country has said practically all she can say
in the way of expressing of opinions and setting
forth our stands. We feel that we have now reached
a point where no further positive action can be
taken by us except to urge the United States to re-
consider her views. We urge therefore that you let
it be known to the United States that our country
is not in a position to spend much more time discussing this matter."

He slid the paper back into its envelope with a
glance at the **Eyes Only** stamp. The special courier
stood close to one side, waiting patiently, the usual
protocol for intercepting the diplomatic traffic sent
via the **Purple** codes. It was Hull's privilege to be
allowed access to Magic intercepts, but he would
never be allowed to keep the dispatches in his own
possession. Once read, they would return to the
intelligence offices.

Hull handed the envelope to the man, who
snapped to attention.

"Thank you, Lieutenant. You may leave. I've seen
what I needed to see."

"Thank you, Mr. Secretary."

The man made a tight pivot, moved quickly out
of the apartment. What is so secretive about what I
just read? Well, of course, it's not that at all. It's that

we're reading this stuff in the first place. Maybe one day, that will win. Don't think on that. You'll sweat all over the paper.

He could hear the clink of coffee cups, knew Frances was in the next room with two of his staff. Yes, my dear, keep them away from me when it's **Eyes Only,** as though they don't already know that. He thought of the dispatch, had tried to look past the words, to find some sort of clue about just how serious the Japanese were becoming, if their internal warnings or instructions meant any more now than they had before. Is it just the embargo? he thought. Do they want war just because they want war? Yes, fine, Grew is right, we do not understand them. But they are not an entire nation of lunatics, murderers, and suicidal maniacs. They are ruled by an emperor, and everything I know of him tells me he is a soft-spoken, conservative . . . hell, a **gentle** man. Surely he still maintains control.

He walked into the next room, all eyes on him. Frances read his silent cue, and removed the cups and saucers, slipping quickly toward the rear of the apartment. He glanced at the clock above his mantel.

"Gentlemen, Ambassador Nomura is due here in ten minutes. I wish each of you to sit in, to make written notes, and beyond that, to keep silent. He has to be coaxed. He is very much the opposite of the German ambassador, who seems intent on stuffing his fist down your throat."

There were low laughs, not from him.

"Let's go into the outer room. I'll tell you where to sit."

They took positions as he directed, and Hull sat in his usual perch, the thick cushions of the chair embracing him. The two men were assembling their notepads when Hull heard the rap on the outer door. He looked at the younger of the men.

"Mr. Herman, please answer the door."

The young man responded quickly, made way for Nomura. Hull could see a change in the ambassador's demeanor, and he stood, the proper formality. Nomura offered the usual bow and Hull said, "Ambassador, welcome. Please be seated. These are my aides, Mr. King, Mr. Herman. I've asked them to observe our discussion, if you have no objection."

Nomura moved to his spot on the sofa, seemed extremely uncomfortable. "I welcome them. Younger men should understand what this world is becoming. I am pleased to see you again, Mr. Secretary. Much has happened since we last spoke."

Hull thought, I know that. But he doesn't know I know that. What will he tell me?

"I am pleased to see you as well. Tell me, what is happening with your government? You have a new prime minister, a foreign minister, a new cabinet. That must be very interesting for you."

Nomura said nothing for a long moment. He glanced down, then looked up at Hull. "My government continues to be most anxious to reach a mutually beneficial agreement, an understanding that will serve both nations."

Hull knew the dance had begun. "I am very interested in that as well, Ambassador. I fear we might be losing patience, and that must not happen. The Japanese government must know that any rash move would have immediate consequences. There is no desire for either Great Britain or the United States to pick a fight with Japan. The uniting of all those who feel themselves threatened by Japanese policy is purely defensive. When there is so much gunpowder lying about, he would be a very incautious man who dropped a match on it."

"I understand your points, Mr. Secretary. There is some concern, however, that the American government's attitude toward Germany could have dangerous consequences. Your president has been most aggressive in his protests concerning German activity in the Atlantic."

Roosevelt had just the night before given a fiery speech regarding Germany, which obviously Nomura had heard. Hull had thought the declarations a tad too strong, designed to placate our allies while offering Germany a clear message that the U.S. would not tolerate any actions against shipping near the American coastal waters.

"Ambassador, what do you believe would be Japan's reaction if the United States and Germany commenced a shooting war in the Atlantic?"

Nomura seemed to digest the question. "Japan would be free to decide her own course of action."

It was yet another nonanswer from a man who seemed to specialize in them, and Hull thought of the Magic intercept, ached to ask just what was really happening inside the Japanese ministry. But no, he thought, Nomura would have no idea. Nomura said, "Mr. Secretary, have you felt I have been honest with you?"

"Mr. Ambassador, since I took office in 1933, it has been my policy to offer absolute candor and trust in my relationships with the diplomatic heads of every nation on earth. I have also maintained the expectation that those diplomats respond the same way with me and my staff. Of course, there have been disappointments. But I have never wavered from that commitment. That being said, I believe you have **attempted** to be honest with me. But your government has chosen another path."

Nomura nodded. "Well expressed, sir. Then I shall be honest with you now. With the change in my country's government, I feel I can no longer serve the purpose for which I was sent here. I have not enjoyed skating around the most serious issues facing us. But I must do as I am instructed." He paused. "I am deeply upset that anyone would think I am fleeing the field of battle. I am a man of honor, but there is much in this position that is not honorable at all. Thus, I have offered to resign my post."

Hull was surprised. "Has your foreign minister accepted your resignation?"

Nomura shook his head. "No. They insist I am doing an excellent job."

There was sarcasm in Nomura's words, and Hull said, "Are you?"

Nomura smiled. "I suppose, if you consider that I have told you almost nothing of what my government is seeking to do, then by all means, I am outstanding. My principal duty has been to communicate to the foreign minister just what the American attitude is toward Japanese activities. In that, I have also excelled."

"I would not be eager to welcome a new Japanese ambassador. I believe you and I have some important understandings. I believe you do not want a war."

"On the second point, you are correct—no sane man wishes for war. On the first . . . again I will be honest with you. In about three weeks, I will have . . . I'm not sure of the word in English. A 'partner'? My government is sending another who will be here to assist me."

Hull knew what Nomura was saying. His government was sending someone to keep an eye on him.

"Do they feel your workload is too great?"

Nomura smiled again, understood Hull's joke.

"Possibly. His name is Saburo Kurusu. His title is special envoy."

"Then he is not a spy?"

Nomura laughed now. "If he is, they have not told me so."

Hull laughed along, thought, Thank God we have Magic. We will find out soon enough.

# TWENTY-TWO

# Biggs

PEARL HARBOR, HAWAII—SATURDAY, OCTOBER 18, 1941

The ball game ended near dusk. The victory for the **Arizona** was one that not even the losing team could complain about. They had played an army team from Schofield Barracks, in a game marked by the usual catcalls and insults fueled by the ever-present rivalry between army and navy. No one took the insults seriously, both sides knowing that if either pitcher was tempted to use his fastball as a weapon, the game could end very badly. But on this day, even the army players offered a show of respect toward the **Arizona**'s pitcher. Against a well-practiced team of Schofield's best athletes, Woody Finley had pitched a no-hitter.

After the final out, the sailors had surrounded Finley with joyous cheers and pats on the back, but the celebration was cut short with a sharp order from Lieutenant Janz. No one had to rub the army's face in it. They all knew what Finley had done.

Biggs's day had been, for him, unimpressive, a single hit that added nothing to the team's 2–0 victory. Throughout much of the game, he couldn't avoid the distraction shared by most of the others, a cause for celebration that had nothing to do with baseball. They all knew the schedule, that in two days the **Arizona** would put to sea again for another tedious and redundant training exercise. But morale had begun to climb as word spread through the ship that in a couple of weeks, the ship would put to sea for a very different journey, this one eastward, across the Pacific to the naval base at Bremerton, Washington. When the rumors were confirmed by the senior command, morale had leapt skyward. Even the men who enjoyed the revelry they could find in Honolulu had applauded the opportunity for a change of scene. Bremerton was not Hawaii, of course, but to many, Hawaii had become something of an isolated prison, a forlorn and empty part of the world.

Like many, Biggs knew almost nothing about Bremerton beyond geography, that it was on the mainland, directly across Puget Sound from the city of Seattle. For a sizable number of the crew, Seattle offered the opportunity for families to visit. Sailors were already writing home, telling anyone close enough to the West Coast to drive or take the train ride west. None of the crew was quite sure just how long this respite would last, but a ship this size would never make such a journey unless the navy had a very good reason. And any of those reasons would certainly consume a week or two, and possibly much more.

The team followed Lieutenant Janz aboard the bus, all of them bathed in the aroma of sweat and dirt. The ride from Schofield took less than a half hour, the bus stopping with a groan alongside a concrete pier. There, the familiar launch waited for the short trip across the water to Ford Island.

Biggs glanced around, saw smiles everywhere. A few men were still offering back slaps to their pitcher, and Biggs couldn't hold back, said, "Hey, Woody. You ever done that before?"

Finley shrugged, said, "Once or twice. High school. Never did it in the minor leagues. I'd always give up a few hits, or worse. Once I really got shelled. A Cincinnati Reds club, the Syracuse Chiefs, hit seven home runs off me, and got about a dozen hits. After they scored the first five runs, I figured they better pull me out of there, and fast. But my damn manager left me in just 'cause he was pissed at me—I kinda threw a kiss toward his daughter. I think I gave up fourteen runs. That game might be the reason why I never got a real shot in the majors."

The catcher, Harrington, said, "I tell you, Woody, you pitch a few more like today, you'll get there. I heard there was a scout from the Cardinals out here poking around. He might have been at the game. There were a couple dozen people watching us."

Finley seemed unimpressed. "I'll believe that when he shakes my hand. That's the biggest rumor you hear in any minor league park: The scouts are everywhere. You might have a crowd of fourteen gray-haired old ladies, and somebody's gonna swear they're from the Yankees. I've got as much chance of signing with them as I had with that manager's cutie of a daughter. I'd rather just do what we're doing now, showing everybody else in Hawaii how good the **Arizona** is."

The coxswain took his position at the helm, the engine revving up, his crewman tossing the lines back to the concrete pier. The engines coughed out black smoke, the boat lurching into open water. They were directly across the harbor from Ford Island, where the battleships were berthed, but Biggs scanned the sites nearby, the clusters of smaller ships and maintenance craft. Around him, even the long-timers stared out, taking in the sheer beauty of the power around them. Biggs saw a line of seaplanes in the distance, the new PBYs, parked alongside what had to be a tender. He searched for the ship's name, hoped it was the **Curtiss,** saw crewmen working on the deck. I'd really like to see Ray again, he thought. Hell, you'd think it would be simple—there's nothing but water between us.

Finley put a hand on Biggs's shoulder, said, "Pretty damn impressive, huh? Hard to believe any stupid damn Japanese would pick a fight with us."

Beside Finley, a man said, "Woody, there ain't a damn thing to all that nonsense. The brass is putting out those rumors so we'll pay better attention to all that malarkey we're doing on those open-water drills. The brass tells us we got a threat, that we're in danger, so we work harder. Nice try. If we're in so much danger, why the hell are we sailing out of here and going back to the States?"

There was no argument to that from any of them. Even Janz let the comments pass. But Biggs was beginning to nurse a healthy curiosity.

"Any of you been to Bremerton before? I heard the ship's been there a few times. Not sure when."

Behind him, the catcher, Harrington, said, "Back in December, we went into dry dock there. I figure that's what we're doing now. We were there most of two weeks. I'll take that. My family's in Montana; ain't seen my mom since before that. Used to have a girl there too, but I think she ran out of hope, so she hitched up with some other joker. The guy's first name is Beezy. Who the hell marries a guy named Beezy?"

Harrington laughed, others joining in. There were more comments about Bremerton, all of them positive, adding to the enthusiasm Biggs already felt.

He looked at Janz. "What do you say, Lieutenant? We gonna have a few weeks there?"

Janz shook his head. "They don't tell me a thing. What I'm looking forward to, even if we only have a single night off the ship, is a big plate of raw oysters. None better than the ones that come out of Puget Sound."

The reaction was mixed, drawing a smile from Janz.

"You boys have no idea what you're missing. You don't want to eat those little jewels, that's fine. Just means there's more for me. That's all I'll say."

Harrington said, "I heard the more of those slimy things you eat, the more the gals will appreciate it. Supposed to kind of **improve** things, if you know what I mean. Sir, maybe I better have me a couple platefuls."

Biggs had never eaten an oyster, wasn't really sure what the fuss was. "I'd like to try some, sir. There a place that sells 'em?"

Janz still smiled. "There are about a hundred places, Mr. Biggs. Tell you what. I'll buy the first half dozen. But you gotta eat 'em. After that you're on your own."

The talk drifted away with the scenery, the launch closing toward Ford Island, eight of the great battleships berthed in a row. Some were tied up side by side, with not enough space for them to line up in single file. Most had crewmen suspended over the sides, wooden platforms supporting the men with buckets and paint rollers.

As the launch drew closer to the **Arizona,** Biggs could see the platforms there as well, a dozen men laboring with the gray paint. He saw one man looking down, saw a quick wave in his direction, realized it was Wakeman. He waved back, the launch sliding past the bow of the ship, maneuvering carefully to the pier, the coxswain showing his experience. The lines went ashore, and the boat was secured, the men climbing up and out. As they walked toward the ladder, Biggs stared up and along the great ship. It was habit now, absorbing the sheer strength, the extraordinary beauty, and he felt the pride in what he saw, and where he lived. The ship was his home.

He had written much of that in a letter to his mother, but no matter the details and his feelings, he knew she'd never understand. His father would certainly have something to say, and Biggs tried not to think of that at all. So I'm a sailor, and maybe I'll be a corpsman. And I get to play ball. And I'm kinda good at it. Damn. This is just about perfect.

He felt a hand on his shoulder. Finley was beside him. "Ain't got too many friends that are swabbies. But you're okay. Hell of a hitter, that's for damn sure. You oughta keep an eye out for scouts too. They ain't only looking for pitchers. You might get a shot at it. Never know." Finley eyed the rail of the ship as they moved past. "We sail out of here, we might not have a ball game for a long time. I hate that, but it's just the way it happens. Not much else I wanna do. Just be a marine, I guess."

"Nothing wrong with that, Woody. Being a marine's gotta be a good career."

"Yep. You're right. What about you?"

"Navy's pretty good place for me to be. Never really thought about playing baseball, not for a real team. I can't even hope for something like that. All of this beats what I got back home, that's for sure."

Finley looked ahead, called out, "Hey, Lieutenant. You think we earned some liberty? We had a pretty good day."

Janz stopped, scanned the team's faces. "Since we're under way in two days, I guess you all earned at least one night ashore. I'll see what I can do. Great job today, Private Finley. All of you."

Janz led them up the ladder, each man going through the usual routine with the officer of the deck. Biggs recognized the man, Janz's friend, the lieutenant who had intercepted the pounding he would have received from Kincaid. The officer looked at Biggs with recognition, and when the formality passed, he said to Janz, "You win today?"

Janz looked at Finley, pointed. "Thanks to one of our stars. Next time it will be the other one."

Janz motioned toward Biggs, the team passing by him, more slaps on the back.

Finley moved away, said, "See you tonight, Tommy. We make it into town, you can buy me a beer."

"You're going on liberty with a **marine**?"

Biggs finished polishing his shoes, said, "Lieutenant Janz said he'd try to set it up for the whole team."

Wakeman cinched up his pants. "Yeah, well, I got liberty for sure. Piece of paper to prove it. Not sure I wanna risk tangling with a flock of jarheads."

Biggs wasn't sure what he could say to ease Wakeman's prejudice against the marines. It was unusual for the two groups to spend much time together, the sailors and marines serving very different functions onboard the ship.

"Look, Ed, Finley's a good guy. Doesn't much matter to me if he's a marine. He's my teammate."

Behind Wakeman, Mahone said, "I'll bet you hired the guy to be your bodyguard, right? You take him to Hotel Street so's he'll take on those mooses they got in the Boom Boom Room, while you make happy time with Maggie Sue. She's a real honey, I'm telling you."

The laughter filled the compartment and Biggs let them have their fun. Biggs leaned closer to Wakeman, lowered his voice, said, "Hey, Ed. You ever been to Bremerton?"

"Of course. We were there around Christmastime. Rained a bunch. But it's a pretty place. Different kind of pretty from here. My family came over, took the train from Sioux Falls. I don't think my mom stopped bawling the whole time. They're scared, both of 'em."

Biggs sat, pulled on his shoes, wrestled with the laces. "Scared of what?"

Wakeman sat as well. "Every damn thing in the world. I'd go fishing when I was a kid and my old man would give me a damn speech about every dangerous thing that could happen. I joined the navy, my mom figured I'd get killed the first week. Ships sink, they said. Ships blow up. Gunpowder and fuel oil. **Boom**. Happens every day, they said. I was surprised as hell they even took the train. My mom gave me a speech about that too. They can run off the tracks, she said. Trains slam into each other. **Happens all the time.** I tried to tell them, hey, you just made a long train trip, and everything turned out fine. Didn't change a thing. They just started worrying about the next trip."

Biggs thought of his father, the speech about ships sinking. "I guess we've all got some of that. My folks might never leave my hometown. My pop always said there's nowhere else to go. I guess that's just being afraid of doing something different."

Wakeman rested one arm on his knee. " 'It happens all the time.' Can't tell you how many times I had to listen to that. I always wondered, How do you know what happens all the time? Neither one ever read the damn newspaper." He shook his head. "Both of 'em probably afraid of getting a paper cut."

Biggs laughed, thought of his mother, said, "I'd give anything to have her come out west, Seattle or anywhere else. It's like her soul's buried in that little town. I hate that. All I know is she's happy for me, she wants good for me. If it's the navy, she'll accept that. My pop's never accepted anything positive about me my whole life."

Wakeman tied his shoes, then stopped, looked at Biggs. "I bet your mom's damn proud of you. That matters most. Don't never forget that." He thumped his chest. "My mom's heart is right here, no matter what kind of craziness I gotta listen to. Yours too."

The voices grew suddenly quiet, all eyes toward the hatch. Biggs turned, expected to see Kincaid, was surprised to see Finley, in his working uniform.

Biggs said, "Hey, Woody. What's up? Did you get liberty?"

Finley looked down through the compartment, a hint of uneasiness. "Uh, no. I've got brig guard duty tonight. First Sergeant Duveene felt bad about it, but said it couldn't be helped. Couple of guys picked a fight, and when Ensign Marsh stepped in, they walloped him pretty good. Lieutenant Smith tried to put everybody under arrest and one of the morons took a swing at **him.**"

Wakeman said, "That's a court-martial."

"At least. They smuggled some hooch onboard in a paint can, best as we can figure. The navy doesn't appreciate that. And, taking a drunken swing at two officers, well, likely they'll be booted out of here pretty quick, and maybe get some brig time stateside."

Wakeman said, "Were they marines?"

Muted laughter spread through the compartment. Biggs cringed, but saw Finley smile.

"Not this time, swabby."

Biggs let out a breath of relief that Finley had a decent sense of humor. But he could tell that Finley was disappointed.

"Well, hell, Woody, I was gonna buy you a beer." Biggs pointed a thumb toward Wakeman. "Now if I get a pass, I gotta depend on him. It's gonna be a crappy night."

"Sorry, Tommy. Maybe some other time. We get to Bremerton, you can show me how the lieutenant eats oysters." He moved toward the hatch, looked back at Biggs. "See you later, slugger."

Biggs looked at Wakeman. "Well, hell. Damn shame. Kinda hoped to find out a little more about being a marine, what that's like."

He expected teasing for that, but Wakeman turned to Mahone, said, "That guy's not so bad, for a marine anyway. I heard he can put a baseball through a tin can without touching the sides."

Mahone laughed, said, "First time a jarhead's ever come in here unless there was a fight to be had."

Biggs said, "Woody won't admit it, not to me anyway. But I know that he really wants to play baseball. He's only twenty-two, and if he works on his pitches, he could make it."

Wakeman said, "What about you, **slugger?**"

Biggs thought a moment, hesitated before giving

them an easy reason to razz him. "Well, it was Woody who kinda put the idea in my head. He said I've got a natural swing, all that kind of stuff. I'd love to stand in against somebody like Bob Feller, just once. He might strike me out on three pitches, and I'd never even see the ball go by. But, still, I'd like to know."

He expected laughs, but the looks were serious, some of the others even nodding.

Wakeman said, "That's good, Tommy. And I bet you'd see that ball." He laughed. "But I bet you wouldn't **hit** it."

The laughs came now, and Biggs played along, stood, swung an imaginary bat, spun himself down to the deck like a corkscrew.

"Well, here's all my babies in their playpen. How sweet."

Biggs saw Kincaid by the hatch, pulled himself upright, noticed a dark scuff on his trouser leg. There was no covering it up, and Biggs waited for the inevitable.

"So, what the hell was a jarhead doing in here? One of you idiots insult his sister? This bunch would be stupid enough to do just that. Had to be you, right, Biggs?"

"No, sir. That was Private Finley. He's the pitcher—"

"Shut your damn mouth. So, he thought he'd hop by here so you could brown-nose him, right? I see the stain, Biggs. You kneel in front of a marine, you deserve a stain."

Biggs fought to keep silent, knew the eyes behind him were squarely on his back.

Kincaid glared at Biggs, said, "I saw your request for leave from that baseball lieutenant you love brown-nosing too. It's not happening. You're ordered to report to sick bay in thirty minutes. You wanna bitch about it? Bitch to your short-arm inspectors." He looked past Biggs, faked a smile. "Enjoy your evening, boys."

Kincaid moved out through the hatch, and Biggs sat heavily. Wakeman said, "Holy cow, Tommy. That's rough. He's got it in for you something awful. He's been a bad-ass ever since I been here, chewing out a bunch of us for no good reason. But he's square on you now. If you could file some kind of complaint maybe he'd ease up."

Mahone said, "Bad idea. He's an old-timer, probably counting the days for his pension. You muck it up for him, he'll do you worse than he's doing now."

Biggs shrugged. "Nah, it's okay. I'll report to sick bay like I'm supposed to. I know he hates my guts. I've just got no idea why."

Wakeman said, "Tommy, I been here nearly three years. I've heard about those kinds of guys, who just need somebody to bust up, take out their anger on. Looks like, for now, it's you. There ain't much you can do. Just try not to piss him off any more than he is right now."

Biggs shrugged. "I'll try. Well, I better get up to

sick bay. The doctors wouldn't have ordered me to report if it wasn't important. There's other days for liberty. Besides, it's just Hawaii. Next time, it'll be Seattle."

USS ARIZONA, AT SEA—WEDNESDAY, OCTOBER 22, 1941

Thoughts of Bremerton were set aside for now, the **Arizona** engaging yet again in sea drills. They moved in convoy as usual, with several smaller ships maneuvering around and behind the **Arizona** and her frequent partners in these drills, the battleships **Nevada** and **Oklahoma.**

Biggs had reported to duty for the late shift, found Dr. Condon there with two of the pharmacist's mates. Condon sat in his office, a book in hand, the other two playing cards. Biggs did his usual job: ran a mop around the edges of sick bay, then through the center of the spaces, the decks beneath his feet brought to a wet shine.

He completed the job quickly, stowed the mop, checked the wetness of the deck, found it already drying. Vaughan came through the hatchway now, wiping his face.

"Man, I never saw rain like this, not out here. The guys on deck have it pretty miserable."

Condon put the book down. "That means we'll have a flock of guys coming in here thinking they're dying of the flu. Mr. Block, Mr. Corey, when you finish your game, put together a tray of various cold medications, the usual drug store stuff. That should solve any of those problems. How bad is the rain, Mr. Vaughan?"

"Coming down in sheets, sir. Worse is the fog, though. That's something new for me. Got to be the darkest night I ever saw. Glad somebody smarter than me is steering this ship."

Biggs said, "What are we doing? I don't hear any firing. Last time it was all the antiaircraft guns."

"No, not now. We're doing ninety-degree turns, other maneuvers. Twisty turning stuff. Don't ask me why."

The alarm bell erupted in the passageway. Condon shouted, "**Collision alarm.** Hang on to something."

The ship lurched hard, no time to react, the men tumbling, rolling across the deck to the port side of sick bay, the deck sloping that way, then rolling back to starboard. Biggs held tightly to the legs of a surgical table, his heart racing, questions roaring through his mind. Around him, the others fought to stand, questions from all of them, a chorus of loud voices out in the passageway, curses and more questions. He rolled over to one side, looked through the table legs. He saw Vaughan sitting on the floor, holding his arm.

"What the hell's going on? Jesus, my shoulder."

Condon braced himself against the table above Biggs, said, "Just sit there. Not sure what happened, but we'll probably have casualties. It felt like we ran aground, but we're in the middle of no place, and it's gotta be two miles deep. If it was a mine or a torpedo, we'd probably smell it. Or maybe not. Mr. Biggs, you all right?"

Biggs pulled himself to his feet. The deck was sloping to port, but the rolling had stopped. "Yes, sir. I'm okay. What do you want me to do, sir?"

"Go up on deck. If you can, find out what the hell happened. If they need stretchers, get back here quickly. Dr. Johnson is on his way here, pretty sure of that. It's gonna be a long night. But it would sure help us to know what's going on."

"Yes, sir. I'll come back quick as I can."

Biggs made his way to the hatch and stepped into the passageway, men moving past him in a rush. He fell in with the flow, reached the first ladder, climbed up with others behind him and one man above. The way cleared, and he climbed the final ladder, emerged onto the upper deck, beneath the massive guns of the first turret. Men were lined up in the rain and darkness along the port side, the ship listing that way. He heard orders shouted out along both flanks of the ship, fought to keep upright, the deck slippery from the rain. He made his way to the rail, saw rainy blackness beyond, but off the port side was a hulking shape, more lights and noise. It was a sight he had never expected. It was the **Oklahoma,** and it was very clear that she had collided with the **Arizona.**

———

The collision had taken place late in the night, in the midst of a drill to avoid submarines—tight turns, zigzag maneuvers. But the rain and the dense fog had added one more challenge to the routine, with visibility cut down to no more than shouting distance. Before the ships collided, the commander of the **Oklahoma,** Captain Edward Foy, had realized what was about to occur. He had ordered his engines to immediate full astern, which lessened the impact and possibly prevented the **Arizona** from sustaining enough damage to sink her. The **Oklahoma** received only minor damage, but the **Arizona** suffered a triangular gash in her port side more than twelve feet long and four feet wide. Though the damage caused the ship to list nearly ten degrees to port, within a short time the starboard ballast tanks had taken on enough water to balance the ship.

Condon ran a hand over his face, let out a breath of exhaustion. "Lots of shook-up people, but I don't want to hand out pills just to calm people down."

Johnson said, "Agreed. That part will pass soon enough. I spoke to Commander Register. He told me how damn lucky we were."

Condon shook his head. "Lucky for the skipper of the **Oklahoma.** If we'd have gone down? They'd have hanged him."

"Let that go. Nobody was killed, nobody knocked overboard. Lousy weather means problems. Always has. If they'd put radar on these boats, we'd all be better off."

Biggs was working with Vaughan, tightening the sling that held his shoulder. "Sir? What's 'radar'?"

Condon said, "It means 'radio detection and ranging.' It's a way of finding out if another ship, or plane, or anything else is out there where you can't see it."

Johnson laughed. "You see, Mr. Biggs? This is why he should outrank me. The younger they are the more they know."

Vaughan flinched, and Biggs pulled his hands away, said, "Oh, sorry."

"Nah, wasn't you. Just hurts like hell. More of a bad bruise than anything busted. Hope so, anyway."

Johnson said, "We'll be back in port soon. It's slow going. And then they'll put us into dry dock. Commander Register said the hole wasn't too bad, considering how we got hit, and it should be a fairly simple repair. If there's any such thing on a battleship."

Biggs absorbed that, said, "Sir, how long's that gonna take, dry dock? We're supposed to head out to Bremerton soon."

Johnson looked at him, and Biggs saw gloom on the doctor's face.

"I love that area, Mr. Biggs. Great place to fish, to eat; the mountains are spectacular. I was really looking forward to seeing it again. But I'm afraid it's not going to happen anytime soon. Commander

Register says the move east has been canceled indefinitely."

Condon said, "For crying out loud, I've got family planning on meeting me there."

Biggs could only guess what this would do to the morale of his buddies. "Wow, sir. That's a shame. Everybody I've talked to was looking forward to it."

Johnson moved back toward the office, said, "I know. Now they'll just have to look forward to spending a whole lot more time in Pearl Harbor."

# TWENTY-THREE

# Yamamoto

THE NAVAL MINISTRY, TOKYO, JAPAN—
SATURDAY, OCTOBER 11, 1941

**H**e was exhausted. The meetings had lasted far longer than he wanted, though as long as he had expected. The debates were mostly tiresome, the senior admirals offering their points of view with their usual flair for self-importance. But there was one surprise, and Yamamoto could not complain. The admirals all seemed eager for the assault on Hawaii to take place at the end of November. There were fears that December could bring storms and dangerously rough seas, a serious handicap for the oilers who were charged with the refueling operations for the rest of the fleet. Yamamoto knew from the beginning that refueling was essential to the assault, and in rough water, what was virtually untested might become impossible.

But the schedule the Ministry had suggested would have compacted Yamamoto's training. The air commanders were already nervous that their pilots were not quite ready. Yamamoto knew that Genda was even more concerned about the usefulness of the torpedo bombers. To Genda, the torpedo was the most valuable weapon they could use against the American fleet, but the technical experts had still not designed an effective way to flatten out their trajectories, allowing the torpedoes to motor toward their targets without plunging too deeply into the shallow waters of Pearl Harbor.

In addition to the headaches and challenges of training so many pilots in the different types of aircraft, Yamamoto also had to put up with the loud boasts of those officers who felt the need to shout their patriotic claims about the inferiority of the American military. When possible, Yamamoto had silenced that. He knew that the wrong words, even from an officer with no knowledge of the details of the Hawaii operation, could offer clues that someone else, an intelligence officer or an American diplomat, might interpret in such a way as to raise alertness in the United States. His weapon against the big talkers was simple and direct. He told them that big words came from small men, that it would be far more useful if the words were replaced by actions. Yamamoto had yet to hear an argument.

The discussion had gone on for so long his voice was fading into a painful hoarseness. But permission for adjournment would come from the chief of staff, Admiral Nagano, and there was no hint from the older man that he had anywhere else to go.

The papers were being shuffled, small speeches still droning past him.

Alongside Admiral Nagano, Tomioka was speaking endlessly, a speech about nothing. With a shuffling of papers and a look of self-satisfaction, he seemed to wait for praise. Yamamoto ignored him, could see Nagano sagging, his shoulders stooped, his eyes closing for a brief moment. Good, he thought. Let us move on, stop this chattering about the glory of Japan. Then he can go off and take a nap. Next time I should send Commander Genda to meet with these biddies, and he can march all over them with the kind of energy they've never experienced. That might even keep Admiral Nagano awake.

Yamamoto was fidgeting, and his impatience pushed him to ignore protocol, to speak out of turn.

"Admirals, there is little more for us to discuss. The air training is going extremely well. The fleet has been engaged in maneuvers required for such a mission. We have challenges, certainly, but all of them are being addressed with great skill. What I require of you is the approval of the date of the assault, the X-Day. I know that the Ministry has proposed the last week of November. I believe it is too soon. We require more time to ready the fleet, to rendezvous the various ships as necessary. There are details being addressed about the types of weaponry we will have available, and we cannot rush those arrangements."

Nagano was more awake now, nodded slowly.

To one side, Fukudome said, "What do you propose?"

Yamamoto was prepared for this. "We have determined that the Americans put the bulk of their fleet to sea during the week, and bring the ships home to roost each weekend. They do this with astounding consistency. Therefore, it is logical to make the attack on a Saturday or Sunday. It is customary for Americans to regard Sunday as a day of rest and rejuvenation. I witnessed this very often in my tour of their country. I am not suggesting that they would all be asleep, but I do anticipate that their posts would be more lightly manned, compared to other days of the week. With that in mind, I believe the most practical time of the assault should be a Sunday, at first light. I would beseech you to approve the attack date of December 8. That would be, of course, December 7 in Hawaii."

Fukudome slid a paper from under his table, smiled at Tomioka, at the far end. He held the paper toward Yamamoto, the smile now directed at him.

"Admiral, it will please you to know that we have considered December 8 to be the appropriate

X-Day for several days now. It was thought necessary to have you confirm our judgment."

Yamamoto was annoyed, repressed the urge to shout at his former chief of staff. He took a deep breath, would not allow his temper to jeopardize their approval, not now. "I am pleased to hear that the chiefs agree. We shall now proceed with the final preparations."

Tomioka said, "Have you made a decision with regard to the use of submarines? There has always been concern that they could easily be detected from the air, and thus endanger the entire operation."

Yamamoto had heard too much of that already. "At first, I shared that concern. But there is risk throughout this entire operation. We are talking about making war, about an aggressive attack against another country's navy. Nowhere on earth could that occur without risk, and certainly, without loss. I have chosen Admiral Shimizu, who commands the Sixth Submarine Fleet, to oversee this part of the operation. I am now convinced that the submarines can be very useful as an additional weapon against any ships that are outside of Pearl Harbor, and the five midget submarines could find a path into Pearl Harbor itself, and cause havoc as well."

Fukudome cocked his head to one side. "Shimizu? When I was your chief of staff, I knew him well. He has little experience in submarines. What does he know of the midgets?"

Yamamoto felt an itch in his back, thought, There was a time when you did what I told you to do. "Admiral Shimizu has an entire fleet of well-trained submariners serving him, including those familiar with the midgets. The most important trait he brings to this operation is his skill as a leader. I have complete confidence in him, as I do in every man in my command."

He eased his chair from the long table, stood slowly, made ready for the usual formalities of adjournment. But Nagano held up a hand, and Yamamoto knew he was expected to sit again.

"Is there something else, sir?"

"You should know, Admiral, that no decision we have made assumes an outcome that will bring us all glory. If we allow the United States to determine our future, as they seem to intend, Japan shall likely perish. Even if we fight a war with them, we may perish, and the Japanese people shall likely disappear from the earth. Therefore, it is our duty to bring a fight to the United States that demonstrates to them our spirit, our love of honor, our love of our country, of our emperor. If we succeed in that, it matters not if we are defeated in battle. The enemies of Japan will recognize that spirit, that willingness to sacrifice, and we shall survive, our children shall survive, to rebuild our nation. I truly hope, as do we all, that there is a solution to our conflicts through diplomacy. But if that is not to be, then we must be prepared for the great fight to come."

Yamamoto was surprised to see tears in the older man's eyes. He pondered the words, sensed confusion in the odd sentiment. He stood again, the air around him stale with cigarette smoke and closed windows, said, "I assure you, Admiral, we shall do all within our power to ensure Japan's survival."

To his right, Tomioka raised a wineglass. "To our diplomats, and the hope for a peaceful solution."

Yamamoto had no glass, could only watch the other two complete the toast. He made his bow, then stepped into the cool air of the corridor, inhaled deeply, tried to wash away the stagnant air. So, he thought, Nagano believes we are to **perish** no matter what we do. Unless, of course, our diplomats talk our way clear, negotiate away all our differences. Yes, diplomacy is a wonderful thing. And if there is a significant agreement, even if our ships are already on the sea, then we shall turn them around, and celebrate the peace.

He stepped outside into a gentle coolness, a fluttering of leaves from the trees. He stopped, still rolling Nagano's words through his mind. He laughed to himself, thought of the new prime minister, Hideki Tojo. I do not believe Tojo or anyone from his command in the army will happily bow to the diplomats. Even my own commanders, those young fliers, the men who train for Genda, even they are filled with the fire. What would a sudden declaration of **peace** do to them, to those who have trained so hard? To extinguish their spirit at this hour would crush their morale. Diplomacy is a wonderful thing, certainly. But it is too late.

OMURA AIR BASE, NEAR NAGASAKI, JAPAN—
    FRIDAY, OCTOBER 24, 1941

The plane was in a steep dive, its speed increasing. Yamamoto stepped back slightly, butterflies in his gut. He watched without breathing, the plane only a few hundred feet above the ground, and Yamamoto began to flinch, thought, No, too low. He saw the dummy bomb released, the target a heavy crate in the field beside him. But he ignored that, his eyes still on the plane as it leveled out, the pilot bringing it closer to the ground than Yamamoto had ever seen a plane fly. Then it rose in a shallow climb, banked in a sharp turn, and flew straight overhead, with a slight waggle of the wings. He felt his hands shaking, laughed to himself. There is a good reason you remain on the ground.

Beside him, he could feel Genda's pride, but even that was overshadowed by the ebullient enthusiasm of Commander Fuchida.

"There, as I promised, Admiral. Lieutenant Hoda has hit the target perfectly. He shall lead one of the dive bomber groups. I have absolute confidence in his abilities."

Yamamoto put his hands behind his back, a show of bored disinterest. There would be no fuel for Fuchida's zeal, not yet.

Yamamoto glanced skyward again. "We are on a hard surface, with little wind. How can anyone say these men will be perfect when the enemy fills the air with fire?"

He could see Fuchida preparing an objection, red-faced. Genda interrupted.

"Commander Fuchida has done exemplary work training these pilots, sir. They are ordered to make as many as six takeoffs each day, navigating to a distant target. This demonstration was for you, to show their improvement in accuracy. No one expects perfection."

Fuchida still seemed anxious for a compliment, and Yamamoto turned to Genda. "I am aware of your numbers and your percentages, Commander. It is not necessary to treat me as some tourist."

Genda dropped his head. "Certainly not, sir. Please forgive me. It is just that I am extremely pleased with our progress, as is Commander Fuchida. Every man in my group shares respect for him. We all believe that you chose the right man to lead the assault."

Yamamoto turned away again, hands still locked behind his back. "I have known Commander Fuchida for several years. He will perform as I anticipate. There is no alternative to that." He looked toward Fuchida now. "Am I correct, Commander?"

Fuchida said, "I am humbled by your confidence in me, sir. I shall not disappoint."

Behind Yamamoto, his chief of staff, Ugaki, said,

"Sir, Commander Genda's staff, and the others, are waiting in the map room."

"They can wait. Commander Fuchida, are the training operations improving to your satisfaction in all areas, or just the dive bombers?"

Fuchida seemed to explode at the opportunity to brag about his pilots. "Quite, sir. The fighter squadrons have been practicing formations, and have become extremely proficient with their carrier landings. The same is true for the high-level bombers. As you know, sir, that is where I shall be, observing from above as the dive bombers and torpedo bombers make their attacks. I am most proud of the men, sir, most proud. Their proficiency has improved each week."

Yamamoto didn't need Fuchida to tell him the obvious. "They are pilots, yes? They were chosen to fly airplanes because they could be taught to fly airplanes. When they learned their lessons, they performed as they were taught. That is the way it should work, yes?"

Genda held a hand out, quieting Fuchida, said to Yamamoto, "Yes, sir. Certainly. I would only like to add, sir, that ever since you chose Commander Fuchida to command the actual air assault, the training schedules of these men have produced the results I had hoped for as well."

Yamamoto smiled to himself. Yes, you are learning, Mr. Genda. One does not need to heap praise on a warrior. He must earn that in his own mind. If he does not have such confidence, he will not succeed. And that is fatal.

He could feel Ugaki moving behind him, the nervous energy of a man who embraces a schedule. Beside him was the naval air base commander, Captain Aki, a stern-faced man who seemed annoyed that the commander in chief was taking up his time. But like most of the officers in the fleet, he kept his grumbling to himself. Yamamoto turned to him. "Captain, we shall retire to your map room. Commander Genda and I have much to discuss, and the others are no doubt tired of drinking too many cups of your tea."

Aki snapped to attention, an unnecessary gesture. "Right away, Admiral. My aide shall escort you."

Yamamoto saw the aide, a young petty officer, wide-eyed, in a stiff pose, nervousness in his face. "Right now would be acceptable."

They stepped inside a block building, a stairway leading down, then another. Yamamoto trod carefully, could feel Genda behind him, heard a whispered voice, Genda speaking quietly to himself, as though rehearsing what he had to say. Yamamoto smiled and thought, I am fortunate to have such passion and such efficiency, talent, and energy all in one man. Perhaps a touch of insanity as well. Perhaps they all should have that.

The aide stood aside beside the open door to a long rectangular room, a dozen men seated around a large table.

The aide said, "Sir, I am at your disposal if there is anything you require. I will remain very close outside the door."

Yamamoto moved past him, trailed by Genda, and Yamamoto turned back toward the young man, said, "Not too close, Petty Officer. One should not exercise his ears where there is nothing to be heard."

The young man seemed to understand, backed away as Yamamoto closed the door. The others rose in unison, offered short bows. The chairs at each end of the table were vacant, and Genda moved to the far end.

Yamamoto took his seat, and said, "Sit down, all of you. I have grown tired of meetings, and I would like this to be a short one."

They resumed their places around the table, and he saw their faces, saw young, ambitious men who were very good at what they did, men who could impress Genda with their skills. He spoke slowly, letting his guard down for a moment. "You know, I miss my own quarters on my flagship, the familiar bed. I admit to missing my own chef. Perhaps many of you shall reach command one day. You will know of these things, you will know that I do not speak to embarrass you, or shame you. When we began to design this operation, a year ago, I knew there would be decisions to be made. But I did not know just how many. You have made many of them for me, and I am grateful."

He ran out of words, admonished himself for

offering compliments to men he barely knew. On the far side of the table, Genda was kneeling before a small safe, twirling the dial.

"Commander, you brought a safe with you?"

Genda stood, a sheaf of paper in his hand. "Oh, no, sir. Captain Aki was gracious in his offer. He understands how sensitive my work is, how careful we must be. It is as you ordered it, sir."

"I know my own orders, Commander. Let's get on with it."

He regretted the words, had no reason to fault Genda. And the decision today was vital to the entire mission.

Genda laid the papers on the map table, unfolded three different sheets of paper. One of his men smoothed out the creases.

"Sir, I believe it is the appropriate time to select the route that our fleet shall navigate on its course toward Hawaii." Genda seemed energized now. He pointed to the first paper, a map of the South Pacific. "Sir, my men and I have narrowed our options down to three potential routes. The two more southerly routes would assume a substantial risk of discovery by American ships of all kinds, from surface to submarines, as well as by merchant ships from every country. The one advantage of those routes is that they offer calmer seas. Another route was considered that would shorten the distance of the journey by aiming the fleet in much more of a straight line from Japan to Hawaii. But that passage too would prove vulnerable to American contact along the way."

He paused, his black eyes burning, and glanced quickly at Yamamoto. "My personal choice, sir, and the one that is now the consensus of my officers, is the northern route. We would depart from the more northern anchorages in the less-inhabited Kirile Islands, thus affording us secrecy from the prying eyes of the general population." He leaned closer to the map, moved his finger along the paper. "This route is least likely to encounter merchant traffic, which avoids this area of the sea during the colder months. The water is simply too rough for most merchant ships."

"But not for warships?"

Genda looked up at him, a demonic smile. "Our warships can take rough seas, especially if they know how this increases our chances of success." He returned to the map. "When the fleet reaches a point approximately here . . . one thousand miles north of Honolulu, the ships would turn due south, and approach Oahu from the north, halting at a point two hundred miles from their target. It is our estimation that even if the Americans are searching the skies with their reconnaissance missions, they would be unlikely to place any priority on the northerly direction."

Yamamoto scanned the map, rubbed his chin with one hand, looked at the others. "Were there significant objections to this particular route?"

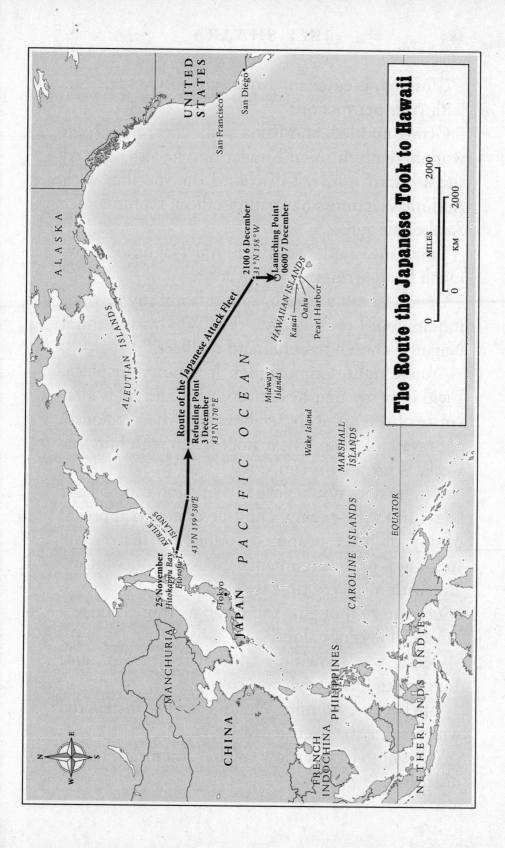

# The Route the Japanese Took to Hawaii

UNITED STATES

San Francisco

San Diego

ALASKA

ALEUTIAN ISLANDS

PACIFIC OCEAN

Route of the Japanese Attack Fleet

Refueling Point
3 December
43°N 170°E

2100 6 December
31°N 158°W

Launching Point
0600 7 December

HAWAIIAN ISLANDS
Kauai
Oahu
Pearl Harbor

Midway Islands

Wake Island

MARSHALL ISLANDS

CAROLINE ISLANDS

EQUATOR

KURILE ISLANDS

43°N 159°30'E

25 November
Hitokappu Bay
Etorofu I.

Tokyo

JAPAN

CHINA

MANCHURIA

PHILIPPINES

FRENCH INDOCHINA

NETHERLANDS INDIES

N
E
W
S

MILES
0        2000

KM
0        2000

Close by, Lieutenant Koba said to Genda, "Sir, with your permission?"

Genda nodded, and Koba said, "Sir, I have been working with Admiral Kusaka, and he also selected the northern route. I discussed the specifics with Admiral Nagumo's navigation officer, Commander Sasabe. He agrees as well."

Yamamoto said, "And Admiral Nagumo? How much hand-wringing has he done?"

Genda let out a breath. "Sir, it is not my place to inquire, but I must address this. Why was Admiral Nagumo chosen to command the fleet?"

"You're right, Commander. It is not your place. I will only say that he has seniority, and he is a favorite of several of those above me who graciously approved this plan. I have not spoken with him this week. What are his concerns?"

"Sir, he does not believe this mission can be kept secret from the enemy. Thus, he offers no approval of any of these proposed routes, no matter the soundness of the arguments. He seems uncomfortable with me every time we confer."

Yamamoto thought, You mean he thinks you're a lunatic? He is not alone.

Genda was showing a hint of frustration, and Yamamoto knew what was coming.

"Sir, I believe Admiral Nagumo must be **instructed** which route the fleet shall take."

Yamamoto let out a low laugh. "You mean, I must order him."

"If you insist, sir."

Yamamoto sat back, scanned the map again, caught smiles on several of the young faces around him. "You are all pilots, yes?"

Genda stood tall, straight, stared at the wall above Yamamoto's head. "They are the finest pilots in the world. They each will lead a significant portion of the attack, as they serve Commander Fuchida."

There was a light rap on the door, and Yamamoto waited for Genda to roll up his papers, then said, "You may enter."

He saw Captain Aki's aide, and another man, the uniform of a lieutenant.

"Sir, please forgive the interruption. This man has a message for Commander Genda."

Yamamoto turned toward Genda, who seemed puzzled.

"Sir, I wasn't expecting anyone . . . Only a very few people know I am here."

The man bowed, handed him a fat envelope, and quickly stepped out.

Yamamoto said, "Might we all know, Commander, why someone knew to find you in a classified location?"

Genda stared hard at the envelope, tore it open, read for a brief moment, and then offered a rare smile.

"Sir, it is from Ensign Kito, of my staff." He sat down, another rarity. "Sir, we had engaged the Mitsubishi company to work on the challenge of constructing a torpedo that would function effectively in shallow water. Please forgive me, sir. I need to examine these numbers."

Yamamoto waited patiently, knew how important this could be. "So, have they succeeded? Or are we doomed to plant our best weapon into the mud of Pearl Harbor?"

"Sir, at your instruction, I approached Mr. Fukuda, the chairman of Mitsubishi, about this problem some months ago. As you know, we are highly indebted to the company for its design and production of our A6M Zero aircraft."

"I'm waiting, Commander."

The smile returned, and Genda said, "Sir, they have tested a mechanism that attaches to the torpedo's fins. When the torpedo impacts the water, the device falls away. But in doing so, it effectively slows the dive, so that the torpedo levels out far more quickly. There are test results here that demonstrate the torpedo to be effective in less than forty feet of water, perhaps a good deal less. They are to begin manufacture of the new devices immediately, and will deliver them as quickly as possible, possibly by mid-November."

"That's a little late, isn't it?"

"Well, sir, they've begun delivering the first few now, so that we may begin our own tests. Sir, this is the best we could have hoped for. They have created a new technology."

Yamamoto thumbed through the documents,

saw graphs, angles of descent, arcs of approach to a target. "So, what kind of device did they come up with? Is it electrical, fuel-driven?"

Genda looked away, seemed hesitant, and Yamamoto put down the papers.

"What kind of device, Commander?"

"Um, sir, for lack of any better description . . . it's a wooden box."

# TWENTY-FOUR

## Biggs

PEARL HARBOR, HAWAII—MONDAY, NOVEMBER 3, 1941

The ordeal of the dry dock repairs was supposed to last only a few days. It had surprised Biggs that the crew stayed aboard the **Arizona** as the ship maneuvered slowly into the great trough. The massive gate closed her inside, then the water was pumped away, leaving the ship fully exposed. But life on the ship went on: the same duties, and often, the same monotony. Biggs had been called to duty with many others to add one more coat of paint to the steel. But this paint was different, a darker gray, while the superstructure was painted a much lighter color.

As the first grueling day ended, Biggs was one of many who had asked the petty officers about the difference in color. The explanation had to do with camouflage, that at sea, the color scheme would make the ship more difficult to see at long distance. Biggs and many others had asked: **Why?** There was no good answer, the crewmen around him assuming it was one more dose of nonsense. Even with the **Arizona** perched high and dry, orders had come down from command that when the ship again put to sea, the drills would be more serious, the casual maneuverings tightening up. For the first time, the newer recruits would run through their drills as though war was very close. At sea, the lookouts would pay special attention to the signs of enemy submarines, and this was not a drill. What no one seemed able to answer was just who the enemy might be.

For Biggs, the urgency of the new duties had spread even to sick bay, both doctors double-checking supplies and instruments, as if preparing for the worst. The worst **what,** he had no idea. His job was to do what he was told. And the doctors knew as little as he did. Their orders were as simple as those given to every crewman on the ship: **Make ready.**

With the ship scheduled to remain under repair for at least several more days, Biggs had secured a liberty pass, and not even Kincaid seemed to care. Rumors had begun to fly that when the **Arizona** finally floated out of dry dock, she would be at sea for perhaps a very long time. Rumors spread that they were going to the Philippines, to Australia. The most optimistic believed the ship would make the journey to Bremerton after all, or to the port of Long Beach, California.

Biggs tried to remember what Dr. Johnson had taught him, that the more appealing the rumor, the less likely it was to be true. He kept his thoughts on his work: painting, holystoning, and more important to him, his duty in sick bay. But functioning out of water had an odd effect on Biggs, as it did on many others. It was as though the **Arizona** was no longer a ship at all, just an enormous steel barracks. Nothing onboard had changed except the view around them, but to Biggs, that was enough. When the opportunity for liberty was offered, he seized it, the treasured pass taking priority over anything else in his mind. He knew that Wakeman was going to town, several of the others as well, but this time, Biggs had his own agenda. He was going to try to meet up with his best friend, Ray.

He saluted the officer of the deck, moving down with a flow of the workmen whose shift had just concluded, men who smelled of smoke and sweat and welded steel. As Biggs stepped onto solid ground, he moved away from the parade of workmen, then looked back to see what he could of the wound in the ship. The next shift of workers had already taken their places, and he could see cranes raising sheets of steel into place. I hope nobody gets hurt, he thought. Seems like it would happen pretty often. How do you treat a man who's crushed? Maybe it doesn't matter. Does anyone survive that kind of damage?

He heard his name, was surprised to see Dr. Condon.

"Headed into town, Mr. Biggs?"

"Yes, sir. You too?"

"I'm having dinner at the Halekulani with a few medical officers. A couple fellows from the **Oklahoma** will be there, so I'm sure they'll buy us a few drinks, and I'm sure we'll get in a few jabs at their skipper's bad driving. I hope they have a sense of humor."

"They're probably hoping **you** have a sense of humor, sir. They busted up our ship, coulda sent us to the bottom. Nothing funny about that."

Condon rubbed his chin. "Very good, Mr. Biggs. Maybe you should come along."

"No, thank you, sir. I doubt your friends would be happy having an apprentice at your fancy dinner."

"Any more than your bunkmates would be happy sitting down to eat with an officer. I guess it's just the world we live in. What are you watching?"

"Oh, sir, just the steel workers. It's pretty amazing how quick they can patch us up. I just worry somebody's gonna get hurt. Looks pretty dangerous, all of it. I'm not sure we could do much for one of those fellows in our sick bay."

"You're thinking like a corpsman, Mr. Biggs. But Dr. Johnson and I have already spoken with the naval hospital over at Hospital Point. What we can't handle, they can. We're just hoping it doesn't come to that."

HONOLULU, HAWAII—TUESDAY, NOVEMBER 4, 1941

The beer was still awful, but it was all he could afford. He was determined to send his pay home, but his mother had protested, wouldn't accept his generosity. Instead, she had assured him the money would be there when he returned home, in the savings account she had opened for him at the one surviving bank in Palatka. He had been surprised at that, still insisted she use the money as it was needed, but she insisted right back, it was **his** money, and certainly, once he left the navy, he would need it more than they would. Biggs had begun to suspect that his father was behind that, that his pride would never let him accept his son's help to pay the bills.

He took another gulp of the beer, forced it down. He didn't know how to tell her, tell either one of them, that he wasn't sure if he'd ever come home, not as a civilian anyway. I love the navy, he thought, and if it works out, it could be a hell of a good career. Compared to . . . what? Palatka?

He glanced to the side, saw Russo staring down into

his bottle. Ray's got it a hell of a lot worse. His whole family needs him. Joining the navy was his idea, but he'll have to go home first.

Russo seemed to rock slowly on the stool, and Biggs said, "Geez, Ray, how many you had?"

Russo responded with a mumble. He let out a loud belch, leaned forward and put his head down onto the bar. Biggs knew he had no business scolding Russo for anything at all. Ray was as close a friend as he ever had, but Biggs wasn't comfortable pushing him to talk about his misery.

He jostled Russo, saw the bartender eyeing them with a hard stare. "Hey, Ray. Sit up. You'll get us tossed out the door. Come on. You can't sleep on the bar."

Ray sat up, blinking, looked at Biggs, smiled. "I'm okay, Tommy. Just kinda thinking about things, you know?"

"Yeah, I know. You tell me when you're ready to head back to the ship, and I'll take care of the tab. They're gonna want these stools."

Russo studied his bottle again, tilted it back, most of the beer finding his mouth. Biggs watched him carefully, a glance again at the bartender. His own bottle was empty, a relief, his gut already churning from the few he had consumed. He wanted to ask just when Russo was planning to ship out, if he would still complete his hitch. But it was a subject neither man seemed willing to raise. He'll be out of here soon enough, Biggs thought, back home to a whole new life he never planned.

He questioned himself often, why he seemed to be different from so many of the others, even the men in his own compartment. So many were homesick for whatever life they had left behind them. He thought of Mahone, the man who wrote a letter to his parents nearly every day, sad, emotional letters about how he couldn't wait to come home. Hell, I write my mom plenty, and if Pop ever sent me a note, any kind of note, I'd answer him. But I don't need to unload every detail on them, every day. A lot of what I do ain't all that interesting. And all the stuff she writes about. That just reminds me I don't want to be there hardly at all.

But, Jesus, all around me, there're so many complaints, every day, so many of us griping about Hawaii, the ship, the duty, the officers. And of course, Petty Officer Kincaid. Biggs shook his head. Now **there's** something to gripe about. The biggest bastard in the navy. Maybe the world.

He leaned closer to Russo. "Hey, Ray, you got anybody on your ship who loves to bust asses just for no good reason?"

Russo seemed to think for a moment, as though he was pushing through a headful of cobwebs. "Nah."

Biggs laughed. "You probably forgot." He looked around, the bar packed with sailors, a handful of marines in one corner, standing like a human fortress. He blinked through the smoky haze, tried to remember the name of the bar they were in, said it aloud, "Blue Moon."

Beside him, Russo surprised him with a sudden burst of clarity. "It's not the Black Cat?"

"Nope. I got tired of that place. Too crummy. Too many fights. And the beer's bad."

"This beer's bad."

Biggs couldn't argue with that, but his bottle was empty and he motioned to the bartender, an older Hawaiian with no teeth. "One more, please, sir."

The old man said, "You better pay up first. Your buddy's had enough. You too, maybe. That's four dollars twenty."

Biggs groaned, knew that all he had was a five, and there was still the cab ride. But he couldn't take anything from Russo, no matter how much beer his friend had consumed.

"Fine. We're done."

He dug the five out of the pocket on his shirt, handed it to the bartender, who seemed surprised, as though he had expected trouble. Biggs felt mildly offended, thought, Look, pal, my buddy's drunk, but he's not a thug. You oughta keep an eye on those marines over there. He suddenly felt guilty for that, had no reason to spout out the same prejudice against the marines that they felt for the sailors. He had become very close to Finley, even if Finley had to suffer ribbing from the marines around him, wondering why he even spoke to a swabby. It's all so ridiculous, Biggs thought.

He put a hand on Russo's shoulder. "Come on, Ray. We're done here and there's guys waiting for our seats. I got no more dough."

Russo slid clumsily off the stool, held himself up on Biggs's shoulder. "Jesus, Tommy. I'm kinda blasted."

"Let's go, I'll get you into a taxi."

Russo followed him outside, the air cool, breezy, a blessed relief from the bar. But the streets were as busy as always, a slow-moving river of white, boisterous sounds coming from the clubs, music and shouting and drunk revelry. Biggs couldn't avoid a feeling of gloom, knew that when Russo went home, he might never see him again.

The rendezvous tonight was a rare success for a general plan they had hatched weeks ago. Neither of them could know when the other had liberty, and there was no way for low-ranking seamen to communicate between ships, but they had agreed that whenever they had a pass, the Blue Moon would be their first stop. If they both had liberty, they would find each other easily. Tonight had been only the second time it had worked, a stroke of luck for both of them.

He held Russo's arm up, checked his watch: nearly ten o'clock. "Come on, Ray, there's a taxi stand over this way."

Russo could barely walk, Biggs supporting him. Men all around him staggered by, some of them as bad off as Russo. Biggs was surprised to see Wakeman, coming toward him.

Wakeman said, "I thought it was you. Hard to pick faces out of this school of fish. So, this your hometown buddy?"

Biggs stared at Wakeman's face, a deep purple stain under his eye.

"Yeah. Ray Russo. He's a little foggy. Ed, holy cow. What the hell happened to you? Marines again?"

Wakeman touched the bruise, flinched. "Ow. Damn. Is it getting bad? You can see it?"

"See it? Hell, Ed, the whole fleet can see it. It's all over your face. What did you do?"

"Look, Tommy, I don't mean to sound insulting or anything. It's just that I can't always understand people from your part of the world."

"Palatka?"

"No, I mean the South. I was waiting for my beer, and heard kind of a ruckus behind me, this big fellow, sailor, pushes into me, says something. He was nice about it, but I didn't understand his accent. He says it again, and damn it all, I got no idea what he's saying, talks with a mouthful of marbles. Well, hell, I guess I pissed him off, and he was pretty tanked, so he swings at me, catches me flush on the face. I ain't ashamed to say that I went down, kinda hard. It ain't been too often I actually saw stars. His buddies helped me up, more mouths and marbles, and one of 'em wanted to buy me a beer, I think. I declined. Figured I'd best get the hell out of there. Then I see the guy who decked me, leaning over the bar, puking. I guess that's what he was saying. Maybe I needed you there to translate."

Biggs fought the urge to laugh, his eyes on Wakeman's glorious shiner. "I might not have understood him either. Down home, we say some people talk with a mouthful of grits. Same idea."

Wakeman prodded the bruise again, said, "Guess I'll be seeing you in sick bay. This hurts like hell."

"I'm heading back to the ship now. I just want to get Ray into a taxi, so he can get out to the **Curtiss.**"

"I'll give you a hand. Looks like you'll need it."

Russo had sagged down to his knees, and Wakeman moved closer, helped Biggs pull him upright.

Wakeman said, "He's a little fellow. Thank God for that. But if he says something I can't understand? I'm getting the hell out of the way."

USS ARIZONA, DRY DOCK, PEARL HARBOR—
    SATURDAY, NOVEMBER 8, 1941

The bundles were lowered by crane and a dozen crewmen unloaded the boxes and crates. The officer, a young lieutenant, called out the contents.

"From the Wing Coffee Company, we've got four thousand pounds of oranges."

Beside Biggs, Dr. Condon stepped forward, selected one large crate. "This one."

The crate was pried open, and Condon eyed the oranges, then gave a nod to the lieutenant, who read from his pad.

"From Wing, twelve hundred pounds of pears."

The routine was repeated, Condon making his own notes, Biggs focused more on the sheer volume of food. Condon examined a huge crate of the pears, stepped back with a nod, and the lieutenant called out, "From Chun Moon Ltd., tomatoes, seven hundred pounds."

Condon chose the sample to examine and the crate was pulled open, a sour stink filling the air. Condon leaned closer, said, "No good, Lieutenant. These have seen better days. There's mold, and some of them are flat-out rotten."

The lieutenant leaned closer, saw it for himself, made a face. "Never understand why these folks think they can stick us with this crap. Okay, hoist it up, get it out of here. Next, from Tai Hing Company, sixteen hundred pounds of apples . . ."


Biggs felt as exhausted as Condon looked, the two men stepping through the hatchway into sick bay. Johnson emerged from the office, laughed at the sight.

"You two have a swell day on the job?"

Condon sat heavily, pointed to another chair, permission for Biggs to sit as well.

Condon stretched his back, said to Johnson, "I learned something today, **Commander.** There's advantage to rank. I suppose that was the lesson. Otherwise you'd have been out there instead of me, smelling rotten tomatoes."

Johnson laughed again. "No need to get all pissy with me, Dan. I've done those food inspections plenty of times. I assumed you'd give Mr. Biggs his share of the fun. How bad was it?"

Condon laughed now. "Pretty impressive, I'll say that. Never appreciated before what it takes to stock this ship. Hell, there was fifteen hundred pounds of grapefruit. I don't even like grapefruit. Four hundred pounds of lemons, for God's sake." He looked at his notepad. "A half ton of sweet potatoes, eight hundred pounds of squash, three hundred pounds of cucumbers, seventeen hundred pounds of celery, five tons of potatoes. **Five tons.** No wonder the boys who have to peel those things hate it so much."

"Any problems?"

"Tomatoes. If we'd have eaten those things, we'd have killed half the crew."

Johnson looked at Biggs. "So, what did you think? The best six hours of your life?"

Biggs shook his head. "Not sure I'd call it that, sir. I sure never seen anything like it. They loaded us with a thousand pounds of ice. I guarantee, sir, that those fellows doing all that hoisting will find a way to grab up some of that. My back hurt just watching them."

Johnson took Condon's pad, looked it over. "Part of the job, Mr. Biggs. One way to fight sickness is to prevent it. As much fresh food as there is to come aboard this ship, it has to be inspected for quality. Can't have any bad tomatoes."

SHORE LANDING, ADJACENT TO DRY DOCK—
   TUESDAY, NOVEMBER 11, 1941

The gift of a party had come to the crew from the gunnery officers and their men, a celebration to honor Armistice Day. It was held near the dry dock, along a stretch of narrow beach.

The gunners had provided the steaks and the charcoal, and enough beer to float the ship. Biggs had consumed the charred beef with the same enthusiasm as the men around him, and the beer was far more palatable than what they had endured in town.

Biggs was in the grass above the rough dark sand, laid flat, staring up at a perfect blue sky. Beside him, Wakeman let out a long happy belch, said, "I guess they're making sure we remember why there's a holiday today. End of the Great War and all. Hell, I bet those poor bastards didn't have a steak dinner."

Biggs turned his head. "Bet they did when they got home. **If** they got home. That was a bloody hell on all sides. Hell, Ed, I don't wanna think about that stuff. I'd rather just lie here, drink beer, and pretend I'm in Daytona Beach."

Wakeman lay flat as well. "You're right. But have you walked out there, right off this little shoreline? Water feels good, but the sand, well, hell, it ain't sand. It feels like walking on pieces of glass. It'll cut you to hell. Not like any beach I ever seen."

"You go to the beach a lot in South Dakota?"

Wakeman laughed. "Went to somewhere in California when I was a kid. They had real sand. Not like this stuff. So, Daytona pretty nice?"

"Never been there. Parents couldn't afford to go. I seen pictures."

Wakeman raised himself to his elbows, looked at Biggs. "You know what we are? Idiots. We're in the navy, and we don't know a damn thing about oceans. I remember the recruiter where I signed up. All kinds of posters of white sand beaches and palm trees. Still waiting to find out where that was."

"It's right here if you wanna hang at the Royal Hawaiian or the other fancy places."

Wakeman stared out into the harbor, a long minute. "They probably bring their sand in from Florida. Those people can afford it. Hell, I'm gonna get another beer. You?"

"Sure."

Wakeman was up, gone, and Biggs heard a new voice.

"You boys doing okay? There's a few more steaks if anybody's still got an appetite."

Biggs sat upright, saw the chief gunner's mate, Isham, hands on his hips, pure satisfaction on his face. No one seemed willing to volunteer for any more gluttony, and Biggs turned, faced him, said, "This was really swell, Chief. You fellows did us a real good thing."

"Thanks. Just part of being a team, all of us. What's your station?"

"Hospital apprentice, sir. Tommy Biggs."

"Well, Hospital Apprentice Biggs, I hope you have the most boring tour of duty of any man on the ship. I kinda hope the same for all of us."

Isham moved away, passing through the sea of well-fed sailors, offering the same good cheer. Wakeman was back now, handed Biggs a bottle, said, "Who was that?"

"Chief gunnery officer. Just making sure we're all fat and happy."

"That man's got maybe the best job on the ship."

Biggs drank from the bottle. "Why?"

"Hell, Tommy, they get to fire all those guns—big ones, little ones. I tried for that duty, couldn't get it. And he's the chief? Lucky son of a bitch."

"Why?"

Wakeman looked at him. "You been lying out here in the sun too long. I said, they get to fire the damn guns. Make all that racket, while the rest of us are pushing a mop. If we ever run into a real gun-shootin' enemy, these guys get to blow 'em to hell. Like I said, it's the best job on the ship."

Biggs settled back into the grass, heard commotion, men starting a football game across the field.

Wakeman was looking that way, said, "We should head over there. Looks like it might be a good game. Hey, how come there's no baseball game? Your team could beat hell out of anybody around here."

"Played day before yesterday. It was good. We beat a team from the **Tennessee.**"

"How bad? I love it when you whip up on the battleships."

"Doesn't matter. We won."

Wakeman lay flat again. "I hate it when you're so damn humble."

Biggs stared into the blue for a long minute, then said, "Eighteen to three. I hit three home runs. Finley struck out fourteen guys."

Wakeman held up his bottle. "I knew it. Salutes to you."

Biggs drank, then lay flat again, staring beyond the blue, his eyes picking out moving shapes. His mind swirled with the same questions from his childhood: Why is it blue? What's up there past the blue part? He pushed away Wakeman's talk about the gunners, all the envy about firing weapons, jumping with both feet into a war. He had kept Dr. Johnson's advice tucked away, reminding himself that no matter the enthusiasm for the adventure of war, there was no escaping the simple fact that if you find joy in shooting those big guns, there might be an enemy out there, taking joy in shooting at you.

When the ship had first moved into dry dock, the scuttlebutt had been that the repairs were due to be completed by the fourth of November. Like so many rumors before, there was no truth to this one either. It wouldn't be until the next day, November 12, that **Arizona**'s great wound would be pronounced healed and, to the delight of the entire crew, the water of the harbor allowed to fill the enormous trough around the ship. Once she was afloat, the tugboats backed her out of the flooded dry dock, positioning her again along her perch against Ford Island. Most of the crew still embraced the fantasy that Bremerton was their next port of call.

After one day's speculation, the orders were issued, and the **Arizona** once again slipped out through the narrow entrance to the harbor. The crew pressed their questions where they could, but there were no satisfactory answers. The orders came for a submarine watch, and with that a heightened sense of alarm among the senior officers, even if no one could communicate to the crew exactly why. And

for all those who still held to the desperate dream
that they would steam gloriously eastward, the per-
sistent fantasy of lengthy liberties in Bremerton
or Long Beach, very soon it was apparent that the
ship was far out to sea for the sole purpose of drills,
training and running around in circles.

# TWENTY-FIVE

# Hull

The Carlton Hotel, Washington, D.C.—
Sunday, November 16, 1941

Stimson drank from the coffee cup, set it down beside him. "I am the head of a department where **confusion** is standard operating procedure. So much authority divided between the services is simply idiotic."

Hull tried to read how serious Stimson was, then said, "Anything you want to talk about?"

"I mean that there are wrestling matches going on all over the military to see who can make the biggest splash with the White House. The army and navy have separate intelligence commands, two groups trying to do the same job, deciphering all the **boogie woogie** that flows through their offices. I've told them to coordinate, to work together, to analyze the information they're receiving from all over the world. If I have to put up with spies and all that under-the-table crap, at least they can try to be efficient about it. Too often it's a damn competition, somebody racing into my office with some dribble of intelligence just so they can thump their chest that they beat out the other guy. Nobody's in charge, and then, everybody's in charge."

Stimson paused. "You know, they don't have this kind of foolishness when there's a dictator. One man runs the show, so one man makes every decision. You tell people what the hell to do, and nobody argues with you."

Hull wasn't sure if Stimson really believed any of that. But he didn't respond, his eyes focused outside, so many of the trees bare of leaves. After a long moment, he said, "You'll make it work. Nobody in the War Department wants you to get mad at them. You're too frightening."

Stimson made a low laugh. "I assume you mean that as a compliment."

"Of course. I don't want you mad at me either." He kept his eyes on the street, people passing by in heavy coats, the first cold weather of the season. "I don't care for this time of year, Henry. I get impatient for spring to get here even before Christmas. Everything just seems so bleak."

Stimson laughed, surprising him. "Of course it's bleak. The entire world is bleak. That's what we're trying to change."

Hull saw a family leading a small dog, the animal wrapped in a sweater. "I suppose that's the diplomat's job. Your job is to oversee the military, make sure everybody has the right boots on, that the tanks have plenty of gasoline. Not much controversy over that, I suppose."

Stimson seemed puzzled, said, "My job's a lot more complicated than that, and you know it. What the hell's eating you?"

Hull turned away from the window, looked at him. He didn't want an argument. "Sorry, Henry. I'm thinking too much, I guess. You want to yell at anyone, you go right ahead. It's the War Department, after all. People expect you to be a grouchy old fart. You do a fine job of it too. My job is to be pleasant to everyone, offer the happy handshake, all the while making sure I'm more clever than the other guy, that I can figure him out first. The worst thing I could ever do is lose my temper. There are times, when some smiling liar is sitting across from me, that I want to kick him in the shins. But nope, can't do that. I'm supposed to make peace with everybody."

Stimson reached for the coffee cup. "I agree, your job is harder. Soldiers and sailors follow orders. **You** can't order anybody to do a damn thing. If some foreign hotsy-totsy gets mad at you, they walk out and raise hell with their government or the newspapers. Don't forget, I did your job once. These days, you can have it. I'm not good at being nice."

Hull scanned the papers on his desk. "You know, the president has pretty much handed me the Pacific, told me to take care of our problems with the Japanese. Churchill has him arm in arm, and their priority is the Atlantic, Europe, all of that."

Stimson sipped from the cup, made a face. "Coffee's cold. Can you have an aide bring me another one? And, just so we're clear, Cordell, the Atlantic is my priority too. The Pacific isn't much more than a bitching contest, whether it's the Japanese, the Chinese, or anyone else who feels trespassed upon. And of course, you can bitch on our behalf as much as the rest of them. In a nice way, of course. But Europe's different. There's a shooting war that's spread out all over the damn place. If the good guys lose . . . well, I don't have to spell it out."

Hull saw one of his young aides leaning past the doorway.

"Mr. Jordan, bring a fresh cup of coffee for the secretary. Then you're excused. Go over to the State Department, see what needs tending to."

The young man disappeared, and there was the sound of a coffee pot, the clink of a fresh china cup. He returned now, said, "I hope this is all right, sir. It's been in the pot for a while."

"Thank you, son. It's not polite to eavesdrop."

"No . . . I mean, I'm sorry, sir. I didn't hear anything. I'll be leaving now."

Hull bristled at Stimson's unnecessary admonition.

It's not his place, he thought. And I trust every one of my people to keep their mouths shut. Well, most of them, anyway.

Stimson looked into the outer room, waited for the aide to leave, then lowered his voice. "You see the latest from Magic? I know the Japanese are your bailiwick, but I do pay attention to what's going on."

"I've seen a number of the **Purple** messages lately. Most are the usual chatter. I'm concerned about the new foreign minister, and the instructions he's giving Ambassador Nomura."

Stimson tested the heat of the coffee, blew carefully, the steam fogging his glasses. He set the cup down, said, "Nomura's being told to bring us to terms, and quick. What do you make of that?"

"It's more involved than that, I think. But you're right, they've told Nomura to keep talking to us, and get us to agree to all the Japanese conditions, and to do it by November twenty-fifth."

Stimson thought a moment, said, "What are you planning to do about that?"

It was an odd question, and Hull said, "I'm going to keep talking to them, of course. There is no alternative I can accept."

Stimson frowned, shook his head. "There are always alternatives. Sometimes you have to do what needs doing, push your buttons before the other fellow pushes his. We have a flock of B-17s designated to be deployed to the Philippines, and they should be there in a few weeks. Let's say MacArthur sends them to fly over Tokyo. No bombs, nothing ridiculous, yet. It's just a little show we give to their emperor, which just might make their **demands** a little more flexible."

It cannot happen that way, Hull thought. It's too easy for him to say that, and he knows better. And you might start a war. Thank God the president understands that.

"I will continue to talk. And listen. It's the only way, Henry."

Stimson shrugged. "For now. Thanks for the coffee, but I need to go. I have a meeting at the Department of the Navy. Knox and Stark are getting a barrelful of bellyaching from Hawaii, from Admiral Kimmel. Seems Kimmel thinks he needs an extra fleet added to the one he has now. Never mind that there's no reason for any fleet to be out there in the first place. I'm considering moving a good number of his ships to the Philippines, adding to the B-17s we've promised MacArthur. It doesn't take a genius to understand that if we're under any threat by the Japanese, the Philippines will be the target that matters most. But Admiral Kimmel's having a tantrum about losing any more ships. He's afraid we're going to move everything he's got to the Atlantic. I'm not completely opposed to that, but I'll see what Knox and Stark have to say about it. Tomorrow, I'll check in on General Marshall, see what the army thinks."

Stimson pulled himself up slowly, struggling

through obvious stiffness in his legs. Hull rose as well, moved to the doorway, waited, held out his hand. Stimson shook it, and Hull could feel the man's weakness. He tried to ignore that, said, "Glad you came by, Henry. Good luck with your admirals."

Stimson moved past him, then stopped, said, "Admirals and generals. They think they know so much more than us mere mortals." He went to the door, stopped again. "Meant to ask you, where's your wife? Mine's always pushing us to get together, dinner or what have you. She makes a murderous coffee cake."

Hull wasn't sure if that was good or bad. "Frances is out gathering up whatever she's planning for Thanksgiving dinner. I know better than to interfere."

"Wise man."

Stimson was gone now, and Hull stared at the closing door. He thought of the Japanese, and all he still had to do, the efforts that had so far been useless. But we **have** to talk, he thought. There is no other way.

The Magic machines had intercepted an unusual message sent via the **Purple** codes, and it immediately crossed the desks of everyone in Washington authorized to receive it. It was an oddly detailed set of instructions from the Japanese foreign ministry to its consulate in Honolulu. The instructions called for the entire area in and around Pearl Harbor to be laid out in a series of grid lines, as though a checkerboard was to be superimposed over a map. The instructions also called for the consulate to designate the types and classes of the warships anchored in the harbor.

Hull's reaction to the intercept was concern, but the cryptologists and the ranking military officers all the way up the chain of command dismissed his worries. They described the message as just one more peculiar example of Japanese attention to detail. Hull had no reason to disagree, and no reason to act beyond what he was told. After all, those men were the experts.

Hull's meetings continued with Ambassador Nomura, the exhausting back-and-forth of proposals and arguments from the Japanese that never seemed to change. Through it all, Nomura kept up the pretense of good humor and pleasant conversation, and seemed completely agreeable to the proposals Hull offered, solutions to the dangerous difficulties that stood in the way of a genuine peace in the Pacific. Hull repeated his cautionary warnings about all that could go terribly wrong, and Nomura accepted them with enthusiasm, insisting he would communicate those warnings and Hull's proposed solutions to his superiors in Tokyo.

But Nomura could relate only the responses that

he was ordered to give, and the responses from
Tokyo were maddeningly consistent. If the United
States would agree to everything Japan wanted, in-
cluding lifting the embargoes, all would be made
well, and surely, the Japanese would embrace the
peace. Meanwhile, the occupation of China would
continue, as would the occupation of Southeast
Asia. There was no guarantee on any level that the
Japanese would end their designs on the Dutch
East Indies, or on the islands spread all across the
South Pacific.

THE STATE DEPARTMENT, WASHINGTON, D.C.—
    MONDAY, NOVEMBER 17, 1941

As Nomura had told Hull weeks before, the Japanese
foreign ministry was sending him an assistant,
or co-worker, or any other euphemism Hull wished
to apply. There was no doubt at all in Hull's mind,
even before he met the man, that the Japanese
government was sending Nomura a babysitter.

Saburo Kurusu was as opposite from Nomura as
a man could be. Unlike the hesitant and slightly
clumsy Nomura, Kurusu spoke perfect English,
likely aided by his marriage to an American woman.
While Nomura continued to display a naive charm,
Kurusu seemed to Hull to be little more than a
snake, a small, thin man, with the narrow mustache
and glasses that gave him an unfortunate resemblance to the most racist stereotype of Hollywood's

version of a **Jap.** But Hull measured the man by far more serious considerations. Kurusu had formerly been the Japanese ambassador to Germany, and as such, had been the signatory of the Tripartite Pact. No matter what other proposals Kurusu might bring to the table, Hull knew it was unlikely Kurusu would negotiate any terms that would upset the Germans.

As they began their first meeting, marked by the usual cheerful politeness, Hull was immediately convinced that he could believe nothing that Kurusu said to him. Beyond that, he simply didn't like the man.

————

We ought to wait and see what turn the war takes and remain patient. However, the situation renders this out of the question. The deadline is set and there will be no change. You see how short the time is. Therefore, do not allow the United States to sidetrack us and delay the negotiations any further. Press them for a solution on the basis of our proposals, and do your best to bring about an immediate solution.

He finished reading the intercept, read it a second time. The messenger waited patiently, and Hull slid the paper back into its envelope, stared at it for a moment, handed it to the man, who said, "Thank you, sir. I must return to the decryption office. Enjoy your day, sir."

The man didn't wait for any acknowledgment, left quickly. Hull heard the outer door close, and now his aides appeared, waiting for instructions. He waved them away without speaking, sat back in the soft chair, turned it toward the window and the gray gloom of a chilly November afternoon. The aides are asking each other what this is about, he thought. Probably do that every time this happens. I would too, I suppose. They're used to messages from the White House, from Stimson, from any of the ambassadors in every part of the world. But the Magic messages are different, so very unusual. This is **secret,** what that messenger with his pistol carries in his sealed folder. I wonder if **he** knows. Is he tempted to stop for a doughnut and scan the decryptions over a cup of coffee? No, it's not funny, none of it.

He thought of the text he had just seen, the obvious message. Japan is telling Nomura that if we don't meet the deadline he's been given, then . . . what? They set off bombs in Washington? In New York? They assassinate someone important? They send their army to invade the Philippines? That's what Stimson thinks, certainly.

He thought of Nomura. A decent man, unless I've been fooled completely. The Japanese offer us the pretense that we are **negotiating,** that it's a give-and-take. Nomura has become a mindless servant, marching in whatever direction they point him. Kurusu is here to make sure that Nomura makes no mistakes. And that we keep our lines of communication open, so that we may avert a war. What happens next? Stimson would push them hard, maybe even threaten. Is that the better course? No, it most certainly is not. Starting a war is never the right thing to do.

I will take both men to see the president, and let Franklin form his own opinion of Mr. Kurusu, and perhaps we will learn a little more about what this "deadline" might mean. But you already know what it means. We sign on the dotted line, or we accept the consequences. How much of that is just bluster or posturing? Have they gone too far, or are they pushing us, to see how far we will go? I know the military people believe we must show Japan that we aren't to be pushed around. But damn it all, this isn't a school yard. Japan isn't simply the latest bully who should be punched in the nose.

He heard sounds in the outer office, the voice of his wife, saw her now, one of his aides relieving her of an armload of bags. "Please put them right over there, Jeffrey. I'll deal with them in a moment."

The young man did as he was told, said, "My pleasure, ma'am."

Hull said to the aides, "You two can go on home. Now that the real chief has returned, I'm the aide."

The young men responded with smiles, brief fare-wells. They were out quickly, and Frances waited for the door to close, said, "What's wrong?"

Hull moved back to his chair, sat. "Did I say anything was wrong?"

"Your face does. Don't hide it, Cordell. I know better."

He felt the usual surrender, said, "Yes, you do. I don't know how else to say it. The Japanese continue to insist that their goal is world peace. And it's a lie. They're testing us, testing how much backbone we have."


For the next several days, Hull, Nomura, and Kurusu wrangled and wrestled over demands from both sides, the sticking points varying from Japan's occupation of China to its ongoing alliance with Germany, from the oil embargo to Japan's occupation of Southeast Asia.

On November 20, Thanksgiving Day, Nomura and Kurusu presented Hull with a new proposal, what they described as the final effort at a negotiated solution to their differences:

Japan and the United States to make no armed advance into any region in Southeast Asia and the Southwest Pacific area;

Japan to withdraw her troops from Indo-China

when peace is restored between Japan and China or an equitable peace is established in the Pacific area;

Japan in the meantime to remove her troops from southern to northern Indo-China, upon conclusion of the present agreement;

Japan and the United States to cooperate toward acquiring goods and commodities that the two countries need in the Netherlands East Indies;

Japan and the United States to restore their commercial relations to those prevailing prior to the freezing of assets, and the United States to supply Japan a required quantity of oil;

The United States to refrain from such measures and actions as would prejudice endeavors for the restoration of peace between Japan and China.

THE WHITE HOUSE, WASHINGTON, D.C.—
THURSDAY, NOVEMBER 20, 1941

"Is this worth a damn?"

Stimson spoke up. "Hell, no. If we were at war with these sons of bitches, this would be our surrender."

Roosevelt seemed impatient with Stimson's comment, looked at Hull. "Well?"

"My people have gone over every piece of this. The Magic intercepts have confirmed what we had believed, that they have no intention of making a withdrawal from China. According to **Purple,** it's not in their planning right now. In other words, some of what you read here is . . . bull. They are requiring us to supply them with as much oil as they declare to be necessary, and nowhere here does it mention ending their alliance with Germany. It is reasonable to assume that we would become an open spigot, providing oil to the entire Axis alliance."

Roosevelt stared down at his desk. "I wonder what Churchill would think of that idea."

Stimson said, "Not much. He'd be fighting German planes filled with American gasoline."

Hull said, "That's certainly a possibility. They offer assurances here that they would not make further forays into Southeast Asia and the South Pacific, though they don't mention Asia, including Russia, Australia, and that part of China not now occupied. We would be compelled to withdraw aid to China, and allow, or even assist, the Japanese to take whatever resources they wish from the Netherlands East Indies."

Roosevelt shook his head. "The Dutch would hate us for decades."

"Yes, sir. Rightfully so."

"How do you intend to handle this?"

Hull glanced around the office, the military chiefs waiting for his answer, Stimson with a look of utter disgust.

"If we were to agree with these proposals, it would mean we condone Japan's most hostile and barbaric actions so far. We would be abandoning our allies China and Russia. It would allow Japan to march roughshod over just about any territory she wishes to occupy. And, nowhere here is there any mention of a pledge to maintain friendly relations with us, nor to respect our sovereignty. In other words, we would be giving all, and receiving nothing. I would like to prepare a counterproposal, spell out exactly what we feel must happen, what they must agree to."

Stimson seemed to growl, said, "Maybe you should tell those bastards to take their demands and put them where the sun . . . the **rising sun** doesn't shine."

Roosevelt ignored Stimson, looked at the others. "Secretary Knox, any thoughts? It's your ships that might get pulled into something pretty damn nasty out there."

Knox looked at General Marshall beside him. "We've been anticipating something along these lines since the last **Purple** intercept. There is no doubt that the Japanese are handing us an ultimatum. We go along, or there will be war. But from all we know of them, they are most likely to strike southward. The greatest threat to us is the Philippines."

Marshall said, "I agree, but I must emphasize that we need time, Mr. President. I believe that once we're up and running, no army on earth can match ours. But right now, it would be a serious challenge to wage all-out war, especially since we have to assume the war would be on two fronts. If Japan declares war on us, Hitler would surely follow suit. As I said, sir, we just need a little time. Our best estimate is that the Japanese will make a move against us next spring. That should fit well with our own planning. For now, I certainly support Secretary Hull's willingness to offer the Japanese a way out, a way for their government to back down from all those threats and still save face. That seems to mean a great deal to those people."

Roosevelt let out a deep breath, sat back. "I suspect you're right. Fine, Cordell, put something together as quick as you can. You know these people better than anyone here. Communicate to Ambassador Nomura and that other fellow that we're still absolutely seeking a peaceful solution to this mess."

Hull said, "The first step is to officially decline their proposal. I'll meet with Nomura and Kurusu immediately. I cannot believe they prefer a war. But their government has backed itself, and us, into a corner. General Marshall is correct: I do believe they will go to war to avoid a loss of face."

Stimson grunted, said, "They will go to war anytime and anyplace it suits them. Saving face has nothing to do with it. The Japanese are notorious for attacking without warning. You can be certain that they will not hesitate to start a war, regardless of how much talking we may do. You can't trust anything those people say, Cordell, and you know that better than anyone in this room."

Hull felt buried by a curtain of gloom. "It is hard to disagree. Right now, the Japanese are in control of this situation. We are not." He looked at Marshall, who showed no expression, staring back at him. "General, if, as you say, we require time to be prepared, I would estimate that they do not. They have been preparing in fact for some time, especially since their alliance with the Germans. I do not believe there is anything further the State Department can do to solve this problem. The word 'peace' is easily tossed around by Ambassador Nomura, and it has no more meaning here than it does in Tokyo. The Japanese are likely to break out at any time with acts of substantial force. While I do not shirk my department's responsibilities, I am convinced that our national security lies in the hands of the army and navy."

Stimson said, "I assure you, Cordell, you may depend on the military to handle any crisis."

Hull saw all eyes on him now, a hint of defensiveness in all of them. "I would only add that any plan from our military leaders should include the assumption that the Japanese might make the element of surprise a central point in their strategy. There is simply too much emphasis from their representatives here that all is well, while they speak privately of deadlines. That's only my opinion, of course. It's all I can offer you."

Roosevelt stared at Hull, then at the others.

"Thank you, Cordell. I pray you are mistaken, that you misread their intentions. I pray you are all mistaken." He paused, thought for a moment, the room silent. "I must do what is required, no matter the difficulty, no matter the gravity of the crisis. But I never expected to be a wartime president. I've thought about what that means, how that has gone in our history. Woodrow Wilson, McKinley, Lincoln, Polk, Madison. None are truly remembered for that, other than Lincoln. But it doesn't diminish the awful responsibility. I know there are some who believe we should take the bull by the horns and preemptively crush the Japanese military. Would that make our lives easier? I will not speak for the young men who would have to carry out that policy. Men would die because we were not patient."

Stimson said, "Men will die whether we're patient or not."

"Henry, I will not be the president who started a war, not while there is any possibility of an alternative. Cordell, you're the champion among us of **talk.** I do not intend that as an insult. Your opinions are noted, but you are still in daily contact with those people. That is still our priority. Offer them what you have to, and demand what we must have. Dammit, find a way."

Hull saw the others' eyes on him, all the military chiefs who seemed to view the situation through a single set of eyes. "Yes, sir. I'll do what I can, as quickly as possible. I want to believe that they aren't interested in killing their young men any more than we want to kill ours. They understand what is at stake here."

Stimson sniffed, glanced at Marshall and Knox. "And if they don't?"

Roosevelt stared at Stimson, said, "Then, Henry, may God have mercy on our souls."

# TWENTY-SIX

# Yamamoto

"By Imperial Order, the Chief of the Naval General Staff orders Yamamoto Commander in Chief of the Combined Fleet as follows: Expecting to go to war with the United States, Britain, and the Netherlands early in December for self-preservation and self-defense, the Empire has decided to complete war preparations. The Commander in Chief of the Combined Fleet will carry out the necessary operational preparations. Its details will be directed by the Chief of the Naval General Staff."

ONBOARD BATTLESHIP NAGATO, IWAKUNI, JAPAN —
MONDAY, NOVEMBER 17, 1941

He had known the order was coming, and was both grateful and skeptical. They will bask in the credit for our success, he thought. Or, they will blame me for getting it all wrong. "Carry out the necessary operational preparations." There is no casual meaning there. If everything goes wrong, then of course it will mean I did not adequately carry out the preparations.

And what do I believe? Is this the opening act of a magnificent victory, glory to the emperor, perhaps glory for **me**?

He stood on the upper deck, staring toward the town, the morning sun still below the horizon. He thought of the young men he had trusted, good minds, fertile with ideas. They will take charge of all this, perhaps very soon. The old men cannot adapt to what a war will do to us. They speak of their own experiences, the legacy of our great victories. But that was forty years ago, a fight with the Russians, and the spoils of that great victory were a few islands in the north. Had we lost, then what? We might have given them a few islands of our own. Now the stakes are higher. We will fight now for survival.

Yamamoto had ordered that those ships and aircraft designated to make the journey to Hawaii go through a detailed rehearsal. There was criticism of that, some of the senior officers in Tokyo concerned that it was only a waste of precious fuel. But Yamamoto knew that the exercise was essential, not just for training, but to build the confidence of the men who had to perform the most dangerous mission of their lives.

The rehearsal had been spread out over three days, witnessed and supervised primarily by his chief of staff, Admiral Ugaki. The armada had been maneuvered into attack formation some two hundred miles out to sea, mimicking the approaches to Pearl Harbor as much as possible. The pilots had gone through their routines, bombing runs and torpedo launches, the Zeros rehearsing their positions high above, then diving low in strafing runs. Yamamoto knew it didn't really matter if the rehearsal ended in success or failure, that nothing would change the plan. Though he had hoped to observe some of the activity, Yamamoto had instead been summoned to Tokyo by the prime minister's office and the army chiefs, who insisted he be included in meetings to discuss the many parts of the war they were preparing to fight.

The most intriguing part of those meetings had been the puzzle of Hideki Tojo. It had been a great surprise when the prime minister singled Yamamoto out for a private conversation. At first Tojo teased him for keeping secrets, since for most of the year, the army had not been informed what Yamamoto was planning to do. The army ministers had only been notified of the Hawaii plan in October, not long before Tojo had taken power. But there was a menace to Tojo, as though the man trusted no one, and regarded Yamamoto as a potential threat. Yamamoto could only guess that Tojo's rise to power had come at the forceful expense of others. And so, he would be correct to fear the next in line, who might be just as **forceful** with him.

There had been another surprise as well. It involved the army's requisition of his own ships to move a substantial number of soldiers southward. The surprise was that the approval had been given by the Naval Ministry without much debate, and the ships were already preparing to receive their human cargo. Tens of thousands of troops were preparing to make the journeys, whose destinations included Indo-China, the Malay Peninsula, Borneo, and Thailand and, to protect the flank of such a convoy, there would be an invasion force designated to strike the Philippines.

No matter all the concerns that had floated through the Naval Ministry about the risks of starting a war with the United States, the army and Prime Minister Tojo had no such qualms. While Yamamoto's Hawaii plan was still shrouded in absolute secrecy, the army seemed unconcerned about hiding these southbound invasion forces; if Japan's enemies learned of the move, so be it. Other than Douglas MacArthur's B-17s around Manila, there was no force strong enough to put a dent in Tojo's intentions.

When Yamamoto was finally able to leave Tokyo,
he returned to the **Nagato,** and for a few days at
least, he was able to enjoy the sanctuary of his own
flagship. Each morning had been the same—awake
very early, enjoying the peacefulness of the open
decks and the chilly air, a precious hour when he
would be unbothered by messages from the fleet or
the usual business from his staff.

He looked toward the sun, the first glow out
beyond the mouth of the harbor, across the wide
ocean. Tojo knows nothing of ships and airplanes, he
thought, but he understands the notion of **attack.**
Perhaps he is one of the few who truly believes in
war, a man with no fear, no hesitation, a man willing to drive a nail into a board with his head. Our
plan has audacity, and so he is happy. How will he
feel two years from now, when the great American
giant has been awakened, when they strike back at
us with a power we cannot yet imagine? And what
of the British? The Dutch? The Australians?

No, do not think on all of that. Tojo is with you.
Most of them are with you. For now, they have left
full command of the Hawaii force with you. Be
pleased with that.

He watched a small fishing boat slide past, an elderly man ignoring the great ship as he moved by.
Yamamoto smiled, thought, What do you know of
our world, old man? Do you believe war is a positive
thing, that your life will be better? Or are we just
an annoyance, my beautiful battleship blocking you

from a good fishing hole? Do you have a young son, a grandson perhaps? To him, our war will be more than an **annoyance.** The young men will fight, they will **have** to fight. It is simply the way.

"Sir?"

He turned to the young officer, realized it was raining, said, "Yes, what is it, Ensign?"

"Sir, you have a guest. She has been escorted to just outside your quarters."

Yamamoto couldn't help a smile, thinking, It has been so long. But he imagined the awkwardness she must feel, standing in a cold passageway, probably with a guard.

"You do not leave her standing there, Ensign. You will immediately allow her entry to my quarters. Is Admiral Ugaki aware of her arrival?"

"I'm not certain, sir."

"Once she is in my quarters, inform him of her presence. I must know well in advance when we are getting under way, so she may leave the ship. She will not accompany us to Saeki Bay."

"Understood, sir. It shall be done."

The young ensign moved away quickly, and Yamamoto blinked through the misty wetness, brushed at the dampness on his coat. Present yourself well, Admiral. She will expect that.

He followed the trail of the young ensign, climbed the first ladder, moved past sailors who watched him with knowing glances. But they said nothing, made no impolite comments he would ever hear. I wonder how she climbed through the passageways, he thought. Somehow she is just there, and there is never a complaint. I should have a talk with the officer of the deck. Perhaps someone carries her. He laughed as he moved to the next ladder. Now, there is a magnificently awful idea. She would no doubt prefer to carry me. And that would not look good to the crew.

His mood had lightened considerably, and he stopped outside of his quarters, caught his breath from the climb. He heard a noise from inside, pulled open the hatchway, saw her bending low beside his bed. He waited as she finished sweeping dust from the deck with a small broom. He cleared his throat and she stood, turned to him, hands now on her hips.

"How do you create such a mess? You make dirt just by standing there. I do not understand how you can tolerate these conditions."

"Sorry, my flower. It seems that you do enjoy cleaning up after me. I like providing you entertainment so early in the morning."

She glared at him, but he knew she was not angry. It was all just a part of their game.

"This is not entertainment, Admiral. It is necessity. You require a healthy place to sleep. Since neither you nor your officers will make that effort, I will."

"Who escorted you here?"

"Your wonderfully kind staff officer, Captain Kuroshima."

"Did he carry you?"

"Am I to laugh at your poor joke? I am quite capable of climbing ladders. And he did not drop a single ash on me from his cigarette."

"Now who makes poor jokes?" He smiled at her, and she bowed toward him. The game had passed, and she returned his smile, the soft warmth of her eyes spreading through him. He caught the flowery fragrance of her perfume, said, "I have suffered long nights without you. I am sorry we could not be together in Tokyo. It was a tedious nightmare. I wanted you here, even if for a short time. This might be the only place I truly feel . . . safe. I am so very happy you are here."

"How long do we have, Iso?"

"We leave for Saeki Bay very soon. I will be informed when Admiral Ugaki has made preparations. I am so sorry to put you through the journey here. I will make it up to you, I promise. How was the train?"

"I had a sleeping car. That is very rare for a woman. Someone surely thought I was important."

"Someone was correct."

There was a soft knock outside the steel hatch, and Yamamoto said, "Yes?"

"Sir, very sorry to bother you, but Admiral Ugaki

wishes you to know that we shall be under way in two hours."

"Thank you. Tell the admiral I acknowledge his message."

He looked at her again, the silk of her dress, realized she was standing taller than he was.

"Chiyoko, if you please. You may remove your shoes."

AIRCRAFT CARRIER AKAGI, SAEKI BAY, JAPAN—
MONDAY, NOVEMBER 17, 1941

He stood in the blustery winds, the flight deck of the carrier lined with more than a hundred men, a mix of officers and many of the senior commanders who would lead the flying squadrons and others who would carry out more details of the plans that he and his officers had designed. He waited, no one speaking, all eyes on him.

"I do not have a written speech for you. You are beyond that. The admirals, the men who argued and debated and added and subtracted . . . those men no longer have meaning to you. What matters now is the heart of this crew, these officers, these pilots. You are going a very long way to accomplish a very difficult mission. It is possible that you will find the path to be without resistance, that we will have achieved the kind of surprise we have hoped for. It is also possible that you will have to fight your way to reach the enemy targets, that they will be expecting us.

"In our history, Japan has faced many powerful enemies—Mongols, Russians, Chinese—but the enemy we will now encounter is the strongest and most resourceful of all. Many of our citizens, and possibly many of you, believe that the Americans are a weak and decadent people. Do not embrace that fallacy. Our goal is to strike, and strike hard, to damage and cripple and kill that powerful foe. But that will not end the war that we seek. It is never that simple, and we must be prepared for whatever follows."

He paused, saw men glancing at each other. "My opponent in this encounter is named Admiral Kimmel. He is a junior grade admiral, and yet he was appointed to command their Pacific fleet. He is surely able, gallant, and brave, and you may be certain that he will put up a courageous fight. It is the custom of the Bushido for the warrior to choose an equal or stronger opponent. On this score, you have no complaint. The American navy is a good match for us. Embrace that."

He paused again, scanned the faces. "I have heard it said that a surprise assault such as we are doing here lacks honor. I have heard that a warrior must stand in front of his enemy and challenge on equal ground. There are those, some in Tokyo, others perhaps on this ship, who would believe that Japan and the United States should be like two sumo wrestlers, equal in size and strength, standing chest to chest, that what we are planning against Hawaii is not . . . proper. I do not agree. Secrecy and deception in war is often how one **wins** that war. And it is my preference that we **win** this fight.

"I will let others judge if we fought with honor. But I will judge you right now. I know how you have trained, I know how much work all of you have done, and I know the dedication you have for completing this mission. If I was a younger man, and I had the skills of the pilot, I would be in a plane, joining you in the attack. And so, I leave it to the younger men here to guide you. I will shake every hand upon your return. And the emperor will salute you. I wish you success, a safe voyage home, and the blessings of God."

He didn't hesitate, walked over to the flight leader, Commander Fuchida, held out his hand. He saw tears in Fuchida's eyes, the man's hand in his now. Yamamoto bowed slowly, his final salute. There was nothing left to say.

The submarines were the first to leave, slipping out to sea on November 18. Five of them carried the midget craft strapped to their hulls. Each of the odd craft carried a pair of torpedoes and were manned by two crewmen. Those men understood that their journey was most likely one-way.

By the next day, the rest of the submarines had begun their journey, some of them to positions around Hawaii, some going even farther, between Hawaii and the West Coast of the United States. Their captains knew that when the war began in earnest, the submarines would seek targets, whether warships or any other craft with an American flag.

As Yamamoto returned to his flagship **Nagato,** he stayed in radio contact with the fleet for as long as the radios were functioning. But as scheduled, those radios soon went silent. For the next few days, the ships designated as the combined fleet moved out of seaports scattered all over Japan. With no fanfare or any public notice, they made their way north. They would make their rendezvous in the Kurile Islands, Hitokappu Bay, far to the north, and far from the eyes of even their own citizens.

By November 23, the ships had crowded into Hitokappu Bay, cruisers and battleships, destroyers and the tankers that would keep them all running. But of the thirty-three ships, the greatest attention was paid to the six aircraft carriers, a full complement of planes on each one. Of the vast quantities of supplies and armament, there was one cargo that held the attention of Commander Genda. As the crates were brought aboard carrier **Akagi,** he anxiously examined the contents, breathlessly aware that this might decide the success or futility of the mission. To Genda's relief, the quantity matched the promises, the ship's crew going to work to install the new equipment, the torpedo modifiers, the oddly simple pieces that would allow the torpedoes to run in shallow water.

ONBOARD BATTLESHIP NAGATO, IWAKUNI, JAPAN—
   TUESDAY, NOVEMBER 25, 1941

It was even earlier than usual for him to be awake; the only crew Yamamoto saw were the men of the night watch. He had gone first to the bridge, acknowledged a guard, then back down the ladders, wandering through one of the massive gun turrets. He was outside again now, walking slowly along the rail on the main deck, his hand hopping along the steel cable. He looked to the east, saw only the first hint of sunrise, shivered, though he wore his coat. I should be sleeping, he thought. No, I shouldn't. I can't anyway, even if I wanted to. I need tea. No, sake perhaps. No, don't be a fool. He stopped, debated what to do next, turned, walked back along the rail, saw faint lights from the town, the early risers, thought, Workers perhaps, starting their day. He looked down to the water, wondered if there were fisherman. Well, of course there are. You eat their fish, don't you? All right, maybe you should go back up to the bridge. The captain should be awake, and he will have tea. Perhaps there, you will find some **calm.**

"Sir?"

**"What?"**

His response burst out with more volume than he intended. He was surprised to see Kuroshima, the man engulfed by the smoke and the smell of his cigarette.

"Sir, I didn't mean to startle you. Very sorry. Admiral Ugaki is searching for you. I thought you might be out here. I rather like the dark before dawn."

**"Why is he looking for me?"** It was too loud again, but Yamamoto made no apology, waited for the response, an agonizing second.

"Sir, the radio signal has come in, as you requested. I am honored to convey the message to you that the fleet has left Hitokappu Bay and has put to sea. It has begun, sir."

Yamamoto turned toward the dawn, felt his heart racing, said, "Yes. It has begun."

# TWENTY-SEVEN

# Hull

As promised, Hull delivered the American counterproposals for the president's approval within twenty-four hours of rejecting the Japanese ultimatum. With Roosevelt's approval, Hull immediately presented the terms of his new proposals to Nomura and Kurusu. Hull's ten points specified the demands and concessions that he had outlined to the president the day before.

Chief among the points were that Japan withdraw its troops from China, as well as Southeast Asia. Hull intended that to be a necessary message to America's allies all over the world that the president would not sacrifice any nation just to appease Japan. Hull also proposed that Japan withdraw from her alliance with Germany, canceling the Tripartite Pact. Through Magic intercepts and other intelligence data, Washington already knew that the Japanese were uncomfortable with that alliance, and that Germany, embroiled in its invasion of the Soviet Union, had little confidence that Japan would offer any substantial assistance. Add to that the air of mutual distrust between the two widely diverse cultures, and Hull believed that the Japanese might welcome the opportunity to pull out of the alliance.

The proposals also included offers to resume trade relations, to eliminate the oil embargo, to support the sagging value of the Japanese yen, and to take other measures to compensate Japan for the loss of resources that she might otherwise take from the weaker nations in the southern Pacific.

As Hull expected, Kurusu had little optimism that the ten-point proposal would be welcomed in Tokyo, though he assured Hull that it would be communicated by telephone to his superiors. This level of urgency suggested to Hull that the Japanese were actually intending a serious response. But to his frustrated disappointment, the face-to-face meeting the next day produced nothing more than the usual smiles and pleasant conversation, punctuated by the regrets of the two Japanese officials that the terms were unacceptable. The explanation offered by Kurusu was a simple definition of the obvious cultural divide between Japan and the United States.

To the Japanese, control and occupation of China, Korea, and any other nation or territory along the Pacific basin was their destiny; the utter inferiority of so many other cultures made that imperative.

Hull could sense that Nomura was not completely comfortable with that kind of absolute justification for going to war, but Hull could plainly see that the ambassador no longer had the authority, beyond his title, to negotiate anything. As he sat beside Nomura, Kurusu was unabashedly in charge, doing most of the talking. And, Kurusu again gave Hull pleasantly worded assurances that the Japanese government would give serious consideration to any additional proposals Hull might offer. But he had heard that before.

THE WHITE HOUSE, WASHINGTON, D.C.—
    THURSDAY, NOVEMBER 27, 1941

The call had been urgent, the president's aide insisting that Hull make the short journey from the State Department as quickly as possible.

The marine guard stood aside, Roosevelt's aide peering into the Oval Office, then back out.

"You may go in, Mr. Secretary."

Hull stepped inside, found Roosevelt rifling through a thick stack of papers, a cigarette jammed into the tight clench in his jaw.

"Sit, Cordell."

Hull didn't like seeing the president in this kind of

foul mood, had been concerned about Roosevelt's health for some time. There was nothing specific, no illness that anyone had diagnosed. But Hull had known him for too many years not to notice that the kind of stress Roosevelt was under had seemed to weaken him.

He sat, waited, wanted to offer something light-hearted, a joke about the mountains of papers, but the president seemed too angry. He attacked the paperwork with a pen, violently scribbling his signature. Hull sat quietly, his eyes drifting around the office, and suddenly Roosevelt said, "Stimson called you."

It was not a question, and Hull said, "Yes, sir. This morning. Asked me where we were with the Japanese."

"I know what he asked you. I know what you told him. I know exactly what those sons of bitches are trying to do."

Hull wasn't sure how to respond, said, "If you mean talk and more talk, yes. They tell us what they want, and we're supposed to give it to them. We tell them what we want and they toss that in our faces."

"So, I guess you haven't been briefed. Good. Some people still know how to keep their mouths shut around here. I wanted you to hear this from me."

Hull felt a jab of alarm. "Hear what, sir?"

Roosevelt shoved the paperwork to one side, still obviously angry. "Our intelligence people in Southeast Asia and the Philippines have verified that, while we were playing patty-cake with that pair of weasels, the Japanese launched a series of transport ships, stuffed with troops, sailing southward from Japan. Their intention, so we believe, is to invade the Malay Peninsula, and most likely the Philippines. There could be other targets as well, but those are the ones we're most concerned about, obviously. The British are scrambling to reinforce Singapore as we speak. We still anticipate an additional invasion force to move northward to the Soviet seaports. Hate to leave the Russians out of the party."

"So, that's why the secretary of war called me."

"Well, we can't slip anything past you." Roosevelt paused. "Sorry. I've got no reason to jump down your throat. But there's a beehive of activity going on right now in the War Department, and not just with Stimson. He's been huddled with the whole gang there all day. They are putting together a serious communiqué going out to the primary Pacific commands. Admiral Kimmel is commander of the whole theater, Admiral Hart's in the Philippines with MacArthur. General Short commands the army units in Hawaii, Admiral Bloch the naval base. You know the chief of naval operations, Admiral Stark?"

"Yes, sir. Betty."

Roosevelt shook his head. "Makes it hard to take him seriously sometimes. Some people think he chose the nickname, but I think I started it. The admiral is a direct descendant of the Revolutionary War general John Stark. There's some legend or myth or whatever about him going into battle and calling out the name of his wife. Her name was Molly, I think. Somewhere it got changed to Betty, and the admiral must have liked it, so he never changed it back. I rather thought it fit him, so he's been 'Betty' for a long time now. He doesn't seem to mind, and I like it better than Harold. Anyway, Stark is putting together a war-warning letter to the naval commands, and they'll be instructed to pass it along to the army. This will damn sure put everybody on their toes, all over the Pacific. If the Japs hit the Philippines, as it seems they're planning to do, Admiral Hart and General MacArthur should be ready to give them a hell of a welcome."

Hull absorbed Roosevelt's mood, the urgency suddenly shifting direction from all the empty talk with the Japanese to something very much more serious.

"Is there anything else you want me to do? Ambassador Nomura is still willing to discuss all of this, I'm certain. Kurusu . . . I'm not really interested in what he's got to say. He might as well be reading the text off our own intercepts. He repeats most of that word for word anyway."

Roosevelt stared at him, jammed the cigarette into an ashtray. "Talk all you want. Those weasel-worded bastards know full well that all they've done is put off the inevitable. They've killed time, a lot of time, while their superiors in Tokyo have charged ahead with what they intended to do in the first place."

Hull looked down, shook his head. "Who hopes for war, who believes it's a good idea to start one? What do they think will happen?"

Roosevelt seemed exhausted, his breathing labored. "There are people in Tokyo who are modeling what they do after Hitler. It seems they haven't noticed that the Germans are getting chewed to pieces in Russia. But there's something very attractive about absolute power, total control. The Japanese won't be happy with your proposal, or anyone else's, until they grab and hold on to every place they've chosen on the map. We don't yet know what that means. The British don't know, and they're bracing for what happens next. That's what we've told Admiral Stark to do—communicate in the strongest language possible that we must be prepared for whatever it is the Japanese will do next. There can be no mistakes, no confusion."

## FROM CHIEF OF NAVAL OPERATIONS ADMIRAL STARK

This dispatch is to be considered a war warning. Negotiations with Japan looking toward stabilization of conditions in the Pacific have ceased and an aggressive move by Japan is expected within the next few days. The number and equipment of

Japanese troops and the organization of naval task
forces indicates an amphibious expedition against
either the Philippines, Thai or Kra Peninsula or
possibly Borneo. Execute an appropriate defensive
deployment preparatory to carrying out the tasks
assigned in WPL 46. Inform district and Army
authorities. A similar warning is being sent by
War Department . . .

# PART THREE

"Does it seem as if a child might be born?"
(Response) "Yes. The birth of a child
seems imminent."

—Japanese special envoy Kurusu,
correspondence with foreign ministry—
November 27, 1941

"[In December 1941] the Commander in
Chief of the U.S. Fleet had been known as
CINCUS . . . This was later thought utterly
inappropriate, as it is (of course) pronounced
'sink us.'"

—Vice Admiral Charles Wellborn Jr.,
United States Navy (Ret.)

"[Japan] cannot attack us. That is a
military impossibility."

—Chicago Tribune, "Navy Day,"
October 27, 1941

# TWENTY-EIGHT

# Rochefort

HQ, 14TH NAVAL DISTRICT, PEARL HARBOR, HAWAII—
FRIDAY, NOVEMBER 28, 1941

The air was thick with the sweat of a dozen men, most poring over the latest radio intercepts from Japanese ships, transmissions that might offer a single morsel of information that would help pinpoint that ship's location. Rochefort sat at his desk, checking the translation of one particular message, scribbling a correction along one edge of the paper.

"Ensign Cabot."

"Sir?"

"Where do you get 'moonlight' out of this? These are literally the symbols for 'after midnight,' but the whole expression translates to an activity scheduled to begin in early morning. The coding indicates a heavy cruiser, which I've been following since they put to sea on twenty-four November. They will probably reach their destination by tomorrow morning, which would put them close to the Philippines. That makes a little more sense, wouldn't you agree?"

Cabot was appropriately chastened, said, "Of course, sir. I'll be more careful."

"You'll do more than that. We have no time for sloppiness in here. I've had to look over your shoulder a half dozen times this week. Can't have that. You understand?"

"Yes, sir. I'll do better."

Rochefort thought, He doesn't take a dressing-down worth a damn. Now he looks like a whipped puppy. But damn it all, we can't be screwing around in here. No patience for that, none. The others had glanced his way, returned now to their work. He had tried to offer encouragement to them all—the old pat on the back, could even toss out a good joke once in a while—but most of the time, any joviality he might feel was overshadowed by his impatience. Dammit, he thought, they know I've got a short fuse, and I'm not a nursemaid to these jokers. Nobody's being especially nice to me.

He could see frustration on some of the faces, weariness on others. A long day, he thought. We're just now breaking the November signal codes. I've got no patience for wasting time.

The air conditioning was haphazard at best, which only added to the dismal environment, but Rochefort had no use for complaints. The workplace for Rochefort's team was called the Dungeon, appropriately named. It was a large room with no windows, down a full flight of stairs beneath one of the primary headquarters buildings for the Fourteenth Naval District. Officially, Rochefort's department was designated HYPO, the navy's way of specifying the location as H for Hawaii. The Dungeon was the best facility the navy seemed willing to offer the cryptanalytic experts, what Rochefort knew was a typical disregard for the men who labored to decode foreign messages.

The Dungeon's working conditions seemed to Rochefort to be a perfectly appropriate symbol for the way Naval Intelligence was regarded by most of the admirals throughout the service. As far back as Rochefort could recall, the decoding and cryptography offices had been treated as a stepchild to the more "important" commands, an attitude that extended all the way to the highest levels in Washington. Even now, the Office of Naval Intelligence, headed by Captain T. S. Wilkinson, had lost a turf war for most of its usual responsibilities, a short-lived feud with Admiral Richmond K. Turner, chief of the Navy's War Plans Division. As a result, the intel officers, who should have been receiving and interpreting all manner of potentially useful intelligence, had seen their duties gutted by an egocentric admiral who seemed more interested in enlarging his own footprint.

Even worse, Rochefort couldn't avoid an instinctive itch that Washington was processing and interpreting considerably more intelligence information than was being revealed to any intelligence office in Hawaii. He had no real evidence of that, and it wasn't the sort of thing to complain about to a superior, certainly not to the admirals who oversaw his department. But the messages Rochefort knew about, those received by Admiral Kimmel and the commander in chief's own intel officers, seemed to be bare-bones at best. It would be foolish, and for Rochefort potentially career-threatening, to suggest that Washington was purposely withholding anything. But Rochefort had always relied on his instincts. The **itch** was something he couldn't escape.

Since Rochefort's arrival at Pearl Harbor in May, he had experienced the frustration that any substantive intelligence uncovered by his own crew would likely be digested only as far up the chain as the senior commanders in Hawaii. After that, it might as well have been tossed in the sea. It showed the chronic disregard for the intelligence service in general, whether in Washington or anywhere else in the field, as far back as Rochefort's service in the Great War. Some of that came officially from Henry Stimson, now secretary of war, who had long ago declared it inappropriate for anyone, even a nation potentially under threat, to open anyone else's mail.

Secretary Stimson's attitude was driven downward, all through the ranks, until finally it had become accepted fact that assignment to intelligence was a dead end to any kind of advancement. Rochefort had accepted this as the price for doing work he truly enjoyed. With a variety of successes decrypting Japanese codes as early as the 1920s, Rochefort had seemed to find his place in a command that others continued to shun. Unlike many of the higher-ranking officers around him, mostly a fraternity of Naval Academy graduates, Rochefort had joined the navy straight out of high school. Yet his instincts for decryption had propelled him to the rank of commander. He knew, as did those who knew him, that as long as his work bore useful fruit, no one would care where he'd gone to school.

Once established at Pearl Harbor, Rochefort found a new challenge. Since no one had any interest in looking over his shoulder, no one above him seemed to care just who had specific authority over the results of his work. Rochefort's superior was technically Captain Irving Mayfield, who answered to the commander of the Fourteenth, Admiral Bloch. But Bloch rarely offered input of his own, simply passing along any meaningful information to his superior, Admiral Kimmel. Along the way, there were various other department heads who had some sort of hazy authority over Mayfield's department and Rochefort's team, though few seemed to pay much attention to what Rochefort was actually doing. To Rochefort, that was just fine.

The most effective and desirable connection that led directly to Admiral Kimmel's office was the fleet's overall intelligence officer, Commander Edwin Layton. But there was more to Rochefort's relationship with Layton than a shared interest in cryptology or code intercepts. Earlier in their careers, both men had spent considerable time in Japan, and like Rochefort, Layton spoke fluent Japanese. If there was a hint of envy that Rochefort felt toward his friend, it was only that Layton had developed a friendship with the man who was now the commander in chief of the Japanese combined fleet, Admiral Isoroku Yamamoto. It required patience from Rochefort, not his most developed talent, to hear Layton tell the story he'd heard dozens of times, how Layton had so often defeated Admiral Yamamoto in games of bridge.

Both men knew that Layton did not quite have Rochefort's raw talent for his job, and so Layton had come to rely on him more than Layton's superiors might respect. But as long as their intelligence was accurate and useful, no one would object. Since he had taken command of HYPO, Rochefort's attention had been focused primarily on radio traffic originating from Japanese ships, the only effective way to estimate their locations from so far away. Though his team had clear interpretations of barely 10 percent of the coded transmissions, his skill at identification could fill in many of the gaps.

More important, he had become familiar with the distinct patterns of messages from many of the ships, and could identify some of the ships by the rhythm of certain keystrokes or other tendencies of the particular radio and telegraph operators. Again, much of that was Rochefort's instincts, not something he could teach to his crew. But he had trained them as much as possible to consider the fragments they could identify as part of a greater puzzle. As time had passed, they were gaining proficiency. Even without a clear interpretation of the bulk of the Japanese messages, Rochefort had developed the ability to locate most of the Japanese navy's most powerful ships. And, as any fleet officer would know, if you locate a battleship or aircraft carrier, you've located a supporting cast of smaller ships to go along with it.

Weeks before, without any scraps of useful intelligence from Washington, Rochefort had been able to confirm what most of the highest-ranking officials were suggesting, that a great part of the Japanese fleet had set sail from their ports in Japan, and were on the move southward toward Indo-China.

The guard knocked on the metal door, and Rochefort pointed, the closest man rising up quickly to respond. Rochefort saw the guard, the man peering in as though expecting to see some sort of demonic behavior in the dingy grubbiness of the room.

Rochefort said, "What is it?" There was nothing friendly in Rochefort's words.

"Sir, there is a driver here, with orders from Commander Layton to transport you to CINCUS. Commander Layton will be waiting there."

"Why the hell don't we ever have any meetings down **here**? We've got a coffee pot that's as good as theirs. I'm a little busy."

The guard seemed puzzled, still peering into the dull light, and Rochefort said, "Relax, son. Jesus, doesn't anybody around here have a sense of humor?"

"Sorry, sir."

Rochefort scanned the room, saw eyes on him, then on the guard. "Yeah, I know. You're all trained to frown. Anybody's caught laughing around here, they ship him to Wake Island. Okay, son, you've delivered your message. I'll be upstairs in a minute." He shoved the most current papers into a folder, rose up from the steel desk, said, "I'll be back quick as I can. Nobody goes to get a beer. Keep working. We're damn close to figuring out the codes for the last period, and I want them completed."

Nobody responded, and Rochefort moved out, the guard leading the way up the steps. He passed by the offices of a variety of fleet departments, typewriters and telephones, then outside, saw several cars parked in the narrow lot. He searched for one with a driver, moved that way, opened the rear door himself, slid inside.

"Okay, what's up? Somebody sink the fleet without telling me about it?" There was no smile from the driver, a face Rochefort had seen before. "You know, you could have opened the door for me. If I was a damn admiral, you'd be out running around here making sure I didn't slam my pinky in the door. How fast can you drive? I have work to do."

"Whatever you say, sir."

The car lurched forward, a hard acceleration out onto the road. Rochefort saw the driver's eyes watching him in the rearview mirror, said, "Fine. That'll do. But keep your eyes on the damn road."

## HQ, COMMANDER IN CHIEF PACIFIC FLEET, PEARL HARBOR—FRIDAY, NOVEMBER 28, 1941

The car slid to a halt, Rochefort's stomach rolling over. He reminded himself, Don't razz the driver. He stepped unsteadily from the car, adjusted his uniform, tucked the folder under one arm. He glanced back at the driver, who nodded to him with a smirk.

Rochefort couldn't avoid the last word, said through the car window, "There's a word for cocky-assed sailors who piss off officers. It's called Guam."

The car drove away with none of the recklessness that had brought him there. He saw Layton standing outside, talking to a pair of young officers.

There was obviously nothing sociable about the conversation, unusual for Layton. The two younger men moved off quickly, into a car of their own, and Layton said to Rochefort, "Let's go inside, Joe."

Rochefort followed Layton quickly up the flight of stairs to Layton's office. Rochefort glanced toward the one window, a clear view of the open water. It was an odd decision to some, Admiral Kimmel moving his office away from his flagship, the USS **Pennsylvania.** The word had gotten around that Kimmel had been annoyed by the inconvenience of his communications flowing from ship to ship. The submarine base was, to Kimmel, a much more practical solution. If any of his officers thought it strange that the admiral of the entire fleet would establish himself in a land-based office, no one mentioned that to Kimmel.

Layton waited at the opening to his office, and Rochefort slid by him, sat in his usual chair.

"You're in a crappy mood, Eddie."

Layton settled in behind his desk, said, "We're getting a raft of information about the negotiations with the Japanese. It's more of the same. Washington seems to know things we don't, a whole bunch of things. I've sent letters to Naval Intelligence, to Admiral Turner, and I've asked Admiral Kimmel to push Admiral Stark. I would think they'd keep us informed of anything involving the Japanese, since we're pretty much on the front lines out here. So far, all I've received is this." He held up a letter.

"Commander McCollum, head of the ONI's Far Eastern Division. He writes a long message in babble-speak that could have been shortened to one damn word: **NO.** They're decoding Japanese messages that we aren't receiving, and they won't tell us why, and they won't tell us what those message are. How pissed off am I supposed to be?"

Rochefort looked at the letter. "Should I bother reading that?"

"I told you what it said. Five hundred words of double-talk, ending with a negative response."

"How's Admiral Kimmel reacting to this?"

"You can ask him yourself. But that's not why you're here. What can you tell me about the location of the Japanese fleet?"

Rochefort wanted to laugh, but Layton's expression didn't change.

"Jesus, you're serious. The whole damn fleet?"

"What do we know? What can we tell Kimmel?"

Rochefort opened the folder, but he knew it wasn't what Layton was asking for. "Here's our latest intercepts. They changed their radio addresses and service identification codes on 31 October, on schedule. That gives us another five months or so to map out who's who, and we're well along with that. We've just about completed identifying their battleships and cruisers, along with most of their submarines, which, for reasons I don't really understand, are far easier to decode. It's as though the Japanese don't care if we know the location of their subs.

"The best that we can determine is that the fleet we previously pinpointed moving to Southeast Asia is still headed that way. The Japanese don't seem to care who knows about it. I suppose, down there, no one's in their way. There are also the transport ships, most likely with cruiser and destroyer escorts moving toward the southern tip of the Philippines, passing to the south of Basilan Island. Again, either they don't seem to care that we know or they aren't aware that we know, which I find hard to believe—as many spies as there are on Hawaii, count at least that many in the Philippines.

"I'll tell you, picking up the main radio transmissions from the bases in Japan is like hearing a mother calling out to her kids. We just have to figure out how many kids she has, and where the hell they are."

"What about the battleships?"

"Most are with the fleet moving south. Likely, there is at least one with the Philippines convoy. Those we have not accounted for are likely in port in Japan. That makes sense, since there is no imminent danger of a major naval battle, and we know they're concerned about their fuel supplies, thanks to the oil embargo. We have also determined that the Japanese submarines are on the move, some of those around their bases in the Caroline and Marshall Islands and along the most heavily traveled shipping lanes, where we would expect them to be."

Layton stared down at his desk. "I have a problem

here, Joe. My people are picking up scraps of intel from local sources, some of that handed over from the FBI, Special Agent Shivers. But Japan's a long way away. That's what frustrates me about the information Washington is sending us. It's as though they're holding back, as though what **they're** doing is the only thing that's important. It's just damn aggravating that they act like it's private, that only Washington is privileged to know what the Japanese are talking about."

"I'm doing the best I can, Eddie."

"You know as well as I do that it's not just about machines and earphones. Your people do a hell of a job, putting together useful information from a five-second crackle on a Jap radio."

Rochefort could feel an odd tension in Layton, said, "Thanks for the compliment, Eddie. But you didn't send for me just to bitch. What the hell's going on?"

"I have to let the admiral tell you, if he's inclined. Don't ask, just do what you're told, answer his questions."

"Jesus, I've met him plenty of times before. He's not all that hard-assed."

Layton reached for a phone, dialed a pair of numbers. "Yes, this is Commander Layton. I have Commander Rochefort here, from HYPO. Is it a good time? Thank you. We'll be right up."

Layton moved around the desk, a hand now on Rochefort's shoulder, then led the way.

The admiral's office was strangely spartan, nothing to indicate who held court there. The chairs were all filled, and Rochefort recognized the faces of those who belonged there, including Captain "Poco" Smith, Kimmel's chief of staff. There were others, including some men Layton seemed to know well, and one army officer, a major Rochefort didn't know.

Kimmel acknowledged Layton with a quick nod, offered another toward Rochefort. But Rochefort could feel that this was more than the usual briefing about intel and fleet movements. Rochefort and Layton stood back against one wall, Kimmel speaking toward them now.

"Sorry there aren't sufficient chairs. My wardroom on the **Pennsylvania** was a palace compared to this place. I'll make this as brief as possible. Some of you have already been informed of the communication I received late yesterday from Admiral Stark. I have a copy here, and if you haven't seen it, read it now. The communication does not leave this office. Poco?"

Smith took the paper and gave a quick glance at the men seated. He moved toward Layton, handed him the paper, said, "Hand it to Commander Rochefort when you're done. The rest of us have already seen it."

Layton read, seemed to stare blankly at the paper for a long moment. He handed it to Rochefort.

**"This dispatch is to be considered a war warning . . ."**

Rochefort finished reading, absorbed the words, tried to interpret what lay between the lines, the code breaker's habit. He looked at Layton, waiting for a reaction, but Layton remained stoic, his eyes on Kimmel, who said, "Commander Rochefort, return the paper to Captain Smith. All right, everyone here has read this message, written or at least sent by Betty Stark. Hell, it could have come from the War Department, or, hell, maybe from the president. And there's the army's version, sent to General Short by way of General Marshall. Major Fleming has delivered us a copy, which most of you have seen, courtesy of General Short. I had a meeting late yesterday with the general and a number of senior commanders to discuss the differences in the two messages. The army's version is not quite as, well, dramatic as this one.

"It's possible, and I say this with utmost respect for Betty Stark, that he is crying wolf. It would not be the first time. We have received similar notes in the past, indicating Washington's concerns about all manner of potential difficulties we might be facing out here. It seems that the farther one gets from the War Department, the greater our dangers must seem to those people. Anyone reading the local newspapers here would believe there is a war breaking out every Sunday. I would imagine the same is true for anyone reading **The New York Times.**"

Kimmel took the paper from Smith, glanced at it. "This message specifically mentions those locales under threat of attack, and none of this is a surprise to us. It is my opinion that, should the Japanese insist on starting a war, our forces in the Philippines are in the greatest danger. Our island bases, notably Wake, Midway, and Guam, are also vulnerable. I have never believed we had any business trying to protect islands in the middle of absolute nowhere, with resources that could be put to better use right here. But I have been overruled.

"For that reason, I have instructed Admiral Halsey to command what we have designated as Task Force Eight. At 0800 this morning, the task force put to sea, led by Halsey's carrier, **Enterprise,** along with three cruisers and nine destroyers. Also included were three battleships. The show of force is partly for any hostile eyes who pay attention to such comings and goings. The task force is very similar in makeup to many of the standard training exercises we have scheduled in the past. Thus, there is no reason for anyone locally to pay any special attention. In fact, when the task force reaches the usual training area, the battleships will hold that position, and by Friday will return to port as per our usual practice. Halsey will keep going, with a primary mission to transport combat aircraft to Wake Island. He will also exercise his own discretion to seek out and destroy any Japanese submarines he may encounter."

Kimmel looked at the lone army officer, said, "All right, Major. Brief these men on the army's attitude about this mess."

The man glanced at the naval officers around him, said, "Sir, General Short is taking this message from the War Department very seriously. He has ordered Alert Number One, to be put into effect immediately."

Kimmel waited for more, then said, "He's told me about his new system. But explain to all of us what the hell that means."

"Yes, sir. General Short has created a system consisting of three alerts. Alert One is to enact a vigorous defense against sabotage, espionage, and subversive activities which do not include a threat from the outside. Alert Two includes the conditions for number one, plus defense against air, surface, and submarine attack. Alert Three is defense against all-out attack. Thus, sir, General Short is taking serious precautions to head off the possibility of sabotage against all our installations. Special attention will be paid to the activities of the Japanese indigenous population of the island, which as you know, sir, numbers some one hundred fifty thousand people."

From the far side of the room, Smith said, "Does the general have any serious indications that there are movements or organizations on the island of Oahu that would engage in acts of sabotage?"

The major stood now with the unmistakable air of a man with something important to say. "We have been working alongside the local FBI office here, as you have as well. We are fully prepared to corral any criminal elements should they attempt to make a subversive or destructive move against any of our installations." He looked at Kimmel now. "I might also add, sir, that General Short is pleased to communicate to the naval command that our training schedule shall not be interrupted or disrupted by the War Department's message. General Short feels most strongly that the ongoing training exercises for all of our forces are the highest priority. The gist of the War Department's message, as you know, sir, is that we be prepared in the event the Japanese should launch an attack against our interests in the Pacific. The most effective means of preparing is training. General Short assumes that you agree, sir."

Kimmel nodded. "Certainly."

"Sir, as well, General Short interprets his instructions from Washington as including two very important conditions. It is imperative that the local civilian population not be pushed toward a panic. In other words, we must not agitate the populace unnecessarily. In connection with that, sir, General Short is adamant that he will not be accused on any level of starting a war. If the local Japanese populace should rise up against us, it could have far-reaching consequences.

"To that end, the general is presently relocating arms and materiel, safeguarding our assets in the event of any attempts at sabotage. The general believes it is essential that we keep a close protective eye on our ordnance. This includes artillery, antiaircraft batteries, and fighter aircraft, including their stores of ammunition. All are being gathered and stored to ensure their readiness should the need arise. As General Short put it, sir, he wants to keep our powder dry and our ammunition clean. And, if most of that is under lock and key, it becomes far easier to protect it against the saboteurs. If we require the ammunition, we will access it on an as-needed basis. I must add, Admiral, that General Short feels the presence of your fleet in port here is an enormous deterrent to the threat from subversive elements."

Kimmel seemed to digest the man's report, then said, "Major, I will not offer opinions on General Short's command or his decisions. He has his duties, I have mine. I'm confident that General Short also accepts that one of the army's primary responsibilities in Hawaii is to protect the fleet when we're in the harbor."

He paused. "Unlike the message General Short received from the War Department, what I was told by Admiral Stark is that we are to assume a 'defensive posture.' Admittedly, I am not completely clear on that meaning, since, as these men know well, in the navy there is no such thing. That is no insult to the army, Major, but at sea, there is no place to dig a foxhole. While I understand General Short's focus on the immediate threat to this island, I am training this fleet for an aggressive wartime footing—thus the orders to Admiral Halsey. In addition, the carrier **Lexington** will put to sea within the week. I wish I could send the **Saratoga** out there as well, but she's going the other way, en route to the mainland for repairs.

"Gentlemen, I have long insisted that we should take the offensive, take the war across the ocean, right into the heart of our enemy. I made that case to President Roosevelt when I was in Washington this past summer. I insisted in the strongest terms then, as I insist now, that the two new battleships coming on line, **North Carolina** and **Washington,** be sent here to strengthen the Pacific fleet. Thus far, I am a voice in the wilderness. However, I am greatly concerned that the president's decision will leave us extremely vulnerable in the Philippines. But at least with our carriers moving that way, we should be better prepared. And we shall prevail."

Kimmel stood, the signal to the others to rise as well. Rochefort felt his head swimming, thought, Get me back to my radios. Beside him, Layton gave him a gentle push toward the door, the others falling into line, filing out. They paused outside the doorway, and Rochefort heard Kimmel's voice, the army major still in the office.

"Make sure you remind General Short of our golf game Sunday—0800 I believe."

"Yes, sir. And he asked me to remind you, sir, that tomorrow is the Army-Navy game."

"He hardly needs to remind me of that. I took ten bucks off the last general I served with. I'll do the same to him."

### HQ, COMMANDER IN CHIEF PACIFIC FLEET, PEARL HARBOR—TUESDAY, DECEMBER 2, 1941

Rochefort pushed the door open, didn't wait for a friendly greeting. Layton sat at his desk, across from Rochefort's immediate superior, Captain Mayfield. Both men seemed annoyed at the interruption, and Layton said, "Jesus, Joe, you can't wait a half minute?"

"No, I can't. Whatever you're talking about isn't as important as this."

Mayfield looked at Layton, said, "He's usually right. All right, Joe, what have you got?"

Rochefort took a deep breath. "The Japanese have changed their radio codes, the call signals for their ships."

He was breathing heavily, waited for a response from either man. Mayfield said, "So? Don't they do that fairly often?"

Rochefort felt a pulsing anger, impatience with the question. "**No, they don't.** They change their codes every six months, like clockwork. These codes were changed after four weeks. That's all. **Four weeks.**"

Both men stared at him, and Layton said, "What does it mean?"

The words came out in a shout. "How the hell do I know what it means? But it means something. It's not like some damn admiral got a bug up his butt and decided last month's codes stunk. If they've figured out that we're listening to them, they suddenly don't want us to know where their ships are going. Logically, it means they're preparing for a large-scale operation. At the very least, they're tightening up their security."

Mayfield said, "If they've figured out we're listening to them, maybe they're throwing a wrench into your earphones. Hell, they're probably listening to **us,** and they decided to put a bug up **your** butt just by changing their codes. It could just be their way of playing with you."

Rochefort was calming down, said, "I don't know. It's just that they've never done this before. They're a very methodical people. There's a rhythm to them, which is why I can pick out the keys coming from several of their ships, like I know the operator personally. This is just . . . out of rhythm. It means something. I just don't know what."

There was a knock on the open door, a young lieutenant.

"Excuse me, sirs. Captain Smith has requested your presence in the admiral's office, right away."

Layton said, "All of us?"

"Sir, to quote Captain Smith, 'Find anybody who knows anything about the damn Japs.'"

Layton said, "I guess that's all of us."

They followed the young officer up the stairs, and Rochefort could already hear Kimmel's voice, loud and angry. The lieutenant hesitated at the closed door for a pause in whatever Kimmel was shouting about. The break came, and he rapped lightly, Smith pulling open the door.

"Gentlemen, take a seat. Sit tight."

At the far end of the office was Captain "Soc" McMorris, the admiral's war plans officer. He gave a silent nod toward the others.

Kimmel was holding a telephone to his ear, said, "Fine. You do that. You find out just where I'm going to find a hundred fresh pilots, and the planes to stick 'em in. I've got Washington pushing me to send aircraft all over the damn Pacific, and I'm not interested in hearing any guff about what we ought to be doing with them right here. Someone decides to give you my job, then you can come up here and run this show. Until then, you'll do what the hell I tell you to do."

He dropped the phone onto the receiver with a loud clatter, stared at it for a long minute. He seemed to realize now that the others were there.

"I am so damn tired of people under my command telling me what's good for my command. We're strapped to beat hell trying to get more of the new PBY flying boats, and Commander Jacobson wants to put them all in the air, burning gas flying circles around Oahu, when we haven't even broken them in yet. Never mind that sooner or later we're going to need those damn things on the far side of the Pacific, never mind that we're short of decent pilots, and never mind that every base from Midway to Manila is screaming for fighter planes. Not only that, he wants to send up just about anything else we've got that will fly, and send them off like a herd of butterflies.

"I keep telling these people, recon is the army's job. They're supposed to be looking out for the bugaboos here. They've got as many planes here as we do, and they're bellyaching because they haven't gotten their B-17s yet. Hell, even I know that there's a dozen or more headed this way, and I'm sure Washington will order them sent on to MacArthur, whether General Short likes it or not. We take our own pilots out of their training routines here, send them off sightseeing, and all we're doing is wasting time and gasoline. I won't have it. And, neither will he."

He seemed to sag, looked at the three intel officers. "I guess having some junior grade shavetail arguing with me is better than a yes-man. I hate yes-men. Don't agree with me just to make me happy. It doesn't."

He reached down into his desk, pulled out a folder, opened it, slapped it down. "Here's another gem. This was received this morning. You familiar with Commander Arthur McCollum, ONI in Washington?" Kimmel didn't wait for a reply. Rochefort knew they were all familiar with McCollum. "He sent this note, obviously something they picked up from a Japanese transmission somewhere. I'm beginning to feel like no one in Washington has any idea what they should be telling us except that the Japanese might do something, or they might not, or we should be afraid, or maybe not. Read this, all of you."

Layton took the paper, passed it along to Mayfield, who handed it to Rochefort.

**"Circular 2444 from Tokyo one December ordered London, Hong Kong, Singapore, and Manila to destroy Purple machine. Batavia machine already sent to Tokyo. December second Washington also directed destroy Purple and all but one code of other systems and all secret documents. British Admiralty London today reports embassy London has complied."**

Kimmel waited for Rochefort to finish, then said, "All right. Three top-flight intel officers sitting in front of me. Can someone tell me, first, what the hell this message is about? Why should we consider this important? And, please, what the hell do they mean by 'Purple'?"

Layton said, "They're referring to a message sent from Tokyo—as you said, sir, number 2444—that apparently went out to their embassies, or operatives in London, Batavia, Hong Kong, Manila, and Singapore. It's an order to destroy . . . well, I don't know what. Whatever it is, their London office has complied."

"What the hell does this have to do with Hawaii, Commander?"

Layton looked at the other two. "I don't see anything about Hawaii, but Commander McCollum must have a reason for sending this to you, sir."

"And again, Commander, **'Purple'** refers to what?"

"Sir, I'm not familiar with the meaning."

Kimmel looked at Rochefort. "You? Either of you?"

Mayfield shrugged, and Rochefort said, "Sir, I have no idea."

Kimmel shoved the paper back into his desk. "Well, maybe one day they'll explain it to us. Now, Commander Layton, there's another reason I called you in here. I've got a big damn map over here, and I've got Admiral Halsey out there with a carrier task force just itching for a fight. And I've got Washington telling me we can probably expect one, sooner or later, somewhere or other. So, why don't you show me where the Japanese fleet is."

Layton stood, leaned toward the map, and Kimmel said, "Not the entire fleet, mind you. I know all about the South Seas and submarines in the Carolines. I just want to know about their carrier divisions, One and Two. That's four flattops, at least. Halsey runs into those fellows, he won't like the odds."

Layton glanced back at Rochefort, who knew what was coming.

"Sir, I do not have that information. For a couple of weeks now, there has been no radio traffic from the carriers. We are confident that they are anchored in their home waters, though I admit, sir, we do not know that with certainty."

Kimmel stood, put his hands on his hips, looked at Rochefort, then back to Layton. "So, you don't have the first idea where Carrier Division One and Carrier Division Two are?"

"No, sir."

Kimmel moved close to the map, planted a finger on one spot. "Do you mean to say that they could be rounding Diamond Head and you wouldn't know it?"

"I would hope, sir, that they would have been sighted before that."

Kimmel sat again, pointed to Layton's chair. "Sit down, Commander. You gentlemen were in this office four days ago, while we gnashed our teeth over the messages we had received from Washington. I cannot speak for General Short and how much gnashing is still going on over there. But I have concluded that this navy is too big and too sophisticated to fall prey to an enemy as weak as the Japanese. It is certainly possible that they will attempt to attack us via the submarine, hitting the fleet when we are out on training maneuvers. I do not intend to forgo that training just to keep us safe and warm in Pearl

Harbor. It is a concern that we do not know the location of the Japanese carrier divisions. My point here was to push you boys just a little harder to do the job. And you will.

"For now, I have a mathematics problem to confront. I am to strengthen the island bases—Wake, Midway, all the rest—while maintaining adequate air strength right here. When Washington's message of the twenty-seventh was being tossed about with General Short and his people, there was concern expressed that Oahu might be vulnerable to air attack from the Japanese." He looked toward McMorris. "The captain here set my mind at ease, certainly. Tell them what you told me, Captain. Is there any chance of an attack on Oahu?"

McMorris looked at the others, said, "No chance, Admiral. Absolutely none."

THE DUNGEON, 14TH NAVAL DISTRICT, PEARL
HARBOR—WEDNESDAY, DECEMBER 3, 1941

The earphones offered nothing but silence, the occasional soft crackle of static. He stared at the ceiling, his hands clenching, felt the aching need to hear something, **anything,** any radio signal that would offer a hint of information. He lowered his head, slid the earphones off, looked across the room, most of the others doing as he had done, searching the silence. The knock startled him, the same cadence he had heard before, and he moved to the door, knew it was the young guard who seemed so enamored of this strangely named place. Rochefort pulled the door open, was surprised to see Captain Mayfield standing on the steps behind the guard. The guard stood aside, and Mayfield said, "A minute, Commander? Outside?"

The guard led the way, Rochefort pulling the door closed, following Mayfield up the stairs. The guard vanished, and Rochefort followed Mayfield out into the sunlight, a stark blue sky, the soft sounds of birds broken by trucks moving past, the green of the army. Rochefort said, "Looks like General Short's busy. We being invaded?"

Mayfield said, "Short's ordered his people to prepare for an uprising. He thinks there's an underground army of Japanese troops here. Those trucks are probably full of ammo, being hauled to some safe place where he can keep an eye on 'em."

Rochefort shook his head. "The invasion's already here. I heard someone speaking Japanese in a restaurant a week or so ago. Must be a spy."

"Laugh all you want, Joe. Speaking Japanese in public might get you arrested before too much longer. We're doing a lot of listening to a lot of people."

"How many of those people speaking Japanese are American citizens, for Chrissake?"

Mayfield glanced around, caution against anyone listening to **him.** "Well, let me tell you about those American citizens, Joe. You know we've been working alongside the FBI, that we've got listening bugs in their consulate."

"Yeah, I know it. The newspapers get wind of that, and you'll have hell to pay."

"Well, the newspapers might get hold of this too. The FBI just passed along something you and Commander Layton ought to know. We didn't have the faintest idea what McCollum's note meant, all that talk about destroying God-knows-what in London and everywhere else. Well, it's happening here. As of this morning, the workers inside the Japanese Consulate are burning their code books and their official papers. They're either making ready to strike us, or they're preparing to run like hell out of here. And you still don't know what's going on with their ships, their carriers?"

Rochefort felt a cold jab in his chest. "All I know is they're not talking. I don't know why."

# TWENTY-NINE

# Biggs

**T**he ship arrived on December 3, the tugboats teasing her to her berth at the Port of Honolulu. She was the **Lurline,** a passenger liner that made a regular run from San Francisco and Los Angeles to Honolulu and back again. For this part of the journey, she carried nearly eight hundred passengers, many seeking a Christmas vacation in the tropical extravagance of Hawaii. Among those who disembarked with wide-eyed expectations were fifty-two college football players, teams from San Jose State, in California, and Willamette University, from Salem, Oregon. They each came for a competition against the team from the University of Hawaii, but as passionate as the athletes might have been for football, the voyage alone had been an adventure.

USS Arizona, at sea—Thursday, December 4, 1941

The man let out a sharp yell, one of the mates, Vaughan, and a corpsman, Hankins, holding him down at the shoulders. Chief Isham stood beside Biggs, anchoring the man's undamaged leg. The other leg was bound against a narrow board, wrapped in gauze, the only way the leg could be held steady. Dr. Condon worked slowly, removing the gauze straps one at a time, but every touch made the man jerk and twitch, and Condon stopped, said to Vaughan, "Ice packs. Bring a half dozen. Wrap them in gauze. Applying them will hurt enough as it is."

Vaughan moved away quickly, dug through the freezer, returned with the packs, handed them to Condon one at a time.

"This will hurt, sailor. But it will numb you up a little, and keep the swelling down. You ready?"

The man looked at Condon, nodded, and beside him, his chief said, "He'll handle it. Tough as nails. Just a little stupid."

Condon looked at the chief, said, "How'd you get him down here? He didn't walk."

Isham kept his eyes on his man, said, "Took four of us. Damn fool was screwing around where we were handling the five-inch shells, and they came loose, rolled right up his leg. How bad is it, Doc?"

"Could have been a whole lot worse. I don't think anything's broken, but his ankle's sprained pretty severely. I need an X-ray to see if there's anything else broken."

"Thanks, Doc. He's a tough old bastard, knows better than to pull a stupid stunt like that. He's been here near as long as I have. Right, you old fart?"

The patient didn't speak, and Biggs could see that the man's fists were clenched against the pain.

"He'll be okay, Chief. A sprain can hurt worse than a broken bone, but the ice will help. And a handful of aspirin. Nothing more for you to do here."

There were thumps from above, a rattle of anti-aircraft fire. Isham looked up, said, "I need to get topside. We've got firing exercises all damn night. Those are my guns, and there's too many recruits up there jerking around 'cause they like to make big noises. I feel like I'm some kind of papa bear sometimes. Thanks for everything, Doc. The rest of you too."

The others offered him a quick nod, and Biggs said, "Sir, I'm sorry about your man, but I wanted to tell you that I remember you, from that steak and beer cookout you did for us. That was really swell. Just want you to know how much we needed that, all of us."

Isham seemed to appreciate the compliment,

said, "Thanks. Yeah, that was good. We'll do it again sometime, maybe next week. I'll mention it to the commander. We could do something on Ford Island. We'll get back to Pearl tomorrow, and we've got a fair amount of maintenance to take care of. We have to overhaul the cannon sleeves, check out the smaller ordnance in case there are cracks or any other damage. All typical stuff, but when it's time, it's time. Can't screw around with that kind of work."

"You mean, like dry dock?"

Isham shook his head. "No, we'll be berthed beside a repair ship. I think it's the **Vestal** this time. Those fellows enjoy all the dirty work."

Biggs thought, Holy cow, so much I don't know. So much other people **have** to know. He could see Isham growing anxious to leave, but he had to ask.

"Sir, I don't understand. The big guns—they have sleeves?"

Isham seemed to animate. It was obviously his favorite subject. "Yeah, like inserts. They get worn out after so many times being fired. Hell, every gun barrel on this ship needs checking—some get replaced pretty regularly."

Biggs absorbed the new education. "I wonder who was the first guy to figure that out."

Isham said, "The first guy who got his ass blown off the ship because a barrel split open. 'Course, that's just a guess. I wasn't there."

He turned to Condon, said, "Thank you again,

Doctor. Can you have one of your people keep me posted on how he does?"

"Sure thing, Chief."

Isham moved out through the hatchway, and Condon motioned for Biggs to move closer.

"Hold his good leg down—don't need him kicking me. Mr. Vaughan, be ready with those ice packs. He's not going to enjoy this one bit. Sailor, if it keeps hurting after this, we could give you some morphine. But I'd rather not. Let's just wrap it up, keep the swelling down. We get back to port, we'll probably send you over to the hospital. You'll like the nurses. A whole lot prettier than these fellows."

Biggs watched Condon wrapping the ankle, checking the leg again for anything broken. Condon worked efficiently, his eyes focused on the leg, said, "You fellows going to the football games?"

Biggs was surprised by the question, looked at Vaughan and Hankins, holding the patient's shoulders flat, a foam pillow beneath his neck. Both men smiled at Condon, and Vaughan said, "Sure thing, Doc. We been looking forward to it. Nice change from the usual."

Condon laughed. "As long as somebody doesn't bring any more busted-up gunner's mates in here, everybody can have a pass." He ran a finger down the bottom of the injured man's foot.

"You feel that, sailor?"

"Yep. Doesn't hurt as much. Thanks, Doc."

Condon said, "You'll not want to do any walking

around for a while. We'll keep giving you aspirin for now. You can sack out right here for the next couple days, since we've got to keep your leg elevated. We've got crutches here when you feel up to wandering around."

He looked at Biggs, laughed. "He won't take 'em. Never saw a gunner yet who'd admit to needing them. They're as bad as marines."

Biggs saw the patient smile, could see he was a good bit older, just like Isham had said.

"No crutches for me, Doc."

"Whatever you say. So, how about you, Mr. Biggs? You going to the game? Hawaii's supposed to be pretty good, though I don't follow it too closely. Never been too enthusiastic about watching two herds of buffaloes ram their heads together."

"Thank you, sir. But I want to go to the shopping area in town. I've been saving up to get my mom a nice Christmas present. I figure Saturday will be a good time, since a bunch of people will be at the game."

He expected teasing from the mates, but they seemed to approve, and Condon said, "Good for you, Mr. Biggs. I'm betting she doesn't need any straw voodoo dolls or snow globes with palm trees in them. There are several nice shops near the Halekulani, and I guess it depends on just how much money you've saved up. But I'm pretty sure you won't have to rub shoulders with a thousand sailors just to cross the street there. Hope you find something nice. Oh, I meant to ask you. What about your next baseball game? Aren't you about done for the year?"

"One more to go, sir. Monday afternoon. We keep hearing rumors about big league scouts showing up. Drives me nuts that people believe that stuff. Why in hell would a big league team send somebody all the way out here? I feel bad for Woody, 'cause I know he wants to believe he's got a chance. He's damn good, and somebody oughta be paying attention to that. We're just too far away."

"I hear you're pretty good too."

Vaughan said, "He is. I hear plenty of chatter about it."

Biggs shrugged. "I can swing a bat okay. It takes a lot more skill to pitch like Woody."

"Well, then I would suggest you go out and play that last game like it really matters. If there's not one single soul watching you, do it anyway. Do it for you."

USS ARIZONA, PEARL HARBOR—
SATURDAY, DECEMBER 6, 1941

He watched Wakeman and the others scrambling to get dressed, some of the men choosing up sides for which team they would root for, how much betting they were willing to do. He laughed as they debated just who would win even though none of them had any idea which teams were better.

The Saturday before, they had listened to the Army-Navy game on a radio set at the YMCA, the crowd nearly all sailors. The soldiers, of course, had mostly been at Schofield Barracks, listening to radio sets of their own. Biggs had been as caught up in the raucous enthusiasm as any of them, especially when Navy won the game, 14–6. That celebration had naturally spilled out toward the bars and entertainment on Hotel Street, and Biggs was grateful that Schofield was several miles away. With so many sailors swarming the usual haunts, it wouldn't be wise for a squad of soldiers to go roaming through the crowd of white uniforms with a chip on their shoulder. Surely the army officers had understood that, and so naturally, rumors filled the ship that the soldiers had stayed home, consoling themselves over their team's crushing loss with whatever dirty water they could drink on their base.

This week was very different. No one had a rabid passion for any of the teams. The sport was enough, the kind of entertainment that most of the men appreciated. The monotony of their schedule had spread to the weekends in port, the **Arizona** sailing into Pearl Harbor nearly every Friday, going out to sea Monday morning. Hotel Street was still a draw for some, but Biggs knew that many of the men were ready to spend a Saturday afternoon doing something more fun than nursing a hangover.

The men began to stream up the ladders, and Biggs could hear their questions, most of them having no idea where the stadium was. With all the mayhem around Biggs, no one had razzed him about his own mission, to buy his mom a Christmas present. To forgo a sporting event for your mother seemed to be a perfectly reasonable excuse.

Those in his compartment began to move out into the passageway, crisp white uniforms over polished black shoes. Men emerged from other compartments, and Biggs hung back, feeling no need to join the crush. It was barely noon, and he had plenty of time for his own mission.

Wakeman moved past him now, slapped him on the shoulder. "Wish me luck, Tommy. I bet five bucks on Hawaii to whip San Jose."

Biggs laughed. "Why?"

Wakeman feigned offense. "Simple. I need the five bucks."

The talk was rowdy as the men disappeared up the ladders, and Biggs felt their enthusiasm. Work and training, he thought, that's about all there is. Drinking too. And the squacks.

He still thought about the girl, but would never go back to any of those places. It was something he'd needed to do, or at least that's what he told himself. It was fun, I guess. I wonder if she'd remember me. Okay, now you're just being an idiot. There might be fifty guys lined up outside. She's a whore, for crying out loud. One of these days, you'll find a real girl, somebody just as pretty—prettier. Somebody you want to have kids with.

He moved out into the passageway, could hear the voices on the deck above, men still crowding the ladders. He put one hand against the steel bulkhead, looked at the steel beneath his feet. I'm not ready for a wife and kids, he thought, not yet. I really like it here. I think I know why guys join the navy and spend thirty years at sea. Maybe every sailor feels this way about his ship. Maybe that's how Ray feels, and it's breaking his heart to leave the **Curtiss.**

The passageway was empty now, the voices quieting.

"Hey, well, look who's still home."

He knew it was Kincaid, felt his pleasant thoughts shatter like glass. He turned, Kincaid standing behind him with his hands on his hips.

"Hello, sir."

"Thought I'd come through here and make a note of what kind of messes you turds left behind. Didn't expect to run into the biggest turd of all."

"I was just heading up the ladder, sir. I'm going into town to find a Christmas present for my mother."

Kincaid tilted his head. "So. A mama's boy. The rest of your buddies are off to a football game, and you're gonna tuck yourself into mama's petticoats. Damn, that's so sweet. You know, Mama's Boy, there's nobody else around here. We're all alone."

Biggs knew he was being baited, but it had happened too many times, he'd been insulted too often by a man who never seemed to do anything else.

"Sir, why? What did I do that you jump on me so much?"

Kincaid stared at him for a long moment. "Because I don't like you. Not one bit. You think you work so hard, you do everything everybody tells you to do, you work in the sick bay with fancy-ass doctors, you dream of **being** a doctor so you'll be better than the rest of us. This is my ship, Mama's Boy. There're sailors here who I put up with, and sailors I don't. And there are sailors who make me want to break their teeth every time I run into them. And that's you." He paused. "I've got three weeks left. That's it. **Three weeks.** For thirty years I've had to put up with **smart boys** like you, and now, they're making me stand down. I can't even get a damn desk job. The captain wants to hang a medal on me for my good service, like that's worth a turd in a snowstorm. Thirty years."

Biggs was surprised to hear a softening in Kincaid's voice.

"I'm sorry, sir. That's gotta be tough." Biggs knew immediately he'd made a mistake.

"Pity from **you**? The day you walk off this ship, you can go play baseball, like you're ten years old. You go back to Florida and lay on the beach, or maybe you get a job at some hotshot hospital, make a million dollars fixing up rich whores. I don't need anything from you, you spoiled son of a bitch."

Biggs had no words, felt as though he was

confronting a different kind of steel bulkhead, immovable, unchanging.

Kincaid leaned closer to him, into his face, too close. Biggs felt his hot stale breath, was suddenly very afraid, tried to back away, pressing hard against a bulkhead. He slipped to the side, past the hatchway into his compartment. He tried to hold himself up, fell backward, his head coming down hard on the deck. Now Kincaid came at him, stood over him, bent low, said, "**Mama's Boy.** You know how we treat mama's boys?"

There was nowhere for Biggs to go, no way to avoid Kincaid's open hand, coming down hard across his face, a loud **slap.** The fear grew now, Kincaid staring at him with a sickening fire.

Biggs forced the words, "I don't understand. I ain't done anything to you."

Kincaid straightened up, towering over him, a foot planted on either side, still nowhere for Biggs to go. "You've done plenty. Get up, Mama's Boy. You wanna get back at me? You pissed off? You wanna play some more?"

"No, sir."

"I didn't think so. Now, you wanna go around talking about this, about what a mean son of a bitch I am, how I beat your ass, how pitiful it is that you turn my stomach, well, you go right ahead. And if you do, I'll smash your skull into the bulkhead, right about there, and won't nobody know who did it or why."

Biggs tried to clear his head, a single word all he could manage. "Why?"

Kincaid ignored him, stepped away, out the hatchway, down the nearest ladder, and gone. Biggs pulled his legs in, one hand on the bulkhead, steadied himself, stood slowly. He was dizzy, a hard knot on the back of his head, his face numb, one thought: **sick bay.**

He kept one hand on the bulkhead, reached the first ladder, started up, voices above him, "Jesus. What happened to you?"

He realized they were officers, two young, one older.

"Sorry, sirs. Going to sick bay."

"What happened to you, sailor?"

"Fell down the ladder, sir."

There was silence, and the older man said, "You know the way?"

"Yes, sir."

They moved past him, and he could feel their eyes on him. He had no idea how his face looked, how swollen, if there was blood. He climbed, knew they were still there, watching him, was relieved when he was out of their sight. He moved forward, down the familiar passageway, stepped inside. He heard the voice of Dr. Johnson, "Be with you in a second."

The doctor came out of the office, didn't show any recognition, then leaned closer to Biggs, said, "Good Christ, Mr. Biggs. I didn't know it was you. What in God's name happened to you?"

He couldn't ignore his embarrassment, looked away, said in a low voice, "Fell down the ladder, sir."

Johnson stood back, moved from side to side, taking in every angle. Biggs could feel his head clearing slightly, could see Johnson's face, an angry scowl.

"That ladder had fingers, Mr. Biggs. You want to try again?"

Biggs looked down. "No, sir. I fell down the ladder."

Johnson slid a chair closer, sat. He looked at Biggs for a long moment, then said, "You been drinking?"

Biggs was surprised by the question, looked up at him. "No, sir. Not at all."

"Who hit you? Or rather, who slapped you? That's a tried-and-true method for kicking someone's ass without blood or busted teeth. Without evidence."

Biggs dropped his head again. "I fell down the ladder."

Johnson crossed his arms, said, "Let me tell you about that ladder. You just listen. You've got a shipmate who's a real ass, a big-mouth. Maybe he's in your compartment. Maybe he's your petty officer. I know you, Mr. Biggs. You're not the type to pick a fight, to open up your mouth and say something stupid. And right now, you're keeping your mouth shut about what happened to you because . . . well, you're scared of what might happen next, or you're ashamed."

"Maybe both, sir. I'm sorry, sir, but I don't want to say any more."

Biggs kept his eyes down. He couldn't look at Johnson, hated himself for lying.

"Have it your way, Mr. Biggs. Either way, I'll fix you up. An ice pack will reduce the swelling—and you've got a hell of a lot of swelling. Not sure if you'll have a bruise in the next couple of days. The ice may help that too." He ran his hand around Biggs's head, felt the lump. "I thought so. An ice pack there too. Aspirin will help. You didn't lose any teeth. That's good. Sometimes it happens. Let me get the ice."

Johnson moved away, to the freezer Biggs had cleaned many times. He returned, wrapped a thin cloth around the ice pack, put it in Biggs's hand.

"Press. You know how."

Biggs put the ice to his face, fought the shock of the cold, kept his eyes down, still too embarrassed to look at Johnson.

"By the way, Mr. Biggs, Dr. Condon told me you were going into town today, to do some shopping. Tell you what, since you're not going to look that handsome wandering around those fancy stores, how about I give you a pass for Monday instead?"

"No, thank you, sir. I don't have a lot of time to mail a package for Christmas. I've been looking forward to just doing something for my mom. I wish I could do more. Maybe even for my pop. They don't have much of anything."

"That's up to you. Hey, I just thought of this, since you know that saxophone player, Mr. Cox.

Tonight is the semifinals of the Battle of Music. You know that our band's right up there. Tonight will decide who we'll compete against. The championship is scheduled for twentieth December. I may be biased, but I think we're the best band in the fleet, and I think the rest of the fleet knows that too."

"I think so too, sir."

"Well, look, I was heading over to Bloch Arena tonight to hear the bands, size up the competition. You want to go?"

"No, thank you, sir. I just want to do my shopping, come on back to the ship. It's gonna be hard enough explaining my face to my buddies . . . Well, you know, sir."

"Yes, well, that makes sense. You'll be pretty sore tonight, so if you need more aspirin, stop by. Dr. Condon comes on duty at 1600. When your start your shift tomorrow, I'll give you the full report about the band competition. It'll be great, pretty sure of that."

Biggs had one mission to accomplish before he made his way to the high-end stores. He was surprised that the crowds were as large and as raucous as they were, the sailors massed along the streets as they always seemed to be. He realized he had been wrong about the draw of the football games, though he still assumed the university stadium had to be a mob scene. But his interest was very different, and within a few minutes of leaving the taxi, he stood in front of the Blue Moon, scanning the faces of the men in white for the one he sought.

"There you are, you ugly bastard!"

Biggs didn't have to see him to know the voice, and to sense that Russo had been there for a while already. He turned, saw the wide smile as Russo shuffled out of the bar, and Biggs said, "Hello, More Ugly. How many have you had so far?"

Russo straightened himself, said, "Damn, Tommy. Nobody's as ugly as you right now. What the hell happened to you? Your face . . ."

"Yeah, I got a face. Took a wrong turn and ran into a pineapple."

"Come on, Tommy. Somebody belted you. You get in a few too?"

"Can we let it go? It's just a little swollen. I really don't want to talk about it."

"I don't care. You're my buddy. Somebody roughs you up, I wanna help. The marines jump you? Those pissed-off soldiers who lost the game last week?"

Biggs looked around through the crowd, leaned closer to Russo. "There's just a bastard of a petty officer, has it in for me. The guys warned me about him, and they were right. He just hates my guts."

Russo studied his face. "Yeah, I've heard about guys like that. I think some guys get more pissed off the older they get. Hell, I don't know. Maybe they're afraid of having to quit, leave the navy. What's a guy do?"

Biggs shrugged. "Don't know. He's about to re-tire, doesn't seem too happy about it. I just try to stay out of his way."

"Okay, Tommy. I just hope you're okay."

"I'm okay. Now, how many beers you had?"

"Oh, just a couple. I'm trying not to do this stuff anymore. I can't go home a damn lush. My mama's already saying a novena for me, and every other prayer she can come up with. If she could, she'd ask the pope to put in a good word."

"So, Ray, you loading up on Christmas presents? I just need one, for my mom. Hell, you got a whole high school worth of sisters."

"Yeah, I've got a few ideas for Mama. Not sure about the girls. They'd be happy with some souvenirs."

Biggs couldn't help thinking of Dr. Condon's teasing about straw dolls and snow globes.

Russo rubbed his chin. "What about you? Where you planning on shopping?"

"I'm gonna hit the fancy shops near the big hotels."

"Well, how-de-do, Mister Big Shot Biggs."

"Yeah, but I've been saving up. Mom deserves something decent for putting up with Pop, and I don't think I ever really tell her how much she . . . I mean . . ."

Russo shoved him lightly on the shoulder. "Yeah, I know. They gave us all they had, and sometimes, there's nothing left for them. I'm damn sorry you don't have it so good at home, not like I did. But you're looking out for your mom. That's great. I'd do anything to bring back Papa."

Biggs didn't know what to say, put a hand on Russo's shoulder. "Look, I'm gonna hop on the trolley, head over to the Halekulani. You wanna go?"

"No, I'll mess around here for a while. You wanna stay for one beer?"

Biggs was tempted, fought it. "I know what'll happen: You'll talk me into six more, and that'll be the end of my money, and my shopping."

"Well, then, as long as I'm alone, I might as well not be **too** alone. The line's not too long over at Mama Hula's. There's a redhead in there—holy cow."

Biggs laughed. "You're completely full of crap. You wouldn't go near that place. Look, if you'll hang around here, I'll come back. If I've got any dough left, I'll buy you that beer. If I don't, you can buy it for me."

The salesgirl had been short and pretty, a native Hawaiian who seemed wary of his appearance. But the size of his budget had cured her uneasiness. She had pointed him finally toward the silk scarves, and he chose the prettiest one in the store, blue and soft pink. The price had given him pause—it was more money than he'd ever spent on anything in his life—but he had cash in his pocket and the salesgirl was just persuasive enough.

As he walked farther down the street, he passed more shops, more possibilities, had to assure himself that his first instinct had been the right one. He passed the Halekulani, was tempted to wander in, maybe buy a drink, but he felt awkward and very out of place. The only sailors he saw going in were officers. The swelling in his face was no help either, was sure to raise some alarm from hotel security. Nope, he thought. Ray's where I need to be. And I could really use a beer.

# THIRTY

# The Spy

JAPANESE CONSULATE, HONOLULU, HAWAII—
FRIDAY, DECEMBER 5, 1941

**H**e woke up to a sharp glare of sunlight, put one hand to the side, the bed empty. She should have stayed, he thought. It is a great honor for her to lie with me. He swung his legs to the side of the bed, yawned, stood slowly. He moved to the window, stared out at the blue sky, his mind already working on the duties that lay in front of him today. He dressed quickly, looked at his watch. It was close to noon, and he thought about where he was going—something new. He glanced skyward again, imagined flying, how different that would be, how much more useful to see beyond the tall gates and barbed wire.

The plane had been chartered by the consulate,

using his alias, **Tadashi Morimura,** as if he were just another privileged tourist, eager to see the beauty of Hawaii from the air. On the floor beside the empty dresser was a pile of clothes, and he shuffled through, chose the brightest Hawaiian shirt, purple this time, what any undignified tourist would wear with pride. He examined himself in the mirror, smiled. Perfect.

Yoshikawa glanced around the cottage, searching for his camera, didn't see it. Never mind. Better without one, even as a prop. They will know that I am so excited to be here by my smile alone, my eagerness to experience the beauty of the island. There is no need for photographs, after all. What I see remains inside my mind, and details on my notepad.

He walked outside, ignored the flowers, the other touches of beauty spread out around the grounds of the consulate. The place meant nothing to him. The main consulate office was a short walk from his private cottage, and he pushed through the door, ignored the rows of secretaries, the other offices where men labored over their papers. He did not hesitate, stepped into the office of Consul General Kita, saw the man scribbling on a pad of white paper.

Yoshikawa said, "I am off to the airplane ride."

Kita pointed to the door, and Yoshikawa closed it.

"Do your people know nothing of my mission here? After so much time?"

Kita seemed annoyed. "What they know or do not know is not your concern. We have completed transmitting your last reports by wire. Tokyo has received them by now. Do you anticipate another report today? If so, I shall have the wire operator stay at his post until you return."

Yoshikawa shrugged. "If there is something to report, I shall report it. They continue to send me questions, and I continue to answer them. It is as simple as that. I do not require assistance." He paused. "And I do not require minions who follow me around, doing the same job I have already completed. It is unnecessary and dangerous. I know I am to obey my superiors in Japan, and I have done so. But I do not understand why they insist that more people in this role will do a better job. I am inconspicuous because I practice the art, because I know my place here.

"So they send me a German as an associate? This man, Otto Kuehn, is nothing more than a lazy pig, who prances about claiming he is related to Heinrich Himmler. That is supposed to earn him respect? Does he do his job any better than I do? Why would anyone in the Naval Intelligence Office believe him to be of value to my work here? He reports nothing useful, has made no observations except that there are occasionally women here who prefer spending time with a German than with any man who possesses a hint of dignity."

Kita was watching him with wide-eyed distress, and Yoshikawa realized his voice was carrying beyond the office.

Kita said, "Please. I am aware of the disadvantages with Mr. Kuehn. But he has influential friends, and they believe him to be of value here."

"I do not. Are you aware that he has proposed that our fishermen put signal lights on their sailboats, flashing code to our patrolling submarines, as though no one in the American navy would notice that at all?"

Kita lowered his head. "Yes, he has presented that idea to me. It will not happen." He looked up at Yoshikawa now. "But what of Seki? He respects your work, and is of service to you in any way you choose."

Yoshikawa sat now, his arms on Kita's desk. "He should clean my room. All he has accomplished is to wander the hillsides, walking in my own footprints, making the same observations I have already sent to Tokyo. He is so ill-prepared for the tasks assigned to him that he had to request a copy of that textbook on American weaponry, **Jane's Fighting Ships.** He would not know a battleship from a tugboat. If these men seek glory, let them find it on some path that I have not already flattened with my shoes."

Kita seemed to struggle with his patience, said, "I respect what you are doing. It is important work, as the foreign ministry tells me. But it does not require genius to count ships, to study airplanes."

Yoshikawa stood again, sniffed. "I will ignore your insult. However, there will come a time when

Tokyo recognizes what I am doing here, in the only way that matters to the intelligence officers. I have not been **caught.** And I shall never be caught."

Kita was worn out yet again by Yoshikawa's speeches. He folded his hands in front of him, tried to guide the conversation back to his own job. "We have observed movement in the harbor, perhaps more than usual. It is not unusual for the Americans to put some ships to sea while others are brought home. But there seems to be much more, and Tokyo has requested more detailed information. As well, there is concern that the Americans are launching aircraft in new patterns, that they are sweeping the skies in every direction, perhaps reconnaissance patrols that extend far from Oahu."

"Or perhaps they continue to train their pilots. I have observed nothing unusual. But I shall continue to find the answers to the questions they sent me three days ago, which is why this airplane tour today will be useful."

"Do you have a copy of those questions?"

"Of course not. I do not always rely on paper. Carelessness could result. I keep a single small pad in my pocket that can be destroyed quickly. I do not take foolish risks. This evening, when I return, I shall eliminate much of the bulk from my files, burning anything I no longer need."

"We have all been ordered to do exactly that. There is danger we will draw the attention of the Honolulu Fire Department."

Yoshikawa shook his head. "Or the FBI. Do you not feel it would be prudent to burn what we are instructed to burn very slowly, creating a minimum of black smoke?"

"Smoke is not dangerous. Coded documents are. It is not necessary for you to teach me my job. I am not so concerned that American security will invade my office." Kita pulled a paper from his desk, handed it to Yoshikawa. "This is the decoded message from December second."

Yoshikawa thought, Keeping these decoded messages in your desk is abominably stupid. But he said nothing about it, leaving Kita to his own consequences. He read the paper.

"Yes, I recall all of this. They are requesting a count of all warships of all types in the harbor, daily, through the next several days. They also wish to know if the American ships are protected by torpedo nets, and if they are employing observation balloons over the harbor." He was feeling impatient now, unwilling to spend any more time with Kita. "My airplane is waiting."

Kita seemed to hesitate, said, "I must say one more thing. I am receiving complaints about your activities, including the performance of your duties in the consulate."

"I have no duties in the consulate."

"Well, yes, I know that. But there is an entire consulate full of capable, hard-working people outside this office who are not aware of just what you are supposed to be doing. Can you not make some effort to disguise your mission by sitting at a desk, or engaging in conversation with them? Some of these people are laboring on your behalf, transmitting and receiving messages, scheduling things for you, including your airplane flight today."

"The fewer people who know my mission, the less that risk. Everything is fine."

"Can you not at least use some discretion with your whiskey bottles? Or the number of women you bring to your cottage? And is it necessary for you to sleep half the day?"

"I will try to be more discreet. But I will sleep as much as I require. Is there anything else?"

Kita seemed defeated, said, "No. Enjoy your airplane flight. Will you be alone?"

Yoshikawa thought a moment. "No. I will appear more the tourist if I have a wife accompany me. I will stop first at Shuncho-ro Teahouse. The geishas are most friendly, and any one of them would enjoy the flight."

The flight was barely thirty minutes, and there were few surprises, beyond the graphic image now in his mind of just how the various bases on Oahu were spread across the island. Civilian aircraft were not allowed to fly over the harbor itself, but there was no difficulty, even from a distance, in mapping out the positions of specific ships, from great to small.

From the air, however, Yoshikawa could make an observation denied him by the gates and fences around most of the bases. For the first time, he had a clear view of the harbor itself, the anchorages around Ford Island, the submarine base and dry docks near Hickam Field, and the way the harbor squeezed down to a narrow passageway at its entrance.

As he flew near the airfields, he was able to sketch out the directions of the active runways, while also noting the configuration of the hangars and other buildings. But the greatest surprise, for which he put pencil to paper, was a change in the positioning of the fighter aircraft, short-range bombers and training craft, at nearly every field. He had no idea what Tokyo would do with this information, and what value it might have. But he had never noticed before that on each of the fields, dozens of aircraft, big and small, were parked together wingtip to wingtip, in long straight lines, as though they were on parade.

He was not at all comfortable handing over his reports to the wireless operator, whose job was to translate Yoshikawa's observations into the latest codes used by the intelligence offices. He preferred to encode his messages himself, before anyone else in the consulate could read them. It was one more element in his shield of personal security that Yoshikawa valued above all else.

The transmissions were something new, born of necessity. It had once been possible, though more dangerous, to deliver the reports to the intelligence officers directly by hand. The Japanese ocean liner **Taiyo Maru** had steamed into the harbor at Honolulu on November 1, just one of several passenger ships flying the Japanese flag that made scheduled voyages to Hawaii. On this journey, its passengers were mostly family members of Japanese-Americans on the islands, and some were Americans emigrating back home from Japan. For them, this journey was a halfway point, most waiting for the next voyage of the **Lurline** to take them to the American mainland.

With the **Taiyo Maru** and many other passenger liners flying the Japanese flag, there was nothing unusual about a ship being visited by the Japanese consul general, and of course, his chief deputies. Though the passengers were observed dutifully by the FBI, the Japanese government officials were given free passage and were never violated by a search. Consul General Kita and his associate, **Tadashi Morimura,** made several visits, ostensibly to discuss various matters with the ship's officers. But once onboard, out of sight of American security, they instead met with low-level crewmen and stewards who were in fact high-ranking Japanese naval and intelligence officers. Yoshikawa's lengthy and detailed reports had thus been delivered by hand directly to those men who would make the best use of the information.

But the growing animosity between the United States and Japan made passenger travel increasingly unwise, especially with anxious submarine commanders on both sides now prowling the sea lanes. On November 5, the **Taiyo Maru** sailed westward from Oahu, severing the last personal link between Japan and the U.S. For Yoshikawa, that link had been a symbolic lifeline, a possible escape route to Japan should American intelligence sniff too closely. So far that had not happened, but merely knowing that he was now alone on an island made his sleep just a bit more fitful.

JAPANESE CONSULATE, HONOLULU, HAWAII—
   SATURDAY, DECEMBER 6, 1941

It was another morning like so many others, a woman and a bottle, but he was up early, a nagging itch that this job was becoming more complicated, and possibly, more dangerous. The wires had been coming steadily from Tokyo, an odd sense of urgency to the frequency of their questions.

Even at this hour, the woman was already gone. He bent down, picked up the whiskey bottle from the floor. Empty. He tossed it onto the bed, knew that someone would clean it up.

He thought of breakfast, knew his request would bring grousing but that they would still serve him. The secretaries do know their jobs, after all. I don't ask them to type or write my letters. All I want is breakfast.

He looked outside again. It was clear and blue, a perfect day for wandering through cane fields, or whatever else they would ask of him. He dressed as always, in another Hawaiian shirt, never the same one in any given week. Again he would play the role of the mindless tourist, wandering aimlessly through the sites, awed by the distant warships. Perhaps now, he thought, I am not a tourist. The passenger ships are gone, after all. Now I am one of **them,** the Japanese Hawaiians who are not Japanese, pathetic lackeys with menial jobs who say they are Americans. I look like them, but I will never behave like them. I'm not sure how I could ever live among them, pretend to do their jobs, even while I do my own.

Since he had been in Hawaii, his cover had included a variety of strange and, to him, demeaning jobs. He had washed dishes at an army officers' club, had performed menial labor, exposed himself to ridicule and insults from co-workers and superiors, all for one purpose. In every case he had been an excellent listener, picking up any piece of information that would add value to his **real** job. On the island of Maui, he had posed as an extravagant businessman, buying drinks for military officers who laughed at the jokes he told on himself. There were still the gates he could not enter, places he could not go, but he pushed through in other ways, flattering the drunk sailor, asking with innocent curiosity what might lie beyond the fences. But now, from a peaceful ride in a small tourist airplane, he had seen it for himself with astonishing ease.

He adjusted his clothing in the mirror, glanced again at the unmade bed. He tried to remember the woman, one of the geishas from his favorite teahouse. What kind of men are there for them here, in this place? Bartenders and gardeners. It is truly a shame I can never tell them what I do here.

He finished buttoning the garish shirt, bright yellow this time, laughed. Perhaps the geishas are agents of the FBI. Surely we are all being watched here, their police with a file on each of us. If they still believe I am **Tadashi Morimura,** then I am fortunate indeed. Or perhaps they are utterly inept.

All right. I'm hungry. He picked up the telephone, dialed the numbers, waited. "This is Morimura. I am ready for my breakfast."

He didn't wait for a response, hung up the receiver. The phone rang and he picked it up, heard Kita's voice. "The wires continue to arrive. Come to my office."

Yoshikawa thought, Well, they can bring me breakfast in his office.

He crossed the open path, entered the main

office, the eyes on him, as always. "You may bring my breakfast in here. But knock first."

He stepped into Kita's office, saw a paper in Kita's hand.

"The wires are growing more frequent. They expect your responses without delay."

"I never delay."

There was a soft knock, and he saw the disgust on Kita's face. Yoshikawa turned, opened the door, took the tray from an annoyed young woman, was pleased to see she had included the morning's newspaper. He watched her as she backed away, said to her, "You would be very good as a geisha. Consider it. I can get you a position."

The woman bowed, moved out quickly, with forced politeness. "Thank you, sir."

Yoshikawa stuffed the seaweed in his mouth, drank the soup in one gulp. He laughed. "She wasn't very appreciative of my offer."

Kita said, "Her husband wouldn't appreciate it either. He is a police officer. I have no authority to tell you what to do. But there are times when you should just be quiet. We do not need the police, **any** police digging around here, especially an angry husband."

Yoshikawa pushed the tray farther onto Kita's desk, wiped his mouth with his sleeve. "My superiors are asking for more of the same information, I assume."

Kita tried to ignore the tray. "As much as possible.

And soon. Here, read this. A list of questions, much as before."

"Why soon?"

"I don't know. And there is no point in asking. Just do your job."

The taxi drove up toward the grassy heights, the reliable and aging Mr. Mikami behind the wheel. The land was very familiar, and he stared out toward the harbor, the tops of the largest ships coming into view. He sat back in the seat, ignored it all, thought, One more time, I will get my pants dirty in a cane field, scuff my shoes in the mud and rocks. I do not understand why they ask this of me every day. Is it so different from a week ago?

The car slowed, pulled off the road, and Yoshikawa climbed out. Mikami sat quietly, as always, patiently waiting. Yoshikawa stepped into the tall grass, the cane spreading down the hill to his left. He kept clear of that, noticed his own tracks, made days before, and days before that. He crested the rise, the harbor now spread out in front of him. It was never as satisfying to be here as he would like, without a close enough vantage point to pick out the details he sought. But he dared not bring binoculars, nothing to show that his interest was any more than that of a sightseer. Across the harbor, he saw the battleships along Ford Island, and he searched now for the aircraft carriers. His brain snapped awake, and he scanned again, so many details, so many of the other ships committed to memory. Where, he thought, are the carriers?

He had seen the **Enterprise** sail out earlier that week, and there was nothing unusual about any one of the flattops leading a handful of smaller warships out to sea. It had become a pattern, surely some training mission, repeated again and again. Like clockwork, they would return, as would every battleship and their support vessels. But for one to leave, he thought, and then, the other two . . . that has not happened before.

He moved quickly up the rise, through the grass, slid into the back seat of the taxi.

"Take me to the tearoom. Fast."

As always, the women greeted him with smiles, but he ignored them and moved upstairs to the sun deck, grateful there was no one there to interfere. He swung the telescope toward the harbor, scanned the ships again, the view here much more detailed. Did I miss the carriers, he thought; are they somehow obscured? He took his time now, thought, There is a reason they want this from me today. They know something about the carriers being gone. Or they don't and they require confirmation. Take your time—no mistakes. He fingered the pad of paper in his pocket, the short stub of a pencil. It's all right out there. They want information, so I will give it to them. I will give it **all** to them.

## SATURDAY, 6 DECEMBER—
## NOW PRESENT IN PEARL HARBOR

Nine battleships
    Three light cruisers, plus four in dry dock
    Seventeen destroyers, plus three in dry dock
    There are no carriers in port
    There is no sign of barrage balloon equipment
    In my opinion, the battleships do not have
torpedo nets
    There is little to no aerial reconnaissance in
operation
    The American military forces show no state of
alert
    I imagine in all probability there is considerable
opportunity left to take advantage for a surprise
attack against these places.

# THIRTY-ONE

# Genda

**"F**rom the beginning, I have been concerned that there are so many pieces to this puzzle that it could simply come apart. I respect Admiral Yamamoto, and I know that he placed great faith in my skills in commanding this fleet. But we are so far from home and so close to our targets, and I cannot just ignore all that could happen, all that could go wrong."

Genda had heard these speeches many times from Admiral Nagumo. He has so much authority over us all, Genda thought. He has been given so much responsibility for the success of the mission. I wish he could feel what the airmen are feeling, that we are the tip of a great spear, a weapon that reaches all the way across this ocean. Genda tried to form words, some kind of argument to blunt the admiral's concerns. Around the long table, he could see Nagumo's staff officers watching him, as though they expected the "lunatic" Genda to erupt like a volcano. Nagumo was silent now, as though inviting Genda to speak. The words came slowly, with painful effort to control his usual manic outbursts.

"Admiral Nagumo, with respect for all of your concerns, I must quote a wise saying. There are times when you must use courage to push yourself up the mountain, even if you know you will not come down from the peak. Often it is the wisest decision to happily jump off."

Nagumo looked at the younger officers, then at Genda. "I am not familiar with that saying. Is it from the emperor?"

Genda had not expected the question. "No, sir. It is from . . . my mother."

There was low laughter around the wardroom table, the loudest from Fuchida, the man who would command the planes over Hawaii.

Genda ignored the good humor of the others, kept his eyes on Nagumo, who said, "Admiral Yamamoto places great confidence in you, Commander. The emperor and the Naval Ministry place confidence in me. We can only rely on ourselves, and neither you nor I are accustomed to the responsibilities we have been given. Neither of us has our superior officer with us, guiding us, judging what we do."

"Sir, the judgment will come from our deeds. We have no control, no influence on what will occur anywhere outside of this fleet. If those men in their fine suits and their well-pressed uniforms agree to embrace peace, then we will as well. But if this is to be war, then there can be no hesitation, no second thoughts, and no fear. The pilots are prepared to die for this fight."

"Commander, I cannot expect you to know what I feel. The ships of this fleet, they are very much like my children. I treasure them all. There is enormous risk in what we do."

Genda tried to find sympathy for Nagumo. This could be his last campaign, he thought. But we cannot wrap ourselves in the fear of **risk.**

"Admiral, respectfully I must say, we are not out here to avoid risk. We are here to damage one American fleet. It is no more complicated than that."

Nagumo stared at Genda, nodded slowly. "Well spoken, Commander. But I worry about the intelligence we have received. What if we have miscalculated? What if the American fleet is much larger than we have estimated?"

Genda smiled. "Then we shall have a great many more targets."

"We are targets as well, Commander. Perhaps when you are older and the weight of these decisions rests on **your** shoulders, you will understand my concerns. We are to attack a great world power. Your confidence is welcome, but I am concerned that we might sail home to Japan with half of what we came with. Perhaps, we may not sail home at all."

Genda looked at the admiral with the hard glare that Nagumo had come to know so well. "Then, sir, they will build shrines to us. I would welcome that, as would my pilots."

A young ensign appeared at the wardroom door. "Sir! Excuse me."

Nagumo looked up, said, "What has happened?"

"The destroyer **Isokaze** reports contact with a vessel, most likely a merchantman, sir."

Nagumo stood up nervously, the others as well, and beside him, one of his officers said, "Sir, we must confirm the identity of the vessel with all haste."

"Yes, of course. We cannot allow them to send any communication. Ensign, instruct the **Isokaze** to prepare to sink the vessel on my command. Let us go topside."

Genda kept his seat as the others flowed out, thought, This is not good, not good at all. There should be no other vessels in this part of the Pacific. A merchantman in disguise, perhaps? Their radios sending warnings back to their navy, setting the trap?

He tried to calm himself, knew his edginess was just one more symptom of the stress of the mission. He let out a deep breath, then another. The admiral's men will do their jobs. They will communicate with that ship, determine who they are and why they are out here, so far from the common shipping lanes. If they must sink a ship that flies a foreign flag, any flag, it could cause Tokyo a great many problems. But Tokyo must worry about those things. We have more important tasks to complete.

He stood, said to his aides, "I will go to my quarters now. Admiral Nagumo and the crew of this ship do not need us in their way." The two men stood at attention, backs against the bulkhead. He stopped at the door, said, "I will brief the flight leaders one more time before they retire tonight. The weather has taken a turn for the worse. I want to test their confidence for those conditions."

He moved out, down a narrow passageway, passed Nagumo's palatial quarters, a guard standing tall outside the door. Genda ignored the young man as he moved by, thought, This is what admirals do, I suppose, flaunt their authority. Or perhaps he fears thieves. He reached his own quarters, stepped inside, stood quietly for a long moment, so many thoughts rolling through him, so many details. He flexed his fingers, trying to relax, took deep breaths. Yes, Admiral, I have my concerns as well.

He sat down at a small desk, covered with stacks of papers—the flight plans for each of the groups, along with target lists and schedules. He sifted through, tried to focus on a detailed map, a smaller version of the scale model now in the operations room. He thought of Yamamoto, the older man eyeing him with the grim confidence of Genda's grandfather. I wish the admiral were here, he thought, to see all of this, to feel the pilots' raw passion for this fight, embracing the honor they will earn. Even now, they are in their quarters, but they're not begging for mercy, for protection. They pray to serve the emperor the best way they can. I wish Admiral Yamamoto could know that.

Or, perhaps he does.

He thought of the flight leader, Commander Fuchida, who would command the first wave from a bomber high above the targets. He has no fear, Genda thought, smiling. He has, perhaps, too much courage. He is arrogant, a joker. He treats this mission as though it will be fun. Even through so much of the training, his enthusiasm and his skills were one of our great strengths. He believes with absolute certainty that his men will fly gloriously over the American navy, that they will rely on their training, and they will destroy their targets. And so, I believe that as well.

He studied the map again, and the thought suddenly rose up inside of him, the great fear he had tried to ignore.

**What if the Americans know we are coming?** What if all the secrecy, the careful planning, choosing my route away from normal shipping lanes has been a waste of all our energy? Now, less than a day before the attack, we must confront some unknown ship? Is that by chance, or by design? Perhaps they have already sent their signal to Hawaii, warning them. Will there be antiaircraft batteries waiting for us, to shoot us out of the sky like so many birds?

**Stop this!**

He tried to grip the wild emotions inside of him, closed his eyes, thought of what he had said to his aides: **Let the admiral and his men do their jobs. That is, after all, why they are here.** Is this why they call you Genda the Lunatic, because you embrace such crazy thoughts? He slid the papers around on the table, searching yet again for details he had missed. He studied the numbers and the descriptions he had memorized and preached so many times before. He knew he was being ridiculous, but it never stopped him from reviewing the details, searching for the single deadly mistake.

The knock came, and Genda said, "What is it?"

The door opened slowly, and he saw his aide, Ensign Noti.

"Sir, identification was made of the merchant ship. It flies the Russian flag, and made no effort to contact the fleet. It seemed to keep a wide berth of us, sir. Admiral Nagumo did not feel it necessary to destroy them."

Genda waved the man away without a word, and the door closed. He stared at the papers, felt suddenly like laughing. There were a dozen reasons why you were terrified of the unknown ship, and none of them were real. Now, it is one less detail for you to ponder.

He looked again to the papers, had a sudden thought, called out, "Ensign Noti!"

The door opened immediately, and Genda said, "Go, find Commander Itaya. I wish to speak with him. Be quick."

The wait was barely a minute, a knock again.

"Yes. Enter."

The door opened, and Genda saw the serious stare of Shigeru Itaya, the commander of the squadrons of the fighter planes most now knew as the Zero. Genda didn't wait for pleasantries.

"Are you completely confident that our fighters are superior to what the Americans can send against us?"

Itaya smiled now, seemed to understand why Genda had called him. It was not the first time he'd been asked this question. "Commander, I am completely confident. In fact, after studying the specifications of the American fighters, I am confident that one of ours can successfully combat **three** of theirs."

"Thank you, Shigeru. Your confidence is welcome. Your fighters will be the first to go airborne, and you will protect the bombers and torpedo planes throughout the assault. If the Americans greet us with significant antiaircraft fire, the torpedo bombers will go to their targets last. They are too slow, too vulnerable to lead the assault."

He saw a wide smile on Itaya's face.

"I believe, sir, we have gone over these details a great many times. There will be no mistakes."

The smile remained, and Genda said, "I know.

Forgive me for being anxious. I agree with Admiral Nagumo that this is a puzzle with many pieces. Admiral Yamamoto has placed his career, his future, his life onto our shoulders. I cannot stop examining the details."

Itaya was serious now, said, "It will be a good mission, Commander. We are prepared, and no matter what awaits us, we will triumph. My squadron chiefs are in the operations room right now, where the scale models have been located. I must say, sir, it has been extremely helpful having such large maps and models of the target area available to us at all times. There is no mystery when we discuss the choice of targets. There will be no confusion."

Genda tried to smile, but it would not come. "Your confidence inspires us all. Now go, tend to your pilots. Perhaps once more, you can go over the details?"

Itaya made a short bow. "We shall discuss details as often as you would like, sir. Will you join us out on the flight deck?"

"Of course."

"Then I shall salute you from the cockpit of my plane."

Genda felt a wave of butterflies in his stomach, could not escape them. "We must have surprise, Shigeru. We must."

Itaya seemed puzzled by the energy behind Genda's words. "Is there any reason to think we will not?"

Genda looked past him, with the odd stare all of

his officers knew well. "I must know if the enemy awaits us, if they are prepared to meet the assault. **I must know.**"

Itaya laughed. "Oh, you will, sir. Tomorrow morning."

AIRCRAFT CARRIER AKAGI, AT SEA—
SUNDAY, DECEMBER 7, 1941, PREDAWN

Genda had barely slept, but was delighted to learn that most of his pilots had slept very well.

The ship was rocking even more than yesterday, and it was one more reason for concern. For most of the way across the Pacific, the seas and winds had been surprisingly peaceful. For Admiral Nagumo, calm seas had eliminated one serious challenge. Refueling any craft in rough seas could be extremely hazardous. Broken fuel hoses and collisions were nearly unavoidable. But to everyone's relief, the refueling had been accomplished almost without incident. Now, with each of the warships fueled, the tankers had been sent away, led by a destroyer that had escorted them back to a predetermined rendezvous position.

Genda thought of asking for tea, but there was too much anxiety swirling in his stomach, and breakfast was out of the question. He moved into the passageway, his aides responding, snapping to attention.

"I shall go to the operations room."

They followed, struggling to keep up with Genda's energetic gait. Behind him, a voice, one of Nagumo's officers. "Commander Genda, a moment. Please. Here is information you requested."

Genda forced himself to stop. "What is it?"

"Commander, we have received a wireless transmission from submarine I-72. They report that there are no American warships at Lahaina Roads. It is most regrettable, is it not?"

Genda stared at the man. "It matters not where the Americans have docked their ships. I have always expected they would be in Pearl Harbor, and submarine I-72 has confirmed that."

"It's just that . . . Admiral Nagumo had said if their ships were in deeper water outside of Pearl Harbor, sinking them would be a simpler matter."

"None of this is a simple matter. But we can destroy the enemy no matter where he sits."

The officer clearly didn't know what to say, and Genda turned, headed again down the passageway.

He passed the radio room, stopped, heard a low hum, saw a half dozen men with earphones. The radio silence had been complete, no transmissions at all going back to Japan. But close by, the battleship **Hiei** had the most powerful receiver among the ships of the fleet. It was that receiver that had picked up the final **Go** message from Tokyo, the confirmation that nothing had changed with negotiations in Washington, and so this mission would continue as planned. Genda had embraced the message with nervous glee, the pilots and their crews cheering the news.

Genda had been concerned that even the one-way wireless communication the fleet received, no matter how coded, could risk interception and provide the location, or even the intention, of the fleet. To address that vulnerability, the radio receivers were tuned to pick up commercial radio broadcasts from specific radio stations in Japan. Otherwise innocuous news and weather reports had been laced with code words and phrases that had been designed to pass a stream of messages to the fleet.

Genda kept going, paused at the operations room and eyed the scale model of Pearl Harbor. But there was no need now for another look. He felt the ship rolling again, said a low curse under his breath, moved up the largest ladder. He stepped out onto the flight deck, followed by his aides. There was nothing of the dawn yet, the stars mostly obscured by a wet haze. Toward the bow, a wave broke high, washing the deck, the spray blowing past him, driving a hard chill into his jacket. Flight mechanics were moving past, some struggling to stand upright. He had the urge to help, saw one man slipping down, another assisting him.

He felt a hand on his shoulder, one of Nagumo's officers, an older man.

"Commander Genda, the admiral has been looking for you. You are certainly welcome to relax in the admiral's wardroom. We have breakfast there, of course. A good place to enjoy the adventure of it all. And there is certainly no need to be uncomfortable. It's a little messy out here, after all."

Genda did not look at him, said, "This is no 'adventure' for the flight crews. My men will not be comfortable in their planes. Do we know what will happen with this weather?"

"Well, Commander, we had amazing weather up until two days ago. What we see now is much more common in this part of the ocean, so I'm told. It shouldn't affect the aircraft. Very soon, we will reach our attack point, and we shall turn all the carriers directly into the wind, while we also increase the forward speed of each ship. This will provide more lift for the aircraft as they move along the flight deck."

Genda stared at the man now, saw him brush wetness from his face with a handkerchief.

"I am aware how airplanes fly. Are the pilots in the briefing rooms? Perhaps you can instruct me what I should say to them."

The officer seemed to miss Genda's sarcasm, said, "Yes, I believe they have gathered. They are in the large operations room, just inside, to the right."

Genda had no more use for this man, talking to him as though he were some kind of sightseer. "Excuse me. I shall go inside then. Please enjoy the admiral's breakfast."

Genda ducked out of the wind, moved down the passageway. He could hear men talking, a joviality that pleased him to hear. He saw Fuchida now, coming toward him in his flight suit.

"Ah, Commander Genda. Look here, allow me to show you." Fuchida tugged beneath his suit, a flash of red cloth. "Red underwear. Lieutenant Murata and I bought the same color, the color of blood. If we are badly wounded, it will be difficult for our crews to notice. We do not wish to upset the others in our aircraft. If one of three is wounded, the other two could panic. We will avoid such a thing, wouldn't you agree?"

Fuchida's energy was overwhelming, and Genda stood silently for a few seconds, then said, "I suggest the best tactic is not to be wounded." He put a hand on Fuchida's shoulder. "We have worked very hard, Mitsuo. I have been honored to stand with you, to train your men. We may never have an experience like this again. It is all in your hands now."

Fuchida lowered his head. "You honor me, Commander."

Genda stepped back, saw more of the pilots gathering, and he stepped away, knew that his role was ending. Fuchida said, "Commander. I know you are concerned, but Honolulu sleeps. It is a peaceful Sunday morning."

Genda asked, "How do you know that?"

Fuchida was all smiles. "I went by the radio room. They were listening to the radio station in Honolulu. Some very peaceful music, the kind you play to keep the people asleep."

Genda headed for his quarters, only for a moment, to retrieve his heavier coat against the blowing wetness on the flight deck. He stepped inside, thought of Fuchida's smile, all the boisterous enthusiasm of the others. It is all good, he thought. It is all so necessary. He started to move back out, stopped, his hand gripping the handle of the door. The butterflies were relentless, and for one long moment he envied the pilots their good fortune, that after so many months and so much training, they would justify everyone's faith in the plan, and in Admiral Yamamoto. He smiled to himself, thought, My job now is to sit and wonder what is happening, and what will happen. Every minute there will be wondering, and then, more wondering. He moved out into the passageway, saw one of the pilots.

"Sir, Admiral Nagumo is searching for you."

Genda looked past the man, saw Nagumo coming toward him, said, "He has found me. Thank you."

The pilot withdrew discreetly, and Genda saw a smile from Nagumo. Genda could see a change in the admiral, a surprising calmness that he hadn't observed through the entire voyage.

They stood together in the passageway outside the larger briefing room, the pilots easing past, the admiral's presence stifling most of the chatter. Throughout the journey, the meetings and conversations between Genda and Nagumo had mostly been terse affairs, admiral to commander, fleet commander to flight trainer. But Genda could feel a difference now.

"Ah, Commander." Nagumo stopped, seemed out of breath. "I wanted to tell you personally that the fleet navigator has brought us to the point of attack. We are two hundred miles north of the island of Oahu. Thus far, Commander, we have been successful in every part of this mission. I now turn that responsibility over to you, and the flying group."

He saw emotion on the admiral's face, another surprise. Genda took a step back, stood straight, said, "Admiral, I am certain of our plan. And I am certain of our pilots."

At 0530, the two scout seaplanes were catapulted off their bases on the cruisers **Tone** and **Chikuma,** each with a simple yet dangerous mission. One would pass over Lahaina Roads, the stretch of open water between the islands of Maui and Molokai, confirming once and for all that the American navy had anchored no ships in that deepwater passage. The other would fly over and around Pearl Harbor, verifying that the American fleet had not suddenly put to sea, emptying the harbor of precious targets.

Both planes made their reports by radio, but there was one additional detail reported that helped ease Genda's twisting nervousness. Flying over the American bases on Oahu, the reconnaissance plane had encountered nothing to interfere with its mission: no intercepting aircraft and no antiaircraft fire. As Fuchida had said, the Americans were asleep.

The carrier had turned directly into the wind, the other five flattops doing the same. With the engines of the big ships pushed nearly to maximum, the violence of the ocean around them seemed magnified, great sprays of white pouring over the wide flat bow and down the flanks of the ship, soaking the flight crews as they scrambled around the planes. Genda felt helpless, ached to be a part of what was about to happen, to climb into one of the heavy bombers, launch a torpedo perhaps, anxious to know how the odd modifications would work in the shallow water of the harbor. He moved from one foot to the other, rocking himself in the buffeting wind, immune to the chill and the wet, every thought on the airplanes in front of him.

The pilots came out now, spreading across the flight deck, each man knowing just where he was supposed to be. Genda watched them, remembering so many details, the bomber pilots who trained so differently than the men who would fly the fighter planes, the magnificent Zero. Genda watched them climb up and into their planes, could see the white cloth wrapped around their helmets, carrying the words **Certain Victory.**

Genda now did as the pilots did: stared straight

upward, his eyes finding the carrier's mainmast in
the hazy darkness. The ship rolled and dipped over
a violent wave, and Genda grabbed a steel railing, steadying himself. He looked back toward the
planes, saw the faces of every pilot looking up, and
he did the same now, his eyes again on the mast.
The salt spray washed across the deck around him,
and he ignored that, kept his eyes on the mast, a
voice inside of him: **Raise it!** As if on command, he
saw the first flutter moving up the mast, the three-
sided flag, bright red with a white ball in the center.
It was the signal the pilots had been training for,
had wanted **now.**

He turned again to the planes, felt the sharp blast
of salt spray, thought, There are no more lessons
now, no more **details.** Nothing matters now but
the mission.

The engines roared to life, the sounds rolling over
him, deafening. The flight deck was bathed with a
new cloud of sea spray, the propellers driving the
pools of wetness back toward the stern. The crews
worked their planes, pulling chocks from the wheels,
pushing tails to straighten the line. Genda stepped
forward, just to be closer, to feel what they were
all feeling, the power of those engines, the power
of their weapons, the power in each man who flew
his plane.

Genda ignored the roll of the ship, blinked
through the heavy mist of the breaking waves, his
eyes on the first plane in line. He saw the man's

face now, Itaya, looking at him, the smile and the confidence that Genda always hoped to see. Itaya raised a hand toward him, his own salute, and now the flight crew in front of the Zero stepped away with a salute of their own. Itaya revved the engine, the air around Genda shivering with a hard blast of sound, the plane quivering in place, Itaya holding the brakes.

It lurched forward now, into the spray, toward the rising bow of the ship. Genda held his breath, watched the Zero leave the end of the flattop, then drop, out of sight, and he felt a stab of horror, **No,** it cannot be. But the plane appeared again, rising.

Genda put his hands on his face, holding away tears, his mind letting go of all the uncertainty and all the doubt.

Close by, the next Zero burst into motion, the others lined up behind it, waiting their turn. Genda watched them all, the fighters followed by the larger horizontal bombers. Genda saw another smiling face, Fuchida, a manic wave toward Genda as the three-man plane moved into position.

The dive bombers followed.

Then, finally, the torpedo bombers.

Genda stayed in place through every takeoff, ignoring the winds and the spray and the tossing of the ship. He realized the skies had lightened, and he checked his watch: 0620. He looked up, the formations of planes coming together high overhead, the good training, **his** training. The planes were already at differing heights, the Zeros climbing high above, the others moving to their assigned altitudes. He heard a new sound, a formation of the heavy bombers flying low, passing over the bow of the ship.

Genda smiled, his heart racing again, knew it was Fuchida. It was the signal they had devised, a last salute as Fuchida took control of the first wave of the mission, 183 planes on their flight path toward Oahu.

Genda stared out to the formations of planes, growing smaller, more distant. He ignored the manic activity of the flight crews around him, preparing their planes for the second wave, and for a long moment, the ship seemed to pause: no movement, no thoughts, no sounds. In his mind, he could see the face of Yamamoto, the old man who offered few compliments, who so rarely smiled. I hope you are smiling now, Admiral. Today we will start a war.

# THIRTY-TWO

# Outerbridge

DESTROYER USS WARD, OUTSIDE PEARL HARBOR—
SUNDAY, DECEMBER 7, 1941, PREDAWN

The sighting had been radioed to the ship just before 0400, by a sharp-eyed observer on the minesweeper USS **Condor.** Even in the darkness, the **Condor**'s watch officer insisted they had spotted a submarine, mostly submerged, moving through an area where no friendly craft should be. The **Ward** had responded, moving closer to the minesweeper, observers and sonar equipment laboring to confirm what the **Condor** claimed was there. After nearly an hour, the search turned up nothing. Men on both ships started to believe that the contact was likely a whale or large fish, the most common source for so many false alarms.

Outerbridge had gone through this before, but

he wouldn't embarrass the skipper of the **Condor** with any pronouncement to the minesweepers that the search was a waste of time. He had ordered the search continued, even as the minesweepers had moved out of the area. Searching for submarines, or for any other unauthorized vessels in the channels outside the entrance to Pearl Harbor, was, after all, why the **Ward** was there. Despite the ongoing search, Outerbridge hadn't communicated any sense of urgency to his bridge crew, because he didn't feel any himself. As the destroyer swept in wide circles through the deep water, Outerbridge went back to bed.

He had tried to relax on the cot, in the small makeshift quarters close to the bridge, had thought about what it was the **Condor** had seen. Since he had been in Hawaii, Outerbridge had made a sport out of whale watching, and like so many others, he knew that the winter brought the whales down from the frigid waters near Alaska. As he lay in the darkness, he thought of the amazing sight the day before, a humpback making a complete breach, a massive splash that reached the main deck of the destroyer. What did we look like to him? he thought. A mate? Or maybe he thought we were the biggest damn whale in Hawaii. And is he out there right now, convincing trained observers that he's a submarine? Careful, my friend. More than one whale has been blasted to hell by a gunner who made that mistake.

He didn't expect more than a couple hours of sleep, but after the turmoil of the last few days, he would take whatever he could grab. For the first time, Outerbridge had been given command of his own ship, a posting he had begun to think might never happen. He had suffered for months onboard the **Cummings,** a destroyer commanded by a skipper Outerbridge despised. As the executive officer, it was reasonable for Outerbridge to hope that someone in the Fourteenth Naval District might take notice of him, consider him for a command vacancy, even on something smaller than a destroyer.

But then the unexplainable workings of the navy suddenly shined a light on him, orders coming for Lieutenant William Outerbridge to assume command of the destroyer USS **Ward.** His first response was overwhelming joy, for both the command and the fact that it was a destroyer. Adding to his celebration, the navy had granted him an escape out from under the miserable boot heels of Captain George Dudley Cooper, his tormentor on the **Cummings.**

There were new curses, of course. The **Ward** was one of the oldest destroyers in the fleet, and thus was nearing the end of its useful life. The ship had gone to sea during the Great War, and seemed to wear that age with less than pride. The old-style four-stack configuration identified her as one of those tubs soon destined for the scrap yard. But not yet; for now, the **Ward** would patrol the waters close around the shores of Oahu, seeking out any kind of craft, big or small, that wasn't supposed to be there.

The other curse was a milder one, and seemed to draw pity to Outerbridge from some of his friends in other commands. Outerbridge was a graduate of the United States Naval Academy, which was not unusual among command officers throughout the fleet. But his crew now consisted of reservists, most of them from the state of Minnesota. Though Outerbridge was teased about the relative inexperience of his sailors, when he assumed command of the **Ward,** his first impression was that despite their relative lack of seasoning, these men at least had enthusiasm for their jobs. It was up to him to prove to them he could be an effective leader. Today, December 7, was his second day in command.

He stared up into the dark, thinking of his wife, Grace. She sent him a stream of letters across the Pacific that brightened every day he received them. Grace was in San Diego, along with their three young sons, and one of the frequent subjects of her letters had been a family reunion, the hope that his ship might make the journey to the mainland. He had sent off another letter of his own, telling her of his new post, and new ship, though he hesitated to tell her that "new" was not a word that applied well to the **Ward.** It was one more bit of abuse he had to suffer from his friends, that the **Ward** might not be capable of making it to the mainland at all; she might simply fall apart. Outerbridge took the ribbing for what it was, knew that those friends who mattered were happy over his new command, a posting similar to what most of them hoped to receive themselves.

But there was another kind of teasing Outerbridge had to endure. It was a secret well protected by his closest friends: He suffered from bouts of seasickness. For the **Ward** to be attached to the Fourteenth was a gift in itself. The **Ward**'s primary mission, as it was for several of the other "old tubs," was to patrol the waters close to the island. Thankfully for Outerbridge, that usually meant pretty smooth sailing.

He had nodded off to the soft hum of the engines, was surprised to hear a loud shout.

"Captain to the bridge!"

The call jolted him, and he sat upright, tried to clear his brain. He reached for a robe, threw it over his pajamas, scrambled out through the hatchway. "What is it? Talk to me, Mr. Goepner."

"Sir, we've been continuing the search, per your orders. But we've received a light message, from the **Antares,** over there, sir."

Outerbridge eyed the ship moving across the **Ward**'s bow, a mile distant. "What message, Lieutenant?"

Goepner had a pair of binoculars in his hands, said, "Sir, the **Antares** is being trailed by something."

Outerbridge stared that way, the faint daylight showing the details of the supply ship and her barge, and now, something distinct in the water between. Outerbridge felt a jolt, a single thought: That isn't a whale.

"Call General Quarters!"

The sharp whistle sounded and the ship seemed to burst to life, the crew emerging from the hatches, moving quickly to their positions.

Beside him, Lieutenant Goepner said, "Sir, is that . . . ?"

"It's a periscope. All ahead full."

They accelerated quickly to twenty-five knots, covered the distance to the **Antares** in minutes. He kept his eyes on the small black object, could see now that it was on the far side of the supply ship, still moving in line with the **Antares** as though pulled along on a string. As the **Ward** drew closer, Outerbridge could make out more details, saw nearly two feet of a small conning tower protruding above the surface.

"Sir, we're on a collision course!"

"Come left, Mr. Raenbig. Slip us between the sub and the **Antares.** I want to see what that fish does next."

Beside him, Goepner said, "Sir, it's like he doesn't even see us."

"I don't care about that, Lieutenant."

He heard the roar of a plane, looked up, saw a large flying boat, a navy PBY, making tight circles over the **Antares.** Two small balls fell from the plane, smoke pots, impacting the water near the sub.

Outerbridge said, "We've got a helper. Thank you, friend, but there's plenty of daylight now. We see him just fine."

Goepner stared out through his binoculars, the sub barely a hundred yards from the **Ward,** making no apparent effort to change course. "She's not very big, certainly not one of ours. What are we going to do, sir?"

Outerbridge eyed the submarine, tried to imagine the crew, incredibly brave or incredibly reckless. Or both. "We're going to sink her. Commence firing."

The first gun erupted, forward of the bridge, and Outerbridge flinched at the sound. A geyser erupted well past the sub, a clean miss. Damn! The sub was closer still, and he could see more details: rust and barnacles, the glint of the glass in the periscope. Now the second gun fired, just aft. The impact was immediate, the shell piercing the conning tower, the sub suddenly veering, rolling to one side.

Outerbridge turned that way, called out, "Signal four depth charges!"

The whistle sounded, four short blasts, and he could only wait, the depth charges rolling into the churning foam from the ship's engines. Almost instantly, the eruptions blew great fountains of water skyward, and Outerbridge heard cheers, the men reacting to the vast pool of oil now boiling up to the surface.

In seconds, one of the chiefs was there, smiling and out of breath.

"We nailed her, sir. No doubt."

"Good job, Chief. Mr. Goepner, we should report this. Encode this message." He looked at his watch. "Time 0651. **'We have dropped depth charges upon subs operating in defensive sea area.'** Take that below, send immediately. Somebody ought to know about this."

"Yes, sir!"

Goepner dropped into the radio room, and Outerbridge knew there would be no delay. But then Goepner returned, seemed concerned.

"Sir, I'm not certain that's the best message. There have been so many false alarms out here, people shooting at every kind of fish. I think maybe we should be more specific. Only if you agree, sir."

Outerbridge stared out toward the oil slick, the **Ward** circling slowly. "All right. Do this: **'We have attacked, fired upon, and dropped depth charges and sunk submarine operating in defensive sea area.'** "

"I think that's better, sir."

"Make sure they go out to the Fourteenth HQ. No delays. I wouldn't bet that fellow was by himself. He was too small. Where the hell did he come from?"

Goepner went below again, and the helmsman, Seaman Raenbig, was looking at Outerbridge with an odd expression.

"Something wrong, Mr. Raenbig?"

"Um, sir, certainly not. I just thought now that things have calmed down a little bit, you might wish to go below and put on your uniform."

Outerbridge followed the man's gaze, looked down. "It seems I may have dressed too quickly. This was to be a gift to my wife, eventually. It was rather dark."

Raenbig looked again to his post, stared out toward the bow of the ship.

"It is attractive, sir. Can't say I've seen a man wear a kimono before." Outerbridge could feel the man stifling a laugh. "Of course, sir, you **are** an officer."

The messages from the **Ward** were received by the intended stations. A flurry of conversation and debates eventually reached all the way to the commander in chief, Admiral Kimmel. After long minutes of chewing over the significance of what the **Ward** claimed to have done, Admiral Bloch, at the headquarters of the Fourteenth, finally made the decision. He ordered that before further action was taken, they would "**await further developments.**"

# THIRTY-THREE

# Elliott

Opana Army Radar Site, North Shore, Oahu—
Sunday, December 7, 1941, 7:02 A.M.

"It's 0700. I'm done. I got letters to write."

Elliott kept his eyes on the oscilloscope, said, "Yeah, maybe. Could use some fresh coffee. Any idea why they only do these shifts for three hours? Seems funny to shut us down so early. Hell, if you're gonna train somebody, train 'em when they can stay awake."

"Hell if I know why they put us out here in the first place. It's the middle of nowhere. I guess we drew the short straw. Or that captain, Jenks, he's got it in for me. Six stations, and we're out in the jungle."

Elliott laughed. "This whole island is jungle. Even Honolulu. Different kind of jungle, maybe. I'd rather be in San Diego." He twisted a knob on the oscilloscope, the image on the screen tilting slightly, as though he was squeezing it.

Lockard said, "Don't do that. Keep the signal straight up and down. More accurate that way, so they tell me."

Elliott twisted the knob again, then another beside it, the signal sharper. "See, Joe? That's why we're out here. So you can teach me stuff. You're the old pro, and I kinda want to learn this stuff. Captain Jenks told me that this stuff could change the whole world, and if you're an expert, you could get a hell of a good job someday."

Lockard leaned in closer to the screen. "You believe him?"

Elliott shrugged. "No idea. But we're here, and it's pretty clear that you're supposed to be teaching me how this gizmo works. Then, maybe you can tell me what the hell we need it for. What happened to using your eyeballs?"

Lockard stood straight, picked up a coffee cup. "Eyeballs don't work in the dark, or see things miles away. This is the new thing, George. Get used to it. The army's coming up with all kinds of newfangled gizmos, and not all of them shoot bullets. They sent you up here to learn, and you're learning, right?"

"Whatever you say, Teacher."


Private George Elliott had come to the army the year before, a twenty-two-year-old from Chicago.

Though not entirely certain just where he belonged, the army had singled him out for training in the new technology of radar, as well as a variety of other electronic tools just being developed. Assigned to the newly constructed radar stations scattered across Oahu, he would serve first as an apprentice, assigned to learn the operation of the new equipment under the tutelage of Private Joseph Lockard, whose experience and expertise was only slightly more advanced than Elliott's. Lockard's seniority came from the training he had already received on the radio aircraft detection device at the Opana station. It was designated the SCR-270, a piece of equipment that was, to most eyes, top secret. Lockard and Elliott had been told it could detect an enemy attack well in advance. Since there had never been an enemy attack with the SCR-270 in use, no one actually knew if what the army was doing might just be a waste of time.

This morning, they had drawn the assignment to spend their shift at Opana. As the radar sites had come into service, General Short had issued the order that the shifts would be brief, that a fully staffed office at Fort Shafter, where any reports would be monitored, pulled the men away from what the general insisted were more essential tasks, including the heightened vigilance against what seemed to be the general's favorite obsession, sabotage.

On Sunday, General Short's office had declared that the radar stations were to operate for only a three-hour shift early in the morning, from four to seven. The young men whose job it was to stare into the round screen of the oscilloscope were usually grateful for the brief turn. Sunday morning followed Saturday night, and if any of these men had enjoyed the good fortune of a night on the town, they'd barely slept before manning their post.

"Hey, Joe, it's after seven. No reason to stick around. I guarantee there isn't a soul at any of the other stations. Most of those guys are ready to bolt out the door by 0659."

Lockard stood, stretched, let out a long low groan. "There's supposed to be a breakfast truck rolling up here. They're always late. I need some coffee that's better than this crap—it's been boiling for an hour. Hang on, I'll be shutting this thing down in a couple minutes, and I'll show you how to do it. There are just a few switches."

Elliott backed his chair away from the screen, said, "Hey, where's my helmet?"

Lockard moved closer to the unit, said, "You weren't wearing it. You must already be asleep. Hey, what the hell is that?"

"What?"

Lockard pointed at the screen, and Elliott leaned in closer, said, "What the hell is all of that?"

Elliott slid in front of the screen, adjusted one of the knobs, sharpening the signal. "This thing's gotta be busted. No wonder they sent us up here. We got nobody to bitch to."

Lockard put a hand on his shoulder, said, "Move. Let me look at this mess. Go to the plotting board and do what I tell you."

"Whatever you say, boss."

Elliott waited, could feel an itch of urgency, Lockard staring hard at the screen. Lockard said, "Mark five degrees northeast of azimuth at one hundred thirty-two miles. Jesus, this is an enormous signal. At least fifty planes."

There was no humor now, and Elliott drew the line on the board, then said, "All right, what now? We call this in to Shafter, the Info Center?"

Lockard sat back, still looking at the screen. "Maybe not. Christ, it's Sunday morning. Their shifts ended at 0700. I bet nobody's home."

Elliott moved back to the screen, stood over Lockard. "Let's call 'em anyway. They like having drills, and this is a perfect test, something they're not expecting. Maybe we'll get stripes for this."

"And maybe we'll get chewed out by the captain."

Elliott stared at the mass on the screen, said, "It's still there. If this is a glitch, it's a hell of a big one. And that can't be seagulls."

Lockard leaned forward, rested his chin on one hand, eyes still on the screen. "God, that looks like fifty for sure, maybe more. I guess it's navy planes. All right, call Shafter. Just be ready to get yelled at."

Elliott picked up the phone, dialed, the answer surprisingly quick.

**"Private McDonald, switchboard."**

"Yeah, this is Opana. Is the controller there? We have a report."

**"Yeah, well, the office is off-duty. The shift here ended at 0700."**

Elliott looked at Lockard, who had not moved from the screen. "Look, Private, our shift ended too. But we've got an unidentified image we need to report."

**"Hang on, let me write this down. Opana, right? Nice up there, ain't it? Wait, damn pen's got no ink. Hold on."**

Elliott looked over Lockard's head to the screen, said, "That getting closer?"

"It's getting closer."

The switchboard operator returned, said, **"Oh, hey, I've got Lieutenant Tyler here. He hasn't left yet. Hold on. Sir?"**

**"This is Lieutenant Tyler. Who is this?"**

Lockard was there, his hand out for the phone. Elliott said, "Lieutenant, please hold for Private Lockard." He whispered as he held out the phone. "It's Lieutenant Tyler."

Lockard took the phone, his eyes still on the screen. "Lieutenant, this is Private Lockard at Opana. Sir, this is the largest sighting I've ever seen . . ."

———

The lieutenant took the report, the details of which seemed overwhelming. But the notion of incoming planes sparked his memory, a report he had received the day before. Like so many others, he had passed the time in the early morning hours enjoying soothing music, courtesy of KGMB radio in Honolulu. Tyler had been told what many of the more senior officers already knew, that when any squadron of planes was inbound, usually from the mainland, the radio station would broadcast its music all night. This would signal to any command on Oahu to expect the planes, while also providing a pleasant welcome to the planes themselves, a homing beacon the navigator on each aircraft could latch onto.

On this night, the army was expecting the arrival of twelve B-17 bombers, making a stopover on their way across the Pacific.

As Lieutenant Tyler digested the report he was receiving from Lockard and Elliott, he eased his own concerns, and theirs as well, recalling the incoming flight of bombers from the West Coast. Despite what the Opana signals seemed to suggest, the incoming aircraft appearing on the screen were nothing to be alarmed about. Lieutenant Tyler's last words to the two men at Opana:

**"Well, don't worry about it."**

# THIRTY-FOUR

# Biggs

USS ARIZONA, PEARL HARBOR, HAWAII—
SUNDAY, DECEMBER 7, 1941, 5:20 A.M.

**H**e woke early, still too dark to see his watch. He heard the usual snoring around him, Wakeman's worst of all. It was a permanent argument in the compartment, the victims of Wakeman's nightly chorus of snorts razzing him about it nearly every day. Wakeman of course denied any offense, and so, the back-and-forth would ensue. Last night, Biggs actually slept fairly well, even with Wakeman nearby. He had no idea why.

He stared into the darkness, knew he couldn't climb down, not yet. Expelling yourself from the hammock was a clumsy exercise, certain to wake up most of the men around you. Just relax, he thought. Dawn will come soon enough.

Last night, he'd watched a movie, shown on a screen on the fantail, **Dr. Jekyll and Mr. Hyde,** with Spencer Tracy. Biggs knew almost nothing about Hollywood, but he'd heard stories from some of the older veterans about how the actor James Cagney had once visited the ship. It was a source of pride, the men around him clearly impressed, though Biggs had hidden his ignorance of just who this Mr. Cagney was. But he knew Spencer Tracy now, and after seeing the film, he likely wouldn't forget him.

He thought of the bizarre images he had seen. How do they do all that stuff? Is every movie like that one? There had been no theater in Palatka, and no chance that a young Tommy would be allowed to go all the way into Jacksonville just to waste money on a movie. He shifted his weight slightly, loosening a kink in his back. You don't know much about anything, he thought. I guess the longer you stay in the navy, the more you'll learn.

Beside him, Wakeman made a loud grunt. Biggs smiled and thought, I wonder what it's gonna be like for Ed's wife, if he ever finds one.

The whistle sounded now, shrill and loud. The compartment came alive, the first lights switched on. It was the usual routine, groggy men emerging from their hammocks, stowing the canvas in the cabinets, making way for the mess tables to be set up. Biggs hit the floor, moved to his small locker, glanced at his watch. It was 0530.

He knew Wakeman had been in town, had listened to him stumbling into the compartment close to midnight. Biggs watched him now, saw a slight stagger.

"Have a good time, Ed?"

Wakeman sat in one of the metal chairs. "I'm starting to think there's no such thing. I pissed off some big lug of a Hawaiian, said something he didn't like to his girlfriend or sister or who knows what. I was just slipping away from that crisis when I knocked a beer out of a marine's hand. **Splash,** right on his shoes. There must have been four hundred of them, like they were coming up outta the floor. I'm lucky I'm alive."

Biggs started to dress, said, "You don't have to go to town, you know. You keep blowing your pay on that stuff, you're gonna be broke forever. And you look like hell."

Wakeman fumbled with his clothes. "Thanks, pal. But if I hadn't run like hell from those marines, I'd look a whole lot worse."

The lights were fully on now, other men going about the task of preparing the compartment for breakfast. Biggs checked his watch again. "Why don't you get a shower? You've got time."

Wakeman tugged on his pants, said, "For the twelve seconds they give you to get the job done, it's hardly worth it. I'll shower in a couple of years, when I've finished my hitch. You can put up with me until then."

Biggs finished dressing, thought of the crew's shower. Twelve seconds was an exaggeration, but thirty? Take any longer than that and some petty officer might grab you and toss you out. Kincaid would probably make you eat a bar of soap just for good measure.

The thought of Kincaid made Biggs probe the pain in his face, the swelling mostly gone. Wakeman was struggling with his shoelaces, looked over at Biggs. "I see you poking around. You look a hell of a lot better than you did yesterday."

Biggs thought of Dr. Johnson's assessment: A slap, no matter how hard, is a good way not to leave evidence. Biggs continued to probe the soreness, said, "Yeah, it doesn't hurt too bad. Let's just drop it, okay?"

"Sure. Nothing we need to talk about. Hey, what's your duty today? Time off?"

"No, I'll be in sick bay. Sunday morning's usually our busy time, when we get all the sailors worse off than you."

"Well, I'm gonna find me a secluded place some-where up top, get me a suntan. Hell, this is Hawaii, and when my time is up, I wanna go home all crusty burnt, so's the gals will know I've been here."

The mess attendants appeared now, with platters of eggs, pancakes, and a heaping stack of fried Spam. Biggs sat in his usual seat, watched as the eggs made their way toward him, followed by the customary ketchup bottle, the only way to add flavor to powdered eggs.

Biggs sipped carefully from the coffee cup, then ladled the eggs and Spam onto his plate, stabbed at a pair of pancakes, coated them with a small ladle of syrup. Beside him, Wakeman said, "Pancakes are extra rubbery this morning. Make good life preservers. Not sure what would happen if you dumped these eggs in the harbor. Don't wanna know."

Biggs ate in silence, listened to the usual chatter from down the compartment, a flood of complaints, as though griping was required. He grabbed an orange from a large bowl, thought of holding on to it for later, but was too tempted, ripped at the peel. He stuffed a section in his mouth, but it was sour and now he had a mouthful of pits. Nothing like back home, he thought. He ate a piece of Spam, savored that, a luxury his parents could never afford. Mom would love making this kind of meal, he thought. The eggs would be fresh and she'd make better pancakes for damn sure.

"Hey, Ed, your family do a big Sunday breakfast?"

Wakeman squeezed the words toward him through a wad of pancakes stuffed in his mouth. "Corn flakes."

Kincaid suddenly stepped through the hatchway, his expression no worse than usual. Biggs expected some kind of nasty comment, or even an acknowledgment of the damage he had inflicted on Biggs.

But Kincaid ignored him, said, "Listen up, worms. At 0755, morning Colors will sound, followed by 'The Star Spangled Banner.' I'm ordered to tell you what you morons already know, so that at least some of you will attend the ceremony on the fantail. I am told that this **suggestion** is so the crew will show support for our band. If you don't show up, I'll discuss that with the admiral, the next time he and I have tea. If you do show up, don't use that as an excuse for being late for your duty shift. Now finish your damn breakfast." He paused, faked a smile. "Ain't the navy fun?"

He spun around, was gone.

Biggs felt a heaviness to the silence, knew that word had spread about the punishment he had taken from Kincaid, some of the evidence still on his face. But no one but Wakeman would speak of it, and then only in a private place. Biggs stood, his plate clean, the mess attendants swarming through, removing the plates and the remnants of food. Others were standing as well, stretching backs, rubbing stomachs.

Wakeman said, "So, you gonna go aft to the fantail and rub shoulders with the officers, or you gonna go to work?"

"Actually, I'm going to see the band. I've met a few of 'em—nice guys. It would be great if they won that contest."

"If you say so. I'm gonna go hide out from

Kincaid, in case he decides he wants me to scrub the head with my toothbrush. Have fun."

USS Arizona, Pearl Harbor, Hawaii—
    Sunday, December 7, 1941, 7:55 a.m.

Biggs breathed in the salt air of a cool, perfect morning. There were sailors along the main deck, some already on duty, manning various stations. He moved past a cluster of junior officers, and realized one of them was Lieutenant Janz.

"Excuse me, sir?"

The men turned to him, Janz lighting up. "Mr. Biggs. One more game tomorrow. You ready?"

"Yes, sir. We're playing the marines again, right, sir?"

"Yep. Good way to end our season. They're tough. So, you'll be on the team again next year?"

"Yes, sir, if that's okay."

"You're not a reservist, are you?"

"Oh, no, sir."

"Good. Wasn't sure. Hate to see you jump ship just when our team was getting really good. Woody will be back, I know that. Several others."

He could see the other officers checking him out, knew Janz would fill them in.

"Well, sir, I'm heading to the fantail. I'd like to see the band, the Colors ceremony."

"See you on the ball field, Mr. Biggs. Tomorrow at 1500. The passes will be with the OOD."

"Thank you, sir. Sirs."

Janz returned to his conversation, a pair of the officers watching Biggs as he moved away. Well, that feels good as hell, he thought. We'll put a decent team together for sure. It had never occurred to him that he might play baseball more than one season. He felt a wave of pride, as though he belonged to something on the ship that had value. Officers knew his name. I wish Kincaid would come to watch a game, just once. No, don't be an idiot. You'd strike out three times, and he'd kick your ass.

He hurried now, hoping he wouldn't miss the music. He glanced out toward Ford Island, saw sailors lining the rail, all of them staring out that way. He heard the rumbles now, saw a burst of fire, smoke rising. Beside him, "Hey! Some jackass is bombing the base!"

"Head aft. Looks like a better view."

The flow of men moved that way, and Biggs saw more plumes of smoke, heard the whine of airplanes, more thumps. All of it seemed to be on Ford Island.

He followed the crowd, curious, more men jogging along the rail, comments around him, "Jesus, what's going on? Some army idiot using live bombs?"

"Hell, it's a drill. Musta needed to blow up some extra stuff."

"Or some dumb son of a bitch got the wrong orders. Leave it to the army."

The men around him had slowed, hugging the

rail, staring out. Biggs looked out toward the fantail, thought of the band. Damn! I'm gonna miss
it. More men were emerging from the passageways
behind him, and now, from the loudspeakers,
**"Battle stations. All hands. Battle stations."**
Biggs looked again toward the smoke on Ford
Island, thought, What the hell is going on? Battle
stations? Men were still rushing past him, both
ways now, some of them angry, one man laughing,
and he heard more jokes about the army's stupidity. He knew he was supposed to report to sick bay,
still hesitated, saw more smoke billowing up from
the island. There was a new sound, screaming overhead, and he looked up, saw the plane, heard a loud
voice: "Jesus, it's a Jap!"

Another plane sped past, moving out past the bow.
The plane seemed to roll over, made a looping turn,
came in fast toward the ship. Biggs could see the
flickers of fire along the wings, sharp whistles in
the air close by, the deck behind him punched and
torn, shells skipping across the steel of the bulkheads.
Men dove out of the way, and Biggs dropped down
against the rail, staring at the splintered deck. He
rose to his knees, his heart pounding, saw the open
hatchway, men crowding inside. He pushed himself
up, made the short scamper into the passageway,
the other men making way. Around him, men were
shouting, all at once, a chorus of angry questions.
He moved farther down the passageway, saw others
moving past, some with helmets, more questions,

cursing. The machine gun fire came again, outside the next hatchway, the pinging of lead against the ship's steel, a man screaming. An officer hurried past, shouted to him, to the others, "Get to your posts! **Now!**"

Biggs ran down the passageway, climbed the ladder, and raced into sick bay. Both doctors were there, Johnson talking with urgency on the telephone receiver, three of the pharmacist's mates and a handful of corpsmen as wide-eyed as Biggs, waiting for their instructions.

Biggs was out of breath, looked at Condon, said, "Sir, what the hell's happening?"

Condon raised a hand, silencing him, pointed toward Johnson, who put down the receiver, said, "We are being attacked by the Japanese. We have casualties throughout the ship. Dr. Condon, take a couple of medical kits, and you and Mr. Biggs go aft. I'll stay here with the mates. Corpsmen, spread out forward and amidships, check all the decks."

Condon said, "Are we sure of this? It's the Japanese?"

Johnson was angry, said to Condon, "Dan, I spoke to the captain. It's the Japanese. No more questions. You and Mr. Biggs make your way aft. There are people down who need our help."

Johnson looked up toward a rattle of popping sounds, shells impacting the steel above them. The deck beneath them suddenly shook, staggering the men, the ship listing slowly. Across from Biggs, Vaughan said, "What the hell was that?"

Block said, "A collision, felt like."

Johnson said, "Don't think so. Something hit low, belowdecks. Christ, could be a torpedo." He looked at Condon. "Go! We'll be doing what we can here."

Biggs followed Condon down a passageway, down a ladder, out onto the main deck, the sounds of airplanes in every direction. The wounded were scattered along the deck, and Condon stopped, knelt down. Biggs saw blood on the deck, saw the man's chest ripped apart, a bloody gash. Nearby, a second man was screaming, rolling side to side, his arm nearly severed. Condon shouted to Biggs, "Bandage! Sulfa!"

Biggs obeyed frantically, Condon working quickly, Biggs watching. He understood that all the doctor could do out here was stop the bleeding. But there was too much bleeding.

Condon shouted something, his words drowned out by the roar of a plane racing past. Biggs felt desperate, didn't know what to do, but Condon grabbed his arm, began to move again. The doctor slowed, glancing at one man out near the rail, but he didn't stop. Biggs looked at the man, saw a piece of his skull missing, the man's blood flowing across the deck, more blood than Biggs had ever seen.

The noise around him was growing louder. There were more planes passing close overhead, more of them farther out, swirling around other ships, some flying low across the water. The machine gun fire came again, ripping through the tower high above, chattering sparks, a row of bright flashes down the side of the ship, men going down on the walkway high above him. A familiar sound came, the ship's own antiaircraft guns. There had been so many drills, so much practice at targets that weren't there. But the targets were all around them now, and the gunners were beginning to fight back.

Biggs followed Condon, kneeling again beside another man, and Biggs strained to hear the guns, the **right** guns. But there weren't many, most of them horribly silent, as though no one was there, as though no one thought they would ever be needed.

Another plane raced past, straight along the ship, machine gun fire pinging and sparking against the steel, men hunkered down. But there wasn't good cover. Biggs saw a man tumble over, spinning from the impact of the shells, blood on his back. Condon was there quickly, rolling the man over, tearing at his shirt, the man's chest ripped apart, hard screams, Condon shouting toward Biggs. "Morphine! Give me a syrette!"

Biggs dug into the kit, his hands jelly, fingers not working, but he felt the syrettes, handed one to Condon. Condon looked at the men huddled nearby, said, "Listen! There's nothing I can do for him now. Stay with him, if you can. One of you keep his shirt pressed into his wound, steady pressure. We'll get stretcher bearers back here quick as we can!"

The men seemed frozen, their eyes panicked. They stared at the wounded man, the flowing blood, another horrible stain spreading on the deck. Biggs felt pure helplessness, watched Condon, saw a flash of anger, Condon shouting at them. **"Do it! Help him! Hold the shirt!"**

The sailors obeyed, crawling toward the wounded man, and Condon rose, stared at Biggs with a furious glare.

**"Let's go,** Mr. Biggs. There's so much more. We can fix all of this later on."

Behind Biggs, a shout, and Biggs saw a corpsman, Hankins, already dropping down to the wounded man. Condon yelled toward Hankins, "Good. Do the job. We're going aft."

Biggs could feel himself shaking, heard more clatter of fire overhead. A plume of water launched skyward close to the ship, farther out in the water.

**"Now,** Mr. Biggs!"

He followed Condon quickly up a ladder, and Biggs felt another hard **bump,** the deck rising up beneath his feet, then settling down, the ship rocking slowly side to side. He wanted to ask Condon, anyone, **What is that?** What does it mean? But the doctor was dropping down to more wounded men, another bloody body. Biggs's eyes were pulled to a man's gut, ripped apart, the man's eyes watching him, tears on his face, and Biggs thought, What do I do? How do you fix this?

"Keep moving, Mr. Biggs."

Biggs saw the same hard look on Condon's face, then the doctor moved away to another wounded man. Out across the harbor, Biggs saw a plane flying low, crazy low, nearly touching the water, a long black bomb sliding off its belly. The plane rose up slowly, just enough to pass over the ship, and Biggs could see the open cockpit, the pilot looking down, looking at **him.** And then, the pilot waved.

The thunder beneath his feet came again, the ship rocking, and nearby, more antiaircraft guns were doing their work. Condon still moved, closer to the fantail, and Biggs saw more wounded men, a fresh horror, a man sliced nearly in two, rivers of blood flowing across the deck, spilling into the drains. Condon stopped, staring for a brief moment, said something Biggs couldn't hear, too much noise, more shouts, the engine of a plane, coming across the water. He felt himself yanked down hard, Condon beside him, the plane machine-gunning the deck, the hatchways behind them. Biggs closed his eyes, bent low, nothing else to do, waited for the plane to pass. He pushed himself up from the deck, realized it was wet, thick and syrupy, looked at his hands, dripping with blood. He felt sick, but his brain kept that away, and he saw the teakwood deck behind him, shredded. He felt himself pulling away, to some other place, thought, This can't be real. He wanted to laugh, someplace opening up inside of him, trying not to see the blood caking on his hand, one thought, I guess there's no more holystoning here.

Condon shouted into his face, "Mr. Biggs! I need you here. **Right here.** Do you hear me?"

The doctor's voice shook him, cut through the fog. He nodded sharply. "Yes, sir."

"All right, let's go. We need all the gauze we've got, and we have to rip bandages from shirts or pants. There's so many men down. Are you okay?"

The roar of the planes was farther away, no danger close by, at least not yet.

"Never seen this before, sir."

"Neither have I. But we have to do the job."

"Yes, sir."

Condon climbed to his feet, his white pants mostly red, a trail of footsteps through the blood. Behind a ladder, a cluster of men were gathered, one man calling out to Condon.

"Doc! Over here!"

The men made way, Condon went down to his knees, and Biggs saw a pair of men, side by side, both with stomach wounds, one man moaning, nonsensical words, the other with wide terrified eyes, looking at Biggs. "I'm gonna die! The Japs killed me!"

Condon took the kit from Biggs's hand. "You're not dying yet." He looked up at Biggs. "Get down here. Hold this fellow's hand. **Do it!**"

Biggs obeyed, knelt in another red pool, took the terrified man's hand, leaned closer to the man's face. "Hey, buddy, you're gonna be fine. The doc, he's the best there is."

The other man was still moaning, delirium and shock, the sound drilling into Biggs, Condon trying to quiet the man, administering a morphine syrette. Condon looked the other way, toward the bow, the direction of sick bay, a long way away.

"Damn it all, we need stretcher bearers and more corpsmen! It must be just as bad toward the bow."

Biggs felt agonizing helplessness, still holding the wounded man's hand, his eyes still looking up at Biggs with terror.

"Don't let me die. I don't wanna go to hell. Help me."

Biggs leaned close again. "You're fine, just a wound. The doc'll fix you up. It'll be okay. Nobody's going to hell." Biggs watched Condon sprinkle sulfa powder in the wound, spread a bandage on the other man's belly. Biggs stared at the doctor's work, his fast hands, precise motion. "Sir, what do you want me to do? Tell me!"

Condon continued to work on his man, the moans more faint. He said, "Morphine's working, bleeding's almost stopped. We get him to the hospital ship, he'll be okay. Okay, let me check your patient."

Biggs realized he was still holding the man's hand, and Condon was close beside him now, put a hand on the man's neck. He let out a breath, said, "You can let go, Mr. Biggs."

Biggs looked at the patient, the eyes calm, the fear gone. The man's face was a light gray, but

Biggs wouldn't let go. He squeezed the man's hand, then again, like a beating heart, his mind telling him it was the thing to do. Condon put a hand on Biggs's arm.

"Nothing you can do. Let go of him."

Biggs released the man's hand, felt tears, heard Condon, "No time for that. We have casualties back here. Let's keep working. I want a quick look all the way aft, see how many more, then I'll move up the port side. I need you to move forward quick as hell to round up any corpsmen and stretcher bearers. We have to get these men to a hospital as quick as we can. Do you understand?"

"Yes, sir. I can do it, sir."

"All right. Let's check the stern, the fantail, then you can double-time it to sick bay, get word to Dr. Johnson to send the stretchers and stretcher bearers, that we've got a couple dozen casualties aft that we can still save." Biggs caught the stink of dense smoke, a black cloud swirling past, and Condon looked out into the harbor, said, "Good Lord, the **Vestal**'s on fire. Jesus."

Biggs said, "What do we do? Can we help?"

"Not now. We have our problems right here."

Biggs heard another plane, heavy and low, another dive bomber roaring past just overhead, then gone. The impact thumped into the ship, the deck just forward, a man shouting, "A bomb—direct hit!"

There was a hush for a long second. Biggs could see the crushed hole in the steel, the men who could move scattering out toward the fantail. But then . . . nothing. Another man yelled out, "It didn't go off! A dud! Thank God! That makes two of 'em."

Biggs looked down between his feet, thought of the bombs sitting somewhere down below. Or maybe, he thought, they went all the way through, right out the bottom of the ship. How the hell could they do that? Why didn't it blow up?

More planes rolled past now, and Biggs ducked down, felt the sharp punch of an antiaircraft gun firing right above him, men shouting, running, more wounded, a pair of dive bombers screaming past. The lull came again, and he followed Condon up onto the fantail, the stern of the ship, suddenly had a clear view across the harbor. There were planes everywhere, some high above, others very low along the water. Plumes of water rose up along several of the battleships, smoke billowing upward from other ships, the **Vestal** close alongside, still burning. Biggs stared at the planes, helplessly waiting for the next one to take aim at the ship.

Condon had bandaged a man's arm, gave him reassuring words, and Biggs moved closer to him, angry at himself. **Do your job.** He followed Condon again, the doctor searching for anyone he could help. Condon seemed to freeze, staring away out beyond the stern, said, "Oh my God. It can't be."

Biggs looked that way, toward the other battleships, that glorious formation lining the quay along Ford Island. Other men had gathered, staring at a new horror. Biggs saw what they all saw, heard Condon, others: "My God. It's the **Oklahoma.**"

Biggs watched as the great ship leaned to one side, then leaned farther, the superstructure tilting toward the water, dropping closer still. In a long sickening minute, the ship rolled over, its hull and keel and one screw out of the water. For that minute, those men on the **Arizona** watched what they knew to be impossible, knowing that no battleship in this fleet could ever be made to capsize. And now, they could see **Oklahoma**'s crewmen, those who could escape as she rolled over, scrambling over the exposed hull of the ship. And they all knew that many more must surely be inside.

Condon turned to Biggs, a hand on his shoulder. "Go. I'll head up the port side, do what I can there. Bring me more kits, bandages, stretchers. Dr. Johnson will know what you need."

Biggs moved down off the fantail, tried to jog his way forward, but there was debris everywhere, more wounded, and the going was slow. He passed one group of men, working one of the antiaircraft guns, a gunner yelling with bloody rage, **"Where the hell are our planes?"**

It was a new thought for Biggs, and he looked skyward, saw more of the same, the red meatballs on the wings of the planes, on **all** the planes. The gun fired, straight up, and Biggs craned his neck, but there was no time for gawking. Another plane was coming in low and fast, straight along the ship.

He heard a splatter of machine gun fire, fell to one side, hard on his shoulder, the deck beneath him like the others, the polished teak now split and shattered, pulled away from the steel beneath it. A hand was on him, helping him up.

"You okay, Mac?"

Biggs stood, eyes on the damaged deck. "Yeah, thanks. That was close."

It was no one Biggs knew, and he was already gone.

He pushed on, tried to avoid the stains of blood, saw a corpsman kneeling beside another wounded man, and then, another dead man, most of his head sliced away.

The deck rolled to the side even more, and Biggs steadied himself against the rail, the nightmare of the **Oklahoma** filling his mind. He gripped the rail, breathing hard, forced himself to let go. **Get to sick bay!** Beside him, a man fired his pistol at a passing plane, useless anger, Biggs watching the plane, a waggle of its wings, another smiling pilot, now racing away.

Biggs was beneath another of the antiaircraft guns, the barrel straight up, firing a round. He was puzzled, looked skyward, saw a formation of planes, very small, very high. The gun fired again, one man cursing, **"Too damn high. We can't reach the bastards."**

Biggs started forward again, stepped through a wide puddle of blood, one more horror spread out alongside one of the ladders. He tried not to see it, made himself think of Dr. Johnson. How bad is it forward, in sick bay? How do we get these people to the hospital? He looked up again, drawn once more to the formation of distant planes, hidden by the clouds, then visible. He was just past the third turret, the great cannons pointing aft, realized that none of the big guns had fired at all. Mighty weapons, he thought, useless now, with nothing but airplanes out here. Where the hell did they come from?

He was not quite amidships, the great superstructure above him and forward of that, the bridge, the command centers, the men who would know what to do. He looked up that way, thought of Captain Van Valkenburgh. He watched me hammer one of Woody's fastballs. What does any of that matter now? He looked again toward the hatchway far in front of him, the ladder up to the quarter deck, thought, What if the captain's wounded? How do we know? We have to help them all. It's what we have to do.

A plane passed over, from Ford Island, out into the harbor, men responding with whatever weapons they could find. Another came now, past the bow of the ship, speeding across the harbor, barely thirty feet above the water, then pulling up, banking sharply, now racing toward the smaller ships farther away. Biggs picked his way forward again, but in the midst of the chattering machine gun fire and the heavier blasts and the shouts of men, he heard an odd sound. It was a whistle from high above, louder now. He never saw the bomb, but felt the impact through the steel deck, up near one of the forward turrets, a shudder beneath his feet. He stopped, one hand holding tight to the rail, saw others doing the same, searching, waiting for . . . something.

It didn't go off?

The ship erupted in front of him, the bow rising sharply out of the water. A blast of fire punched him backward, a crushing fist that drove him against the bulkhead. He put a hand over his face, reflex, fire blowing all around him, flames sweeping over him. There were no other sounds but the thunderous roar, more blasts blending together, a deafening chorus of hell. The deck collapsed downward, and he fell with it, one arm gripping a ladder, the heat searing every part of him. His hand was still clamped on his face, the only protection he had. He looked down, the wood of the deck torn away, the heat torching the back of his hand across his face, a breath of fire tearing at his skin, burning his scalp. The roar of the fire was relentless, engulfing him, and he covered his face with his arm, let go of the ladder, pulled himself away, sliding on his backside, then crawling, one leg after the other. As he moved away from the worst of the fire, he heard other sounds, the screams of men suffering the burns, blind and limbless, the terror and the pain from an explosion that was destroying their ship.

As he moved farther away, he heard impacts

around him, smacks on the deck, on the steel beside
him. He hugged against the bulkhead, nowhere else
to go, tried to open his eyes, saw a man's arm, no
blood, pale white, a naked bone at the shoulder.
There were other pieces of men, blown high with
the blast, coming down onto the ship, some too
grotesque to identify. Limbs were hanging on the
rail, tumbling slowly down the ladder, like pieces of
mannequins. Across the deck, he saw a man's head,
a white skull, the eyes burned out. He turned away,
the image immediate and terrifying. There was
other debris, not all of it human: shards of steel,
pieces of burned equipment, the leg of a table beside the leg of a man.

Biggs crawled again, the fire driving him from behind, pain on his back, his legs. The harsh burn on
his scalp was growing worse, and he probed lightly
with a finger, testing. His hair was gone, the touch
agonizing, and he screamed from the pain, no one
to hear but the bodies around him, and behind
him, the great maw where the fire boiled up. He
turned toward the fire now, a quick glimpse, saw the
entire bow engulfed in flames and smoke. He turned
away, slid along the deck, blessedly farther from the
flames and the suffocating smoke that engulfed
the bow of the ship, the smoke flowing past him,
seeming to swallow the entire world.

He kept moving, a glance upward, saw the towers,
knew he was amidships, aft, could see the dense
black smoke drifting in a massive cloud outward,

above the harbor. The blistering heat still followed him, and he crawled again, saw others, men appearing through hatchways, horrible burns, some bathed in their own blood, some with skin falling away from bones. Some, like him, were escaping the fire any way they could. He heard a shout, a man staggering past him, his pants burned away, the skin on his legs snow white. The man stumbled close to Biggs, then rolled onto his back, his face a mask of suffering, the flesh on his chest burned away, bare ribs. Biggs stared, nothing he could do, nothing the doctor could do, no medical kit, no morphine. He wanted to tell the man something, soft words, try to help, to offer a minute of comfort. But the man seemed to stiffen, his back arching upward, and he let out a whining sound, and then, relaxed. Biggs looked down, thought, He doesn't hurt now. What else could I do?

The heat still shoved at him from behind, carried on a swirl of breeze, and he put his hand on his face again, a desperate effort to protect his eyes. The deck was becoming blistering hot, and as he crawled, his hands began to burn. He tried to ignore the pain, passed another piece of a man, one leg, half a torso, and again, the bones stark white. He forced himself to keep moving, tried to stand, realized now that his shirt was mostly torn away. His chest was bright red, a brief thought of Wakeman, wanting a sunburn. **Wakeman.** Oh God, where is he?

His feet were soaking up the scalding heat from

the steel below him, and he moved more quickly, other men doing the same. Many were dazed, staggering, wrapped in the shock of the blast. Some had obvious wounds: a grotesquely broken arm, a bloody neck. Biggs slowed, the heat not as blinding, tried to blink through the goo in his eyes. Around him were more pieces of debris spread out on every surface, dropped by the blast, which had thrown everything skyward. There were more pieces of men—a single leg bone, another skull—and he glanced over to the water, thought, How many are out there? He stared back toward the stern, the fantail, not as much smoke there, more of the crew, men working with fire extinguishers. His brain seemed to roll over, the raw stupidity of that. **Fire extinguishers?** What about hoses?

He saw a man in a helmet, his dungarees and shirt perfect, as though he had just come aboard. The man was holding a fire extinguisher high, a small stream shooting into an opening in a bulkhead. Biggs felt a sudden need to kill the man, screamed, "What are you doing? It's up there, the bow! Don't you see the fire?"

The man stepped back from him, said, "Easy, pal. There's no water. The hoses are gone. This is all we've got. We can't do anything about the bow. There are small fires everywhere."

Biggs backed away, every part of him shaking. The man watched him, then returned to whatever job he was trying to do. Biggs continued aft, past men and bodies and shouting, every hatchway alive with men coming out, some with burns they would not survive, finding the open air only to die on the deck. There was a new horror now, an awful mystery. As he moved past the scorched and charred men, a sickening smell rolled over him. He flinched from it, but there was no escape, and he understood now. It was them—the burned men, their burned flesh.

Biggs pushed past them, fought tears through the gooey crust in his eyes. He passed a man vomiting; no wounds he could see. The man was bent over a corpse, white bones and black burned flesh. But the face was there still, recognizable, and Biggs had to turn away, knew that this man had found someone who mattered to him. He pressed on, past the astounding carnage, sights and smells.

Biggs could see the fantail now, smoke rising beyond, from fires on other ships. He pushed himself that way, fought the misery of the burning pain in both feet, the soles of his shoes partly melted, sticking to the deck. He slipped the shoes off, felt the heat in the deck beneath him, but he could move now. His mind was clearing, appraising, nursing the burning in his lungs, trying to avoid the searing pain on his face, much worse on his scalp. Only his legs seemed undamaged. He leaned on the railing, away from the men who were working, the gunners and firemen.

He thought of Condon. He sure as hell needs

help, he thought. It's my job. **My damn job.** He looked toward the fire again, shielded his face, staring into a furnace. His tried to see the first turret, thought of sick bay beneath it, the familiar passageway, the hatchways and ladders. The pain of the heat still ripped at his face, his eyes burning, his hand only a meager shield. He stared for a long moment, but the heat was swallowing him again, and he could not stay, had to keep going, get to the stern. He danced slowly, lifting his feet from the scalding heat of the steel deck. Beside him, a man stood silently, his clothes burned away, then another, his arm hanging like a bloody piece of rope. There were others still, all along the decks, the dead and horribly wounded, burned and broken, some curled into black heaps, some of the wounded staring at their own bones, their own guts.

Biggs could offer them nothing. He shared the shock of those who could still understand, the least injured knowing they had to back away, that every second could bring another blast. Some of the men looked above them, toward their own duty stations perhaps. They all understood that those crewmen, those commanders who had been on the bridge, or forward of the bridge, in or beneath the forward gun turrets, those men were simply gone. As they moved away from the immediate danger of the fire, some, like Biggs, turned again, staring toward the fiery abyss, absorbing the raw shock of what the Japanese had done to their ship.

For Biggs, there was one vision he could not accept. But his mind latched onto the horror, no matter how much he tried to keep it away. He knew
that somewhere **down there,** in the midst of the
boiling storm of fire, was the doctor who would
know what had to be done, who would have done
everything to help the wounded, who would have
sent the medicine and the bandages and the men
with the stretchers.

# THIRTY-FIVE

# Kimmel

RESIDENCE, MAKALAPA HEIGHTS, PEARL HARBOR—
SUNDAY, DECEMBER 7, 1941, 7:50 A.M.

He dressed hurriedly, angry at himself for having overslept. He would never be tardy to this particular appointment with General Short. It was one show of personal pride he could demonstrate to the army, since it was a near certainty that when it came to golf, Walter Short would usually win. Try as he might to improve his game with lessons and practice, Kimmel could never seem to gain any proficiency. Short was sporting about it, and never gloated. But the same message was always there for Kimmel to chew on, that the army would nearly always win this particular battle.

He tied his shoes, still sitting on the soft bed, not quite ready to start the day. Still, he thought, It's

only golf, and it's Walter Short. He can wait if he
has to.

He stood, checked himself in the mirror, straightened his collar. Thank God for golf, he thought.
There's no predicting how long I'll have to enjoy
this job. You've already made one mistake: showing
too much anger toward the president. That can't
possibly be a good idea. He knew very well what Jim
Richardson had done, thought, He spit too much
angry mouthiness into too many prominent faces.
But damn it all, I'm right. The president probably
knows I'm right, but he has to keep everybody in
Washington happy, Knox, Stimson, Marshall, and
God knows who else.

There's something to be said for having a command thousands of miles from those kinds of eyes.
And yet, all those men in their exalted positions,
too far away to understand the vulnerabilities we're
facing out here. Fine, we should be concerned about
the Philippines. But our defenses there are strong
and getting stronger. They're well equipped and
well led. Even the president is in the fog about all
the islands I have to worry about—Wake, Midway.
Hell, I can't even remember half of them without
looking at their little dots on a map, places that
are an asset because they happen to have enough
sand to build a runway. How the hell would we ever
fight a war by sticking a handful of fighter planes in
the middle of absolute nowhere?

Like his staff, like the intelligence officers he

respected, he found it very difficult to believe that the Japanese would be so absurdly stupid as to strike out and purposely start a war with a power as strong as the United States. The navy alone, he thought, our carriers and battleships could reduce that country to rubble in short order. Admiral Halsey believes that, and he's right. Surely the Japanese know that.

He looked at his nightstand, a copy of the Honolulu **Advertiser,** folded to its editorial page.

**"Japan is the most vulnerable nation in the world to attack and blockade. She is without natural resources . . . She has a navy but no air arm to support it . . ."**

He tossed the paper aside and pulled his white jacket off the wooden hanger, slipped his arms through the sleeves. He tugged it tight, took another look in the mirror, began to work the buttons, looked toward the black telephone.

The morning's first phone call had accomplished what his alarm clock had not, jarring him from some pleasant dream about palm trees. The call had been from Commander Vincent Murphy, Kimmel's assistant war plans officer, who happened to be on duty when the report of the **Ward**'s contact with the unknown submarine had worked its way up the chain of command. Kimmel barely knew the **Ward**'s skipper, Lieutenant Outerbridge, and was completely skeptical of the report that the destroyer had actually sunk a submarine. There were too many of those kinds of sightings, and Kimmel knew that along the shores of Oahu, the broken carcasses of whales were testament to the runaway imaginations of overeager ship captains and their gunnery officers.

For the second time that morning, the phone rang. "What is it?"

**"Commander Murphy, sir. Another report from Destroyer** Ward, **sir. She reports a sampan in the area of their submarine contact. They're escorting it out of the area, to deliver him to the Coast Guard."**

"A sampan?"

**"Fishing boat, sir. The** Ward **says the thing had no business wandering into the area."**

Kimmel was annoyed now. "What about the sub they sank? Is there confirmation?"

He heard a sudden commotion on the other end of the line, voices, a man shouting, and Kimmel said, "What the hell is happening there, Commander?"

**"Sir, the Japanese are attacking the fleet, all across the harbor. Sir, this is no drill."**

Kimmel heard a rumble, then another, what seemed to be a long drum roll, the cascading thunder of a distant thunderstorm. He glanced outside, the early morning sun showing only puffs of white clouds. The thunder came again, closer, then farther away, and he dropped the phone, ran quickly down his main stairway. The thunder was continuous now, and Kimmel ran outside, stood in the yard of his home. His fingers still fumbled with the buttons on his jacket, his eyes fixed on a scattering of aircraft, all directions, all altitudes, smoke rising from every part of the harbor he could see.

He realized he wasn't alone, his neighbor, Captain Earle's wife, staring silently. Kimmel moved toward

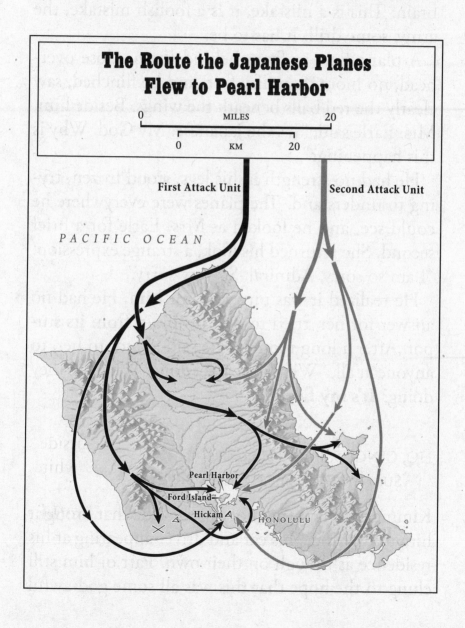

## The Route the Japanese Planes Flew to Pearl Harbor

0      MILES      20

0      KM      20

First Attack Unit

Second Attack Unit

PACIFIC OCEAN

Pearl Harbor

Ford Island

Hickam

HONOLULU

their yard, a clearer view. The woman stood frozen, soft words, "What's happening?"

He tried to comprehend what he saw, planes in a steep bank, diving low across the water, others straight overhead. The words rolled through his brain: This is a mistake, it is a foolish mistake, the army, some drill. It has to be.

A plane flew in from behind them, close overhead, no more than fifty feet, and he flinched, saw clearly the red balls beneath the wings. Beside him, Mrs. Earle said, "It's the Japanese. My God. Why is this happening?"

He had no strength in his legs, stood frozen, trying to understand. The planes were everywhere he could see, and he looked at Mrs. Earle for a brief second. She returned his look, a strange expression. "I am so sorry, Admiral. So very sorry."

He realized it was pity, pity for **him.** He had no answer for her, tried to pull his brain from its stupor. After a long moment he said aloud, to her, to anyone at all, "What have they done? What are they doing? **It's my fleet.**"


HQ, CINCUS, PEARL HARBOR—
  SUNDAY, DECEMBER 7, 1941, 8:05 A.M.

Kimmel had little memory of the ride that brought him to his office, his car and driver appearing at his residence as though on their own. Part of him still clung to the hope that this was all some god-awful dream. But there was no hiding from what was so very clear. From the second deck of his headquarters building, he could see it all, the panoramic view he had always enjoyed. Now there was smoke and planes, shattering explosions and plumes of water. The battleships were the most clearly visible, including the astounding horror of the **Oklahoma** rolling over, its hull no more now than the belly of a dead whale.

His office had filled with other officers, their low comments adding details he didn't need to hear. He heard Commander Layton behind him, nervously chattering, another man calming him. No one spoke to Kimmel, no one breaking the spell he could not break himself.

They all jumped at a sudden explosion that blew a fireball a thousand feet in the air, black smoke rising in a dense cloud, hiding the ships that lay beyond, far across Ford Island. They could see the specks of debris, sprinkling the water, showering the ships close by, and Kimmel said in a soft voice, "What was that? What ship?"

Beside him stood Admiral Pye, the man who commanded the battleship fleet.

"The **Arizona.** Jesus. Just like that. How can that be?"

"And the **Oklahoma**'s capsized?"

Pye seemed to gather himself, no one else speaking. "Yes, sir."

"Why didn't we know they were coming?"

Kimmel knew there was no answer. He knew as much as anyone that they had ignored the answers to questions none of them had bothered to ask. "Do we know where their carriers are?"

Behind him, Murphy said, "No, sir. We'll find them, sir, if you order it."

Kimmel turned, was surprised how many of his staff were there.

An aide said, "Sir, you and Admiral Pye should not be here together. A shell could do great harm to this command. You understand, sir."

Kimmel looked at Pye. "He's right, Bill."

He felt himself surfacing, as though finally coming awake: the job, the duty. He put a hand on Pye's shoulder. "Bill, let's do what we can. Right now. Get our planes in the air, get Short's planes in the air. Find those damn carriers. They can't be that far from here, and they can't escape us if we locate them quick enough. Radio Halsey to get the **Enterprise** back here, use his planes. He'll find them."

Murphy spoke again. "Sir, I would suggest we spread recon patrols to the south and west. That's the most likely position, the most likely route they took to get here."

Kimmel felt anger shooting through him. "Then why in hell didn't we find them before they did . . . this? Didn't General Short have his planes out there? Isn't that the army's job?"

Behind him, McMorris. "Sir, I've spoken to General Short's aide. I'm sorry, sir, but it seems that the army believes that reconnaissance was the navy's job."

Kimmel kept his eyes on the swirling formations of planes, more hits rocking the larger ships, small blasts rocking destroyers, some of those near the dry dock close by. He lowered his head, closed his eyes, but the sounds pulled him back. A plane sped past, close overhead, met by a chorus of firing from the ground.

There was a loud crack, and Kimmel staggered back, felt a sharp pain in his chest, the window in front of him punched with a jagged hole. Men held him, urgent voices, and he touched his chest. But there was no wound, only a black stain on his shirt. He saw the mashed fragment of a shell on the floor, and one of the aides picked it up, said, "Fifty-caliber, sir. A spent shell. Are you okay, sir?"

Kimmel took the shell from his aide, rolled it over in his fingers, and looked again through the cracked glass. He saw another great blast near the dry dock, pieces of a smaller ship blowing apart, pieces of the men who served her. He felt the lead in his hand, said, "It would have been merciful if it had killed me."

# THIRTY-SIX

# Biggs

USS ARIZONA, PEARL HARBOR, HAWAII—
SUNDAY, DECEMBER 7, 1941, 8:55 A.M.

hough the roar from the fire hadn't subsided, the men who had survived the initial blast had begun to work together. Most hadn't noticed, but the word was spreading that the planes were gone. The only sounds now came from the great fire and the screams of the wounded men. Biggs kept his eyes skyward, many others noticing now the empty skies, wondering just where the Japanese had gone. To those survivors on the **Arizona,** who could only count the damage closest to where they stood, it seemed obvious that the Japanese had accomplished exactly what they had set out to do.

From the fantail, what seemed to be the safest place on the ship, those men not working in rescue parties belowdecks could make out bits of details from the other battleships along the quay. The most obvious casualties were **Arizona** and **Oklahoma.** Some of the ships had been berthed side by side, and the ones closest to Ford Island, **Maryland** and **Tennessee,** had been shielded from the worst assaults by the ships beside them. But none of the great ships was undamaged.

Already, rescue boats were swarming around any ship that had been struck, including ships on the far side of Ford Island, and others across the harbor itself, some in and around the dry dock, where **Pennsylvania** had absorbed its own share of punishment.

With none of the medical staff to be found, Biggs was doing as much as he knew how, lining up the wounded beside each other, making his own appraisals of their status. Finally, a pair of corpsmen appeared, one man carrying wounds of his own. They did as much as the conditions would allow, Biggs offering his help in any way he could. He tried to ignore his own misery, could see that some of the men spread along the deck were in far worse shape, and that certainly, many of them would not survive. He had done most of his work on the starboard side, something inside him keeping him close to the open water. The fire still engulfed the forward half of the ship, the searing heat relentless, small pops and blasts adding punctuation marks to the utter destruction.

He leaned back against the rail, easing the cramping in his back, shifted the weight on his stinging feet, curled over, trying to escape the boiling heat. He looked forward through a break in the smoke, saw the repair ship **Vestal** still in place close to the side of the **Arizona**. He stared, realized there was no fire. The **Vestal** had been engulfed by a blaze of its own, but men now swarmed over the decks, rescue boats working around the ship. If they put out their fire, why can't we?

A voice in his head scolded him. **Shut up.** We have to get the hell off this ship, and damn soon.

Sailors emerged from the closest hatchway, one man helping another with a bloody wound, the man's leg bent in a grotesque shape. Biggs moved that way, said, "Put him down right here. There'll be a doc here soon."

It was a lie he had to tell, the only comfort he could offer.

He knelt by the wounded man as he had done with so many others, the two corpsmen working farther along the deck, too many patients of their own. Biggs saw terror in his patient's eyes, and tried to speak calming words. But there was no calm, and no words. Biggs was now gasping through the burning in his lungs, suffering though the agony on his head. He stood, staggered by the pain in the soles of his feet, aimed for the rail, easing down with the slope of the deck. He looked out to the water, tried to take a deep breath, to clear the smoke, but the burning was digging too deep, his scalp still too painful to touch, his face red and aching.

I can't help anybody, he thought. But I'm alive. Maybe Dr. Condon is too. Maybe. I could use him right now. Names rolled through his mind, Wakeman, Vaughan, Lieutenant Janz, Woody. God help us, God help them. He looked around at men still coming aft, more survivors escaping the massive fire. Some were taking charge, officers he guessed, sharp voices, some barely dressed, skin burned away, faces red and blistered, hairless scalps. Others were trying to help as he was, laying men flat, pulling them to one side of the deck, allowing the others to pass. Biggs watched with angry helplessness as more men emerged through the passageways, some with hands wrapped in bundles of cloth, the steel railings and bulkheads below too hot to touch. He heard the begging of men too burned to walk, trying to persuade others to go below, to rescue a friend, pleading with others to return to the hellish place they had barely escaped. And through it all was the relentless smell, some of that carried on the breeze from the great fire, smoke and roasting flesh, a kind of hell that was impossible to avoid.

Biggs eased down to his knees, the weakness and the pain winning the battle.

"Hey, sailor, come on, lie down over here."

He looked up into the eyes of an older man,

sensed the man was an officer. But there was no uniform, just shorts and one shoe.

"I'm sorry, sir. I can't stand for long—my feet. Sir, I was forward."

"Yeah, sailor, we all saw it. Some were closer than others. You're lucky to be in one piece. Anybody who wasn't on deck felt it below. There's a bunch of men still down there. If you feel up to it, pitch in with one of the rescue parties. We need to go below and get those people out. We've got to clear this ship quick as we can, get the casualties to the mainland."

The officer moved away, and now the familiar sound returned, rising up above the deep rumble of the fire. Biggs saw the plane dipping low over the hull of the **Oklahoma,** leveling out, flying directly over the fantail. He heard the machine guns, the faint flashes from each wing, the impact tearing along the deck, across the legs of the burned men. Biggs curled up tightly, nowhere else to go, the pops and scrapes of the shells close past him.

Other faces were watching the harbor, one piercing voice, "They've come back! You bastards! **You sons of bitches!**"

There was more shouting now, wounded men screaming profanity at the departing plane. But the planes were swarming above them again, sweeping over the harbor. Biggs felt paralyzed, his arm still over his face, the only protection he had. He tried to hide his sobs, the burning in his eyes made worse by the tears. The agony of the burned men around him became noisily worse, men whose skin was blistered, enduring fresh wounds from machine gun fire. Others were silent now, their bodies punched and ripped by the new assault.

More planes sped along the row of smoking battleships, machine gun fire and dive bombers. Biggs looked skyward, high above, saw another formation like before, the high-level bombers making their own run. He was surprised to hear the antiaircraft guns, what sounded like a great many guns in a beautiful chorus of firing. Immediately, he saw the result, a dive bomber plunging straight into the harbor. He heard brief cheers, **Arizona**'s guns opening up again, and more all along the quay, sprays of fire that punched the planes out of the sky. A man hobbled across the deck, steadied himself on the railing.

"That's better. Now we're ready. No more surprises, you Jap bastards!"

Biggs tried to feel the man's enthusiasm. He fought the pains that gripped him so hard, the pain in his lungs growing worse. He looked for the officer he had spoken to, felt a desperate need to help, to do **something,** but he knew the help might be for him.

The antiaircraft guns continued their fire, another plane spinning out of control, splashing down. Biggs struggled to control himself. The pain was overwhelming, and he fought for some kind of sanity, angry at himself. Dammit, you want to be a corpsman? Then be a better patient. Do something. You're alive, right? It was like two voices inside his head, one of them sane, calm, the other in a furious rage. Okay, how bad are you? Breathing's tough. Damn tough. You've got your pants, so your legs are okay. No shirt, a hell of a sunburn. No, it's worse than that. Hair's gone. Scalp hurts like hell. And my face feels like it's been peeled off. He touched his face, a mistake. He felt watery blisters, no eyebrows, his lips cracked. He sat, leaned against the rail. You can't do this. You can't act like a little boy. Men are dying. **Do something!**

He looked skyward, the second wave of Japanese planes strafing all over the harbor, the island, the mainland. One skimmed low over the **Oklahoma,** the survivors on the ship's hull flattening out, the plane spraying them with machine gun fire, one more insult. From the dive bombers dropping low across the harbor and those at high altitude, the bombs continued to fall, bomb blasts large and small in every direction. But the slow-moving dive bombers and torpedo bombers made fat targets for the antiaircraft guns. Biggs and the others around him watched planes falling, shattered and ripped by hundreds of guns from every ship, the unprepared now fully armed and fully manned, eager for a target.

Across the deck from Biggs, one man with bloody hands shouted, "Why the hell aren't we standing out? We gotta get the hell out of the harbor.

We're sitting ducks. Where the hell's the captain? The officers?"

Another man moved closer to him, responded, "Seaman, I am an officer. I'm sorry, but we're not going anywhere because half this ship is gone and sitting on the bottom of the harbor. We've likely lost the captain. He was on the bridge, and the bridge is gone. Now, are you hurting? I can give you something. But we have to stay right here until somebody in command tells us what to do. How about you help me with that man over there? He needs a pal right now."

Biggs sat up, his back still against the railing, felt a gasp of relief. "Dr. Condon, it's Biggs, sir."

Condon turned, looked at him, surprised. He seemed to flinch at Biggs's appearance. "Mr. Biggs, thank God. I thought you were . . . Well, I sent you forward . . . I thought you were in the blast."

"I was pretty close, sir."

"I can see that. Burns on your face and scalp. I don't have much of anything left for treating burns." He lowered his voice. "There are fellows up here who lost all their skin. Just peeled off. Never seen anything like that. Poor devils don't have a chance. And I ran out of morphine."

**"Plane!"**

Biggs curled up again, and Condon dropped down beside him. The machine gun fire pinged across the railing, chattering off the bulkhead, one man in the hatchway suddenly collapsing. The plane was gone in a few seconds, and Condon cursed, moved quickly to the hatchway, Biggs struggling to follow. The man was ripped apart, another pool of blood. Around them were more moans, mindless yelling, a new chorus of fear and pain and misery rising up from the men spread all across the deck.

Biggs leaned in close to Condon, one hand on the doctor's shoulder for support. "What do we do? We gotta help 'em, sir."

"Mr. Biggs, go back over there. Sit down. You're hurt pretty bad. There's nothing much I can do for any of these men except wrap up their wounds." Condon lowered his voice to a whisper. "I expect we'll hear the abandon-ship order anytime now. The Japs don't seem to be done with us, and the rest of us could get blown to hell at any time. There's not much else we can do for the wounded except get them off this ship. I don't know how many corpsmen survived, or where they are. But the harbor's filling up with rescue vessels, and we'll be able to leave here pretty soon. Go, sit."

Biggs obeyed, limped past the wounded and burned men, saw antiaircraft guns firing above him. More men came up from below, helped by others, escaping the deepest bowels of the ship, some with burns, others choking from the smoke.

He heard a sound, high above, a high-pitched whistle. He looked skyward, saw the distant planes above the clouds, mostly hidden by the smoke.

The bomb impacted the deck on the port side,

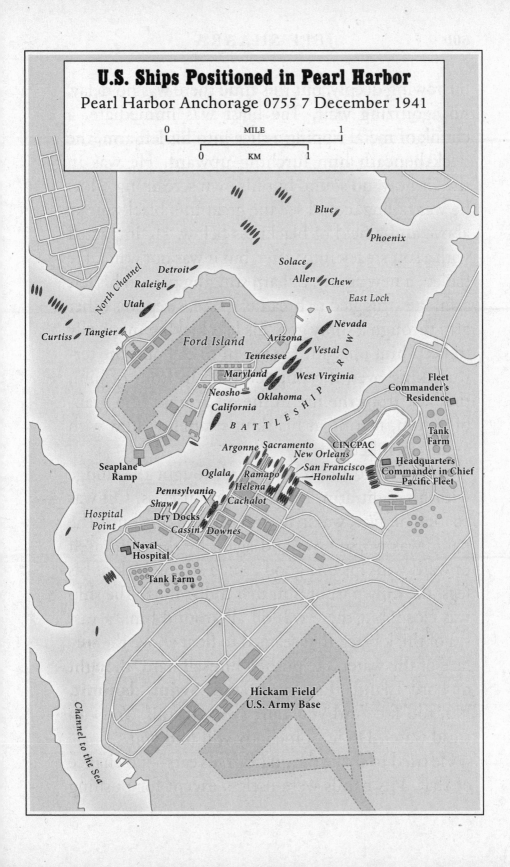

# U.S. Ships Positioned in Pearl Harbor

Pearl Harbor Anchorage 0755 7 December 1941

burrowing deeply, but this time there was no delay, no agonizing wait. The blast was immediate, a chunk of metal ripping a slice into his left arm, the deck beneath him lurching upward. He was in the air now, no sound but his own screaming. Now he was falling, could see the great fire, black smoke above and a field of blackness below. He impacted with a soft smack into water, but it was not water. He flailed, a new agony, a sharp stinging pain in his left arm. He struggled to breathe, to see, swept his other arm through a slimy goo, his legs kicking manically to keep him upright. He began to call out, the terror taking over, the ship looming in front of him, the heat from the fire in the oil around him grabbing him, tearing at his skin, strangling him with an oily blanket.

Biggs kicked himself upward, fought the sludge with his right arm, his left nearly useless. Oil was coating his face, was in his mouth, choking him. The panic was worse now, and again he thrust himself upward with his one good arm, a strong kick of his legs, the only part of him that didn't hurt. The ship was close, but there was oil all around him, a vast sea of thick black that seemed to float above the surface of the water. He pushed himself hard, thought of Ford Island, the closest land. **Swim, dammit.** No, too far. And you can't swim in this. You can tread water. Do it. Somebody will find you.

He tried to shake the oil from his ears—no chance of that. His hands were useless except for pushing the oil away from his face or creating a small open area around his body, but the spread of the oil was relentless. His burns were their own fire, raw screaming pain, and he tried to focus on breathing, swept his arm over the water's surface, could feel that the oil was several inches thick. The stink was overwhelming, a different kind of burning in his lungs and throat, his painful breathing sucking in more of the sickening fumes. He felt himself weakening, panic returning, a new fear. **I'll suffocate.** Okay, keep pushing up. Go! He kicked hard again, bobbed above the oil, tried to shout, choked instead, his stomach curling up with nausea. The effort was draining him, his breathing harder still, ripping agony in his lungs.

He kicked upward once more, his eyes catching the rolling ball of fire that spewed out of the forward half of the ship. But now there was a new horror. As he thrust upward again, his energy fading, no strength, he stared toward the shattered bow of the ship, and could see that the fire wasn't confined to the ship: It was on the water. The oil was more than a hell of stinking fumes and choking—it was a carpet of flame.

**Swim!**

He began to flail through the oil, his legs working rapidly. But the oil was covering him, tearing at the burns on his face and head, choking and blinding him, a new torture from the open wound on his arm. His good arm jutted forward, and he felt a different pain, a collision with something hard, and he draped his arm over a piece of debris larger than a man, fat, with a skin of wood. Deck, a piece of the deck! He held on tightly, tried to ease his breathing, every breath stabbing him, boiling nausea. He couldn't hold it back, vomited violently, the oil unyielding, thick in his nose. He gasped for air through his mouth, then vomited again, forced himself to hold on to the floating debris, his lifeboat.

He looked back toward the fire, saw the flames spreading slowly across the water's surface, black smoke blending with the great roar still boiling out of the ship. His eyes cleared just a bit, and he saw more smoke, smaller fires, could see **West Virginia** close to **Arizona,** and to the left of her, the naked hull of **Oklahoma.** There was smoke from the other big ships, **California** and **Tennessee,** and all across the harbor, in the dry dock, where **Pennsylvania** was moored, another large column of smoke.

The blasted piece of decking had become his life preserver, the only chance he had. He rested his right arm, tried to feel for the wound on his left, but there was no letting go. Beneath him, his exhausted legs hung loosely, and he tried to calm his breathing, took short breaths to slow the pain in his lungs. But the fire was moving toward him, driven by the soft breeze, stinking smoke passing close overhead. **You've got to move!** Kick, get out of the oil. He tried to find open water, but the oil seemed to expand as far as he could see. Just get away from the ship. It's got to be clear farther out.

The smell of the fire blew over him again, and he couldn't control the instinct, gagged, more oil seeping into his mouth. He tried to spit, gagged again, wrapped his arm tightly around the piece of debris. Just kick, he thought. Away from the ship.

His legs obeyed, but the movement was slow going, the debris putting up too much resistance against the deep layer of oil. Maybe climb up, he thought. Wave your hands. If there are boats, they've gotta see you. He started to kick, was bumped by another piece of debris, thought of bringing it closer, adding to his lifesaving raft. He forced his left hand outward, a punch of searing pain, wrapped his fingers around tiny handles. He tried to pull it in, then stopped, his hand pulling back, a shock. He could see now that what he had grabbed were toes. It was a leg.

He turned away from the sight, kept his arm draped over the piece of debris, fought to breathe, kicked again. He used every bit of energy to push away from the ship. His brain scolded him: Don't think about anything, don't look, don't smell. Just kick. They'll find you.

The plane came in low above him, and he froze, but the attack was focused on the wounded ship. He heard the bomb, and even the water beneath him vibrated. He didn't want to see, but his heart turned him around, and he saw the tower of flame near the stern, one more bloody strike on a ship that had nothing left. He heard splashes, muted by the oil, thought of the severed leg, began kicking again, and now, a voice.

"Help! I'm hit! Help me!"

And now, another, "I can't swim!"

The voice was familiar, and Biggs twisted around, tried to see, to bring them, any of them, to his raft. He tried to call out, a beacon for anyone else, but the oil was strangling, the smoke from the creeping fire swarming over him. He closed his eyes, tears pouring through the oily burn in his eyes, the man's voice still in his ears: **I can't swim.** I can't help you, he thought. It's a blessing for you, pal. Just go down, stop the pain.

He felt his hold loosening on the raft, woke up to that, tightened his grip. He took several breaths, as deep as the crushing heat in his lungs would allow, tried to shout, "Anyone? Over here! I got a raft!"

He choked on the last of the words, could muster no more volume. He closed his eyes, thought, Do it again. Help them, for Christ's sake! He glanced at the fire, closer still, no time to rest. He began kicking again in a slow shove against the oil. There was something floating to one side, a body, facedown, bobbing with the sea of stinking goo. **I can't swim.** Was that you? Or were you dead when you hit? He tried to focus his mind. What the hell difference does it make? He continued to kick, forced out the words, "Anybody. This way!"

Another voice came now, different. "Help. **Hello?**"

Biggs stopped kicking, turned, tried to see— nothing but the oil. "Hey! Here!"

"Help! I can't breathe!"

Biggs swept away the fog of the pain, held his breath, looked around, searching. He saw the man's arm go up, splashing through the oil, a lump of black bobbing up, the man's head. Biggs kicked himself around, shouted, "This way. Over here. I've got a float."

"I can't see. I'm wounded. The fire's coming!"

Biggs propelled the makeshift raft toward him, the man's arms manic, splashing into the oil.

"Where are you? I can't see."

"Here. You hear me? Swim toward my voice, this way. It's not far. Ten feet away."

The man was struggling, but his arms were cutting through the layer of oil. He was choking, as Biggs had choked, and Biggs said, "Come on! Hold out your hand, I'll pull you in."

"The fire's coming. We've gotta move."

"I know. You help me; we can kick together. Gotta get to deeper water, let a boat find us."

The man's hand was close enough, and Biggs forced his wounded arm out with an agonizing scream. He felt the man's fingers slipping, made another grab, his fingers wrapping around the man's wrist.

"Gotcha! Here, grab this debris. It floats. Rest a minute. Then we'll kick the hell away from here."

The man draped his arms over the raft, gasping for air, his head soaked with the oil, vomiting, a familiar sound now. There was nothing Biggs could do, waited for the man to calm down.

"We're okay, but we gotta move away from the fire."

The man laid his head down on the makeshift raft, choked violently, wiped at his face. "I got blown clear. Damn Jap bomber. Sons of bitches. Look what they did to my ship."

Biggs stared at the man, his face still obliterated by oil, but the voice familiar, even through the choking.

"Yeah, I got blown clear too, near the stern."

The man said nothing, stared down, ran one hand over his forehead, trying to clear away the thick coating of black slime. He shouted, jerking his hand away. "Gah! I'm burned. Oh Jesus. I don't want to die this way. Not like this."

Biggs moved his legs, said, "Look, there's no time for crying. We've gotta get out past the oil. That fire's spreading pretty good. We need to kick like hell."

The man nodded, coughed, wiped again at his face, and now Biggs saw why the voice was familiar. It was Kincaid.

The rescue boat picked them up within minutes, adding them to a dozen men with burns or wounds or both. As the boat pulled out into open water, the three-man crew scooped up buckets of clean water to try to wash off the oil. On some, the oil hid the worst of their burns, Biggs and some of the others reacting to the sudden bath of salt water with agonizing screams. And the painful bath had exposed the size of the gash in Biggs's arm, a slice from his hand to his elbow. He tried not to look at it, but the pain was brutal, made far worse by the invasion of oil. Still, no matter his suffering, he understood that the oil had filled the wound, and might have kept him from bleeding to death.

With the oil rinsed away, the blood came, one of the crewmen wrapping his arm with a rag. Biggs clamped his good hand on the cloth, the only thing to do, slowing the flow of blood as much as he could.

He laid his head back, staring now at the **Arizona,** beside him Kincaid doing the same. He could see a nasty wound on Kincaid's left leg, blood oozing through the oil, nothing the crewmen could offer him. Biggs wanted to say something, but he was too broken up himself, the searing pain on his head now taking over, his lungs feeling torn apart. He coughed the words. "There'll be doctors. We'll be there pretty quick."

Kincaid said nothing, a slow nod.

Biggs scanned the row of battleships, saw smoke on every ship. A crowd of small boats moved quickly past the oil, the surface fire spreading with the breeze, closer to the other battleships, a new fear, but there were tugboats moving nearer, fountains of water aimed at the many fires. Thank God, he thought. Nobody's alone here.

The boat slowed suddenly, the engine idling, the boat rocking, and behind Biggs the boatswain called out, "Hello? You okay?"

Another of the crew said, "He's done for. At least he's whole. I'm damn sick of looking at pieces of people."

"We oughta fish him out. Jesus, can't just leave him out here."

"Yes we can. You know the orders. We'll retrieve the dead later. Let's get these fellows to the ramp, and find out where they want us next."

The engine revved again, the boat moving forward, each wave sending a shock through the wounded men. Biggs fought the nausea, the film of oil still in his mouth, down his throat. He wanted to ask where they were going, knew it didn't really matter. He had never thought he'd ever need a hospital, and besides, there was always the sick bay . . .

He looked out again to the **Arizona,** felt a different kind of sickness. He wouldn't think of who was still out there, who all those **pieces** belonged to. He looked at the others in the small boat—no one he knew.

Beside him, Kincaid said, "They've taken my life away. My home. It's all I know, all I wanted to know. I'm a plank owner, and I thought I'd die that way. Maybe I have."

Biggs didn't know how to respond.

Kincaid coughed, a groan of pain. "She's gone, Biggs. Maybe we all are. No telling what the Japs are gonna do now." He paused, another cough. "I had three weeks. I thought my life would be over—I couldn't be a civilian. I don't have to worry about it now."

Biggs fought for the right words. "We'll make it. Both of us. We've been rescued."

Kincaid sat silently, the boat cresting a wave, a jolt of pain through them all. "**You've** been rescued, Biggs. Go on, enjoy what you've got. Maybe you'll become a PO, bust some kid's whiny spoiled ass. What I had . . . **all** I had was right out there. Now it's gone."

There was nothing Biggs could say, but he looked skyward, saw something new.

"Hey. There's no planes. The Japs are gone again."

Others looked up as well, heads turning, the boat's crew calling out with enthusiasm.

Beside Biggs, Kincaid said, "What the hell's the cheering for? They're not done. For all we know, they flew back out to their carriers just so they can reload. Bastards."

Biggs looked at him, said nothing, thought, He probably knows.

He felt the boat slowing, and behind him the boatswain said, "Here we go, fellows. The nurses will take over now. You're in good hands. Prettier hands too."

Biggs turned slightly, flinching from the burning pain in his face and the agony in his arm. There were men in white, women with them, stretchers and wheelchairs, a concrete ramp that led up to several buildings. One by one, the men were led or lifted from the boat to the shore, every touch bringing a scream from the burned, careful hands aiding them along. Biggs wanted to step out of the boat on his own, but his feet betrayed him, the pain of the concrete landing shocking him. He staggered, hands quickly under his arms, a woman in a clean white uniform in front of him, guiding a pair of men to carry him to a stretcher. He was lowered, laid flat on soft cloth, and she leaned down close to him, said, "Just stay put, sailor. I'm Lieutenant Fox. I'm a nurse. My job's to make sure you walk out of here better than you came in."

Biggs settled onto the cloth stretcher, saw her still looking down on him. "Ma'am, what happens now? Oh, God, I can't breathe. My face hurts. It's still on fire, feels like. My arm . . ."

She turned away, called out, "Tourniquet here. Left arm." She looked down to him again. "From the looks of you, you walked through a blast furnace and drank a gallon of oil." She knelt beside his feet, put a hand out slowly, probed one foot.

"Ah! Damn, hurts like hell. Oh, I'm sorry, ma'am. I'm a hospital apprentice—I'm not supposed to say that. But, it hurts bad. And I can't breathe hardly.

Feels like I can't hardly move my arm without it falling off."

Fox waved to a corpsman, then looked down at him again. "Don't worry, Hospital Apprentice, we'll treat your burns, and the doctors will do what they can to help your breathing, and your arm. You'll be parked out here, outside the building for now. No space inside. We'll fix that soon enough."

He heard a fresh chorus of screaming, blending with the sound of another boat pulling close. There were loud voices, manic activity, rushing corpsmen, more screams close around him. He knew not to look, that there was nothing else for him to do; for now, his duty had ended.

The rush of movement was all around him, a mix of sharp sounds, burned men reacting the only way they could. The boats continued to come, some moving back out, more men and more of the dead to fish out of the bay. And **pieces,** he thought. They'll pick those up too. Men need to be buried, remembered, not just left for the crabs to eat. The thought sickened him, his horrors all flooding though him; the man's leg in the oil, sailors torn in two, the terrified voice, **I can't swim.** And Kincaid, the man's utter lack of what . . . life? So maybe I saved him. Does it matter?

The screams seemed to grow quieter. The boats had moved back out into the harbor, the sounds of the engines fading, but more were growing close, a steady caravan.

Close to him, stretcher bearers were carrying their patients past him, oil soaking through the white cloth, oozing over the sides, the awful cries of agony. He tried not to cry, said in a low voice, through the burning pain in his lungs, "I tried to help 'em."

He was surprised to see Lieutenant Fox looking down at him again.

"Well, Hospital Apprentice, that's **our** job now. There's just a whole lot of you, and more are coming. We'll give you a half grain of morphine. That will help, I promise. Once the more serious cases go in, we'll get to you. Oh, hell, here's two more. Corpsman! Two more boatloads. Pretty bad. Get the doctor if he's free."

She was gone now, a quick jog toward the concrete ramp, the sounds of boat engines, and still the screams. He closed his eyes, didn't see the nurse suddenly kneeling beside him. His eyes opened: white uniform, curly brown hair, a needle jabbing his arm. He saw her hand, something silver. She leaned close to him, said, "Your forehead's not burned too bad. I've got to do this, to prevent mistakes."

He felt her rub something on his head, the pain dulled by the quick effects of the morphine. He was fading quickly, said, "What was that?"

"Lipstick. I drew an M on your head. Tells the doctor you've had the drug."

He wanted to say more, even a thank-you, but the drug was taking everything away. He felt himself floating higher, the pain left behind, a dream sweeping him to another place, a cradle, soft, comfortable, enormous, beautiful, his mind still backing him away, a boat carrying him across the harbor, the men around him, so many others, arms and legs burned and blackened, so many whispers and so much sadness, and Kincaid's words, **All I had was right out there.**

# THIRTY-SEVEN

# Hull

The message had been intercepted first by the navy's listening post near Seattle, then was forwarded to Washington, to be decoded and translated through the usual Magic resources. The fourteen-point message from the foreign ministry in Tokyo to Ambassador Nomura and Washington spelled out in specific terms how and why the Japanese were completely rejecting the proposals Hull had presented to Nomura in late November. The message seemed to up the ante, making demands that were so provocative it might seem that the Japanese were actually promoting a war.

Throughout the negotiations with Nomura, Hull's primary goal had been to bridge the yawning abyss that separated the points of view on each side. Whether or not the ongoing impasse was frustrating or even infuriating to Hull, he had to continue to try to find common ground.

This new message, which Hull could assume would also be delivered to him by Nomura, was at best a disappointment. At worst, it spelled out all the reasons the Japanese were terminating any further discussion and negotiation, as though they were deeply offended that the United States or any other nation would intrude into their internal affairs. It seemed not to matter to the Japanese that those "internal" matters included their ongoing war inside of China, their invasion of Southeast Asia, and their continuing alliance with Hitler's Germany. Now, this latest message was either an all-or-nothing negotiating ploy by the Japanese that Hull accept their outrageous demands no matter what, or they were issuing the final word, that there would be no more talk. The tone of the Japanese fourteen-point message was direct, the meaning clear enough. The Japanese were telling the United States to go to hell.

The Magic decoders had picked up other nuances that had seemed unusual. The Japanese were ordering Ambassador Nomura that as the transmitted message arrived and was decoded, he would present it to the secretary of state with appropriate formality, typed out neatly on official embassy letterhead. But Nomura was ordered not to use any of his secretarial staff, none of the usual typists who would prepare such a message. Even more unusual, Nomura was instructed in the strongest possible terms that he present the message to Hull on Sunday, December 7, at precisely one P.M. There was no explanation why.

As the final pieces of the lengthy message were received by Nomura's own decoding machine, his greatest challenge was to obey the instructions to prepare the typewritten message by his own hand. As a typist, Nomura was very much of the plodding two-finger variety. Struggling to complete the transcription of the message, he simply ran out of time. As one o'clock came and went, Nomura telephoned Hull's office, requesting the meeting be delayed for forty-five minutes, to one forty-five. Even that did not give him enough time to complete the work. By the time he and Kurusu reached Hull's office at the State Department, it was after two o'clock.

Hull had gone into his office early that morning. There were too many headaches that seemed to be erupting from every corner of the world. He knew if he stayed at the hotel, his wife would make every effort to defuse his frustrations. But there were too many annoyances, and he would not wrap her up in any of that. None of his anxieties had anything to do with her, and he would rather carry his foul mood to his office at the State Department. There, it seemed right at home.

He sat at his desk, hands folded, staring toward the portrait of Andrew Jackson. To one side sat one of his experts on the Far East, Joe Ballantine. Hull checked his watch, 2:20 P.M. Nomura's tardiness was adding to his foul temper. He continued to look at the portrait, said, "Do you think our predecessors had to deal with these kinds of people?"

Ballantine chuckled. "Certainly, sir. All day long."

Hull nodded. "I know. I hate to think that duplicity and double-talk are simply human nature."

"Perhaps it's just the nature of government."

Hull looked at him. "Not this government. At least, that's what I want to believe."

The phone rang in the outer office and was picked up by his aide, Logan Cook.

Hull said, "I wonder if Nomura needs even more time. Perhaps he's having a long lunch, and cannot be inconvenienced."

There was a knock at the door.

"Sir, that was reception downstairs. The two Japanese ambassadors are here. They're in the outer waiting room."

"Mr. Cook, there's **one** ambassador. The other fellow . . . I'm not certain what we call him. Never mind. Have someone escort them to the diplomatic waiting room. We'll bring them in shortly. They made **me** wait."

He heard the phone ring again, and the young man appeared again at the door.

"Sir, it's the president."

Hull looked at Ballantine, thought, **What now?** He picked up the phone, said, "Good morning, Mr. President."

There were no pleasantries, Roosevelt's words precise and grim.

**"There's a report that the Japanese have attacked Pearl Harbor."**

Hull felt a cold chill. "Has the report been confirmed?"

**"No."**

"Do you believe it to be true?"

Hull could hear Roosevelt breathing, an anxious pause.

**"Yes, I do."**

Now Hull let out a breath, his heart pounding, his fingers with a hard grip on the phone. "I have the Japanese ambassador in my waiting room."

**"Cordell, handle this as you feel is best. I'm working now to receive confirmation."**

The phone went dead, and Hull placed the receiver down slowly. He said to Ballantine, in a low voice, "The president has an unconfirmed report that the Japanese have attacked Pearl Harbor." He chose his words carefully. "I'm reasonably certain I know what Ambassador Nomura is doing here. They're rejecting the terms I offered them on November twenty-sixth." He paused, looked at

Ballantine. "It is also possible that they are here to tell us war has been declared." He stood and paced around the office.

Ballantine said, "What are you going to do? Why see them until the president gets confirmation? We don't have any facts."

Hull stopped at the wide window, stared at a gray sky. "I'm rather inclined not to see them at all."

Ballantine leaned one arm onto Hull's desk. "You said the reports are unconfirmed. What if they're flat-out wrong? The president isn't immune from receiving reckless misinformation."

Hull wrestled with his instincts, shook his head. "Confirmation or not, the president wouldn't make that phone call unless he knew more than he was telling me. But I suppose if there is one chance in a hundred that the report isn't true, then there's a chance we'll still talk." He paused. "In that case, I should see them."

"Yes, sir. I think that's the correct decision."

"Do one thing, Joe: Take notes. Write down what is said. I want no mistakes, no misunderstanding. Sit back there, beside the door. You'll be behind them, and they won't be as squirrelly about you taking notes."

He stood, moved toward the outer office, said to the aide, "Go get them, Mr. Cook. I'm ready."

He returned to the desk, Ballantine now in the far corner, a pad on his knee. Hull sat again, hands folded in front of him, fighting for composure. The two men stepped into his office, Kurusu first, always in the lead. They offered him the customary bows, Nomura with his usual smile. Hull stared at them for a long silent moment, saw Nomura glance to the chairs beside Hull's desk, but Hull offered no invitation to sit.

Nomura stepped forward, an envelope in his hand. "Mr. Secretary, thank you for receiving us on a Sunday. I have been instructed by my government to deliver this document to you. I was to deliver it by one o'clock, and I regret the delay. There was some difficulty in decoding the message from our government's transmission, and regrettably, neither of us is a proficient typist."

Hull fought hard to control himself, speaking through clenched teeth. "Why was it so important to deliver this into my hands by one o'clock?"

Nomura seemed surprised at the question. "I do not know. That was the instruction I received."

Hull looked at Kurusu, who shrugged, no change in his expression. Perhaps he knows precisely why one o'clock was so very important. And he will never say.

Hull took the envelope from Nomura's hand, slid the papers from it. He knew immediately what the document would say, the words already familiar from the intercepts. He read it anyway, could tell that Nomura was fidgeting, as always, the man supremely unhappy with the job he had to do. Hull slid the papers apart, the pretense of studying them with a thoughtful eye. He stopped now, had confirmed in his own mind that these were the same points he had seen that morning. He shuffled the papers, tried to slide them neatly into their envelope, but his hands were shaking, roaring anger in his mind.

He glanced at Ballantine, thought, So, they are not here to declare war. But there might be a war anyway. Do they know? Is Nomura so much more devious than I've believed? Or is his government so deceitful that they would deceive their own ambassador? He looked again at Nomura, thought, He is still smiling, as though he is my friend.

Hull looked again at the envelope in his hands, struggled to hide his boiling anger. "I must say that in all my conversations with you during the last nine months, I have never uttered one word of untruth. This is borne out absolutely by the record. In all my fifty years of public service, I have never seen a document that was more crowded with infamous falsehoods and distortions, on a scale so huge that I never imagined until today that any government on this planet was capable of uttering them."

Hull forced himself into silence, could not say anything to them about the president's call. He ignored Kurusu, stared hard at Nomura, who seemed ready to cry. Nomura raised his hands slowly, as if to respond. Hull held up one hand, **Stop.** He motioned toward the door, a sharp nod, the message clear: **Get out.** Kurusu turned quickly, as though he expected to do precisely that. Nomura hesitated, then bowed his head, and without speaking followed Kurusu out the door.

Hull's hands were still shaking, and he closed his eyes, then said to Ballantine, "Did you get it?"

"Every word, sir. Why didn't you tell them that you knew about their attack?"

Hull looked at him. "Because they don't know about their attack. It does no good to accuse someone of something they don't know they have done."

"But if it's true, if the president gets confirmation, do you think they knew? Did they come in here pretending all was well, and that this was merely some diplomatic conflict?"

Hull leaned back in his chair and turned to look out the window, a dismal gray sky, the leafless trees. "Nomura doesn't know, even now. I'm certain of it. He is too inept as a diplomat to hold a secret like this inside. Kurusu? We may never know the answer to that. And it really doesn't matter."

Later that day, the Japanese foreign ministry delivered an official message to the American embassy in Tokyo. It was delivered by a low-level staffer, and so, according to protocol, Ambassador Grew instructed his own staffer to receive the message.

**"Excellency, I have the honor to inform Your Excellency that there has arisen a state of war between Your Excellency's country and Japan, beginning today."**

THE WHITE HOUSE, WASHINGTON, D.C.—
SUNDAY, DECEMBER 7, 1941, 3:00 P.M.

Roosevelt had summoned him immediately after the Japanese officials left. Hull was not surprised that Roosevelt would meet with him alone, in the Oval Office. It was as though the president needed time alone with a friend.

"What did you think of those two birds? What was their purpose? Did they think we were so stupid that we wouldn't know what their country was doing to us?"

Hull could see Roosevelt's fury, knew he was there to help defuse that. "No, I truly believe they did **not** know. It's entirely possible they don't know even now."

"Perhaps we should tell them."

"Not necessary, Mr. President. In a few hours, the entire world will know."

Roosevelt slid a piece of paper from the desk beside him. "I never heard a word from the emperor. Grew did his job, right?"

"Absolutely. Your letter was delivered, with assurances from their foreign ministry that the emperor would receive it. No mention was made if he would respond."

"Was mention made by those deceitful bastards that their emperor would sit quietly by while his damned navy destroyed our fleet?" Roosevelt motioned with both hands. "I'm sorry, but am I supposed to be calm about all of this? This nation has been brutally assaulted. We don't have numbers yet—they're barely picking up the pieces out there. But the casualty count could be higher than any nightmare. And we will have to explain that to the American people."

Hull wasn't sure there was anything he could say. After a moment, Roosevelt seemed to calm himself, said, "I had hoped that communicating directly to the emperor would bridge the gap between us, that it might be the best chance we had to stop all those threats from their generals and politicians, that I could appeal to a man who is supposed to be peace-loving. Isn't that what we've always heard about him? Hirohito? I was wrong yet again."

Hull said, "I agreed with you. I thought the letter might work, for all the same reasons."

"Well, it didn't. Tonight, I'm calling in all the military chiefs, the cabinet, leaders of Congress. In the meantime, I want you and your people to get the word out to every embassy across the globe, to make sure every one of our people in every country in the world knows what has happened."

"I'm already working on that. As well, we will notify every merchant ship under our flag that they could become a target for any of the Axis powers. I will also ensure that the Japanese embassy here will be given protection. I don't believe those people are completely innocent, but we are not barbarians. It's important that we do not commit any acts of retribution against Japanese civilians or officials. I have already sent a cable to Ambassador Grew, urging him to protect himself and his staff as much as possible, and for him to communicate to the Japanese foreign ministry our sincere hope they will safeguard our embassy as we will theirs."

Roosevelt looked at him with utter sadness. "I wanted you here before the circus begins."

"I don't know what you mean."

"Tonight, all those generals and admirals and congressmen will start dancing around this office, preening for me, preening for reporters. There will be so much damn noise; the finger-pointing and excuses will flow across this place like maple syrup. This is not the time for that kind of foolishness, but there will be plenty of it. Everyone has to leave here tonight understanding that this is so much more serious than getting quoted in the newspaper. The world just changed, and everything we thought we knew has been jerked out from under us."

"I think your mood will set the tone. I can't see any of the people you've mentioned going off like a rocket, not in here. This is a catastrophe for the military, but it's a tragedy for a great many American people. Lives have been lost, and families have been affected. Everyone **must** know that. And if they overlook the magnitude of that, you must remind them."

Roosevelt shook his head. "That's one more reason why you would have been so very good at this job. You are a voice of reason, and right now, reason has been stamped beneath the feet of dangerous people, murderers, and today, they have become our enemies, in the most graphic sense of the word. It is our duty to fight back, it is our duty to do to them what they would continue to do to us."

Hull had debated saying anything, but he was spurred on by Roosevelt's words. "Mr. President, how were we taken so by surprise? Everything we have gone through at the State Department, for most of the past year, has pointed unmistakably to Japanese aggression, to their deceitfulness, duplicity, and backdoor actions. We knew exactly what they were doing in Southeast Asia, in the Netherlands East Indies, in China. We had access to their diplomatic communications, we have outstanding people in our intelligence offices, both army and navy. How could this have happened?"

Roosevelt stared ahead, past him, drummed his fingers on the desk. "We believed we knew **everything** they were thinking. Those Magic intercepts made us feel invulnerable. No, a better word is 'cocky.' Arrogant. Their diplomats are chatting back and forth with Tokyo about the weather, or the color of their new Cadillacs, while their military put a plan together to kick us in the teeth. We thought we knew everything. We didn't."

"You're right, of course. I assumed that knowing what the foreign ministry was saying would give us all their secrets. Yes, it was cocky. We were aware that they were burning documents in every embassy around the Pacific, and they had done the same thing here. We knew that Nomura had been ordered to destroy or otherwise eliminate one of his two decoding machines. We knew that the Japanese government had ordered their merchant fleet to withdraw from foreign ports and return to Japan. We knew that Nomura was ordered to deliver to us a message that we had already read, a final rejection of our proposals, that he was to deliver that message exactly at one o'clock. I'm familiar with the time zone in Hawaii. It's five and a half hours behind us. One o'clock was seven-thirty Hawaiian time. When did the attack begin? Do we know?"

"Close to eight."

"So, Nomura was told to deliver that fourteen-point message to me a half hour before they attacked us. He failed to do that, because he had only one decoding machine. And, apparently, he can't type."

Roosevelt seemed to slump in his chair. "Does it matter? Cordell, you're talking about a diplomatic nicety, a violation of protocol. It doesn't make much difference what they meant to tell us, or when. Events have pushed all that away."

Hull looked down, his hands clasped together, his typical position. "You're right, of course. But it's what I do. Protocol is part of my job. I just . . . I would have thought the military, particularly in Hawaii, would be paying attention to details, just like we were. Reconnaissance, radar, all that business."

"We will have those answers in time. I'm hoping that by tonight, we will find out what went wrong and how we were so deaf and blind. But I know damn well that all those generals and admirals will be pointing their fingers at each other and everyone else on the planet. The questions are easy to ask. How could the Japanese bring aircraft carriers close enough to launch planes? How could those planes fly right into Pearl Harbor without being noticed before they got there?

"And the most terrifying question of all, the one we will have to explain to the American people: How many of our boys died? How many ships were sunk? And what the hell happens now? All we have is questions. Why were we so blind? The only answer I have applies to me as much as it applies to every military and intelligence man, here and in Hawaii. It's less about what we knew than about what we **assumed.** We thought we knew the Japanese, we thought we knew what they **could** do, not what they **would** do."

He reached into a drawer beside him, said, "Here it is. A perfect example of who we are and what we thought of the Japanese. It's a letter I received, maybe two weeks ago. I get a lot of mail, but this one bothered me. I hung on to it. He's some fellow in Ohio. Says he voted for me, that I owed him to listen to him."

He unfolded the paper and read.

**"Why are we so concerned about the bug-eyed Japs? They can't see, they aren't bright, their airplanes are not anything like ours, they're too scared to be in submarines, and their ships might as well be made of paper. A single one of our B-17s, one battleship, or even one tank could do to those funny little fellows what it could have done to Lee's army at Gettysburg."**

He put the letter in the drawer. "I heard this sort of ignorance from some of my generals, and I tried to put a stop to it. I failed."

"We've all failed, sir. I should have been able to read through all that verbiage they fed me. My God, we're at war."

"And I need you to help me say that to the American people."

Hull folded his hands between his knees. "Yes, sir. We'll work on a draft this afternoon. Do we declare war on Germany and Italy as well?"

Roosevelt shook his head. "No. I've given that some thought. It's inevitable they'll go along with their Japanese friends and declare war on us. Let's keep the focus on just what has happened, and what we're facing. Sure as hell, that's enough for the American people right now."

"And then what happens?"

Roosevelt sat back, and Hull saw a look of solemn agony.

"And then, my friend, we will send a great many young men across the ocean, and they won't really understand what we're asking them to do. And they won't know the price they'll pay. But we will."

By nightfall, word began to come into Washington from other American outposts, most notably the Philippines, Guam, and Wake Island. Reports came as well from the British, that the Japanese had also launched major offensives against Hong Kong and Malaya.

Even with all the attention that had been paid to the likelihood of a strike against the Philippines, American aircraft there, including a fleet of B-17 bombers, were caught by surprise. As had happened at the bases around Pearl Harbor, they were destroyed on the ground.

THE UNITED STATES CAPITOL, WASHINGTON, D.C.—
    MONDAY, DECEMBER 8, 1941

Roosevelt's speech began at 12:30 P.M., addressing both houses of Congress, and was broadcast via radio to the American people.

Yesterday, December 7, 1941—a date which will live in infamy—the United States of America was suddenly and deliberately attacked by naval and air forces of the Empire of Japan.

The United States was at peace with that nation and, at the solicitation of Japan, was still in conversation with the government and its emperor looking toward the maintenance of peace in the Pacific.

Indeed, one hour after Japanese air squadrons had commenced bombing in Oahu, the Japanese ambassador to the United States and his colleagues delivered to the secretary of state a formal reply to a recent American message. While this reply stated that it seemed useless to continue the existing diplomatic negotiations, it contained no threat or hint of war or armed attack.

It will be recorded that the distance of Hawaii from Japan makes it obvious that the attack was deliberately planned many days or even weeks ago. During the intervening time, the Japanese government has deliberately sought to deceive the United States by false statements and expressions of hope for continued peace.

The attack yesterday on the Hawaiian islands has caused severe damage to American naval and military forces. Very many American lives have been lost. In addition, American ships have been reported torpedoed on the high seas between San Francisco and Honolulu.

Yesterday, the Japanese government also launched an attack against Malaya.

Last night, Japanese forces attacked Hong Kong.

Last night, Japanese forces attacked Guam.

Last night, Japanese forces attacked the Philippine Islands.

Last night, the Japanese attacked Wake Island.

This morning, the Japanese attacked Midway Island.

Japan has, therefore, undertaken a surprise offensive extending throughout the Pacific area. The facts of yesterday speak for themselves. The people of the United States have already formed their opinions and well understand the implications to the very life and safety of our nation.

As commander in chief of the army and navy, I have directed that all measures be taken for our defense.

Always will we remember the character of the onslaught against us.

No matter how long it may take us to overcome this premeditated invasion, the American people in their righteous might will win through to absolute victory.

I believe I interpret the will of the Congress and of the people when I assert that we will not only defend ourselves to the uttermost, but will make very certain that this form of treachery shall never endanger us again.

Hostilities exist. There is no blinking at the fact that our people, our territory, and our interests are in grave danger.

With confidence in our armed forces—with the unbounding determination of our people—we will gain the inevitable triumph—so help us God.

I ask that the Congress declare that since the unprovoked and dastardly attack by Japan on Sunday, December 7, a state of war has existed between the United States and the Japanese empire.

# THIRTY-EIGHT

# Genda

AIRCRAFT CARRIER AKAGI, NORTH OF OAHU, HAWAII—
SUNDAY, DECEMBER 7, 1941

The earliest radio signal they had received came just before eight A.M. It was Fuchida's first signal to his pilots, **To To To.** The order to begin the attack had jolted Genda, and had elated everyone else gathered within Admiral Nagumo's radio room. For a brief moment, there had been noisy celebration, but Genda had silenced that with a sharp wave of his hand and the hard and dangerous stare they had all seen before. There had been a far more important concern for Genda, the one variable he had been obsessing over. He still didn't know if the Americans knew they were coming. If they had prepared to confront the assault, this entire operation could be a disaster.

As he stood alongside Admiral Nagumo and his staff, there was silence, all of them nervously eyeing the radioman and his receiver. Genda knew they were watching him, wondering, if the news from Fuchida was bad, just how Genda would react, if the **lunatic** would explode in some bizarre way. He ignored all of that, cared not at all for what his reputation might be.

The radio room was small, and Genda stood silently with clenched fists, staring at the radio receivers, as if willing them to speak, aching for Fuchida to broadcast the next signal. He ran the possibilities through his mind, the usual disease of detail he could not avoid. If Fuchida remained silent, it could mean that he was in a fight for his life, along with the planes in his command. Genda had fought with himself if he should even remain by the radios, or go topside to the flight deck, to see for himself if Fuchida had returned prematurely. The thought had rolled through his mind in a sickening wave that he was such a fool to believe this operation could succeed as he had planned. Lines on a blackboard and scribbles on a map meant nothing at all until you faced the enemy.

But finally, the radio had crackled, Genda jumping a step closer to it, leaning low beside the receiver, the operator frantically adjusting the volume. The words had come, simple and magnificent, the signal that the attack had moved toward the targets without resistance, without interference. The signal had been chosen for its meaning, the great symbol of strength, the tiger, the words now spoken by Fuchida. It was the message Genda needed to hear, that Fuchida's planes had arrived over Pearl Harbor without any response from the Americans, that the attack was a complete surprise. Genda could hear the enthusiastic joy in Fuchida's voice, the same joy communicated to his pilots, to the admiral, to every crew on every one of the carriers and the ships that supported them.

**Tora! Tora! Tora!**

AIRCRAFT CARRIER AKAGI, NORTH OF OAHU, HAWAII—
SUNDAY, DECEMBER 7, 1941, 10:10 A.M.

Genda shivered against the harsh wetness of the sea spray, the wind blowing so much harder than earlier that morning. The ship rocked violently, and he steadied himself on a low railing, saw the aircrews keeping close to their shelters. He knew that on the bridge, the helmsman would be straining to hold the bow of the carrier directly into the wind, but the rising seas would add one more challenge to any pilot bringing his plane down on the decks of the carriers. Genda looked toward the bow of the flattop, dropping hard into a massive spray from another great wave, then rising up again, skyward.

He wanted to check his watch, knew it didn't matter. They will come when they come. Another great wave washed over the bow, a shallow lake spreading down along the deck, spilling over the side with the motion of the ship. They are well trained, he thought. They will know how to handle this.

"Commander!"

He saw one of Nagumo's staff, the man's hand clamped down on his hat to keep it from becoming airborne. "Yes?"

"Commander, the admiral has invited you once again to his wardroom. You may wait in comfort. With the wind gaining strength, it is likely the weather could be turning against us. Would you be more comfortable inside?"

Genda kept his eyes on the sky. "I am quite certain I would be more comfortable inside. I prefer to remain here."

"As you wish, Commander."

Genda didn't watch to see if the man had gone, but his eye caught several of the flight crew, some moving closer to him, staring as he was, eyes on the broken blue skies to the south. No one spoke, the wind buffeting them all, and now he saw them, like a swarm of insects, disappearing into the clouds, then appearing again, closer. There were more behind those, and the men near him began to call out, arms waving, cheering with relief and joy. Genda watched the planes grow larger, like black birds now, the formations nearly intact, the squadrons splitting up, moving toward their designated carriers.

The first group came over the **Akagi,** dive bombers and torpedo bombers, lining up for their landing. Genda held tightly to the railing, steadied himself against the vicious roll of the sea, watched as the first plane touched down. The flight crews went to work immediately, the plane pulled aside, the second coming in close behind, quick efficiency by the crews again. The third came in, bounced hard, the roll of the ship working against it. The plane spun halfway around, the landing gear collapsing, the plane's belly ripped open. Genda knew to keep away, knew his crews were trained for this. He watched as the pilot was pulled free, the man offering Genda a hearty wave, as the crew shoved and twisted at the plane, tumbling it over the side.

He watched them all, Fuchida's groups coming in first, then the second wave, led by Commander Shimazaki, coming in close to twelve o'clock. As expected, Fuchida's was the final plane to appear. His mission had been to observe the entire attack, both waves, from high above. As the last to land, he was offering yet another signal to Genda and everyone else. The attack had ended.

As Genda counted the incoming aircraft, the numbers had seemed staggering, far more aircraft returning than he had ever expected. But he knew to be cautious, that his eyes could have deceived him, that he would wait for a final count from all six carriers.

His one show of unbridled enthusiasm was for

Fuchida, a laughing embrace as Fuchida climbed out of his plane. It was a rare display for Genda, tempered only by the awareness that Fuchida had one more responsibility: to present his report on the damage he had inflicted on the Americans.

Fuchida met first with his flight leaders, overseeing several radio conversations between the carriers, the flight leaders comparing their tallies, all of them knowing the importance of accuracy. With the accounting complete, Fuchida arrived in Admiral Nagumo's operations room, the joy and pride on Fuchida's face obvious to Genda. Genda sat on one side of the long table alongside a handful of the admiral's staff officers, the walls around them draped in huge maps. He could feel the skepticism from Nagumo's officers, as though it was necessary not to allow Fuchida too much self-satisfaction. At the head of the table, Genda could see, Admiral Nagumo was the biggest skeptic of all.

Fuchida stood at the far end of the table, hands behind his back. He seemed to pulse with the information he was so pleased to share. Opposite him, Nagumo offered no pleasantries, no congratulations at all. His words were short and quick. "The results. What are they?"

Fuchida didn't hesitate. "We sank four battleships. I observed that myself. Four more were damaged. To our regret, there were no aircraft carriers to be found. We sank a number of smaller craft, including one cruiser, and at least four destroyers and other service ships."

Fuchida seemed to expect applause, but Nagumo pushed him again. "What of aircraft and airfields?"

"Sir, we destroyed a significant number of fighter planes, bombers, and their flying boat craft. We also destroyed hangars and other maintenance facilities, barracks, and a large number of other buildings."

"I am not interested in buildings, Commander. Do you believe that the American fleet can come out from Pearl Harbor in less than six months?"

Fuchida seemed nervous now, made a quick glance at Genda. "Sir, I do not believe the Americans can launch their fleet within six months."

Genda nodded toward him, **Yes, very good.** Fuchida seemed to relax, and even Nagumo smiled. Beside Genda, one of Nagumo's staff officers, Admiral Kusaka, said, "What do you believe the next targets should be?"

Fuchida looked again at Genda. "Dockyards, fuel tank areas, any undamaged ships. I would strike immediately, while they are unable to resist us."

Kusaka did not share Fuchida's enthusiasm, said, "Shouldn't we expect the Americans to attack us here? Would they not be aggressive in seeking out our fleet, and taking their revenge?"

Fuchida seemed nervous again. "We destroyed many planes, sir. But I cannot say we destroyed them all."

Nagumo said, "Where are the American aircraft carriers?"

Fuchida seemed to swallow hard. "I do not know, Admiral. I can only assume they are training at sea, which explains why they were not in Pearl Harbor."

"Is it not likely that they have received word of our attack?"

Fuchida's enthusiasm was gone completely, and Genda said, "It is reasonable to assume that the carriers will be seeking our location. If the enemy comes, all the better. Our fighters are virtually undamaged, and our pilots are eager to confront the enemy. We will shoot the Americans from the sky. Their planes are no match for ours."

Nagumo turned to Genda. "Your confidence in your aircraft is admirable, and it would be hard to dispute what you say. Do you propose that we attack the Americans again?"

Fuchida seemed to come alive, and Genda knew him well enough to understand why. Yes, he would take off again, right now.

Genda calmed Fuchida with a brief stare, then said, "We cannot attack again this afternoon. Refueling and refitting the weapons will require time, and our pilots would have to fly after dark, which they are not trained to do. I propose that we keep the fleet in this area for several days, sending out patrols to locate the carriers. I do not believe it is wise to attack Pearl Harbor again without knowing where those carriers may be. In any event, the element of surprise is now gone."

Nagumo rubbed his hands on his face, seemed exhausted. "Commander Genda, will you confirm the reports I have here as to the number of aircraft we lost?"

Genda had already seen the numbers from Fuchida and the other crews. "Yes. I was concerned there might have been inaccuracies, but the numbers are confirmed to my satisfaction. From three hundred fifty-three aircraft engaged, we lost a total of twenty-nine. Less than ten percent."

Fuchida said, "Those numbers **are** accurate, sir. It only suggests that we should renew the attack, strike them again, destroying targets we did not hit this time. I know it can be done, sir. Not tonight, certainly, but by tomorrow morning we will be prepared again."

Nagumo ignored Fuchida, looked at Genda again. "You would have us remain in this area until we engage the American aircraft carriers, yes?"

"Yes. If we have the tankers come to us here, we can maintain the amount of fuel we would require."

Nagumo looked at his staff officers. More than one of them wore the kind of smirk that made Genda want to throw them overboard. After a long minute, Nagumo said to no one in particular, "Commander Fuchida cannot confirm that the Americans have not launched a massive number of dive bombers that are, even now, closing in on our position."

He looked at Genda with a patronizing smile. "Commander, you have done a magnificent thing here. Despite my gravest doubts, you have carried out Admiral Yamamoto's plan with admirable success. Why not be satisfied with that?"

Genda knew Nagumo too well by now, knew that the admiral had resisted every part of this operation. No argument he could make would be good enough to change Nagumo's mind.

"I believe, Admiral, that there is still more we can accomplish here. We can inflict even greater destruction on the enemy."

Nagumo looked at his staff again. "Commander, you remind me of the fisherman who catches a huge fish. Instead of carrying his trophy home, to enjoy the glory of his accomplishment, he continues to fish, hoping to repeat his success, or to catch an even greater fish. With respects to you, Commander Genda, it is not wise to be greedy."


Fuchida was pacing, and two of his flight leaders were staring at Genda with hot anger. Fuchida said, "Why would he take this from us? My pilots do not understand why, after such a triumph, they are not allowed to do it again. The enemy is where he was before, and he remains vulnerable."

Genda spoke in a low voice, as though concerned about unfriendly ears. "Mitsuo, we do not choose who commands us. The admiral believes that we have accomplished the mission we came for and that the enemy is now better prepared against another assault. We do not know where the enemy's aircraft carriers are. It is Admiral Nagumo's decision."

Fuchida still paced, said, "What would Admiral Yamamoto say to all this? What would he say of Nagumo's meek decision?"

Genda thought a moment. "Admiral Yamamoto would say that Admiral Nagumo does not enjoy gambling. I suppose that is why they are not friends." He paused. "Go now. Tell your pilots what I am telling you. It is time for us to return home. We have achieved a great victory. But now, we must prepare for what lies ahead."

# THIRTY-NINE

# Yamamoto

BATTLESHIP NAGATO, ARIAKE BAY, JAPAN—
MONDAY, DECEMBER 8, 1941

He was astonished that **Nagato**'s radio receiver
had picked up Commander Fuchida's sig-
nal, his order to begin the attack, the **To To To.** It
was as though a hypnotic spell had been broken,
the staff around him reacting with utter jubilation.

Within minutes came the next signal, not as clear,
cut by static. It was Fuchida's magnificent message,
**Tora Tora Tora.** Again the men cheered, everyone
but Yamamoto. His chest ached, and he kept to his
seat in the operations center, would not let them see
the weakness he felt, the sudden swell of emotion.
His thoughts stayed on Genda, the young lunatic,
the eyes that tore holes wherever they stared. As the
boisterous calls echoed out past the radio room,

spreading through the ship, Yamamoto could think only of the young man's worst fear, the fear that Yamamoto had shared, that the Americans would be waiting for them, fully armed, hundreds of planes waiting above. He could never have admitted any of that to those old men in the Ministry, who would have grabbed any excuse to deny this mission from ever taking place. But the fear would not leave, even when he heard Fuchida's signal. Some part of him still held back in disbelief. How can it be so easy?

For a brief minute, Yamamoto had wished he was out there, feeling what Genda felt, and Fuchida, and all the rest. The young are in command now, he thought. All they lack is wisdom, and that will come. This week, they will have gained a great deal.

Yamamoto knew little of weather predictions and wind charts, was told only that Fuchida's signals had been received by a stroke of incredible good fortune, atmospheric conditions that Yamamoto could only guess at. He kept his odd gloominess to himself, would not interfere as the good cheer spread quickly through the officers and crew on the ship, the same enthusiasm that he knew would be spreading through Nagumo's fleet as their planes did their work.

The silence returned, the hypnosis once more settling down on his staff. They huddled again, close to the radio room, but Yamamoto knew there would be nothing more to hear, not unless it was a complete disaster. He would not sit quietly to wait for that. He went first to his quarters, a chaos of bed linens and paperwork. He knew that Chiyoko would come soon, would scold him and plow through his mess, and that in minutes his quarters would be respectable again. He kicked lightly through a pile of undergarments on the deck. *If this mess will bring her here forevermore, I will make a mess forevermore.*

He thought of a nap, but the aching in his chest continued, binding him together. *I must breathe,* he thought. He left his quarters, afraid to hear any reactions from his staff. *They will cheer or they will cry. In time, I will know which. I'm just not ready for that right now. I will wait for Admiral Nagumo to make his report. That is how it must be, not wild impatience for a scrap of information, a scrap of rumor.*

He moved toward the open deck, a hard chill in the air, the skies gray, the land beyond the harbor a dismal brown. He pulled his jacket tightly around him, but it wasn't enough. He checked his watch. It had been nearly five hours since Fuchida's first signal. *It must be over,* he thought. *They should have completed the mission.*

He turned to escape the cold, moved toward the hatchway, nearly collided with his chief of staff. The anger on Ugaki's face drove an icy stake into Yamamoto.

"What has happened?"

Ugaki made way for Yamamoto to move inside, leaned closer to him, said, "We received a transmission from Admiral Nagumo. He sent it on open frequency. He has broken radio silence. It is an outrageous breach of protocol."

"What is the message? Has the attack been successful?"

"Sir, Admiral Nagumo has informed the entire planet that the fleet has turned away from its targets, and is now returning to Japan."

"Was the attack successful? Did he report the figures, our losses, the damage to the American ships?"

"We are told that the enemy fleet, particularly their battleships, sustained heavy damage. Our losses in aircraft and pilots were surprisingly low. Now Admiral Nagumo fears reprisal by the Americans. He is moving the fleet out of danger, will rendezvous with the tankers and set a course for home."

Yamamoto wrestled with what Nagumo must be thinking, said, "Are the American aircraft carriers in pursuit of the fleet?"

Ugaki seemed to struggle to hold his anger. "We have not located the carriers, but the American planes are no match for our own. No, sir, from all we can gather, there is no immediate threat to the fleet. There is no reason for Admiral Nagumo to scamper away from the fight, like a terrified rabbit."

"Into my wardroom, Admiral. There is no need to display your concerns to the crew."

Ugaki followed him, Yamamoto wearing a cheerful expression for whoever happened to see them—no need to embarrass his chief of staff. They stepped into the wardroom, Yamamoto's orderly setting out a pot of tea. Yamamoto was surprised, said, "Omi, what are you preparing for?"

Omi bowed, said, "Admiral, this is for you. I thought you would have your officers in here, after what has been reported by Admiral Nagumo."

Yamamoto looked at Ugaki. "So, Admiral, I cannot say if you were correct that the entire planet has learned of our plans. But I feel confident that this entire ship knows, and by tomorrow, the entire navy. Thank you, Omi. You may leave."

Now that Nagumo had ordered the fleet westward, the cheers had turned to gloom, as though Nagumo had twisted his victory into failure. Yamamoto understood the emotions of his staff, as much as he understood their pride. But protest was dangerous, even as dangerous as Nagumo's amazing lack of discretion in announcing his withdrawal order to his fleet.

But Nagumo had one priority: the safety and preservation of his ships. Despite the anger of the younger officers around him, Nagumo was taking his fleet out of harm's way.

Ugaki sat at one end of the table in his usual position, and across from Yamamoto sat the foul-smelling

Kuroshima, empty seats on either side of him. Omi had thoughtfully provided an ashtray, which Kuroshima ignored. Yamamoto said, "It is apparent that our operations against the Americans were successful. As you are all aware, Admiral Nagumo has exercised his authority to withdraw the fleet. I will hear you, your views. Admiral Ugaki?"

"He has made a catastrophic mistake. He has run from the fight just when he had secured victory. That is the mark of a timid man, a man with no heart, a man who does not have faith in his own sword." Ugaki lay both hands out on the table, red-faced.

Yamamoto said, "Continue. Say what you must."

Ugaki forced himself to be cautious, as though he knew he had crossed a line. "Sir, I am aware that Admiral Nagumo is my superior. He has great support from high places. They will no doubt drape him with flowers, medals, perhaps arrange a parade in his honor. But I believe, and I will always believe, that his judgment is in error. I must add, Admiral, that if I had commanded the fleet, I would not now be sailing home. There would still be a fight to be had, even if the Americans attempted to oppose us. I am certain that Commander Genda would agree. Is that not true, sir?"

Yamamoto waited for more, but Ugaki would wait for him to speak.

"Admiral Ugaki, you are most certainly the most able chief of staff ever in my command. Your words echo much of what I would have said at one time. I understand youth. You are a good deal younger than I, as is Commander Genda. Admiral Nagumo is my age. Something happens to a man when he goes to war at a late age. He is not so eager to jump both feet and both fists into the fight, to strike out until his enemy is dead—or he is dead himself.

"The young have the luxury of believing that war is simple, that when there is success, they should embrace their triumph, with no worries about what will follow. The greater the triumph, the greater the glory. That is certainly true. Do I believe that Nagumo should have pressed his assault? Has he made a mistake in returning home so quickly? Perhaps so. Should he have located the American carriers? Perhaps.

"But consider what would happen if, right now, I issued an order to Admiral Nagumo to turn the fleet around, to steam back to Pearl Harbor, to engage the Americans again. I would strip away the honor that Nagumo has earned. I would be telling everyone, from my staff to the Naval Ministry and every pilot and crewman in the fleet, that Admiral Nagumo has made a mistake that I had to correct. I will not do that, not to a man who has commandeered a great victory. The shame of that would be more than he could bear.

"Admiral, this plan was not created so that we might **destroy** the Americans, or **destroy** Pearl Harbor. This was not to be all-out war. The report that Admiral Nagumo has sent shows that our planes did precisely what we intended them to do. The Americans have been crippled. It will take them perhaps six months to put a sizable fleet to sea."

He paused, tried to show a burst of energy that he didn't feel. "We have enjoyed success. We must not forget that."

BATTLESHIP NAGATO, ARIAKE BAY, JAPAN—
FRIDAY, DECEMBER 12, 1941

He heard his name, the aide making the announcement through the closed door of his quarters, even as Chiyoko was beating him at a game of chess. He did not want to leave her, but the aide knocked now, an annoying insistence that this was something Yamamoto had to address. He stood, said, "A small matter, I'm sure. I will return shortly."

She smiled at him, said, "Go on. I shall still be here. Your shirts are wrinkled, stuffed together like rags. I shall have plenty to do until you return."

He pulled his jacket on.

"I would rather stay. I must rescue my game. You have threatened my queen. I trust you not to move any of the pieces."

Still she smiled, her beauty pulling him toward her.

"I do not have to cheat, Iso. I'm doing just fine. Hurry back so I may defeat you."

He hesitated, but the knock came again. He had the sudden need to strangle the aide, but he knew that no one would interrupt him here, with her, without a very good reason. He buttoned his jacket and opened the door, saw a look of terrified anguish on the face of the young aide.

"Sir, I am so sorry. But Admiral Ugaki insisted I bring you up. Sir, the prime minister is here."

Yamamoto said, "Are you certain? Why would he come here? Is he in the wardroom?"

They were moving now, the aide seeming to drag Yamamoto behind him, as though hurrying him without hurrying him.

"No, sir. He insisted on meeting with you on the bridge."

"The bridge? Why?"

"I don't know, sir. I'm just delivering the message. Admiral Ugaki insisted I convey its urgency."

"Well, you did."

They climbed a ladder, then another, and Yamamoto stopped at the hatchway to the bridge, the young man beside him.

"You may go. You've done your job."

He could feel disappointment from the young man, but for now, it was not a concern. The aide moved away slowly, and Yamamoto would not scold him for that, thought, *It's not every day our prime minister visits a ship. He's an army man. Perhaps he's testing himself for seasickness.*

He thought of knocking, but the hatchway was open when the ship was in port, and he laughed at himself now. *Dammit, it's your ship.*

He stepped onto the bridge, saw a handful of his officers lined up to one side, as though terrified. They seemed to welcome his arrival, gave a quick glance in his direction, then back to the man standing at the glass, staring out intently at what seemed to be nothing at all. Yamamoto understood. He's waiting for me to welcome him.

"Excuse me, Mr. Prime Minister. Please, welcome to my flagship."

Tojo turned slowly, as though enjoying the ceremony of it all, said, "I am greatly pleased to visit those of our military who have struck the first blow."

There was nothing of sincerity or friendliness in Tojo's voice.

"If you wish, we can retire to my wardroom."

"I rather like it right here. Perhaps you can order your crewmen to allow us some time alone?"

Yamamoto saw the odd mix of fear and disappointment on their faces, but he made a sharp motion with his hand, the men filing quickly off the bridge.

Yamamoto said, "I am certainly happy to comply with your wishes, though it is fortunate we are in port. Vacating the bridge at sea is not a wise idea."

Tojo smiled now. "You will understand that I have not spent much time on the bridge of a magnificent vessel such as this. It has not been a part of my routine."

"Perhaps you should change your routine, Prime Minister."

Tojo smiled again. "In Tokyo, I am accustomed to toadies and yes-men. A great many seem to surround me. But you seem to have no fear of my position."

"Should I?"

Another smile. "Not after this past week. I will admit to you that I was even more skeptical than the Naval Ministry that your operation would have the faintest breath of success—and we are both aware just how skeptical **they** were. But now, we may share a hearty congratulations for a week that shall become a triumphant part of our history. In case you are not aware, while your aircraft were crushing the Americans in Hawaii, we successfully executed a significant air strike on the Philippines. We will be landing a formidable infantry force there within a few days."

Yamamoto chose his words. "I was aware of these operations, though perhaps not in detail."

"Certainly you were aware. My point in coming here was to express to you, in person, that I am dismayed by the reports I have received that Admiral Nagumo opted for the safe result in his decision to, well, **cut and run** from Hawaii. I am aware you were not pleased with the admiral's inability to make the aggressive move. I am also aware that the Naval Ministry and the Chiefs of Staff have approved Admiral Nagumo's decision, and that, even now, as your fleet returns, they are preparing a lavish welcome. No doubt he will receive some extravagant medal, a medal more deserved by your Commander Genda and others."

"With respect, sir, you are 'aware' of a great deal. I'm not sure what you want me to say."

"This is not an interview, Admiral, nor is it a test. I am not courting your favor, nor granting mine to you. We are both warriors on the same field. I am merely saying that I am not at all pleased that there are men who hold seats in the Naval Ministry who approve of halfway measures. There is no patience these days for hesitation, for the meek and mild to supervise our decision-making. I thought you should hear it from me directly that, with world events as they are progressing, the emperor is depending upon us to do everything in our power to crush our enemies, as your people crushed them at Pearl Harbor. It is our supreme hope, and the emperor's expectation, that all of us work together energetically to achieve victory."

"Mr. Prime Minister, we did not 'crush' the Americans at Pearl Harbor. We wounded them. The attack on Pearl Harbor was meant to accomplish only that. They will heal. They will fight another day, and they will not be timid. I am pleased to allow the young men in my command—Commander Genda, Fuchida, all the rest—to embrace our victory, to believe, as you say, sir, that we have crushed the enemy. But I fear that all we have done is to poke and prod a great power. And now, that giant has been awakened."

"As have we, Admiral. And every day we are stronger, we have more and better aircraft, we are training a great number of troops, we are building ships. It is clear to me, and I know it will be clear to you: The events of this month and the months going forward shall propel the empire higher in the eyes of the world, propel us directly to the top of the mountain."

Tojo turned away, and Yamamoto stared at the man's back, his words rolling through Yamamoto's brain, along with the response he could not say to the man.

**From the top of the mountain, there is only one way to go.**

# FORTY

# Biggs

**T**he morphine had been enough, allowing him to sleep past the agony of the burns on his head and the horrifying wound on his arm made so much worse by the oil. Some around him did not sleep, their suffering far beyond what the doctors could offer them, men whose bones lay bare, flesh stripped away by the fires and the violent confrontations with bombs and the shrapnel they created. The men riddled with machine gun fire were much more fortunate, housed now in a vast number of aid stations and hospitals, and if their vital organs hadn't been ripped through, it was almost certain they would survive. For the burn victims, nothing was certain but the torturous pain they would

endure. Throughout the first night, many did not endure, cries and screams growing silent, the doctors,
nurses, and corpsmen removing those men from
the ward, adding to the death toll that no one could
yet compute.

For Biggs, the forced sleep provided one more
gift: oblivion.

Throughout the early evening, machine gun
and antiaircraft fire had sprayed over and around
Pearl Harbor. It came from nervous gunners, men
with jittery fingers on so many triggers, waiting
for the next inevitable attack by the Japanese. The
rumors had spread through Oahu with the speed
of a typhoon, that Japanese invasion parties had
been spotted to the south, Japanese ships sailing
close, local Japanese citizens already plotting a wave
of sabotage.

From the ocean to the west, Admiral Halsey's
aircraft carrier, **Enterprise,** had received word of
the attack, and Halsey had ordered several of his
own planes to fly to Oahu, seeking more specific
information, adding at least a token of firepower to
Oahu's defense. But those nervous gunners on the
ground saw what they wanted to see, and Halsey's
planes were shot out of the sky, killing three of the
pilots, while the men on the ground convinced
themselves they had thwarted another attack.

Not all the gunfire was skyward. Around every one
of the military installations, whether the Japanese
had struck it or not, guards had been posted,

frightened men staring into darkness, more nervous fingers on so many triggers. The shots rang
out toward any sound, or any suggestion of sound,
real or imagined, whether the wind, a reflection of
moonlight on the water, or the unfortunate dog
that happened past. And when one machine gun
fired, many more responded, adding to the panic,
the determination that this time, there would be
no surprise. And so, the toll increased, men struck
down by friendly fire, some of it from deadly foolishness, some purely accidental.

Rumors came from Honolulu as well, that the
Japanese had launched part of their attack straight
at the city, committing atrocities against civilians. It
took artillery experts days to examine the evidence,
to realize that Honolulu had also been the victim of
friendly fire. Around the harbor, American antiaircraft guns were aimed high, and if the shells didn't
impact or explode, they fell back to earth. Some fell
harmlessly into cane fields, or into the harbor itself.
But a great many tumbled onto random targets in
the city. And so, there were civilian casualties, some
of them the Japanese citizens that the more para-
noid had come to despise.

By morning, most of the rumors had been put to
bed, as the happy machine gunners examined their
prizes only to find shredded trees, slaughtered goats,
or, more often, nothing at all. Most were too embarrassed to admit that they had simply panicked.
The rumors of another Japanese attack had quieted

as well, none of the "definite" sightings proving to be anything more than fishing boats. As a measure of calm returned to Oahu, the officers took command, restoring order, and in some cases apologies were issued for so many hysterical mistakes. For the three pilots who'd flown in from the **Enterprise** and lost their lives, there could be no apology.

Biggs awoke to the smell. It seemed to swallow him, sickening and raw, and he turned his head, a painful mistake. But the stench was overpowering, very much as he had experienced on the ship, but different, a blend of other smells from wounds and antiseptic. Above him was a dull white ceiling, a pair of lights to one side, and he had a flicker of memory. **The hospital.** He tried to call out, but the sharp jab in his throat squeezed away the sound. Sit up, he thought. Try. He moved his arms, one wrapped in a thick blanket of bloody gauze. He tried not to look at that, pushed himself up with his good hand. But he was too weak and the effort was useless. He lay back, enduring more pain from the soft pillow. He raised his head slightly, easing the sting, settled back again, slowly, carefully, surrendering to the white cotton. He felt himself breathing heavily, every breath a knife jabbed into his throat. He tried to relax, but the mystery and curiosity were giving way to fear. The words came out of him, his voice a low-pitched gargling. "Am I gonna die?"

He was startled by voices, close by.

"He's awake. This one over here, Doctor."

"I knew he'd make it. Not nearly as bad as some. No, sailor, you're not going to die. Not today, anyway. Nurse, how's the bandage holding?"

"Which one?"

"I don't need jokes, nurse."

"It's not a joke, sir."

Biggs eased his head sideways, but his eyes wouldn't focus, his mind drifting through a soft mist, like rain, distorting the figures, a man and woman, both in white. The voices continued, and he thought of a radio show, a comedy that wasn't funny. He saw a face above him now, l eaning over, startling him again. "Change the dressing on the arm. I don't know how long he spent in that oil, but it took them an hour to clean it out. With all of that, plus the water in the harbor, there is likely to be infection. Clean it out again, then bandage it up. All right, tell me about this one over here."

The voices seemed to move away, silencing words that meant something, something about **him— his arm.** He raised it slowly, looked at the thick wrapping of white, his fingertips barely visible. He tried to flex them, an immediate mistake, cried out. The faces appeared again, hovering, both of them. The man's voice was older, in command, like Dr. Johnson.

"Give him another quarter grain. We have too

much to do here. The worst burns are more than I can . . . Well, let's not talk here. Go ahead with this one. I'll get another nurse."

"Yes, Doctor."

The woman came back, hovering again, holding his right arm, and he felt the quick jab of a needle.

"This will help, sailor. Your burns probably hurt the worst. Don't touch the bandage on your head. Well, don't touch anything. We'll keep checking on you."

She pulled away, and he felt sick, overwhelmed by the awful stink.

"Nurse, come back."

She was there, but his mind was clouding over from the morphine, her voice far away.

"Ma'am. What's that smell? It won't stop. It's making me sick."

She stood over him for a few seconds, and he held on to her image, wouldn't let go, fought the drug.

"You're in the burn ward, sailor. It's just . . . what it smells like. It's hard for all of us . . . No, I didn't mean that." She paused, and he thought he heard a cough. "I have to go outside. I'll be back. Sleep now."

He felt her hand on his, soft, wonderful. His mind faded with the morphine, her hand a dream, all of it—the stink, the screams, the fire and oil and water—a dream. A very bad dream.

———

He woke to the soft hands, gently removing the bandage on his head.

"Oh, you're awake. Sorry if I woke you."

Biggs tried to see her face, blinked through the haze he was getting used to. "No, ma'am, it's okay. It really hurts. Worse now."

His own voice surprised him again, like flowing gravel, stinging pain in his throat.

"I know. I have to apply a salve to the burned areas, then I'll bind it up again. You lost most of the skin on your scalp. We have to protect it from infection."

**That word again.**

She worked quickly, even her soft touch bringing more pain. He fought the need to flinch, to cry out, to resist what she was doing. She seemed to know what he was feeling, said, "Almost finished. Hang on."

He closed his eyes, his right hand curling hard on the sheet beneath him, short breaths, unable to help a soft cry.

"I'm sorry. There. It's treated, wrapped again. I'll stop now. I'm sorry, I have to go out for a minute."

She was up and gone quickly, and Biggs wanted to bring her back, the soft hands, taking away the agony. The stink was there still, but he was growing used to it now. It was more than the nausea it brought him. It was memory: the bodies, the pieces, black skin, bleached white bones. He tried to push that away, pulled himself up a few inches off the pillow, saw a row of beds along the far wall, another row spread out on both sides of him. He couldn't stay up for long, dropped back down, the effort forcing him to breathe more heavily, the familiar misery in his throat.

He braced himself, pulled his right arm in under him for leverage, pushed up again. He could see the men, like him, wrapped in white bandages, hiding faces, arms, and legs, some bandaged over most of their bodies. There was a growing chorus of sound, some of the men waking up, nurses appearing, doing whatever they could for the worst of the suffering. But with the waking came the louder cries, and then, the screams. He lay back down, closed his eyes, tried to keep it away, but there was no escaping the agony of so many of the men around him. He heard a shout for the doctor, a woman's voice, the nurses moving past quickly. He didn't need to know what was happening, tried to find some comfort in the soft pillow beneath his head.

Close beside him, a man began to cry, no words, just sobs, loud and piercing, driving into Biggs like a knife. He clenched his teeth, put his one good hand up to his ear to shut it out. But there were more cries, more men across from him, the nurses moving past, tending to as many as they could. The sobbing beside him stopped, a low groan now, and Biggs focused on that, wanted to see the man, talk to him, try to help. He raised up, could see a nurse beside the man, helping him, and Biggs thought,

Morphine. It has to be. Give him plenty. Nobody should hurt like that.

The nurse moved off, and Biggs propped himself up on his good arm. He held his breath as much as he could, braced himself against the pain in his throat. "Hey, buddy. You'll be okay. We're all pretty beat up. But we'll be okay."

There were bandages across the man's chest, gauze covering his face and head, a small hole for his mouth. Biggs didn't know what he could do, thought, Talk to him, ask him questions. Maybe take his mind away. "Hey, pal. It's gonna be okay."

The man responded, a surprise. "Can't see you. I need a favor."

Biggs felt relief, as though he might actually be able to help. "Sure."

"You got a forty-five?"

"Uh, no. I'm like you, I'm in bed."

"Well, find one. And shoot me."


NAVAL HOSPITAL, HOSPITAL POINT, OAHU—
    TUESDAY, DECEMBER 9, 1941

The second morning rolled over him with more screams, men calling for help, for God, for their mothers. It had been that way most of the night, even the morphine not keeping away the agony. Some of the men cried out in their sleep, having nightmares no medication could prevent.

As he lay in the first light from the windows, Biggs

realized he could see more clearly, the white coats and dresses moving past him with faces he could identify. It was obvious that they were moving with urgency, that the stink of so many horrible burns meant constant attention, dressings changed, medication administered. From his own training, he knew that burns were the worst kind of injury, the nerves under the skin the most sensitive. It was a curiosity to him that broken bones seemed much less painful, the men he had seen coming into sick bay supporting their own twisted arms.

I don't know enough, he thought. How do you help this much pain? How much morphine can you give a man? How long does it take burns to heal? And the scars . . . The thought stung him, and he put his hand on his scalp. Will my hair grow back? He was angry with himself now. Is that the worst of it for you? These fellows are screaming for reasons I'll never understand. I'm lucky, no matter how much oil I swallowed. Don't forget that.

He saw an older doctor coming closer, trailed by a nurse, young, pretty. The doctor read from a clipboard, then looked down at him, said, "I think you're ambulatory now, Mr. Biggs."

"You sure, Doc? I can't hardly breathe. It hurts to talk. And, I can't hardly move my arm, sir."

The doctor smiled. " 'Ambulatory' means you can walk. I need you to move as much as you can with those places that don't hurt so much. You're luckier than some. It's obvious that wherever most of you had clothes on, the burns weren't as severe. Some of these fellows had every piece of clothing ripped off 'em, and they got it the worst. You must have lost your hat, so, you lost your scalp. Your legs were covered, but your arms weren't. Something sliced into your left arm pretty well, shrapnel, most likely. That's my biggest concern right now. It took off a piece of soft tissue from your forearm, exposed the bone. The oil played havoc with the wound. But, the good news is that your legs and feet aren't too badly burned, so I need you to take a walk, work your muscles. Nurse Powell here will help you out. Excuse me, I've got . . . Oh, hell."

The doctor was gone quickly, a dash to the far end of the ward, his white coat following him like a cape. Biggs saw nurses flowing that way, and he looked at the nurse beside him, her eyes on the far end as well. She turned to him now, said, "Let's sit up first, then move slowly, stand up. If you feel weak or unsteady, I'll support you."

She was staring still toward the far end of the ward, and Biggs said, "I'm a hospital apprentice, ma'am. I wish I could help some of these fellows. Tried to on the ship, before she went up."

He had pulled her attention away from whatever crisis was happening, and he saw red eyes, a glance downward.

"I'm sorry, sailor. It's all been . . . I was never taught to expect anything like this. Can you sit up by yourself? I can help you from behind."

He pulled himself up, pushing with his right hand, sat upright, swung his legs off the side of the bed.

"It's okay, ma'am. My chest hurts, my throat. I just gotta breathe slow."

"All right, let me help you stand."

His legs betrayed him immediately, a surprising weakness, but she had him under the arms, said, "This is why you have to walk. Your muscles don't like sitting still."

He was up now, slightly dizzy. He could see all down the ward, the cluster of nurses gathered around a patient with the kind of urgency he knew not to ask about.

She held his good arm, said, "Let's move out this way. If you're comfortable with the idea, we can go to another ward. It's not like this in the other wards. I mean, the burns . . . Oh God, I'm sorry. I have a hard time working here. It's not just the burns . . . but the smell. Even the doctors can't take it for very long."

Biggs felt his legs steadying, took a single step, then another. "I'm doing fine, ma'am. Just hurts to breathe."

She seemed to appreciate the change of subject. "Well, sailor, it would be a bad idea for you to stop breathing."

Biggs realized she had made a joke. "I don't intend to. Just don't expect me to blow up any balloons."

They reached the door to another ward—more

beds, but it was different, the men not as ghost-like. The bandages were more for wounds, broken bones, shrapnel and bullet wounds, more of the horrors he had seen during the attack. He saw most of the men turning his way, then realized they were looking at her.

"Hey, sweetheart, I wanna go for a walk too."

"Can I get a back rub, sugar pie?"

Biggs felt uneasy, said in a low voice, "We don't have to be here."

She hooked her arm in his. "It's okay. It's just what they do."

Biggs called out to them now, with as much wind as he could muster. "Hey, you goons. This here's my wife."

The catcalls abruptly stopped, and she squeezed his arm, a silent **Thank you.**

They moved through the ward, Biggs scanning the faces—no one he recognized. She seemed to read his mind, said, "What ship were you on?"

The faces were on him now, and he had no reason to hesitate.

"The **Arizona.** I got blown into the water. Well, into the oil."

The ward went deathly silent, and Biggs wondered if he had said something wrong. Down the row, one man said, "That's tough, sailor. The battle-wagons caught the worst of it, and I hear **Arizona** worst of all."

Biggs had not thought to ask the question until

now. "How bad? Anybody know? I thought **Oklahoma** got it worst, rolling over and all."

Another man said, "That's my ship. I made it up to the hull as she capsized. We were pulling people out of the water. A damn Jap strafed us, and there was nowhere to go. Caught both my legs. Even then, we could hear the poor bastards hammering inside the hull, letting us know where they were." He paused, and Biggs saw him staring down at his wounds, his hands shaking. "They were trapped in the black dark, water and oil and God knows what else. And we couldn't do a damn thing for 'em. They're still there. Oh, Christ." He put his hands to his face, no one speaking, no one interrupting the man's emotions. Biggs saw the others looking away, those who already knew what the man had been through.

He looked at Biggs with red eyes, still with the quiver in his voice. "They tell me there's a chance I won't lose my legs. Don't hardly matter. I'd give 'em both away to see those fellows pulled out safe." He paused. "I been hearing that they're still pulling guys out. I know better. It's been two days. Them that survived, they mostly made it to Ford Island." He paused again, still looking at Biggs. "I don't think there's anybody they can pull out of your ship. Sorry, sailor."

Biggs's emotions caught him off guard, another piece of the nightmare he hadn't known until now. He needed the nurse's support now, felt weakness in his legs, said in a low voice, "I don't know how to ask, don't know how to find out. I wanna find out who made it out. And, I guess, who didn't."

The first man said, "Talk to the officers. They can find out anything. A bunch of 'em are in the houses across the yard, so I been told."

The nurse said, "That's right. You feel up to the walk? How're you doing?"

Biggs felt energized, suddenly had a new mission.

"Let's go." He caught himself, looked at the men in the beds. "I'm sorry for you guys. I guess we all lost somebody who mattered."

Another man responded, "Yeah, give me a chance. I'll make those damn Krauts pay."

There was a chorus of groans, and Biggs was confused. "I thought Krauts were Germans, right?"

The man ignored the derision coming from the men around him. "Damn right. And I'm a hundred percent certain that's who flew those planes. No damn Jap can fly like that, hit targets like that. They ain't got an airplane good enough to stay in the air for more than ten minutes. It was the Krauts, sure as hell. They paint damn meatballs on the wings so's to fool us. Well, I ain't fooled a bit. And neither are the boys I heard about, who shot one down. They say it was a Kraut pilot, Kraut uniform."

To one side, another man, "You bring me that Kraut uniform. What I saw was Japs. Saw 'em looking right at us as they flew over. There wasn't a blond-haired, blue-eyed jackass in the bunch. And I saw 'em up close."

The argument continued, obviously a familiar one to all concerned. The nurse tugged at his arm, moving them out through the door, down a short hallway with offices, then outside. He felt the sun on his face, ached to take a deep breath. He turned to her, said, "Hey, what's your name, if you don't mind me asking?"

"Loretta. But if any of the doctors are around, it's Nurse Powell."

"You seem kinda young, not like some nurses I saw."

"Old enough to bandage you up, sailor."

"Tommy. Or, Mr. Biggs, if the doctor's around."

She stopped, seemed concerned. "I'm sorry for what I said before. My job is to take care of anyone who's hurt, no matter how bad. But the burns . . . there's nothing like that. I know that's why the doctor sent me out here with you. I can't stand it in that ward for more than a half hour, maybe less. Most of us feel the same way, but we've got to do the job."

"Why'd you get assigned to the burn unit? You volunteer for that?"

"We didn't have any choice. Nobody can pick and choose what kinds of patients they want to help. There are just too many of you."

"How many?"

She put a hand to her face, took a deep breath.

"I don't know, exactly. But this is just one hospital. There's a base hospital at Hickam, the medical facility on Ford Island, on Tripler, the marine medical facility, and a half dozen other makeshift hospitals. Then there's the hospital ship, **Solace.** People are saying the attack could have been worse, but I don't see how. One boat came into the landing full of limbs. Just limbs. There were corpses soaked in oil, you couldn't make out if they . . ."

She stopped, her face in her hands.

"Hey, it's okay."

She looked at him. "No, it's not. It's war. There's going to be a lot more of this. Even the doctors are talking about that. My mother was a nurse in the Great War, in Belgium. She won't talk about it, not a word. She hated it when I said I wanted to be a nurse. Warned me how bad it can get. It didn't matter. Now . . . I'm here." She seemed to gather herself, gripped his arm again. "We can go over there, where they've got some of the officers. You sure you want to do that? The doctor didn't want me to take you very far."

"I guess I kinda like walking with you, no matter where we go. If it's okay I say that. I'm not good at saying the right things."

She gave a small laugh, like music. "You're doing just fine, Sailor Tommy."

Biggs felt her hand on him now, as though for the first time. He wanted just to stand there, swallowed by the sunshine, by her voice.

"I can't keep you out here for too long. You can't take much of the sun on your head, even with the bandage. And, they'll need me to change dressings on some of the other patients. The doctor tends to be impatient. Do you still want to see the officers?"

He looked across the green lawn toward the other buildings, where men might **know.**

"I have to, I guess. I had buddies on the ship." He thought of Russo now, a cold jab in his gut. "I had buddies on other ships too. My best buddy. I gotta know if they're okay."

She led him slowly across the green grass, and he saw the harbor now. Columns of smoke were still rising, small boats in motion in every direction. He didn't want to see any more, but the largest plume of smoke came from his own ship, and he stopped, stared for a long moment.

"That's her, the heavy smoke. It's wrecked. It's sunk. How did anybody get off her?"

"How did **you**?"

"I didn't have much choice. A bomb threw me off."

"You're alive. That's something. Hold on to that."

Biggs looked at her, the sun on her face. She had soft brown eyes, and he realized just how pretty she was, prettier still.

"You're staring at me, Mr. Biggs."

"You're staring back, Nurse Powell."

They walked on toward a large house, a guard appraising them, then opening the door. The smells returned, but they weren't as brutal as in the burn ward. Another guard met them inside, made a leering examination of Loretta, then stood aside. Biggs stepped inside, saw nothing different, nothing to distinguish these men from any of the sailors he had already seen. She tugged at his arm, said in a soft voice, "Go ahead. Most of them are awake. Keep it in a low voice, but ask what you need to ask."

Biggs felt completely tongue-tied: no words, too many questions. There was a noisy commotion down the row of beds, nurses gathering, a doctor. The doctor turned, walked toward Biggs, ignored him, moved past, said, "Worst damn patients in the world. **Doctors.**"

The nurses spread out now, tending to other patients, and Biggs stepped farther into the room. He saw gray hair, a few men watching him. Their wounds were no different: thick white bandages, heads covered, arms and legs and entire bodies. He searched carefully, hoping to see a familiar face, Lieutenant Janz, or Dr. Johnson. **Doctors make the worst patients.** He looked to where the commotion had been, walked more quickly, Loretta keeping up. He saw the face turn toward him now, both men letting go of a smile, the first for either man since that awful morning.

"I'll be damned. Hello, Mr. Biggs."

"Hello, Dr. Condon."

"To be honest, Mr. Biggs, you look like hell."

"I'm alive, sir. The rest of it doesn't much matter."

Condon looked down. "Well put, Mr. Biggs."

Biggs eyed the bandages, one arm wrapped to the shoulder, another around his chest. "How'd you get hit? You go in the water?"

"No. Bullet hit my arm. Soft tissue, thank God. If it had hit bone, it would have taken the arm away. I fell against a hand rail, broke three ribs. I keep arguing with them that this bed should be used for somebody who needs it worse than I do. That doctor over there, Brubaker, stubborn pain in the ass." Condon looked up at Loretta now. "Sorry. I'm sure he's a great doctor. I just don't like being a patient."

"None of us does, Doctor."

The voice came from the next bed, and Biggs turned, saw an older man, a look of seniority. Biggs stepped back, stiffened, said, "Sorry to disturb you, sir. I worked for Dr. Condon on the **Arizona.** Hospital apprentice."

The man stared at Biggs for a long moment, said, "Your skipper was a good friend of mine. I'm sorry, son."

Biggs turned to Condon, said, "The captain is dead, sir?"

Condon nodded. "Along with Admiral Kidd and most of the senior staff."

Names rolled through Biggs's mind, and he wanted to ask, saw the older officer close his eyes, turning away.

Biggs bent closer to Condon, whispered, "What about sick bay, sir?"

Condon stared at him, no words, slowly shook his head.

They came in the backs of trucks, packed into cars and taxis, some brought by their bouncers or madams, some on their own. They had answered the desperate call for blood, and when the civilians on Oahu responded, so too did the women who had relied so completely on the money they made from the sailors. They lined up at the various dispensaries, the hospital wards, anyplace the blood banks could be thrown together. To the surprise of many of the doctors, and especially their patients, the prostitutes from Hotel Street offered the gift these men most needed now: blood.

But the women didn't simply return to their trade. Some stayed on the bases, assisting the nurses, offering help with even the worst kind of duty, from washing sheets to disposing of soiled bandages, and much worse. Their efforts freed the nurses for far more important jobs—offering relief to the overtaxed doctors. From the earliest days that the navy had anchored its ships in Pearl Harbor, the women of Hotel Street had served a function that the sailors appreciated with lusty gratitude. Now the gratitude was of a very different kind. The doctors knew, even before any of their patients, that these women were saving lives.

# FORTY-ONE

# Biggs

"You have the maggots?"

"Yes, Doctor."

Biggs stared at the small tin. "Is that really . . . You're gonna put those things on me?"

The doctor glanced up at Loretta, a look that showed Biggs he had heard this before. "Mr. Biggs, you're hoping to train in medicine. One lesson you'll learn pretty quickly is that when you're dealing with infection or decaying tissue, maggots can be a lifesaver. They only eat dead tissue, and leave the healthy tissue alone. It's called 'maggot debridement therapy.'"

Biggs looked away while the doctor unwrapped his arm, the familiar smell turning his stomach.

"You ought to watch what I'm doing, Mr. Biggs. Just view the arm as though it's detached, belongs to another patient."

The gauze was removed, and Biggs forced himself to look at the wound, a gash more than a foot long, elbow to wrist. But worse, he could see decayed flesh and the signs of infection, what the doctors had cautioned against from the beginning. The doctor had a small scalpel, looked at Biggs.

"Before we start the MDT, I'm going to cut away some of the dead tissue. It'll hurt a bit, but like I said, it's dead, so it shouldn't be too bad. I'll be quick about it. I don't want to give you any morphine, not for this. We have to be careful how much of that stuff you're administered."

Biggs looked away. He clenched, felt the blade, a sharp pain tearing through his arm, down to his fingers.

"That's it. Got most of what needed to come off. I can't treat the wound with anything that will harm the maggots, so you'll have to tough it out. The pain should fade in about a half hour." He took the small box from Loretta, removed the top, began to pour the tiny larvae into the open wound. Biggs stared at the wound now with a mix of horror, nausea, and fascination, distractions from the pain.

"How long's it take, Doc?"

"As long as it takes. But this is the best way we have to treat the kind of problems that wound is giving us. All right, nurse, you can wrap it up. I'll check on you later, Mr. Biggs. Keep the arm as still as you can."

The doctor moved away, another nurse calling him to another patient. Loretta was on the edge of his bed now, gently wrapping the arm, a glance toward him.

"You're staring at me again, Mr. Biggs."

"You're welcome to stare back, Nurse Powell. Just be careful of our little squirmy friends."

She kept working, and he could see she was trying not to smile. She unrolled another strip of gauze, said, "I know they're useful, but these maggots are pretty disgusting. Like the doctor said, they're larvae. I don't know what would happen if they were allowed to hatch. Some kind of nasty creature, I'm sure."

"Gee, nurse, you're really good at comforting your patients."

She seemed embarrassed now, said, "You're not going to lose the arm. That's the most important thing. The doctor wasn't so certain of that a few days ago."

Biggs felt a bolt of alarm. "He didn't tell me that."

"No, he didn't. Unless he knows for certain, he won't say. It wouldn't have done you a bit of good if he had told you there was a chance of amputation."

Biggs closed his eyes. It was a word he hoped never to hear again.

"Hey! I found you! Son of a bitch!"

Biggs pushed himself upright, knew the voice, the smile, heard a scolding **hush** from one of the nurses.

"Yeah, you found me. Now pipe down. Damn, you're still ugly."

Loretta finished with the arm, stood, and Biggs knew she was waiting for an introduction.

"Nurse Powell, this is Ed Wakeman, the stupidest, laziest idiot I ever met. And if he bends over, I'll kiss him on the lips."

Wakeman scowled, shook his head. "He must be on some really heavy drugs, huh, miss? Damn, it stinks in here." Wakeman glanced around, then lowered his voice, the good cheer wiped away. "My God, this is the burn place. I never thought to look for you over here. I checked the other bases, Ford Island mainly. A lot of our guys ended up there. They're putting together the list of casualties, but they're stingy with the details."

"You find anybody else from the compartment? Mahone?"

"Not a word. I did hear . . ." He stopped, looked down.

"Heard what? Come on, Ed. We're all gonna know sooner or later."

"Tommy, I know you were buddies with some of the musicians. They didn't make it."

"Which ones?"

"None of 'em. All twenty-one guys, the whole damn band."

Biggs let out a breath, felt Loretta's hand on his shoulder. "Jesus, Ed. How does that even happen?"

"It doesn't get any better. A bunch of the marines

didn't make it. Not sure which ones. They're already announcing that over a thousand men were lost with the ship. The whole forward section, plus a whole lot more."

Biggs lay back down, stared at the ceiling. "Sick bay."

Wakeman said, "Yeah. Guess so."

"Dr. Condon's over in officer's country. He may be the only one who made it."

"And you."

"That doesn't feel so good, Ed, not like it should. I guess I'm supposed to be grateful. I am. But, good God. I wonder how long it's gonna be before we learn who survived." The name burst into his brain. "Oh, Kincaid's here. He was burned up pretty good. I found him, or he found me, in the oil. Guess we got blown off the ship about the same time."

He looked up at Loretta. "Do you know where he is? He came in with me, same boat."

"Petty Officer Jack Kincaid?"

"Yeah. He probably got wrapped up pretty tight. He was burned over most of his body, and had a bad wound in his leg. If they wrapped his face, I wouldn't know he was here."

She moved away, checked the clipboard on the far wall.

Wakeman leaned low, said, "Hell, I didn't know his first name was Jack. Did he save your life or something?"

Biggs thought a moment, couldn't find the anger

he had held on to for so long. "I guess I saved his. We were both in the oil. I found debris, used it as a raft, helped him to it. Pretty sure he'd have drowned."

Wakeman put his hands on his hips. "Well, what do you know about that?"

Loretta was back now, and Biggs could see the answer in her face. She said in a low voice, "I'm sorry, but Petty Officer Kincaid died two days ago. The burns were too severe. It's been this way, some of the men just dying in the middle of the night. I'm so sorry." He saw her hopelessness, reached out for her hand. "They scream and cry and beg for their mothers, and there's nothing we can do. It's the hardest part of this job. I remember Mr. Kincaid. He knew he was going to die, told the doctor to leave him be. Said he never should have been pulled out of the water."

Biggs looked at Wakeman, knew they were sharing the same thoughts, a smoldering hatred that had now become something very different. Biggs wanted to say more, to tell Wakeman more about Kincaid's unhappiness, his hopelessness so unexpected. He looked up at Wakeman, said, "He was set to retire end of the year. Didn't want to. I guess that's why he was so pissed off."

Loretta whispered, "I'm so very sorry. So, he was your friend?"

Biggs looked at Wakeman, expected a wisecrack, but Wakeman just shook his head.

"No, miss. He was in charge of our compartment.

He was real tough on us, Tommy most of all. Maybe that's why we're still here and he isn't."

NAVAL HOSPITAL, HOSPITAL POINT, OAHU—
WEDNESDAY, DECEMBER 17, 1941

She had walked with him every day, his legs getting stronger. His feet and hands had healed completely, and his scalp was no longer bandaged. For the first time since the attack, he had been given a mirror. The bald, scarred head had been a shock, but she had laughed, her effort to lighten his feelings. She encouraged him that in time, the hair would grow back. And, if it didn't, he was a very distinguished-looking bald man. He didn't believe her.

But the pain in his lungs and his throat wouldn't leave, his breathing still labored. The doctors feared it might develop into something even worse. There was even more concern over the ugly wound in his arm, that the attention they could offer might be no substitute for a difficult surgery.

Her arm was around his, but by now, both of them knew he didn't require the support. He had visited Dr. Condon as often as he could. It was an excuse for Biggs and Loretta to spend even more time together, but Biggs could feel that Condon needed the visits, the doctor greeting him with almost too much enthusiasm, as though needing to be reassured that someone he knew had made it out alive.

She led him into the officers' house, where they put on a good show for the guards, the damaged sailor and the helpful nurse, as though he needed support for every step. Biggs hated the way they looked at her, but it was a game she was used to, and once more, she reassured him that it got them where they wanted to go without any annoying questions.

Condon seemed to be waiting for them again, with the usual smile. "How's the arm?"

Biggs raised the bandaged limb toward him. "About the same. The maggots have helped keep the infection down, but closing the wound is another problem."

"Exposed the bone. Pretty tough bit of surgery."

"Yes, sir."

Condon looked at Loretta, smiled. "How are you, Miss Powell? He as annoying a patient as I am?"

"I enjoy being annoyed by him, Doctor."

Condon smiled again, said to Biggs, "You know, not every sailor here gets his own private nurse. Not even the officers." He leaned over, past Biggs. "Right, Captain?"

Biggs looked that way, saw the older officer reading a magazine. "I won't need a damn nurse if they let me out of this place. It's just a bullet hole, for crying out loud."

Condon was serious now, said, "A bullet that damn near severed your spine. Let it heal, Doug. You know that."

"Whatever you say, Doc. Bad enough I have to

listen to those fellows in the white coats—I get one in the bed next to me." He looked at Biggs. "Son, you might have your personal nurse, but I've got my personal physician."

Biggs felt an opportunity. "Um, Captain, do you know where they'll post casualty lists?"

The old man got serious. "You in a hurry to know?"

Condon said, "I told you, Doug, he was with me on the **Arizona.** He's got a right to know."

"Yeah, I suppose so. You can reach my aide at the Ford Island air station. There's a card with my name and such, there, in that bag on the floor. If you happen to notice a pint of Scotch in there, keep quiet about it. From what I've been told, most of the known losses are being compiled at the naval station on Ford. Not sure how long it'll take for the unknown, the missing. We may never know, especially on the **Arizona.** Process of elimination. Take the official crew manifests, subtract everybody we can account for. The rest . . . Well, that's how it's gotta be."

The question came now, pushed out by a nervous fear Biggs couldn't avoid. "Sir, besides the **Arizona,** are there lists from other ships, not just battleships?"

Condon said, "What ship, Mr. Biggs?"

"The **Curtiss,** sir. Seaplane tender . . ."

"**Curtiss** is my boat. Who's asking?"

Biggs looked toward the voice, several beds away. A younger man was sitting up, heavy cast on his leg. The older captain said, "Go ahead, son. Find out what you need to know. But I'll warn you, he's the only man in here grouchier than me, and he's half my age."

"Thank you, sir."

The captain waved him away, and Biggs moved toward the **Curtiss**'s officer, Loretta still on his arm.

"Excuse me, sir, but my best friend served on the **Curtiss.** I want to make sure he's okay. I'm not sure how much damage you took, or anything."

He knew he was babbling nervously, the younger officer waiting for him to finish.

"What's your friend's name?"

"Ray Russo, sir. Seaman second."

He felt Loretta's hand squeeze his arm, a reflex of emotion. He stopped talking, saw what she saw, the look on the officer's face.

"We lost a few, but only a few. We got off easy. Not like you boys." He paused. "We took two hits, the worst a bomb that cleaned off a chunk of the deck, knocked us to hell, busted my leg in three places. But we're still floating."

Her grip was relentless, and now the voice in his head. **Say it!**

"Seaman Russo was your buddy?"

**Was.**

His response came in a quiver, his gravelly voice cracking. "Best friend, sir."

"I'm sorry, sailor. Seaman Russo was killed when we took that bomb. Never knew what hit him, if that matters. He was a good fellow. I'll miss him."

Biggs put his hand on Loretta's, still wrapped around his arm. He had nothing left to say. So far, his own wounds had been agonizing and inconvenient, his world confined to a single burn unit in a single hospital, one part of a greater whole. As he turned away from the young officer, his eye caught the window, a view to the harbor. The fires were out, the wrecked hulks of so many ships being swarmed over by mechanics and salvage crews.

He had not even told her about his nightmares, would not make this some kind of drama. Nearly every night, the dreams took him back to the bloody wounded, the bomb blasts and the oil and the smiling face of the Japanese pilot. Every morning, it was all swept away by the comfort of white sheets on a soft bed, and thoughts of her. But he could never tell her that even she couldn't erase it all, that being awake was a nightmare still: the stink of the burn ward, patients beside him dying in the night, his constant pain and the tedium of healing his body. All around Pearl Harbor, men were mourning shipmates and friends—what the reports said were thousands. But still, those were just words and numbers, until now, just one more part of the unending nightmare. But nightmares aren't real. Except now, Russo was dead. Now it was real.

"It's confirmed. You're one of twenty-four men here who will make the trip."

The words came from a young lieutenant, and Biggs looked at the doctor beside him.

"I really don't want to leave, sir. This is kinda like home."

The doctor shook his head. "Nobody ever wants a hospital to be home."

"No, sir, I mean Hawaii, Oahu, Pearl."

The two men glanced at each other, and Biggs knew what was coming. The lieutenant said, "Apprentice Biggs, you no longer have a ship to report to, no posting here. But with the war there will surely be one, assuming you can be made whole and judged fit for duty."

The doctor seemed annoyed with the officer, said, "Look, Mr. Biggs, what this man is so **discreetly** trying to say is that you require the kind of attention we cannot give you here. There is an entire convoy of ships that will be carrying a great many wounded men to the naval facility on Mare Island, near San Francisco. You are fit for travel, so you're on the list. Most of the craft will be destroyer class, perhaps a little larger."

The lieutenant couldn't seem to contain his expertise. "The destroyers will be extremely useful should you encounter Japanese submarines. We'll make them wish they had stayed home."

Biggs saw a look on the doctor's face that suggested indigestion. He said, "Mr. Biggs, the ships are being outfitted to accommodate patients. A number of nurses are traveling with you, so it will be more or less like a fleet of floating hospitals."

The lieutenant started to speak, but the doctor was already pulling him along to the next patient who'd make the journey.

Biggs lay back in the bed, one desperate thought suddenly pushing everything else away. **Will I ever see her again?** He closed his eyes, tried not to let anything else seep in, no thoughts of **Arizona,** or of all that was lost. But Russo was there, always, the worst loss of his life. So many others, he thought, friends, brothers. I don't have the right to feel so damn awful. Now, they're gonna ship me off to some place I don't want to be. And the one good thing that's happened to me, the one thing I look forward to . . . Jesus, I'm gonna lose her, too.

He knew the sound of her shoes, the muffled rubber of her heels, the rhythm of her walk.

"Hey, sailor, I hear you're going for a boat ride."

He opened his eyes, was amazed to see a smile he couldn't return.

"Yeah. I just got the orders. God, I'm gonna miss you. I haven't said this, and now, I may never get the chance. Maybe I screwed up not telling you . . . well, how I feel. I wanted to let you know . . . to tell you . . . I've never felt like this. I really want to be with you, I mean like, a whole lot."

She whispered, "Not now, Tommy. We've got an audience here. Too many ears. I'd rather you say nice things to me when we can enjoy it. We can go for a walk tonight. It's beautiful outside, should be a nice sunset. That sound all right? I promise you, I'll enjoy whatever you want to say." She laughed now. "I know how you feel, even if you're not very good at saying it. I don't know that I'm any better at it, but I'll try."

"I don't know when any of that's gonna be. I don't know how long before I can see you again."

"Well, I have a surprise. You see, I requested a transfer to serve the convoy. It was approved. They don't need nearly as many nurses here now. And, I think the doctor knows just how important **morale** is. Yours. Maybe mine too."

Biggs sat up, a wide smile. He squeezed her hand, but a thought broke in, and he said, "Oh, I forgot to ask the doctor. When do we ship out?"

She sat down on the bed beside him, and he could feel her pressing against him, caught a hint of some kind of perfume, utterly delicious.

"We sail . . . Oh God, is that the right word?"

He laughed. "It's one of them. 'Standing out' is a little more up to date."

"Well, we 'stand out' day after tomorrow, the nineteenth. An officer told me the trip will take five or six days, but he told me the route is top secret, since there are supposed to be submarines out there. The bad ones."

He wanted to wrap his arm around her, knew

they had to show some decorum around the other patients.

"Yes, I heard about the submarines. If there's a flock of destroyers, we'll be fine. Five or six days? That's pretty quick. I guess most of us don't need to get our wounds tossed around too much. We'll be on smaller craft, and that can be some rough water—it was when I came out here."

She leaned away from him, staring at him, serious now. "We're going home, Tommy. The mainland. We'll be safe. And you know what else? If what that officer said is true, we'll arrive on Christmas Day!"

He tried to feel the hopefulness he saw in her eyes. He wanted so much to enjoy everything they could have, everything they might explore together. For her, there would always be the job; perhaps by now she had seen the worst of it, and could focus more on the healing than the dying. Biggs could feel **himself** healing, knew that the doctors at the Naval Hospital had saved his arm and his life. The journey to Mare Island would be the last stage in his recovery, and if the surgery there worked as well as the doctors had told him it would, he might be fit for duty in several weeks.

He had never said anything to her about what he still needed to do. He wanted the navy, the ships. He was a sailor, and if he didn't have a ship, in time he would find one. He could never forget Kincaid's helpless fury, that the **Arizona** wasn't merely his home, but his life. Biggs understood that now, knew that no matter his next posting, the **Arizona** had been his home as well, that she would always be, that he could never forget the agony of her death, the violent catastrophe that wiped away so many lives and so many friends.

He knew that what he and Loretta were sharing was **romance,** the best feeling two people could enjoy. But he also knew there was one very large, very black reality that neither of them could escape. As long as he was healthy, he would not quit, would not walk away, could not settle down to the kind of happy times that Russo and the sick bay staff and so many others could never know.

Before he could embrace the happiness she was offering him, he would have to go back to sea. He had to fight a war.

# AFTERWORD

**N**o account of the attack on Pearl Harbor can ignore the astonishing cost to the Americans, and the astonishing **lack** of cost to the Japanese.

The Americans lose 188 aircraft, with another 159 damaged. Almost all of these aircraft are struck while they are on the ground. In contrast, the Japanese lose a total of 29 aircraft, one submarine, and five midget submarines.

The total number of fatalities for the Japanese is estimated to be between 60 and 80 men. American deaths total 2,403, with an additional 1,178 wounded, most of whom are sailors. Losses also include soldiers, marines, and 68 civilians.

Eighteen naval ships are either sunk or damaged,

including eight battleships. Eventually, **West Virginia, Pennsylvania, California, Nevada, Tennessee,** and **Maryland,** despite varying degrees of damage, are all repaired, and all return to action during the war.

Through an extraordinary feat of engineering, the capsized **Oklahoma** is righted, and placed into dry dock. Determined by the navy to be too obsolete and too damaged for further service, the ship is destined for salvage, but passing through a squall while being towed to San Francisco, she sinks, several hundred miles from the mainland. Today, the Oklahoma Memorial on Ford Island is simplicity in design, emotional tribute to the 429 men lost on a ship that capsizes, trapping most of those men inside.

The **Arizona** is a total loss. By far the worst disaster that day, the ship suffers 1,177 dead, with only 335 survivors. Among the dead are **23** sets of brothers. Of the 88 marines onboard, only 15 survive. It is estimated that more than 900 of those lost sailors are entombed on their ship. Thus are they still **on duty.** Today, the USS **Arizona** Memorial in Pearl Harbor continues to serve as a poignant reminder of **why** we went to war, **how** we went to war, and just **who** went to war.

Within hours after the disaster, the finger-pointing begins, in both Washington and Hawaii. Conspiracy theories explode to life, as some, including members of Congress, fail to comprehend how the United States could have been caught so unprepared, that surely there were dastardly deeds committed, or treasonous plots involving everyone from the officers in Hawaii to the president of the United States.

However, as a variety of hearings and investigations later determine, the high command in Hawaii, Admiral Husband E. Kimmel and Lieutenant General Walter C. Short, simply did not consider the Japanese to be a threat, and made no efforts to deploy reconnaissance aircraft or ships. They paid little if any attention to the deployment of the new technology of radar, ignored reports from their own intelligence officers of spurious communications (or lack of communications) regarding Japanese ship movements, and paid no heed to the suspicious activities in the Japanese Consulate in Honolulu, particularly when documents within the consulate were suddenly burned, only days before the attack.

In Washington, evidence of culpability is equally damning. Though the Magic decoding machines are invaluable for eavesdropping on diplomatic traffic between Tokyo and its embassies all over the world, they offer no direct insight whatsoever into military communications or strategic planning.

Worse, it is a foregone conclusion in Washington—among Secretary of War Henry Stimson, Secretary of the Navy Frank Knox, Army Chief of Staff George Marshall, and Chief of Naval Operations

Harold Stark—that Admiral Kimmel has his own Magic machine in Hawaii, and thus is privy to the same communications they are. Later, the hearings and investigations reveal that not only was there no Magic machine in Hawaii, but that neither Kimmel nor Short had ever heard of Magic (or of **Purple**). In other words, those in Washington were mistaken in their belief that their commanders in Hawaii were as well informed of Japanese attitudes and belligerence as they were.

Valid reasons to lay blame on both Hawaii and Washington can be expanded into a book (and there are plenty of those). Suffice to say that the greatest single flaw that the commanders and their intelligence officers in Hawaii share is their complete failure to anticipate the possibility that the Japanese might actually attack Hawaii. There is no comprehension of the importance of the Japanese government's warlike mindset, or that Japan is building its military toward a war it considers inevitable. All suggestions of Japanese military aggressiveness convince Hawaii and Washington only that such a war will spread into Southeast Asia. Hawaii is thought to be an impregnable fortress.

Though Washington carries its share of the blame, there are significant clues about Japanese planning that are communicated to Hawaii, and for the most part simply ignored. The "bomb plot" message intercepted by Magic ordering the Japanese spy Takeo Yoshikawa to impose a checkerboard pattern on a map of the harbor, cataloguing the ships where they are moored, is given little regard in Washington. In Hawaii, it is completely ignored, attributed to "Japanese efficiency." The "war warning" messages, sent in late November to both Kimmel and Short, are disregarded as well.

As any military commander knows, a message that begins **"This is to be considered a war warning"** should be considered exactly that. Apparently, not so in Hawaii. General Short's response is to heighten his vigilance against sabotage, presumably by the Japanese-Americans already in Hawaii. Thus are American aircraft lined up in the open, closely together, where guards can better observe them. And antiaircraft ammunition is locked away for safekeeping so it cannot be stolen or used by possible saboteurs. There is virtually no useful communication between General Short and Admiral Kimmel regarding the deployment of reconnaissance aircraft, each man assuming the other has that responsibility.

In another area of this tragedy where blame can be tossed in a multitude of directions, the military leaders in Hawaii logically and correctly assume that the Japanese have made their attack from the decks of aircraft carriers. An urgent search is launched to locate those carriers in the direction that the navy believes to be the most logical for the Japanese to have come: from the southwest.

But Commander Minoru Genda has previously

dismissed that approach as being too dangerous. The Japanese fleet sits, in fact, in the opposite direction from the navy's search. It is never located. It is also reported by various stations along Oahu's North Shore that a large mass of planes is flying northward after the assault. Some of those observations are made with the naked eye, various troops watching the planes as they pass over, heading out to sea. No serious attention is paid to those reports.

> "The Pearl Harbor investigations will hear 3,649 witnesses, fill countless volumes with testimony, and ultimately reach the conclusion that the Japs caught us unprepared because we were unprepared."
>
> —JACK TARVER, COLUMNIST,
> **THE ATLANTA CONSTITUTION**

During congressional hearings late in the war, and to this day, there are conspiracy theorists who insist that President Roosevelt knew of the attack in advance, and withheld this critical, lifesaving information from Hawaii. Those people are wrong. The lengthy list of co-conspirators necessary to carry out such a plot would fill a book of its own. Those who would have had to participate in this conspiracy include most of the cabinet and dozens of military and intelligence chiefs, not all of whom are fans of Roosevelt. In a great disservice both to

history and to the men involved, one congressional
hearing that seeks "the truth" devolves into nothing more than partisan bickering between those
who support Roosevelt and those who despise
him. Very little light is shed on the importance of
the intelligence and communications breakdowns
that so delude the American government and its
military into believing that the Japanese are but a
minor threat.

In any significant historical event, the luxury of
hindsight opens all manner of doors into cries of
conspiracy. **Now that we know what happened,
there should have been those who saw it coming.**
This very often devolves into **There were definitely
those who knew in advance.** Despite numerous
claims to the contrary, there is no conclusive or
convincing evidence to support any conspiracy,
in either Washington or Hawaii, that existed prior
to December 7, 1941.

"As any great athlete knows, there is no greater
disgrace than to be defeated by an opponent you
have publicly and frequently denigrated. This is
one reason why the psychological wounds of Pearl
Harbor have cut so deeply. It also explains why the
rumors of sabotage by local Japanese Americans,
and allegations that Roosevelt conspired to with-
hold crucial intelligence from Kimmel and Short,
continue to be widely accepted, despite convincing
evidence and arguments to the contrary. They are,

after all, excuses and explanations for a defeat that is otherwise inexplicable and humiliating."
—THURSTON CLARKE, HISTORIAN

"No joint action to provide radar reconnaissance, no joint action on air reconnaissance, no joint action to create an aircraft identification center, no antiaircraft ammunition deployed to the army gunners. Above all, there was no effective, systematic liaison by either Short or Kimmel, between the army and the navy. This was the complete opposite of what Washington had expected the two commanders to achieve."
—HENRY C. CLAUSEN,
WAR DEPARTMENT INVESTIGATOR

"The signals that seem to stand out and scream of the impending catastrophe are the ones learned about only after the event."
—ROBERTA WOHLSTETTER, HISTORIAN

The Japanese are not without errors of their own. For years after, there is debate in Japan about whether Admiral Chuichi Nagumo's decision not to attack Pearl Harbor for a third time fatally damages Japan's chances for success in the war. Though Admiral Yamamoto himself questions whether Nagumo's decision is a grave error, ultimately neither Yamamoto nor anyone of prominence in the Japanese high command officially faults Nagumo.

He does, after all, deliver a stunning blow to the American fleet, and escapes virtually unharmed.

However, contrary to lore on both sides of the ocean, the assault is far from perfect, in many ways. By focusing so much of their attention on the battleships, many planes ignore other extremely valuable targets. A number of the dive bombers, whose payloads are effectively useless against the heavily armored battleships, nevertheless expend their bombs, tempted by the size of those targets. Those bombs could have wreaked havoc in a number of other areas, destroying smaller warships, and most important, igniting a massive fire that could have destroyed the military's enormous fuel depot, which sits close beside the harbor.

As Yamamoto has predicted, the attack on the American fleet is a wound that the Americans can heal. But his goal of crippling that fleet for six months is nearly met. If there is one disastrous outcome for the Japanese, it is the failure to locate and assault the American aircraft carriers, what Yamamoto and Commander Genda always believe to be a major priority. That failure will begin a chain of events that will alter the history of the war.

"It would be a mistake of the first magnitude to credit the success of the Pearl Harbor operation solely to American errors. We have seen how meticulously the Japanese perfected their planning, how diligently they trained their pilots and

bombardiers; how they modified weapons . . . how
they dredged up and utilized information . . . They
balked at no hazard, ready to risk a wild leap to
achieve their immediate ends."
—GORDON PRANGE, HISTORIAN

"Whatever the answers, one thing was certain. The
enemy came completely undetected, struck with
devastating strategic and tactical surprise, left without being followed or found, and left Pearl Harbor
and military airfields on Oahu in shambles."
—BILL MCWILLIAMS, HISTORIAN

## SECRETARY OF STATE CORDELL HULL

Despite the stain of blame that covers so many
in Washington for their blindness toward the
events leading to Pearl Harbor, there is little if
any recrimination directed toward Hull. In negotiating with the Japanese, Hull makes every attempt
to create a dialogue that will ensure peace. After
December 7, Hull's feelings about the duplicity of the Japanese government are confirmed—
that despite the apparent decency of Ambassador
Kichisaburo Nomura, the Japanese were never
negotiating in good faith, and that war was the
inevitable outcome.

In 1943, Hull and many of his staff assemble the
drafts and details for what will become the Charter
of the United Nations. In recognition, Hull is
awarded the 1945 Nobel Peace Prize. He remains

in Roosevelt's cabinet until November 1944, and thus becomes this nation's longest-serving secretary of state. He retires, suffering ill health, and continues to endure a variety of ailments, including several heart attacks. He dies in Washington, D.C., in 1955, of a stroke, and is buried in the Washington National Cathedral.

## HOSPITAL APPRENTICE 2/C
## THOMAS "TOMMY" BIGGS—USN

The surgery on Biggs's left arm is successful, but the healing process takes longer than he expects. He is finally released from the hospital at Mare Island, California, in March 1942, and undergoes weeks of physical therapy to regain mobility and strength. Despite pronounced scarring on his scalp, his hair does indeed grow back.

Though he and nurse Loretta Powell continue their close relationship, he will not propose marriage to her as long as he is expecting a return to service. Knowing all too well the cost of war, he will not leave her potentially a widow. She accepts the relationship for what it is, and they are both pleased when she is offered a permanent nursing position at Mare Island.

As weeks pass, the couple enjoys exploring San Francisco, while Biggs continues his therapy. When officially approved for return to duty, he presses hard for assignment to a warship. His service on the **Arizona** opens emotional doors with some in command, but his position as hospital apprentice is limiting. He is offered the opportunity for corpsman training, and accepts, returning to Great Lakes, Illinois. Loretta remains in California, and the separation is difficult for the young couple.

Completing his coursework in August 1942, Biggs is certified as a navy corpsman the following month. He asks for, and receives, a posting to the Pacific, and serves on the newly refitted battleship USS **Colorado.** He is eventually promoted to chief petty officer and serves as corpsman throughout campaigns that include the island-hopping fights for Tarawa, Tinian, Saipan, and Guam. In November 1944, he takes part in the difficult fight in Leyte Gulf, the Philippines, and is wounded severely when struck by shrapnel from a Japanese kamikaze attack. He is evacuated, along with more than two dozen others who have received the most serious wounds. Transported by hospital ship, he eventually returns to San Francisco. But there is no joyous reunion with Loretta Powell. Unable to cope with his lengthy absence, she marries a doctor who is stationed at the hospital.

He remains hospitalized with severe shoulder and chest wounds, and is finally released in July 1945. But with the war drawing to a close, there is no opportunity for him to return to service. He accepts his fate, especially with the inevitable downsizing of the navy. Given his medical training and his rank, he receives numerous offers from former naval officers, including Dr. Daniel Condon, now a civilian. Biggs weighs the offers, and accepts a well-paying position at Provident Hospital in Chicago as a physician's assistant. In 1948, after a brief courtship, he marries Eileen Jordon, a nurse. They have one daughter, whom they name Kimberly.

Biggs continues to dream of playing baseball, but is realistic about his age and the lingering effects of his injury. He never pursues any potential opportunity.

In 1951, Biggs's father dies of a heart attack, and his mother dies a year later. Biggs returns to Florida only long enough to attend the two funerals.

He and Eileen live outside of Chicago until his retirement in 1988, at age sixty-seven. He dies of a stroke in 2011, at age ninety. She dies in 2018, at age ninety-five.

On the official recommendation of Dr. Condon, Biggs is awarded a Bronze Star for his efforts during the attack on the **Arizona.** He is also awarded two Purple Hearts.

Though invited often to the reunions at Pearl Harbor for survivors of the **Arizona,** he will never attend.

## LIEUTENANT J/G
## DANIEL CONDON, MD—USN

Condon is released from the Naval Hospital in January 1942. But his wounds cause severe difficulties with mobility, and he is forced to retire from the navy. He returns to his home—ironically, in the state of Arizona—and becomes medical examiner for Maricopa County. He is soon regarded as one of Arizona's leading experts in polygraph examinations.

His expertise in legal medicine and postmortem examinations earns him respect from Hollywood, and he serves as a consultant to author Erle Stanley Gardner, who creates the Perry Mason legal series.

He dies in 1992 at age seventy-seven, and is buried in the National Memorial Cemetery of Arizona, in Phoenix.

### SEAMAN 2/C
### EDWARD "ED" WAKEMAN—USN

Escaping the destruction of the **Arizona** without significant injury, Wakeman accepts an assignment to serve aboard the heavy cruiser USS **Portland.** On November 14, 1942, he is killed when the ship is torpedoed by a Japanese submarine during the Naval Battle of Guadalcanal. He is twenty-four, and is buried in his hometown of Sioux Falls, South Dakota.

### ADMIRAL HUSBAND E. KIMMEL—USN

Kimmel is relieved of command on December 16, 1941, replaced temporarily by his subordinate, Admiral William Pye. Within two weeks, Kimmel's permanent successor arrives in Hawaii. He is Admiral Chester Nimitz.

Kimmel endures the torturous process of testifying before various boards and inquiries, steadfastly insisting that his greatest errors could be blamed mostly on Washington and that his removal is uncalled for. But the American people seek scapegoats, and Admiral Kimmel is front and center. On December 18, the **Chicago Tribune** prints, "It is a military maxim that there is no excuse for surprise . . . If commanders prove themselves unequal to their tasks they must be replaced at once lest greater harm befall the nation." He is determined by the first major inquiry to have been in "dereliction of duty." Those words, while not ensuring a court-martial, effectively destroy any opportunity Kimmel has for further service.

That judgment is considered excessively harsh by many who have served with Kimmel, and subsequent hearings back away from such a severe verdict. On February 7, 1942, it is made public that Kimmel has submitted his retirement. Many who push for a court-martial are disappointed, as though the great secrets will never be made known. One enormous incentive for the government to avoid any kind of public trial is that, while the war still rages, there can be no revealing the existence of the Magic decoding system, which is still top secret, and still in use to monitor Japanese communications.

Kimmel is subjected to considerable abuse, in both newspapers and Congress. He responds by keeping a low profile, returns to his home in Henderson, Kentucky. In July 1942, he accepts a position with the Frederic R. Harris Shipbuilding Company, in New York City. In 1947, he leaves the company, moves to Groton, Connecticut, where his son Thomas is an instructor at the navy's submarine school. Another son, Manning Kimmel, dies in 1944, when his submarine is sunk by a Japanese ship.

Because of his decades of service to the navy, Kimmel would, to most of his subordinates, be entitled to retire into a peaceful postwar life. But he cannot ignore the verbal punishment and condemnation he suffers from a public still out for blood. Worse, for those who attempt to support him, he will not apologize for his errors, refuses to show contrition for his failures that led to the events on December 7.

Late in his life he mounts a somewhat irrational attack on men who are no longer alive, and thus unable to respond. He accuses President Roosevelt, the secretary of war, and many other senior officers of deliberately withholding information from his command in Hawaii, as though they knew that an attack by the Japanese was imminent. Other than the bitterness of Kimmel's passing years, there is no basis for these charges, though the claims provide even more fuel for conspiracy theorists.

He dies in Groton, Connecticut, of a heart attack in 1968, at age eighty-six.

## LIEUTENANT GENERAL
## WALTER C. SHORT—USA

Like Kimmel, Short is relieved of command on December 16, 1941, replaced by Lieutenant General Delos C. Emmons. Short goes quietly, and submits his retirement early in 1942. Like Kimmel, he is called to testify at various hearings, by the army, navy, and Congress. But he does not have Kimmel's polish in public speaking, and his manner is somewhat awkward. Thus it is not difficult for others to judge, rightly or wrongly, that perhaps he is not entirely truthful in his version of the details.

Short makes no effort to hide why he took certain specific actions, such as ordering his people to focus more on the threat of local sabotage rather than on any dangers from the outside. He unwisely suggests that the "war warning" message he received from Washington didn't seem important or meaningful as it related to Hawaii. He also suggests the belief that it was the navy's job to protect the island, never quite admitting, or showing any understanding, that it was the army's job to protect the fleet inside the harbor.

Unlike Kimmel, Short seems to accept his place in the history of Pearl Harbor, as though the energy required to defend himself to his many critics is more than he has to give. Behind the scenes, his wrath is aimed at the War Department, including Henry Stimson and General George Marshall, who he believes have offered him to the public as a sac-rificial lamb in order to disguise their own mistakes.

After the war, Short and his wife retire to Dallas. He occupies his waning years with a passion for gardening. Stricken by pneumonia, Short remains in ill health until his death in 1949, at age sixty-nine. He is buried in Arlington National Cemetery. According to his son, Major Walter D. Short, "He laid all the facts about Pearl Harbor before the con-gressional committee. There was no book for him to write, nothing more that he could say."

> "The fact of the matter was that our commanders and their forces were both caught with their pants down . . . According to law, [Short and Kimmel] appeared to be guilty of criminal negligence and dereliction of duty.
> —HENRY C. CLAUSEN,
> WAR DEPARTMENT INVESTIGATOR

> "[General Short] had narrowed his vision to the point where the whole military power at his command—and it was considerable—stalked a mouse, while the tiger jumped through the window."
> —GORDON PRANGE, HISTORIAN

> "To cluster his airplanes in groups . . . that they could not take the air for several hours, and to keep antiaircraft ammunition so stored that it could not

be promptly and immediately available, and to use [radar] only for a very small fraction of the day and night, in my opinion betrayed a misconception of his real duty which was almost beyond belief."
—Secretary of War Henry Stimson,
referring to General Short

## Commander Joseph J. Rochefort—USN

Unlike some of his superiors, Rochefort feels enormous personal guilt for the shocking surprise of the assault on December 7, and vows to raise the level of his department's usefulness so that nothing like it can happen again.

He continues to work in his Dungeon near Pearl Harbor, painstakingly decoding any useful pieces of Japanese communication he and his staff can detect. The level of urgency increases with the coming of the war. Instead of plodding through what had seemed to be a mystery, his department is now becoming a critical weapon in the growing fight against the enemy. In May 1942, Rochefort and his team make an enormous breakthrough, intercepting Japanese military orders for the occupation of the Aleutian Islands.

But a different link in that chain of communication carries even more weight. The Japanese code suggests plans to attack another target. Using a process of elimination, and a brilliant piece of deception by his own signals to the Japanese, Rochefort concludes that the Japanese are aiming toward

Midway Island. The decoded message indicates Japanese intentions, direction of approach, and entire battle plan. Though there are skeptics above him, the information Rochefort decodes results in the kind of preparedness completely missing from the Pearl Harbor attack. Laying a trap for the Japanese, the Americans engage in a critical battle both at sea and in the air, in what is known as the Battle of Midway. The results of that battle change the history of the war.

Admiral Chester Nimitz recommends that Rochefort be awarded the navy's Distinguished Service Medal, but Rochefort refuses the honor, feeling that such attention would only backfire, since he continues to feel responsibility for Pearl Harbor.

He dies in 1976, at age seventy-six, and is buried at Inglewood Park Cemetery in California. The medal he refuses is awarded to him posthumously. Other posthumous awards include the Legion of Merit and the Presidential Medal of Freedom.

## SECRETARY OF WAR HENRY STIMSON

Despite having been a lifelong Republican, Stimson serves as secretary of war through Roosevelt's final term and remains in the job through the end of the war, serving under another Democrat, Harry Truman. He is a strong advocate of the development of the atomic bomb, and at the war's end he strongly opposes some in the administration who wish to see Germany carved up into nation-states.

To Stimson, it is fuel on a dangerous fire, the kind of punishment inflicted on Germany at the end of the First World War.

Stimson is a principal architect of a mechanism for punishing German officers and officials, at what becomes the Nuremburg trials. With the surrender of the Japanese in September 1945, Stimson feels his time has passed, that nothing which follows the war will be as challenging. He retires from President Truman's cabinet at the end of that September.

His leadership at the War Department contributes greatly to the astonishingly high level of American wartime industrial production. He pushes the Truman administration into working toward a mutually trusting relationship with the world's other great power, the Soviet Union, going so far as to suggest that the United States willingly share the secrets of the atomic bomb. The president does not agree.

Upon Stimson's retirement, Truman awards him the Distinguished Service Medal.

Early in the war, Stimson makes plain his opposition to placing black troops under black officers, claiming that they can only be effective if led by white men, that social equality is effectively impossible. That argument has been made by many others, though none have Stimson's influence as secretary of war. With Stimson's retirement, that policy is changed, and President Truman eliminates official segregation of the military.

In February 1942, Stimson pushes hard for the government to adopt another position of his that emphasizes safety over civil liberties. He displays unbridled racism toward the Japanese, is gravely concerned that younger Nisei, who are in fact American citizens, pose a genuine danger to America through spying or espionage. He insists, with some support in Washington, that the Nisei should be part of a wholesale evacuation and internment of Japanese peoples. He says, "Their racial characteristics are such that we cannot understand or trust even the citizen Japanese."

Despite strenuous objections from the Justice Department, Stimson convinces the Roosevelt administration to issue Executive Order 9066. In February 1942, some 110,000 Japanese-Americans are ordered into internment camps. In a self-congratulatory statement, Stimson says that the order represents "a long step forward towards a solution of a very dangerous and vexing problem."

Thus is Stimson's admirable and extensive public service badly tarnished by two philosophical themes that in many ways erase the good.

He dies in October 1950, at age eighty-three, near his home in West Hills, New York.

### LIEUTENANT WILLIAM OUTERBRIDGE—USN

In sinking the Japanese midget submarine outside the entrance to Pearl Harbor, the skipper of the destroyer USS **Ward** likely strikes America's first blow against a hostile enemy in World War Two. Long after the attack on Pearl Harbor, Outerbridge's superiors recognize their enormous mistake in not appreciating the significance of his report of the encounter with the submarine. None of that is a comfort to Outerbridge.

In 1942, Outerbridge is transferred to Washington, assigned to the office of the chief of naval transportation. With the war expanding, he pushes again for sea duty, and finally, in 1944, is assigned to command the destroyer USS **O'Brien**. His first duty is in support of the Normandy landings, but his time in the Atlantic is limited. By the end of 1944, Outerbridge and the **O'Brien** are back in the Pacific, where his ship adds support for the Battle of Leyte Gulf, in the Philippines.

He works in close proximity to a ship he knows well, the destroyer USS **Ward.** Outerbridge is appalled to see the **Ward** struck by a Japanese kamikaze attack. Damaged beyond repair, the **Ward** nevertheless continues to float. Outerbridge receives the order that, once the crew is removed, he is to fire upon the stricken ship and sink her, thus preventing possible salvage by the Japanese. There is no written account available to describe what he must feel, especially since the date he sinks his former ship is December 7, 1944.

After the war, Outerbridge continues to command destroyer- or cruiser-class ships, and teaches at the Naval War College and the Industrial College of the Armed Forces. His final posting is at the transportation and petroleum branch of the chief of naval operations.

For his service, he is awarded the Navy Cross and the Legion of Merit.

He retires in 1957, as a rear admiral, moves to Florida, and becomes a schoolteacher. He dies in 1986, at his home in Tifton, Georgia, at age eighty.

## LIEUTENANT KERMIT TYLER—USAAC

The lone officer who receives the first radar reports from the Opana Radar Site indicating the incoming Japanese attack, Tyler reflects often on his failure to appreciate the significance of those signals. Like many others on or before December 7, he is one of an enormous number of commanders, observers, and planners who could not grasp the meaning of the clues they were given, and like many, Tyler carries that as a source of lifelong guilt. In Tyler's defense, early on December 7, he is assigned to command the Intercept Center with no training or instruction, and no supervision or support staff to guide and assist him. In a broad sweep that seeks to assign blame, Tyler is targeted by the Naval Board of Inquiry. But once the details of his posting are revealed, including the relative inexperience of the two privates who are assigned the enormous responsibility of manning the new technology of the radar station, Tyler and both privates, Lockhard and Elliott, are exonerated, and there is no disciplinary action recommended against them. Nonetheless, Tyler displays enormous regret, as though offering a lifelong personal apology for his fateful words, "Well, don't worry about it."

Tyler serves in the United States Air Force until his retirement as a lieutenant colonel in 1961. He moves to San Diego, becomes a real estate broker, and dies in 2010 at age ninety-six.

### COMMANDER MINORU GENDA—IJN

Along with his commander, Admiral Yamamoto, Genda is the chief architect of a transition from the old-style ship-to-ship fighting to a greater emphasis on the use of tactical aircraft. It is a practice that will greatly help determine the outcome of the war.

Genda is chiefly responsible for the energy behind the effort to modify the torpedo so that it can be effective in shallow water. That design proves to be the single most damaging weapon against the American fleet at Pearl Harbor. Operating under the intense pressure of Yamamoto's timetable, Genda succeeds in training pilots who will fly four different tactical missions: high-altitude bombing, dive-bombing, torpedo bombing, and fighter support (the Zero). To judge by the astonishing lack of Japanese losses in both aircraft and pilots, Genda's lessons have been well learned. But Genda is the first to admit that it is the surprise achieved by the attack that ensures its success. He understands, as do his pilots, that had the Americans been ready and waiting, with fully equipped antiaircraft guns, the outcome would have been a catastrophe for the Japanese.

Like his admiral, Genda appreciates the enormity of the mistake in not locating the American aircraft carriers. He supports Yamamoto's plan to return to the central Pacific, to aggressively attack those valuable ships once more.

His service as a pilot and air planner continues throughout the war, and he logs more than three thousand hours of air time, including numerous combat missions. In December 1944, Genda assembles an elite air unit, the 343rd, to fly the most modern and what he considers the greatest fighter aircraft of the war. However, the Japanese high command is instituting a very different kind of program, that of the kamikaze suicide flights. Genda is outraged, believing his planes can overmatch anything the enemy is flying against them. But his voice is not heard, his efforts too late in the war to turn any tide.

After the war, he continues to serve in the much-reduced Japanese military, but there is little to challenge a man with Genda's drive. He finally retires in 1962, pursues politics, and is elected to the Japanese House of Councillors, where he serves for twenty years.

In 1969, Genda is invited to speak at the United States Naval Academy in Annapolis, Maryland. Though he is welcomed by his audience, there is substantial opposition to his appearance among members of the Pearl Harbor Survivors Association, as well as among family members of many of the veterans. Genda offers a forthright and enlightening talk, though he unwisely offers the opinion that had the Japanese developed the atomic bomb more quickly than the Americans, they would have used it without hesitation. The audience seems to accept that view as a legitimate one, but not so in Japan, where the uproar over his remarks forces him to resign from his own political party (the Liberal Democrats), though he continues to hold office.

A staunch advocate for Japan's re-militarization, in 1974 he speaks openly about Japan's potential need for its own stockpile of nuclear weapons. It is not a popular position.

He dies in 1989, at age eighty-five, on the anniversary date of Japan's surrender, August 15.

### ADMIRAL KICHISABURO NOMURA— AMBASSADOR TO THE U.S.

Immediately after events are clarified from Hawaii, Nomura is taken into custody by U.S. law enforcement. Released in August 1942, he returns to Japan. Publicly shunned, he is nonetheless privately popular, and is offered a discreet position as an unofficial advisor to the government, though he is never clear on just what he is to advise. Near the war's conclusion, he is selected as a member of the Privy

Council, but with Japan's defeat and its government virtually in tatters, few positions have meaning.

Despite the stain of his service as ambassador, he is still considered to rank as an admiral in the Imperial Navy. That respect opens the door to a position with the Matsushita Electric Industrial Company (now Panasonic), one of many companies working to rebuild Japan.

In 1954, he runs for office and is elected overwhelmingly to a seat in the House of Councillors. He strongly resists invitations to join with those who favor a re-militarized Japan, insisting that any military should be controlled by a civilian government.

He remains in political office until his death in 1964, at age eighty-six. Throughout his life he strongly disputes any suggestion that he was aware of the attack on Pearl Harbor prior to December 7. "I myself became acquainted for the first time with the attack upon Pearl Harbor by the radio news." There is no hard evidence to support a contradiction of that statement.

## TAKEO YOSHIKAWA

Yoshikawa can best be described as Japan's most efficient, and thus most damaging, spy in Hawaii. As a member of the Japanese Consulate, he is arrested shortly after the attack, along with several others. He is then included in a routine prisoner exchange and returned to Japan in August 1942.

The U.S. authorities have no idea what his role has been, and when he reaches Japan he makes every effort to avoid notoriety.

With the American occupation of Japan in 1945, Yoshikawa develops a healthy paranoia, believing he is under threat of arrest yet again, this time as a war criminal, and subject to lengthy imprisonment. He disguises himself in various ways, including as a Buddhist monk and as the nameless proprietor of a candy store.

As the years pass, the danger of reprisals by the Americans decreases, and he emerges from hiding to open a gas station, but those who know him are aware he served as a spy, and he is always under suspicion, even among his friends.

In 1960, he opens up his life in a book, detailing his activities in Hawaii as a **master spy**. He revels in the newfound attention, and negotiates a position teaching espionage to corporate managers. But he is never officially acknowledged by his government, the label of "spy" carrying far too much dishonor. As one high-ranking official states, "The Japanese government never spied on anyone."

He dies in a nursing home in 1993, at age seventy-eight.

Even if most Americans are never aware of Yoshikawa's unquestionable importance to Pearl Harbor, they are treated to a revealing interview of him on television, openly discussing his role in the attack. The interview is part of a CBS News documentary that is broadcast on the twentieth anniversary of the Pearl Harbor attack, December 7, 1961. The interviewer is Walter Cronkite.

## ADMIRAL ISOROKU YAMAMOTO—IJN

"Pearl Harbor was more than one of the most daring and brilliant naval operations of all time. It was one of the turning points of history."
—GORDON PRANGE, HISTORIAN

"I don't see what there is to get so excited about somebody's sinking a handful of warships."
—ISOROKU YAMAMOTO, LETTER TO HIS SISTER, DECEMBER 18, 1941

Ever the gambler, Yamamoto accepts the success at Pearl Harbor for what it is. The gamble had been extraordinary, and the results outstanding, based on the lack of damage to the Japanese fleet and the minuscule number of downed aircraft. But overall, Yamamoto understands that an enormous opportunity has been lost, potentially the most important result of the attack. The inability to locate and destroy the U.S. aircraft carriers is the one failure he laments above all the success. As a champion of the evolution of the airplane as a key weapon, he knows that the Americans are still as strong as they ever were. As Yamamoto has predicted, the great victory at Pearl Harbor is a temporary one.

Lauded as a great national hero in Japan, Yamamoto continues to work with Naval Ministry officials, as well as with the army and its planners, to push forward with all that must follow. While Pearl Harbor captures the attention of most of the world, Japanese forces continue to prioritize their need for petroleum and other materials.

Their original strategy of a strong invasion into Southeast Asia and the South Pacific has not changed. With the navy's support, the army quickly invades the Philippines, after destroying most of Douglas MacArthur's fleet of B-17 bombers in a bombing attack that rivals Pearl Harbor for its level of surprise to American commanders. In early 1942, the Japanese army and navy launch attacks against Singapore, and in the process sink two prized British warships, the battleship HMS **Prince of Wales** and the heavy cruiser HMS **Repulse,** a loss that deeply affects British morale at home. By the end of February 1942, Singapore is over-run and occupied by the Japanese army, as are the Dutch East Indies. A lengthy list of islands in the South Pacific are occupied, including posses-sions of the Americans, British, and Dutch. By May, the island of Corregidor in the Philippines is over-run, the surviving American forces there captured en masse.

For Yamamoto, the successes against the major world powers have been uncomfortably easy, with no significant damage to Japanese forces throughout the campaign area. In Japan, the high commands weigh their next options, though Yamamoto presses for an effort to negotiate some kind of peace with either the British or Americans that would take them out of the war. That effort gains no traction with either nation, who have learned not to trust Japanese entreaties.

Despite the grand pronouncements by many in the Japanese military that the war is becoming a monumental Japanese victory, Yamamoto continues to believe that these triumphs, including his own, will be short-lived. One option that he begins to champion is a return to Hawaii, possibly to capture the islands themselves, eliminating the most significant American base in the entire Pacific. But others in authority have their eyes on Southeast Asia, and are developing plans to drive into Burma, possibly all the way to India. The lure of the wealth of natural resources in that part of the world is more power–ful to the planners than Yamamoto's arguments for Hawaii.

That changes in April 1942, when the Doolittle Raid strikes Tokyo. Sixteen American B-25 bombers are launched from the aircraft carrier USS **Hornet,** a one-way gamble that the planes can drop explosives on Japan, then find safe landing on mainland China. Though the raid does not result in extensive damage or significant casualties, the message to the Japanese is shockingly clear: **Our aircraft can reach you.** It is precisely the message Yamamoto had been preaching prior to Pearl Harbor: that Japan cannot assume the war will always be elsewhere. For the first time, the high command, deeply affected by the raid, begins to listen. A new priority suddenly rises—to destroy the American ability to strike from the air. While Yamamoto dives into that planning with customary energy, he is graphically reminded of the great mistake, the lost opportunity at Pearl Harbor.

Yamamoto plans for an invasion of two islands in the Aleutian chain, off the coast of Alaska. At the same time, the Imperial Navy will move a formidable force of carriers and other ships toward the island of Midway, northwest of Hawaii. The goal is to draw American forces out of Pearl Harbor, especially the carriers, assuming they will steam northward to rescue the Aleutian Islands. Yamamoto believes he can set a carefully timed trap for the Americans as they approach Midway Island. The resulting fight is described by most military historians as the turning point of the entire war.

But that is another story.

"The fact that the Japanese did not return to Pearl Harbor and complete the job was the greatest help to us, for they left their principal enemy with the time to catch his breath, restore his morale, and rebuild his forces."

—ADMIRAL CHESTER W. NIMITZ

"The treacherous attack by Japan, and the declarations of war by Germany and Italy, instantly united us . . . [The United States'] spirit was no longer troubled; their soul was no longer divided; they knew at last what they must do."
—THE NEW YORK TIMES, DECEMBER 21, 1941

# ACKNOWLEDGMENTS

**T**he following officers and crewmen from the USS **Arizona** lost their lives on December 7, 1941. They are listed here because they are all characters in this book, and for that, their contribution to this story is immeasurable.

## MAY THEY REST IN PEACE

Commander Samuel Earle Johnson, MD
Lieutenant Clifton T. Janz
Captain Franklin Van Valkenburgh
Pharmacist's Mate 2/c Ivan Block
Pharmacist's Mate 3/c Ernest Eugene Corey
Pharmacist's Mate 2/c William Frank Vaughan

Machinist's Mate 1/c Kenneth E. Cockrum
First Sgt. John Duveene—USMC
Seaman 1/c Keith H. Harrington
Chief Gunner's Mate Orville A. Isham
PVT Woodrow (Woody) Wilson Finley—USMC
Musician 2/c Gerald C. Cox
LCDR Paul J. Register

The following have created memoirs, diaries, or
other firsthand accounts that were crucial to the
writing of this book.

Secy. of State Cordell Hull
Secy. of War Henry Stimson
Donald Stratton (USS **Arizona**)
Theodore C. Mason (USS **California**)
ADM William F. Halsey
ADM Husband E. Kimmel
CDR Edwin Layton—USN
LTC George W. Bicknell—USA
ADM Matome Ugaki—IJN
Seaman Stan Johnston—USN
ADM/Ambassador Kichisaburo Nomura
Ambassador Joseph C. Grew
CDR Mitsuo Fuchida—IJN
CDR Minoru Genda—IJN
VADM Shigeru Fukudome—IJN
RADM William W. Drake—USN
ADM Chester W. Nimitz—USN
Harold Shimer (USS **Helena**)

I am deeply grateful to the following, who generously furnished material for my use, often firsthand accounts from their own families. Thank you all!

David R. Johnston—Greensboro, NC
David Palluconi—Fairfield, OH
Sam Evangelisto—Cary, NC
Tom Ellsworth—Hot Springs, AR
David Hoffert, PhD—Warsaw, IN
Ed Walsh—Alexandria, VA

The following historians have created published source material that was extremely useful in my education on this subject, and thus most helpful in the writing of this story. I am deeply grateful to all of them, and I recommend their books to anyone who seeks valid information about the Pearl Harbor attack. Listed alphabetically, they are:

Hiroyuki Agawa
Gwenfread Allen
Thurston Clarke
Henry C. Clausen and Bruce Lee
Ronald J. Drez
Donald Goldstein and Katherine V. Dillon
Molly Kent
Walter Lord
Bill McWilliams
Lawrence Rodriggs
Henry Sakaida and Koji Takaki

David F. Schmitz
Michael Slackman
Ronald H. Spector
Paul Stillwell
Steve Twomey
Roberta Wohlstetter
Alan D. Zimm

When it comes to the details surrounding the attack on Pearl Harbor, there is no more respected or appreciated historian than Professor Gordon Prange. His **At Dawn We Slept** is must reading for anyone with any interest in the events leading up to and including December 7, 1941, and provided me with enormous fuel for the factual and historical details in this story. Professor Prange passed away in 1980, and though his scholarship and attention to detail are sorely missed, his work lives on through so many other historians (including most of those listed above). To quote those who worked closely alongside him: "He knew more about the Japanese attack than any other person. He interviewed virtually every surviving Japanese officer who took part . . . as well as every important U.S. source. The scope of his research is without equal."

I have saved the best for last.

I have been extremely fortunate to become well acquainted with Daniel Martinez, the National Park Service Chief Historian for the WWII Valor in the Pacific National Monument, which includes the USS **Arizona** Memorial at Pearl Harbor. Dan is a wellspring of substantial information and insights and, for me, a source of both knowledge and research material without which I might have severely fumbled this effort. Dan offered me a substantial amount of his time, which is a gift of generosity that cannot be overestimated, since he is one of the busiest people I've ever known. Thus is this book dedicated to him. Thank you, Dan.

# ABOUT THE AUTHOR

JEFF SHAARA is the **New York Times** bestselling author of **The Frozen Hours, The Fateful Lightning, The Smoke at Dawn, A Chain of Thunder, A Blaze of Glory, The Final Storm, No Less Than Victory, The Steel Wave, The Rising Tide, To the Last Man, The Glorious Cause, Rise to Rebellion,** and **Gone for Soldiers,** as well as **Gods and Generals** and **The Last Full Measure**—two novels that complete the Civil War trilogy that began with his father's Pulitzer Prize–winning classic, **The Killer Angels**. Shaara was born into a family of Italian immigrants in New Brunswick, New Jersey. He grew up in Tallahassee, Florida, and graduated from Florida State University. He lives in Newtown Square, Pennsylvania.

jeffshaara.com